"Will you not grow tired of a wife always intruding into what you think of as a man's affairs?" Sybelle asked nervously. "Perhaps I am not as beautiful or clever—"

"Shame!" Walter cried, laughing and interrupting her. "Oh, shame, to throw out so plain a lure for a compliment. You know quite well that you are the most beautiful woman I have ever seen. But surely a clever girl could have found a more subtle way to induce me to tell her what she wished to hear."

Sybelle could not help laughing, too, but amid her amusement there was a treacherous warmth, an insistent desire to return Walter's embrace, to taste the mouth smiling down at her.

"I am cleverer than that, Sir Walter," she said, twisting out of his hold.

is the sixth book of the magnificent romantic saga, **THE ROSELYNDE CHRONICLES.** Once again, the medieval tapestry of passion and power are brought to life—this time by fiery heroine, Sybelle.

Other books by ROBERTA GELLIS

KNIGHT'S HONOR
BOND OF BLOOD
THE SWORD AND THE SWAN
THE DRAGON AND THE ROSE

The Roselynde Chronicles

ROSELYNDE
ALINOR
JOANNA
GILLIANE
RHIANNON

The Royal Dynasty

SIREN SONG
WINTER SONG

Sybelle

Roberta Gellis

A JOVE BOOK

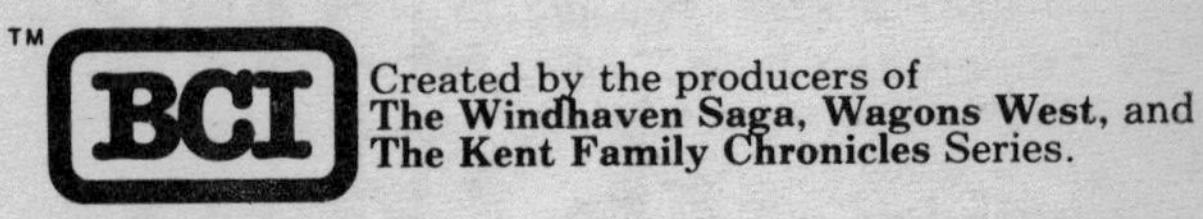

Executive Producer: Lyle Kenyon Engel

SYBELLE

A Jove Book / published by arrangement with
Book Creations, Inc.

PRINTING HISTORY

Jove edition / September 1983

ISBN: 0-515-07128-5

Jove books are published by The Berkley Publishing Group,
200 Madison Avenue, New York, N.Y. 10016.
The words "A JOVE BOOK" and the "J" with sunburst
are trademarks belonging to Jove Publications, Inc.

PRINTED IN THE UNITED STATES OF AMERICA

To my loyal readers, who are as much a part of the Roselynde clan as Alinor, her children, and grandchildren.

CHESTER
N
ABER
MOLD
BANGOR
RUTHIN
SHREWSBURY
SEVERN
WALES
KNIGHT'S TOWER
WYE
CLIFFORD
CLYRO
BUILTH
HAY
HEREFORD
CRASWELL
FOY
GLOUCE
1
2
BRECON
USK
3
ABERGAVENNY
ST. DAVID'S
USK
4
THORNBU
5
CAERLEON
MARGAM ABBEY
BRISTOL
DEVIZES
PEMBROKE
SALISBURY
1 GROSMONT
2 GOODRICH
3 MONMOUTH
4 CHEPSTOW
5 GOLDCLIFF
SOUTHERN ENGLAND AND WALES C.1230
RON TOELKE '82
© BOOK CREATIONS INC. 1982

RICHARD MARSHAL, EARL OF PEMBROKE

CHAPTER 1

Lady Alinor raised her head from the letter she had just read and stared blankly at her husband. From the expression on Lord Ian's face when he first read the letter, she had been prepared for disconcerting though not tragic or dangerous news. But now Ian looked back at her, his surprised disbelief already melting into exasperated amusement.

They sat, as they often did these days, in a wall chamber rather than in the great hall of Roselynde keep. Although the hearth was small and could not accommodate the huge logs that roared and spat in the fireplaces of the great hall, the small room was also free of sweeping drafts. In good measure this was owing to the brilliant tapestries that covered the walls. In addition to providing the chief beauty of the room, for the jewellike tints of the cloth showing the hunting scenes relieved the gloom and gave an impression of warmth to the eyes, the tapestries actually did keep out the damp chill that oozed from the rubble-filled stone walls while they reflected heat from the dancing fire.

There was a sense of peace in the small chamber, of protection from the winds of November that lashed the sea into great breakers, which crashed against the cliff below the enormous stone walls of Roselynde. There was also protection from the noise and bustle of activity in the great hall. As they grew old together, Alinor and Ian prized more highly whatever time of quiet they could seize. There was not much. The fits and starts of King Henry III kept England in turmoil and, at the present time, had brought many powerful barons into open rebellion.

"Is it a jest?" Alinor asked, holding up the letter.

"Oh, no," Ian replied. "It is signed and sealed officially. It is no jest. That is a formal invitation to the wedding of our son, Simon, to Rhiannon, daughter of Llewelyn, Prince of Gwynedd.''

Alinor slammed the letter down on the small table beside her so violently that the goblet of wine on it jumped several inches. Ian's lips twitched. Alinor's temper, although somewhat mellowed by sixty years of life, was still volatile.

''Then the old man is losing his grip on his wits,'' she snapped. ''One does not make a wedding in the middle of a war when the families of the bride and groom are on opposite sides.''

''Llewelyn is no older than I,'' Ian reminded her, laughing, ''and I wish my wits were ever as sharp as his are now.''

Immediately, Alinor's expression softened, and she rose to embrace her husband affectionately. ''There is nothing wrong with your wits,'' she murmured. ''It is your heart that is at fault, my love, from being too soft and easily moved.''

Ian returned his wife's embrace and kissed her. ''Well, heart or head,'' he said cheerfully, ''there is nothing wrong with Llewelyn. In a way it is not so ill a time for a meeting.''

''I think you are as mad as he.'' Alinor laughed. ''Have you also forgot that the barons of the southwest are in active rebellion?''

Ian sighed. ''I wish I could forget it. No, but just think. That surprise attack of Llewelyn and Pembroke's on Grosmont has left the king with hardly a stitch to clothe his men, an ox to feed them, or a penny to pay them. He is sitting at Gloucester, but what can he do? The vassals have withdrawn, and the mercenaries are grumbling and rebellious. At the moment, Henry is helpless.''

''Perhaps, but he is screaming that he will have his revenge. Could it be,'' Alinor asked thoughtfully, ''that Llewelyn believes he can embroil us in the rebel cause?''

''He knows me too well for that.'' Ian smiled. ''Of course, Llewelyn would not object if my going to Wales for my son's wedding increased the king's anxiety. But it is safe for us, Alinor. Henry gave us permission for the marriage. And even more important, I think even the Bishop of Winchester is growing frightened now. Certainly, he will not move against us. Most likely he will simply look the other way and say nothing, to avoid alienating us further.''

''Then why did Llewelyn decide to have the wedding now? Is it pure mischief?''

"An expensive piece of mischief. No, what Llewelyn really wants is news."

"Nonsense," Alinor replied irritably. "What news can we give him? We have not been near Henry since last summer. Llewelyn must know that even Geoffrey has avoided the king since Henry broke his oath to Richard."

"I do not think Llewelyn needs news of Henry," Ian pointed out. "I am sure he has spies in that area, perhaps in Gloucester keep itself, to tell him what Henry says and does. What Llewelyn wants is news of England, of the temper of the barons and of the clergy." He grinned, looking for a moment boyish despite the marks of advancing age. "Llewelyn wants to know how much longer he has to stuff his coffers with the loot of raids before the king offers Richard peace."

Alinor's hand rested on her husband's shoulder. The sparkle of green and gold went out of her fine eyes, leaving them dark. "Will there be peace soon, Ian?"

He covered her hand with his own. "Soon? That I cannot say, but I have hope, dear heart. As you know, Henry is not one to stick to a purpose when it becomes dangerous or even uncomfortable to do so. Moreover, he fears the disapproval of the Church."

"Not with the Bishop of Winchester to assure him constantly that he is doing right." Alinor dropped a kiss on her husband's temple and went back to her seat.

"But I think the choice of Edmund of Abingdon to be Archbishop of Canterbury will change that," Ian said. "Edmund is no man's creature, and he will not fear to speak out urging conciliation on both sides—"

"Which every bishop who is not Winchester's henchman has been doing for near a year," Alinor interrupted impatiently, her eyes sparkling again.

Ian smiled at her. "But Henry's belief is strong, and Edmund will have the primacy of the Church about him even if he has not yet received the pall."

"So Edmund is holy," Alinor agreed, "yet he cannot be more holy than the Bishop of London, and Roger has not been able to bring about a reconciliation."

"Because Roger is a bishop as Winchester is a bishop," Ian said. "In the king's mind, neither is closer to God, although it must be apparent to the whole world else that

Roger will go straight to God's knee when God sees fit to call him to heaven."

"And Winchester will go straight to the devil," Alinor snapped.

Sadness filled Ian's eyes. "No," he sighed. "Despite all the trouble he has caused, Peter des Roches is not evil. There is no evil intent in him. God would not damn a man for lack of understanding."

"He was once your friend, and you will never cease to love him," Alinor said in an exasperated voice. "But Winchester has been no friend to this realm these two years past. It was he alone who set the notion into Henry's head that a king must be all-powerful and rule without the advice or consent of his barons, regardless of law or custom. And it was Winchester who deliberately forced Richard Marshal to rebel, thinking that if he could break the Earl of Pembroke, the rest of us would bow meekly and allow the king to have his own will in all things."

"But Winchester meant it to bring peace and order to the land," Ian pointed out soothingly.

"He meant it to bring the land resistless into *his* hand," Alinor snapped, and then, seeing the trouble in her husband's face, she jumped up, kissed him again, laughed, and went back to her seat. "Very well," she continued, "I will credit Winchester with good intentions. I will only wish him purgatory instead of hell, but I hope it is for as many aeons as he has caused us years of misery."

That made Ian laugh also. "Your notions of mercy, my love, chill my blood. But what I wished to make clear is that you need not fear that Winchester will cry anathema on us when we go to Builth for the wedding."

To Ian's surprise, his wife did not answer. Instead, she looked away to the doorway leading to the great hall of the keep. Ian also turned his head. Instantly, the trouble that had lingered in his eyes despite his laugh vanished into a warm smile of welcome to his eldest grandchild. He had long since stopped reminding himself that Sybelle's mother was his stepdaughter and not his own get. He knew Alinor remembered her first husband with love, but she did not resent Ian's calling Joanna his daughter and Sybelle his granddaughter.

Sybelle dropped a kiss on the top of her grandfather's head as she passed, but she made direct for Alinor, holding out a stalk of flax. "I think this has soaked long enough," she said.

Alinor took the stalk in her hand and teased at it with her nails, then felt the fibers. "Yes," she agreed, "but send one of the maids to tell the women to get on with the work. I want you to write to your mother and father and tell them that Ian and I will leave for Wales in five days' time."

"Wales?" Sybelle repeated, her beautiful amber-colored eyes widening. "Is something wrong with Simon?" she asked in a frightened voice.

"No, no," Ian assured her, and, simultaneously, Alinor said caustically, "Aside from his being even more insane than usual, I do not believe so."

Sybelle looked from one grandparent to the other. "Whatever has Simon done now?" she asked apprehensively.

Simon was Sybelle's favorite, a dearly loved playfellow in her youth; although he was her uncle he was only six years older than she, and now he was her dearest friend and confidant. However, there could be no doubt that Simon was a sport, an unusual growth in a family dedicated to the expansion of its lands, wealth, and power. Thus, Simon was often in disgrace with his parents, more particularly with his practical and hot-tempered mother. However, rather than showing signs of rage, Alinor's bright eyes glittered with laughter.

"For once he has done something right," she said, "since we have just received a formal invitation from Prince Llewelyn to Simon's marriage to Rhiannon."

"Oh, wonderful!" Sybelle exclaimed. "I knew he would convince her." But then her eyes widened again. "But why do you go to Wales now? Surely—"

"Surely Lord Llewelyn is as full of mischief as a dog is of fleas," Alinor remarked tartly. "Unless it is Simon who has conceived this lunacy—a wedding in the middle of a war! The date is the first day of December."

Sybelle smiled again. "That is not lunacy. It is superstition. Simon always said he would marry on the day you did, Grandmama. He said it worked for my mama and papa, for surely they are very happy together."

"Happy marriages are not made by the date of the wedding," Alinor replied, but her expression had softened and her voice was softer, too, as she went on. "Happy marriages come of goodwill, good sense, and honest desire on both parts. In any case,'' she continued with a lift of her brows, ''as things are between Simon and Rhiannon, the wedding could have been left until December first of next year when, please God, our going to Wales would not tempt the king to cry treason.''

''Come, Alinor,'' Ian protested, grinning at her, ''you are only being contrary. You know this is none of Simon's doing. Agreed that Simon wished to marry on December first, he would have been content to take Rhiannon before any priest with a few witnesses and be done with it. And Rhiannon would not care. The wedding must be Llewelyn's idea. I have told you his probable purpose.''

Sybelle had not really been listening to this exchange, and her bronze-gold brows were drawn together in a frown. ''May I go with you?'' she asked. ''I do not know whether Papa will be willing to go—not that he would not like to, but I know he does not wish to hurt King Henry more than he has done already. But I . . . I would like to see Simon married and to see Rhiannon again.''

''And to see Walter de Clare, perhaps?'' Alinor asked, and then added, ''No, I am not teasing you, Sybelle, I am asking you a serious question. Whenever Walter has come among the family, his eyes sought you out. True, there is no certainty that he will be at Builth, but he was with Richard Marshal when last we heard of him. Richard will certainly be invited to Simon's wedding, and it is likely, if Walter is with him, Walter will come also because he and Simon have known one another since Simon went for fostering. I know your father would like the match between you and Walter. He likes Walter, and the lands are what we need.''

''Alinor,'' Ian said sharply, ''do not press Sybelle with talk of Geoffrey's preference and Walter's estates. Roselynde is rich enough and strong enough. We need no maiden sacrifices.''

''I am not pressing her,'' Alinor protested. ''I am asking her—or warning her, perhaps. It is my feeling that Walter will ask for her as soon as he sees her again. I believe he would have asked Geoffrey for her sooner, except that Walter feared he would be named a rebel and disseisined at any moment.''

''That is most reasonable,'' Ian pointed out. ''It was wise and honest not to press his suit. I must say that I believe Walter de Clare to be a man of strict honor.''

Sybelle, as was proper, had said nothing while this discussion of the man who might become her husband had taken place. She had listened with interest, of course, but without anxiety—in which she was different and more fortunate than most girls. In general, marriage was not a matter of liking or loving but of political alliances and transfer of property. The opinions and desires of the women involved were seldom consulted. Sybelle, however, did not fear being forced into a hateful and terrifying marriage. She had, in fact, already refused many matches that had been suggested.

Nonetheless, during the past year, Sybelle had noticed that the expressions of relief her parents had worn when she first turned away suitors had changed to concern. She began to realize that, at sixteen, it was overtime for her to be married. It was also true that she had found Walter de Clare attractive. This had puzzled her a little, for she was surrounded by very handsome men and Walter was not especially handsome.

Not that there was anything distasteful in Walter's appearance. He was as tall as Simon or Ian and as heavily built as her uncle Adam. Still, compared with Simon's breathtaking beauty, which he had inherited from Ian, and even Adam's superlative good looks, Walter was plain. As Sybelle thought the word, Walter's face appeared in her mind's eye: a strong, square chin; a wide, mobile mouth, which looked good-natured and always smiled at her but which she thought could be both hard and cruel; a high-bridged beak of a nose; blue eyes. Sybelle's thoughts paused. The eyes were really nice. They glinted with humor and intelligence.

"Oh, I believe so, too." Alinor laughed, agreeing with Ian's description of Walter's strict honesty. "He is as bad as you, Ian—and I do not say that as a compliment. No, really, he is worse. He is like Simon—I mean my first husband," Alinor said to Sybelle, who had looked surprised. "My Simon was a great one for being so honest he would run his head into a stone wall."

But Sybelle had not looked surprised because she had confused Alinor's son with her first husband, both of whom were named Simon. She was surprised because she realized for the first time that Walter de Clare was, from what she had heard, like the grandfather she had never known. Her mother's father had been thirty years older than his wife and had died when Joanna was nine years old. Much as Joanna loved her stepfather—and she adored him—she had been determined that her own father's memory should not die. Sybelle had been told everything that Joanna remembered of her father's appearance and personality.

Much of what Joanna had told her daughter was idealized, of course, but Sybelle did not realize that. And although Alinor spoke less frequently of her first husband, what she said confirmed Joanna's tales. Sybelle, too, adored Ian, but a powerful admiration for her natural grandfather had been driven into her. Alinor's identification of Walter with her first husband meant more to Sybelle than her grandmother guessed. However, the connection between the men made Sybelle feel oddly shy, and she took refuge in avoiding the subject.

"But you always say it is Grandpapa who is so honorable that he runs his head into stone walls," Sybelle teased.

"It is Simon who was your grandfather, Sybelle," Ian reminded her. Although Ian thought of Alinor's children from her first marriage as his own, he had been Simon's squire and best friend. He did not wish Simon's memory to die, either.

The double reminder brought a faint flush to Sybelle's cheeks, but she only said, merrily, "Yes, I know. Mama often talks of him. It is comforting to have three grandfathers—two here and one in heaven. No matter how wrong I am, I always have someone to take my side."

Alinor raised her brows as she watched her granddaughter's lovely face. Perhaps the faint flush of color had some special meaning, but perhaps it was only a result of the memory of some piece of mischief. Sybelle was a perfect blend of mother and father in appearance—Joanna's brilliant red hair and Geoffrey's light brown mingling into a glowing bronze, Joanna's milk-white skin, and Geoffrey's golden mingling into a soft, lustrous, creamy complexion. However, the eyes were all Geoffrey's, and, unfortunately, the sense of humor was all Joanna's. Sybelle, too, would butter a path to see someone carrying an armful of eggs slide down.

"Now, mistress," Alinor said with mock severity, "you may distract your grandfather into talk of other subjects, but I am not so easy to befool. It is both good and bad to have a man like Walter, who will live and die by his honor. God knows it has cost me much pain and worry to have husbands of that kind. I must warn you that Walter de Clare is not the man to turn aside, even from a disaster staring into his face, if honor bids him go forward."

"So it *must* be," Ian said strongly. "Where there is no honor, there is no man. There is only a beast that walks on two legs."

"Oh, tush!" Alinor exclaimed, using her late husband's favorite expression. "There is no lack of honor in Geoffrey, but he does not go about butting walls down with his head—at least, not often. But what brought Walter de Clare to my mind in the first place was what you said, Ian, before Sybelle came in, about Winchester finally taking fright and not wishing to make more enemies. If Walter also feels Winchester will stop urging the king to vengeance, he will almost certainly come to an open declaration of his intention. Or, if it is not now, it will be soon. Thus, Sybelle must know what she wishes with regard to him."

Sybelle's color, which had gone back to normal, rose again. "But I do not know."

"Do not talk like a silly chit," Alinor said sharply. "You must know whether or not Walter is to your taste."

"Alinor!" Ian exclaimed. "If Sybelle is undecided, we can put off Walter."

"That is not fair to him," Alinor pointed out, gratefully noting that Sybelle was looking at her and had not noticed the expression of astonishment followed by cynicism on Ian's face.

Ian knew that it was most unlike Alinor to worry about what was fair to others when her own family's interests were involved. Alinor could be kind and just—and mostly she was. However, to her, the interests of Roselynde and those bound to it by blood were paramount, and everything else was subordinate. Although Ian was not given to seeing beneath the surface of things, over twenty years as Alinor's husband had sharpened his perceptions. He realized that it was Sybelle, not Walter, about whom Alinor was concerned—and yet that was not completely true. Seemingly, Alinor wanted Sybelle to choose Walter, and once he came into the family he, too, would be "hers, to her," someone to be cared for with devotion. While these thoughts ran through Ian's head, Alinor had continued speaking with calm thoughtfulness.

"At least, if the answer is more likely to be no than yes, I think Sybelle must tell us now so that we may warn Walter that a contract is unlikely. I am not asking Sybelle to commit herself absolutely, only to say whether Walter does or does not appeal to her as a possible husband. It is clear enough that she likes the man, but a woman *can* like a man without the smallest desire to lie with him—in spite of what most priests think—and that would not serve for a marriage."

"It serves for many marriages," Sybelle remarked. Her voice was indifferent but she did not have equal control over her complexion, and her color was high again.

"Not for a woman of this family," Alinor said firmly, and then laughed. "It is only love that tames us of Roselynde."

"And not too well, even so," Ian retorted sardonically.

"How can you say that?" Alinor exclaimed, widening her eyes with a totally false expression of injury. "Have I not always been most meek and obedient to your will, my lord?"

Ian groaned and covered his eyes with his hand, and Sybelle giggled. "Grandmama!" she protested. "Consider poor Father Edgar. You know he is not so young, and that stool in the confessional is very hard. He will be forced to sit on it for *hours* if you claim to be meek and obedient."

"There is no need to confess meekness and obedience," Alinor remarked with deliberate miscomprehension, her eyes sparkling with laughter. "And, you unnatural child, you should first consider the discomfort for your grandmother's rheumy knees in kneeling rather than that of Father Edgar's well-padded posterior."

"Rheumy knees!" Sybelle exclaimed. "There is nothing rheumy about your knees when you want to mount a horse. They only become rheumy for kneeling, which you detest."

"Did I not say she was unnatural?" Alinor complained to Ian. "Such disrespect for an aged and enfeebled grandmother!"

"There is nothing unnatural about it," Ian replied with mock gravity. "Were you not only now saying that her grandfather Simon was more honest than diplomatic? It is perfectly natural for Sybelle to have inherited that honesty."

"She also seems to have inherited his ability to divert me from my purpose," Alinor said wryly, but she put out her hand and touched her granddaughter affectionately. "But it will not do. If you wish to come to Wales with us, Sybelle, my love, you must at least be ready to say no at once. I am sure that if Walter sees you in the suggestive atmosphere of a wedding, he will be catapulted into a declaration."

And if he is not, Ian thought, *Alinor will arrange it,* but he said nothing. He, too, had noticed the varying color in Sybelle's face; he, too, liked Walter and thought the marriage would be most suitable. There would be time enough to interfere if he found that the pressure being put on Sybelle was making her unhappy. And Sybelle's answer to her grandmother's prodding confirmed his decision.

"I do not wish to say no," Sybelle admitted. "I know I must marry soon, and Walter is attractive to me, but . . . but I am not sure he will make a good husband."

In Hemel two days later, Sybelle's parents, Lord Geoffrey FitzWilliam and his wife, Lady Joanna, also were discussing the subject of Simon's marriage to Rhiannon. They had received both their daughter's letter, informing them that Ian and Alinor would attend the wedding, and Prince Llewelyn's invitation within an hour of each other.

It was just dusk and the torches along the walls of the great hall had already been lit. Hemel was old, and the narrow slit windows, deep-set into the thick walls, provided little light even on a sunny day. Covered with thin, scraped, oiled skins to keep out the worst of the wind and cold, the windows might just as well not have existed in a November dusk.

However, the lord's place by one of the great hearths was cozy enough. A huge fire roared and leapt in the fireplace, tall wrought-iron candlesticks holding fat candles of real beeswax gave light without smoke or stench, cushioned chairs provided comfortable seating, and carved footstools raised the feet above the drafts that swept along the floors. Nonetheless, many of the servants seated on stools or even on the thickly strewn rushes that covered the floors were more at ease than their master and mistress. Their lives, if not necessarily happy, were at least simple. They had only to obey; they were not troubled by divided loyalties or theoretical questions of right and wrong.

Joanna watched her husband anxiously. She knew the contents of the letters he had just read, and she wanted very much to see her half brother, Simon, married, for she loved him dearly. Because her mother had been as deeply involved in political affairs as her stepfather and usually traveled with him wherever he went, when Joanna was a girl she had often had the care of Roselynde and of Simon. He was as much eldest son as youngest brother in her heart.

Nonetheless, Joanna did not feel she could urge Geoffrey

to go to Wales. In the conflict that the Bishop of Winchester had engendered between the king and his barons, Geoffrey had been torn by divided loyalties. His every instinct—and his intelligence—bade him side with Richard Marshal, Earl of Pembroke, and uphold Magna Carta. However, Geoffrey was blood cousin to the king, although through two generations of illegitimacy. Even more important, Henry had been very good to Geoffrey.

Until the advent of Winchester, Geoffrey had been a trusted councillor, and he controlled many royal castles. Moreover, Henry had stubbornly resisted Winchester's desire to strip Geoffrey of his honors and holdings, despite the fact that Geoffrey had opposed Winchester's advice and Henry's fancies. The king's trust demanded loyalty, and Geoffrey had given that loyalty, however much it went against the grain for him.

Then came the debacle at Usk. Again against advice, not only of Geoffrey but of every baron knowledgeable in Welsh affairs, the king had listened to Winchester and had attacked Pembroke's keep at Usk with a mixed army of English levies and foreign mercenaries. But the attack had been doomed to failure even before it started. Raids by Prince Llewelyn's Welsh bands on the baggage train had destroyed siege instruments and deprived Henry's army of essential supplies of food and weapons. And the scorched-earth policy Richard Marshal had learned from his Welsh vassals had made it impossible for Henry's men to live off the land or to restore what had been lost, which precluded a protracted siege. Several direct assaults had been resisted with far greater loss to the king's army than to the defenders at Usk.

To save the king from retreating like a whipped cur with his tail between his legs and looking like an utter fool, a truce had been arranged. Pembroke yielded his castle on the terms that it would be returned in fifteen days, undamaged and with supplies intact, and that the king would then call a council in which the complaints of Pembroke, Gilbert Bassett, and other barons would be considered. Geoffrey, the Bishop of St. David's, and several other churchmen and noblemen had gone surety that the king would keep his word and Usk would be returned to Richard. Instead, a trap had been set to catch and imprison the earl for the "crime" of demanding that Henry obey the terms of the truce.

Richard escaped the trap, and Usk fell back into its master's hands with hardly a drop of blood shed. In fact, Pembroke could have demanded that the churchmen use their powers of excommunication against the king and that the noblemen who went surety bring their retainers and fight against the king's forces to regain Usk. But the earl did not go so far as that, although his craw was full of Henry's deceit and treachery. When Henry brought a second army to Wales to punish Richard for his "treachery and insolence," Richard agreed to a surprise attack on the king's encampment at Grosmont, which his ally Prince Llewelyn planned and led. The attack had stripped the king's army naked, although there was little bloodshed.

Because the Bishop of Winchester had alienated the whole barony of England, both by his sneers and his attack on Magna Carta, which defined their rights and privileges, few of the lesser vassals would respond to the levy called. Because they were either sureties for the fulfillment of the king's oath to the Earl of Pembroke, which absolutely precluded fighting against him, or were simply so disgusted with Henry's behavior that they would condone it no longer, most of the great vassals also refused to answer the levy.

Thus, the king's second army was made up almost exclusively of foreign mercenaries under captains from Poitou. The only exceptions were Roger Bigod, Earl of Norfolk, and William Longespee, Earl of Salisbury—Geoffrey's father. Roger Bigod's attendance was owing to a combination of youth, inexperience, a passionate love of fighting for the sheer joy of it, and the fact that he was the king's brother-by-marriage, having married Henry's sister Isabella. The Earl of Salisbury's presence was a different matter entirely, and it was owing to Geoffrey's father's presence at Grosmont that Joanna did not need to hint, even indirectly, that she would like to see Simon and Rhiannon married.

Geoffrey looked up from Prince Llewelyn's letter and met Joanna's anxious eyes. "Yes," he said, "we will go to the wedding." His lips were thin and bitter when he spoke.

There was a brief pause while Joanna continued to examine her husband's face. "You are always so good to me, Geoffrey," she said slowly. "I do wish to see Simon married; you know that. Nonetheless . . ."

Geoffrey uttered a mirthless bark of laughter. "There is nothing you would ask of me that I would not do, Joanna, but

I am not doing this for you. Partly I am doing it to give Henry and Winchester an additional fright. If they were honorable men themselves, they would know that I would do nothing and say nothing in Wales to their detriment, and therefore their hearts and minds would be at peace. However, they are such fools and so little believe in men's honor that they will doubtless think I intend treason because I go to see my brother-by-marriage wed."

"But will that not be dangerous?" Joanna asked.

Her husband's expression softened. "Do you mean to William and Ian? My love, you cannot think I would do a thing that would endanger my sons just to teach any man a lesson. The boys are at Oxford. We will take them with us. What could be more natural than that they should attend their uncle's wedding?"

First Joanna looked delighted, but almost immediately a thoughtful frown replaced the expression of pleasure. "Will that not be going a step too far—to take the boys without permission? You do not really wish to break with the king, do you?"

To Joanna's surprise, Geoffrey did not immediately assure her he would be faithful to his cousin the king. He acted as if he had not heard her questions. "How could I wait for permission and still come in time for the wedding?" he asked cynically in return. "I shall, of course, write to the king and explain what I have done." For a moment the bitterness disappeared from Geoffrey's face and his eyes glowed golden with mischief at the thought of Henry's probable reaction to such a letter, but the amusement did not linger. Still, his eyes did not dull but grew more brilliant with anger. "And I hope he flies into such a rage that he does cry treason. Let him come here and gnaw at Hemel's walls while Ian and Adam come at him from behind. Between us, we will—"

"Geoffrey . . ." Joanna leaned forward and placed a hand over his, which had formed into a clenched fist. "You know you do not mean that. And you know Henry will not cry treason unless you force him. For all his kicking and screaming like a spoiled infant, he loves you."

"Does he?" Geoffrey asked tightly. "Does he? It was only to spite me, to hurt me, that he ordered my father to lead his own men. Poor Papa, he is so crippled he can barely ride. It costs him such pain. . . . That was cruelty, naked cruelty!"

"But was it Henry's?" Joanna asked. She was grateful and relieved that the subject had come up in this natural way. She had tried several times to soothe Geoffrey's anguish, but he had, as was his unfortunate habit, closed his bitterness inside himself. "Henry is fond of your father," she continued. "To me, it appears more like a move Winchester might suggest, thinking that to spare your father you would violate the oath you made to Richard. And I will add this: I do not think it beyond Winchester's duplicity to have summoned your father on his own, telling him that he must speak and act as if his coming to the king was his own idea and desire."

"But why would Papa. . . . Oh, God! Very likely you are right, Joanna. Of course, that snake would have written to Papa and said that the king was greatly angered—which, I must say, must have been true—and that if Papa would come with his men, Henry would be appeased and do neither me nor my sons harm. Bishop! That one should be a bishop in Satan's church, not God's."

"Well," Joanna temporized, "we do not know which man was at fault, and very likely we will never know. Having given his word, your father will stick to it, buckle and thong, that it was his own idea—you will see."

Geoffrey nodded, his gaze abstracted. Plainly he was reconsidering his plans in a light less owing to a raging fury with the king. Watching his face, Joanna could have wept for joy. Ten years in age seemed to have lifted from him and an aeon of bitterness. Unlike Ian, Geoffrey was not suffused with love for all mankind—nor womankind, either. Geoffrey regarded humanity in general with a jaundiced eye, and he saw clearly the defects even of those he loved best. Nonetheless, those he loved, he loved hard, despite their imperfections. There were not many outside of his father and stepmother, their children, and his relations by marriage, but prominent among those were King Henry and Henry's brother, Richard of Cornwall.

If Geoffrey was often irritated by Henry's fits and starts, the enthusiasms that went too far, the way Henry pushed blame on others, and his occasional temper tantrums, he was also closest to the king in his love of music and art. Geoffrey truly appreciated the soaring cathedrals Henry was having built and the marvelous sculptures with which they were being decorated. Henry had made Geoffrey rich, and Geoffrey gave lavishly of those riches to the king's artistic pursuits—

men and money and his own labor to carry hods of stone on his back and set them in the mortar with his own hands. Geoffrey thought less of his soul and God at such times than he thought of pure beauty, but he felt God would forgive him.

In all the years, despite all the rages and petty spites that were characteristic of him, Henry had never done anything to hurt the cousin who shared his love of beauty. The fact that Henry had been cruel to his aged father had shocked Geoffrey and had shaken his faith in his friend and cousin. Thus, Geoffrey had reacted too strongly to the summoning of his father when he himself, who had acted as Salisbury's deputy for years, had refused to be part of the second unjust attack on the Earl of Pembroke.

Joanna had divined all of this. Geoffrey did not speak of it, but she knew him well. In fact, Joanna did not particularly believe what she had said about Winchester being at fault in the summoning of Geoffrey's father to war. She was not herself really fond of Henry. Had he been her child, he would have been taught to curb himself and apply himself to the business of kingship instead of designing cathedrals and admiring statues and pretty songs.

Nonetheless, she was well content with the suggestion that blamed Winchester, for it had lifted part of the burden of her husband's unhappiness. Joanna hoped that the country, or at least the government, would soon be rid of Winchester. The lack of success of Winchester's plans might easily make Henry turn on him. On the other hand, Henry might well be king for a very long time. If Geoffrey were going to bear a grudge, it had better be against Winchester than the king.

Her eyes dwelt on her husband fondly. At the moment Joanna felt only tenderness, but she was well aware that a turn of his head or a particular glance from his eyes could in a flash transform fondness into passion. Then, because she had thought of it, the warmth of desire flicked her, together with a sense of joy and gratitude that passion had lasted between them. As if she could not want him without his knowing it, Geoffrey looked at her. Immediately, Joanna's color rose; her skin was normally so white that even the most delicate flush was obvious. Knowing that her complexion had changed made it worse, of course; Joanna blushed harder and lowered her eyes.

Worry pricked Geoffrey when he first saw that Joanna was

blushing. Although she did not lie, it was not unknown to him that Joanna could bend the truth to suit her purposes with all, or more than, her mother's skill. He had wondered which part of what she had said to him should be subjected to severe examination, and then he had almost laughed. When Joanna shifted the emphasis on facts so that they added to a new and different sum, she always looked as innocent as an angel. It was then, as Joanna's eyes dropped, that Geoffrey connected the flush, the momentary unwillingness to meet his gaze, and Simon's wedding. All anxiety left his face, and he chuckled softly.

"I think I am going to enjoy this trip to Wales—if I survive," he teased. "If thinking of a wedding has this effect on you . . ." He rose suddenly and limped to the back of her chair—long step, short step—and put his hand on her neck. "We do not need to wait for the journey," he said, and the laughter was gone from his voice, which had deepened and thickened.

There was a palpable hesitation before Joanna shook her head slightly and tilted it back so that she could meet her husband's eyes. "They are setting up the tables for the evening meal already," she murmured.

"After the meal, then, O shamefaced maiden? And shall we go up separately to our chamber so that we do not shock the castlefolk?" Geoffrey was teasing again, but his lips were fuller than usual and his eyes were bright.

Joanna laughed. "After the meal," she agreed. "It would be too much to think of them all staring at the food on the tables and waiting for us." She lifted an eyebrow. "I do not like to be rushed."

"I promise not to do that," Geoffrey said softly, and ran his fingers over the back of her neck as he removed his hand.

CHAPTER 2

''Have you thought, my love,'' Geoffrey remarked lazily, ''that one wedding often makes another?''

Although it was common for each to sleep after making love, this time only a soft, pleasant languor had followed, despite rather violent climaxes for both. Geoffrey was lying on his back with his hands laced behind his head, staring upward at the elegant embroideries of the bed curtains. He could just make out the gleaming threads, red and gold against the blue background, because they had not pulled the curtains closed. Both liked to watch what they were doing during foreplay. Joanna's head rested on Geoffrey's bare breast, and she was idly pulling the sparse golden curls of his chest hair up through the thick masses of her own flaming red tresses, which trailed across his body. Both colors were muted in the candlelight.

''Walter de Clare is with Pembroke,'' Geoffrey continued, ''and Sybelle said in her letter that unless we had some objection, she would accompany Alinor and Ian. If Walter sees Sybelle in the atmosphere that will surround Simon and Rhiannon, it seems to me that he will offer for her.''

''I thought he would offer for her when we all met in London, early last month. When he did not, I wondered whether that quarrel they had over raiding the farms near Kingsclere had put him off. Sybelle has a temper and does not guard her tongue sufficiently when she is angry.''

While she was speaking, Joanna bent one of the curls on Geoffrey's chest over several strands of her own hair, making them prisoners. Sometimes Joanna still thought of love as a prison, although she did not now regret the deep joys, nor even the pains, of that imprisonment. Still, the thought of her daughter entering that prison disturbed her.

Clever as he was, Geoffrey had never divined this particular problem. He frowned, pulled his arms from behind his head, and pushed Joanna's face up so that he could see it. The movement freed all the strands of hair that she had interlaced, and she smiled. Then she sat up beside her husband to ease the strain that looking at him had put on her neck.

"He almost did offer, but you sound as if you were pleased that I stopped him," Geoffrey said. "Do you have some objection to him? I must accept *some* offer for Sybelle soon. She is already sixteen, and she should have been at least betrothed two years ago. My excuses are running thin."

"I have no objection at all," Joanna replied, "or, rather, only a mild reservation. I am not sure that Walter will accept our terms. They are . . . unusual."

"To say the least," Geoffrey agreed, grinning. "But they are a sure guide to a man's feelings. Any man who agrees to marry, knowing that his wife will hold her own lands during his lifetime, desires the woman, not the land or the wealth that comes from it."

"So my mother and I hope," Joanna said. "But I wonder whether Walter will understand that this is a real thing, not a polite fiction."

"If he does not know after Sybelle chased his men back to his camp, burned off his ears for his carelessness and inefficiency in controlling them, and threatened that if it happened again she would have out the entire garrison of Kingsclere and hang him, personally, by the heels, he is far stupider than I believe him to be."

"Not stupider," Joanna demurred, running a hand down Geoffrey's hard-muscled chest. "He wants her. One can see that in the way his eyes follow her and in the difficulty he has looking elsewhere when she is in the chamber. Men lie to themselves when they want something. They forget the thorns while reaching eagerly for the rose."

"Women, too," Geoffrey pointed out, imprisoning her hand in his own.

Her caress was beginning to excite him, which he suspected was her purpose, and he wanted this subject thrashed out once and for all. Of all the men who had hung round Sybelle, Geoffrey preferred Walter. Despite her words, he sensed Joanna's reluctance to apply the pressure he felt should be applied to Sybelle to make her agree to marry Walter.

Geoffrey loved his daughter and would not for a moment have considered forcing her into a marriage distasteful to her, but from what he had seen, Sybelle liked Walter. He and the rest of the family also liked Walter. His properties were situated in locations peculiarly satisfactory with respect to the family property as a whole, and since Sybelle had to marry someone, Geoffrey felt that she should be pushed in Walter's direction.

"Sybelle's letter does not mention Walter," Geoffrey continued, "but I cannot imagine Alinor did not tell her he would likely be at the wedding. If she did not wish to see him, she could have chosen to stay at Roselynde. I have the feeling that Sybelle wants Walter. Am I wrong?"

"No. I think she does want him," Joanna said slowly, "not from anything she has said but from the very fact that she has said nothing. You know her trick of ridiculing the young men who have courted her. She has never ridiculed Walter." She sighed. "I suppose you must consider seriously any offer he makes, but I wish he were younger."

"He is only twelve or fourteen years older than Sybelle," Geoffrey protested, "and scarcely an old man. And I feel strongly that it is partly his age that attracts her. I do, indeed, know the way she ridicules her younger suitors. The point is, there is nothing to ridicule in Walter. He is experienced enough not to give way to extravagant words or gestures."

"Yes." Joanna's voice was flat. "But that has another side. Sybelle will brook no infidelity. Will Walter understand that? He is fixed in a pattern of life, Geoffrey. That is why I said I wished he were younger. It will be hard for him to break his pattern. Sybelle is not, I hope, a jealous woman, but she must be first."

"I know about such unjealous women." Geoffrey chuckled. "What would I lose first if *I* were unfaithful—my head or my shaft, O wife without jealousy? Sybelle is not the only one who must be first. But why you should doubt that a man can change his pattern I do not know—look at Ian and Adam and Simon, too."

"It is not the same," Joanna said doubtfully. "Ian had always loved my mother, ever since he first saw her at seventeen. The women who came between, while my mother and father were married, were nothing. No one can expect a man who looked like Ian to be a celibate saint." A smile came to Joanna's lips. "Women would come near to wrestling him to the ground and raping him right in front of my mother's face. Before my father died, when Ian had no hope of gaining Mama, why should he have resisted? And Simon and Adam are different, too. They have been raised from childhood with Ian as their mentor. He drummed it into their heads that a man may play—indeed, that he should play—in his youth so that he will know what he wants in a wife and then be content only with her. You, too, my love, learned from Ian."

Geoffrey's mouth twisted with distaste. "I did not need his lessons. I had seen too much of the other side of the coin already at King John's court. But what makes you doubt that Walter knows what he wants? I will say to you plainly, my love, that if Sybelle is willing, I would welcome the match. And there is another advantage, also. We would not be swamped with an army of dubious relatives. The de Clares have had bad luck in this past generation. Walter is the last of the cadet branch, and there is no one in the senior branch except young Gloucester."

"That is a good thing," Joanna agreed readily, with a spark of enthusiasm. "All the lands are his, and he will have best claim to the earldom of Gloucester if something should happen to young Richard—God forbid it should, for he is a sweet boy. More important, I think Walter will cling to us. He is lonely for a hearth and home."

"Yes, which is another reason I think he *will* make a good husband to Sybelle," Geoffrey insisted. "And I do not think you need to fear that he will wander. She will know how to hold him once she has him—will she not, my love?"

"You are right," Joanna said with a little more confidence. Then she smiled and reached down and tickled Geoffrey in a very sensitive spot. "Or, if she does not, then it is your fault and you are different from other men. I could not teach my daughter what I did not know, and all I know I learned from you."

Geoffrey made no verbal response to his wife's challenge. He had a more interesting and exciting use for his mouth than talking, and, he thought, as he sighed with pleasure and felt Joanna shiver with delight, a better way of convincing his wife that the joys of marriage should not be longer withheld from Sybelle.

• • •

Although it was much closer to Builth, Prince Llewelyn's invitation did not reach Pembroke keep any sooner than it reached Hemel. This was because Richard Marshal had kept the letter for several days before sending it on to his wife, Gervase, with a covering letter of his own, ordering her to come to Brecon to meet him. Even if Richard had been at Pembroke keep himself, the wedding invitation would not have had the same effect on him and Gervase that it had on Geoffrey and Joanna. The truth was that Richard had little love, or even liking, for his wife.

Of course, Richard Marshal had not married for love; he had married the eldest daughter of Alan, Comte de Dinan and Vicomte de Rohan, for the lands and titles that would come to him on her father's death. However, Richard had married in good faith, intending to love and honor his wife as his father had loved and honored his mother. Unfortunately, Gervase was nothing at all like Isobel, late Countess of Pembroke. She was young and self-centered and had been raised in a different tradition than Richard's.

If Gervase had had a child, that might have drawn them together, for both desired children and they would have had some interest in common; however, Gervase miscarried several times, and that increased the tension between them. Soon they found each other's company so distasteful that chances for conception became few and far between. After several years, Gervase's father died, and the lands, as promised, came to Richard. This, however, only pushed the couple further apart. Gervase had expected some special recognition, a great celebration, a swearing of the vassals. But Richard took the lands in hand without reference to her at all—because he did not trust her.

Then the situation was exacerbated by the death of the husband of Gervase's sister, Marie de les Maures. Because the sisters' father was dead and they had no brothers, Marie became Richard's ward when her husband's younger brother, who had inherited her late husband's lands, stated firmly that he would not keep her. Perhaps if Richard could have done so, he would have fought for Marie's dower rights as she demanded.

Unfortunately, Richard's older brother William had died without heirs, and it was imperative that Richard go at once to England and take hold of the vast territories of *his* inheritance.

As it was, the delay caused by Marie's problems and by Gervase nearly precipitated a catastrophe. Hubert de Burgh, Chancellor of England, had seized Richard's lands in the name of the crown, and Richard had to threaten civil war before the lands were disgorged.

Naturally enough, this seemingly contemptuous dismissal of Marie's right to her dower property did not endear Richard to her. He had tried to make her understand that he was aware of the uncomfortable and unhappy situation of a portionless woman. He had assured her that she would not be, in fact, portionless, explaining that her property was so insignificant in comparison with that of the earldom of Pembroke that he would make up to her—for the present—in money or in purchased land what her brother-by-marriage had withheld. In the future, if he had time and resources, he would reclaim her property from les Maures.

Although Marie was not dissatisfied with this arrangement at first, she soon began to think of it as a deceitful trap. Richard had placed her and Gervase for safety in Pembroke keep, an isolated spot far away from the English court or, indeed, any social life. There they remained for something over two years. Marie began to believe that this was Richard's way of escaping his obligation to her; Gervase began to wonder whether she had been brought to a foreign country where no one knew her as a first step to disposing of her. Each sister fed the other's fear and discontent.

The truth, however, was far less dreadful. Richard had serious political troubles and had simply established the women where they could not be seized and used as hostages against him. After that, he had pushed the very minor and disagreeable problem out of his mind. He had used the brief halcyon period after he had been invested with the earldom of Pembroke to visit Ireland and see what his younger brother Gilbert was doing with the Irish estates. But hardly had Richard returned when Henry dismissed de Burgh as chancellor. After that, the Bishop of Winchester had been named chancellor and Richard's political troubles had multiplied in geometric progression, far too fast for him to give a thought to two women he did not like. Even if he had thought of Gervase and Marie, he could have done nothing for them. Soon he was, essentially, an outlaw. He had neither the contacts nor the money to satisfy their craving for brilliant social lives.

Late in 1233 the rebellion, of which Richard was the unwilling head, had changed from amorphous, uncoordinated, and sporadic attacks and had taken form. A definite treaty of alliance had been sworn between the Earl of Pembroke and Prince Llewelyn of Gwynedd, and their first concerted action had resulted in a brilliant victory for the combined Welsh-rebel force against the king's army at Grosmont. Stripped of weapons and supplies, the king's few English supporters had gone home in disgust, and the king, with his nearly helpless mercenary force, had retreated to Gloucester.

To Prince Llewelyn's mind, this was the moment to take accounts and make plans for the next stage of the campaign—and when Llewelyn took accounts, he took account of everything. The Earl of Pembroke might have forgotten that he had a wife, but Llewelyn had not forgotten. Thus, when he wrote an invitation to Richard for Simon's wedding to Rhiannon, he added a specific request—in the politest of terms—that Pembroke bring with him his wife, whom Llewelyn had never met, and, of course, any ladies she wished to have accompany her.

Richard had held the invitation for two days, trying to decide between the relative dangers of letting Gervase and Marie loose in the Welshman's court, where they were sure to offend half the people by their contemptuous attitude toward "barbarians," and the danger of rousing suspicions in Llewelyn's very untrusting mind by refusing to bring his womenfolk with him. At last Richard admitted to himself that bringing Gervase and Marie was definitely the lesser of the two evils. Having gone so far, honest man that he was, he acknowledged that he had only hesitated so long because of his reluctance to endure Gervase's nagging and Marie's whining.

When this unpalatable truth had been absorbed, Richard sat staring—as he thought—into space. However, his blind gaze had passed over the table on which he was leaning, crossed the width of the hall, and had really been fixed on Walter de Clare. After a few minutes, Walter became aware that Richard was looking at him, excused himself from the men with whom he had been talking, and came to ask what Richard wanted.

Jerked out of his unpleasant thoughts, Richard at once knew why his staring eyes had fastened on Walter. Walter was another problem, almost as unpleasant as Gervase and

Marie. Not that Walter nagged or whined—indeed, Richard was very fond of Walter and enjoyed his company—nonetheless, his presence at this time distressed the earl. Walter was an adherent who hurt Richard's too-delicate conscience.

In one way or another, all the men gathered under Richard's aegis had been injured or offended by the king or his ministers—barring, of course, the Welsh, who were allied for their own purposes. The Welsh, however, were not and never had been, except for special circumstances, King Henry's vassals. Walter was the king's vassal; moreover, he had suffered no injury that could justify his defiance of the king. Walter's attachment to Richard's cause was on purely theoretical grounds.

Richard's own rebellion also had a theoretical basis—that the king and Peter des Roches had violated the terms of Magna Carta, to which Henry had sworn. Nonetheless, the earl shrank from involving any other man who had not sustained personal injury for which restitution could be expected if the rebellion was successful. Walter's desire to join Pembroke was therefore a weight on the earl's heart, since the young man had everything to lose and nothing to gain. Thus far, Richard had successfully dissuaded Walter from crying defiance and forcing Henry to proscribe him. However, there would soon be more fighting, Richard knew. If that fighting took the form of an offensive against the king and Walter was involved in it, honor would make him formally abjure his fealty to Henry.

Suddenly, a solution to both problems leapt into Richard's mind. "Yes," he said to Walter, "I have a task for you. I do not know whether or not you will like it."

"I am yours to command," Walter assured him, somewhat puzzled by the qualification Richard had made.

The only thing Walter could think of that could make Richard speak of "liking" was an order to spy. Walter knew he was peculiarly well suited to such a task because he had free entrée into the household of the king's brother, Richard of Cornwall, who had married Walter's eldest brother's widow. Before Walter could think whether he could force himself to accept such a duty, however, Richard burst out laughing. Walter blinked. He knew Richard. A need to urge a companion into a dishonorable duty might wring tears from him, but never laughter.

"I have here," Richard chortled, pushing the parchment

across the table toward Walter, "an invitation—which amounts to an order—from Prince Llewelyn to bring my wife and her ladies to Simon de Vipont's wedding. I have held it two days, wondering which offense would be more deadly—to bring Gervase or not to bring her."

"What do you mean?" Walter asked, also smiling. Richard's obvious amusement made nonsense of the mention of deadly offense.

"I am half-serious," Richard said, sobering. "Obviously, I cannot refuse to bring my womenfolk to Builth. That would imply a distrust in Lord Llewelyn, which, in fact, I do not feel. On the other hand, Gervase and her sister, Marie, are very nice in their ways. They are accustomed to the formality and elegance of the French court, and I do fear that they will tend to sneer at Welsh manners and customs. Since bringing them is unavoidable, I would like you to go to Pembroke keep and escort them to Brecon, where I will meet you."

"Brecon?" Walter repeated, surprised. "Have you taken de Bohun's keep?"

"No, of course not," Richard replied. "Let us say it is lent to me, since it is too far from Hereford's other lands to be useful at this time. Thus, the lands do not suffer raiding. But about Gervase and Marie: If it is possible for you to impress them with the necessity of behaving with the greatest civility, I will bless you. If you cannot," Richard's voice was suddenly dry and hard, "I will not blame you. I know Gervase all too well. She is not always amenable to reason."

"I will do my best, my lord." Walter did not think it his place to question Richard's management of his personal affairs, but his doubt must have shown in either face or voice.

Richard smiled at him wryly. "You are wondering why I do not go myself, since there is no immediate expectation of action and, obviously, there will be no planning until I meet with Llewelyn again. You think it can only make my wife angrier and less willing to accommodate me if I send a stranger to escort her." He sighed. "We are far beyond that. If I ask Gervase to mind her manners, she will only take offense."

Walter opened his mouth and then closed it again. If Richard was in the habit of telling his wife to mind her manners when she was a woman accustomed to court life, it was not surprising that she lost her temper.

Unaware of what he had betrayed about himself, Richard continued conscientiously, "I do not mean to say that Gervase or Marie—Marie de les Maures, a widow in my ward, my wife's sister—are shrews or . . . or not good women. Doubtless our disagreements are as much my fault as theirs. They are unhappy immured in Pembroke keep, but I could not take the chance that they would be seized by the king. Perhaps this chance to visit Builth will relieve the tedium for them."

Pembroke stopped speaking awkwardly, and Walter hastened to ease him by assuring him he would be glad to act as escort for Lady Pembroke and Lady Marie. The earl shrugged and sighed.

"I am grateful to you," he said. "I only hope Gervase and Marie do not take some fancy and decide to punish you for my sins. I will write to Gervase—"

"Please, my lord," Walter interrupted with more haste than diplomacy, "do not say any more about me than that you have bidden me escort them and have confidence in my ability to do so safely."

Richard looked at him, then shrugged again and agreed. He was no fool and realized that Walter felt his attempt to smooth the path would do more harm than good. Probably it would, he acknowledged, but he could not understand why, beyond the fact that the women seemed to be totally irrational and unreasonable. Richard heaved a great sigh of relief. He would be spared at least a week of Gervase's company, and Walter would be safely out of mischief for at least two weeks.

CHAPTER 3

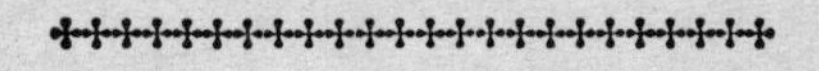

The next morning, at first light, Walter led his troop west. Despite Richard's warnings, he was pleased with his errand. It was a relief to have something that demanded his immediate attention, for Walter had two personal problems that had occupied his mind fruitlessly and somewhat painfully for many weeks.

The first of these was the lands that he had inherited upon the death of his brother Henry seven months earlier. There was a question of whether or not the lands were his. Walter had loathed his brother and thus had never visited him, so he knew virtually nothing of the estates or the castellans who held them. Moreover, Henry had died rather mysteriously, shot by an arrow during a hunt attended by all those castellans—every one of whom swore that the others had been visible to him and therefore innocent of the shooting of their overlord.

Since Walter was no novice at hunting, he knew that it was most unlikely indeed that all the men should have been in sight of each other while engaged in the chase. Conversely, at any other time there was no reason to loose an arrow. There was nothing Walter could do about *that* problem, however, since the king had been at Gloucester at the time, holding his Easter court, and had already accepted the testimony of the castellans. Nor, to speak the truth, was Walter eager to prosecute his brother's murderer—if Henry's death had not been an accident—since he was quite sure Henry had deserved death ten times over.

Walter's real problem lay in the delicate political situation and the fact that he had no way to enforce his overlordship if the castellans wished to resist him. His own estate of Goldcliff, inherited from his mother, was small and could supply neither enough men nor sufficient gold to hire an army with which to conquer any castellan who defied him.

Under the circumstances, Walter had done no more than send letters to the castellans of Foy, Barbury, Thornbury, and Knight's Tower announcing that he had succeeded to his brother's honors. He had not appointed any time for the men to do homage, nor had he suggested making any visit to the strongholds that were technically his. Thus, although he had not taken possession, neither had he provoked the castellans into rejecting him. Walter would not mind at all if they did—once he had a strong enough force to smash them immediately upon refusal. He did not particularly wish to avoid battle; all he wished to avoid was the appearance of pettishly demanding what he had no power to seize at his will.

Walter also wished to keep his dealings with his brother's castellans a private matter. He did not want to owe his control of his property to the favor of the king or even to men he trusted far more, like Richard of Cornwall or the Earl of Pembroke. But this was no problem. All he needed to do was to marry into a family powerful enough to provide him with the strength to overawe or, better, overpower the castellans. Since the marriage would be a blood bond, there could be no question of favors given or received.

There was no need to search his mind for a suitable family, either. Walter had been squire to William Marshal, the previous Earl of Pembroke, when Simon de Vipont came as a page to the household. Everyone loved Simon; it was impossible not to do so—except during the frequent times when one wished to kill him for some outrageous piece of mischief. But even the mischief was loving and harmless, a result of liveliness and good humor rather than spite, so one forgave Simon readily. Nonetheless, he had to be punished, and as senior squire, Walter was often the instrument of that punishment. Yet, despite this and all the castlefolk to choose from, Simon had attached himself to Walter.

A natural result of Simon's predilection for Walter's company was that Walter had heard a great deal about Simon's home and family. At the time, Walter had paid the tales little heed, but they had left a deeper impression on his mind than he realized. When the successive deaths of his parents and his eldest brother had stripped him of a family—since he did not consider any closer relationship with his brother Henry than was forced on him—Walter had often thought of the turbulent but happy and loving Roselynde clan Simon had described. Still, he had no claim on them, and Walter believed a man with one small, unprofitable estate on the south coast of Wales could not present himself as a suitor to a daughter of that wealthy and powerful family.

His brother's death had changed Walter's status. If he could take hold of the estates, he would be a good match for any woman in England. Conversely, with the backing of the Roselynde clan, no castellan in his right mind would stand out against him. However, Walter was not prepared to take a girl sight unseen for the sake of profit. Nor did he know whether there was a suitable girl available, and he was not willing to wait five or ten years for a girl to grow to marriageable age. He wanted a hearth and home he could call his own.

Thus, within weeks of his brother's death, Walter had presented himself to Simon's parents as a friend of their son's. He was warmly welcomed, since Simon had been as free with talk of Walter de Clare at home as he had been with talk of home to Walter. Any faint doubts that Walter had about Simon's tales representing an idealized family picture painted by homesickness were instantly put to rest. The picture sprang to life, and it was true as gold.

Now, what Walter had intended was to investigate delicately whether he would be acceptable to the family and whether they had a marriageable girl uncontracted—and then he had seen Sybelle. That he did not offer for Sybelle within five minutes of his first sight of her was because there was no one to whom he could present such an offer. Neither of Sybelle's parents was in Roselynde keep, and that check reminded Walter that he could not make an offer anyway until he had stated clearly what his own situation was.

Unless he explained to Sybelle's father that his side of the bargain might be worthless, he could not ask for an alliance. But having started to think about a possible marriage, Walter immediately began to suspect his own impulsiveness. Desire stimulated by great beauty was not, in Walter's opinion, a sound basis for marriage. It would be necessary, he told himself, to determine Sybelle's character and her fitness to be his wife. Walter lingered for several weeks in Roselynde keep, spending as much time as possible with Sybelle.

It took that long for the gentle amusement of his host and

hostess to penetrate Walter's preoccupation with their granddaughter. Lord Ian and Lady Alinor had been very polite. They had patiently repeated questions or remarks he had not heard while his eyes or thoughts were fixed on his lodestar, and they had never laughed at him—at least, not in his presence—although sometimes there had been a certain rigidity in their expressions or a rather choked quality in their voices. Of course, it was not until after Walter had realized he was head over heels in love and had promptly removed himself from Roselynde that he also recognized the symptoms of Ian's and Alinor's amusement and associated it with his premature courtship of Sybelle.

The immediate retreat was necessary because Walter could not, in honor, court Sybelle before he had her father's permission to do so, even if her grandparents' attitude had given tacit permission. Although Walter knew he had not said a word or made a gesture that overtly indicated or invited love, he was neither such a knave nor such a fool as to believe that overt words or actions were necessary. All he could do was leave Roselynde in haste and hope the aura of longing he now realized he must have been displaying had not affected Sybelle. It would be a quite dreadful crime to engage a girl's affections and then discover that her father did not approve the match.

Walter blamed himself bitterly for carelessness and stupidity. He could not imagine why it had taken him so long to realize how deeply he was entangled, or that he might be entangling Sybelle. It was ridiculous that he had not recognized what he felt to be love, but after he had mentally subtracted his violent sexual craving from his feelings, it seemed to him that only a pleasant friendliness remained. True, his loins tightened and heated every time he laid eyes on Sybelle, or, for that matter, every time he thought of her, but that had happened to him with other women.

Certainly, he felt none of the symptoms celebrated so widely in songs and poems and romantic tales. Not once had he felt faint or unable to speak or felt himself in the presence of a being infinitely above him. He enjoyed Sybelle's company enormously; she was the most rational girl he had ever met and was most eager to talk about sensible things, like land management and cattle breeding. And it was true that he was aware of missing her when she was not present, but there were no fierce pangs such as those fictional lovers experienced.

Actually, Walter wondered how long it would have taken him to realize how deeply he was in love if Lady Alinor had not jestingly spoken of Sybelle as being already past her first ripeness as a marriageable maid. Walter's immediate reaction, a mingling of rage and terror at the thought that Lord Geoffrey might, at that very moment, be making a contract for his daughter, removed the scales from Walter's eyes.

He left Roselynde the next day, saying nothing beyond farewell to Sybelle, although he told Lord Ian that he was going to Hemel. Unfortunately, Geoffrey was not there, but had joined the king. Walter followed, knowing he would be welcome to lodge with Richard of Cornwall. He reached Oxford just in time for the abortive council of 24 June and was horrified to learn how much the political situation had degenerated while he was idling away the weeks at Roselynde. As the danger of a violent breach between the king and his barons became clear, a bitter struggle ensued between Walter's desire for Sybelle and his knowledge that his common sense, ties of affection, and bonds of honor all placed him strongly in support of the Earl of Pembroke and against the king.

Lord Geoffrey's obvious dissatisfaction with the king's behavior emboldened Walter to go so far as explaining his problems about taking his lands in hand. Geoffrey agreed that he had done the right thing and that it would be wise to make no further move until the present crisis was over. But Geoffrey was clearly interested, and Walter's hopes rose. He therefore gave a very painstaking delineation of his properties and what they would be worth. Tactfully, Geoffrey did not laugh. He was aware of Walter's sojourn in Roselynde and of Sybelle's catastrophic impact on him. Lady Alinor had written very picturesque letters.

However, when Walter went on to describe his political position, Geoffrey drew back somewhat. He did not, as Walter had hoped, encourage him to make the offer for Sybelle that was trembling on his lips. Instead, Geoffrey made it clear that however little he approved of the king's actions, however strongly he would advise Henry to come to terms with the Earl of Pembroke, if a break between them came, Geoffrey would side with the king.

Nonetheless, Geoffrey had not been able to resist completely the pleading in Walter's eyes. Although he had said that this was no time for talk of marriage alliances, he had also made it clear that he welcomed Walter's friendship regardless of the political differences they might have in the future. On the one hand, that prevented Walter from making any offer, but on the other, it had implied that Geoffrey would not entertain any other man's offer for Sybelle, either.

Unfortunately, the crisis did not dissipate in a spate of harsh words and subsequent reconciliations, as Walter had hoped. Nor, no matter how hard he tried, could Walter convince himself that the oath he had sworn to the king when he was invested with his lands was more binding and important than the principle the Earl of Pembroke had espoused. In fact, Walter did not have the lands. Walter knew where his duty lay, and with much pain he put aside his desire for Sybelle to do it. He offered his own sword and the men of Goldcliff—all he had—to Richard Marshal.

Richard did not refuse him, but he urged caution and, if possible, the avoidance of an open break with the king. The fewer men for whom he had to bargain with Henry, Richard pointed out, the easier it would be to make peace. He suggested that Walter play a defensive role, that he help protect the properties of proscribed men against the attacks of opportunists who went about looting for profit, even though they claimed to act in the king's name. Walter's heart leapt with joy. He could not offer for Sybelle because there was still danger that the king would proscribe him without overt offense on his part, but until that happened, he could visit Sybelle's family and, if she happened to be there, see her.

There were, in fact, several meetings. Walter found occasion to visit Hemel after the council called for 9 July, for which the entire upper nobility was absent to show its displeasure with the king's actions and with the ministers he had chosen. And in August, at third summoning, when a trap was laid for Richard from which he barely escaped, Walter saw Sybelle in Oxford. Those meetings were not of unalloyed pleasure. Walter found that Sybelle was as deeply interested in politics as in estate management.

In addition, Walter discovered that the men of the Roselynde clan allowed their women unusual freedoms. Sybelle spoke her mind in no uncertain terms, and her father, uncles, and grandfather not only permitted it without correction but listened and responded just as if she were a man. If they rejected her arguments, which was surprisingly infrequent, it was not on the grounds that it was not her business to speak at all or that the arguments were womanish nonsense, but because she was young and had insufficient experience in the subject. Most shocking of all was that Walter had to admit to himself that, for the most part, Sybelle spoke as good or better sense than any man.

Walter was badly shaken by this experience. It was outside what he had always accepted as normal behavior. No woman he had known ever joined, unasked, a political discussion in a room full of men. However, this shock was nothing compared with the next one he received.

The king's contemplated treachery against the Earl of Pembroke, whether or not it was inspired by the Bishop of Winchester, had ended any expectations of a peaceful solution to the crisis. Disorder multiplied as dishonest men used the excuse of the proscriptions to attack and loot anything they desired. Walter was engaged in protecting some outlying farms east of Upavon. There were men in the district who, while they would not support Pembroke's adherents openly, were sufficiently sympathetic to his purposes to give aid in terms of supplies of food, firewood, and similar items. Thus, Walter had sent out several small troops to obtain these commodities.

Unfortunately, one of the troops decided to engage in a little free enterprise. Instead of merely taking what was freely given by allies, they ranged even farther east to see what they could pick up for themselves. In so doing, they first killed a sheep and then buffeted the shepherd who protested. Then they headed for the richest nearby farm. The men were not native to the area, of course, and did not know they had infringed upon Kingsclere territory.

By the time they had invaded the farmhouse and stolen whatever trinkets and plate the bailiff's wife had, the shepherd had cried warning. The garrison rode out of Kingsclere keep, but the band had already met a severe check. Sybelle, with ten men-at-arms to protect her, had been inspecting the crop of wheat only a few fields away. She and her men naturally came charging to the rescue as soon as they heard of the disturbance.

Her troop would have been satisfied with driving away the invaders, for they were slightly outnumbered and their first concern was, of course, the safety of their lady. However, with the arrival of the men from the castle, Sybelle decided to catch the malefactors so that she could force them to disgorge what they had stolen and then hang them in chains at various places to warn other thieves. Thus, she ordered the troop to follow at all speed.

Knowing what lay in store for them if they were caught, Walter's men fled more directly than they had come, hoping to elude their pursuers or to reach their master and explain their "mistake" so that he would protect them. They were not able to achieve either aim completely. Although they were not caught, they did not outdistance Sybelle and her men sufficiently either to escape or to explain. The troop from Kingsclere came thundering into Walter's camp hard on the heels of the malefactors. It was very fortunate for everyone (except Walter himself) that Sybelle recognized the de Clare colors and that Walter's master-at-arms, Dai of Goldcliff, knew Sybelle and came rushing forward to ask what was wrong. At least a pitched battle between the two groups was avoided.

Walter, who had been out all night fighting off a raid to the north, came stumbling from his tent half-naked and half-awake, and, most unfortunately, the woman who had been with him darted out also, whimpering with fear, looking for a place to hide. What Sybelle said after that was neither delicate nor civil—nor was it true in a general way that Walter was so wrapped up in his lecheries that he had no time to give to overseeing his men. What was true was that Walter had turned a blind eye to small infringements here and there on the property of men faithful to the king. Perhaps he should have delineated more specifically what was forbidden territory, but it was certainly not lechery that had caused him to overlook giving the instructions.

Having disgorged her spleen on Walter, Sybelle realized she could not demand the hanging of twelve or fifteen trained men-at-arms who might be needed for serious business. Properly corrected, such men would not again violate Kingsclere property; they were not masterless rogues and could be controlled. Thus, Sybelle looked down her nose at Walter, who could believe neither his eyes nor his ears and stood, perfectly mute, staring at the goddess of wrath who was castigating him. Then she demanded forcefully that the stolen goods be returned.

"I will leave the punishment of the men in your hands," she added coldly, "although God knows whether you are honest enough, or even competent enough, to manage so simple a matter."

"What are you doing here?" Walter finally managed to get out.

"Protecting my property from my enemies—and, it seems, also from so-called friends, who cannot control their henchmen because they are too busy futtering whores."

But Walter was incapable of reacting to this new insult. He was still too stunned to see Sybelle apparently leading a troop of armed men into battle. "Here! I mean, what are you doing in the midst of an armed troop? Why are you not safe inside some keep?"

"Are you going to return my property?" Sybelle asked indignantly. "It is none of your affair what I do in defense of my land. Must I order my men to fight for what is ours? You, at least, seem ill-prepared to retain your men's ill-gotten gains by force."

This was all too true, as Walter was clutching a loose, unbelted bedrobe about himself with one hand and holding his sword in the other. If Sybelle had not seen the woman, she might have explained that her presence with the men was an accident, a combination of having been caught up in the excitement of the chase and not wanting to cause any delay in the pursuit by ordering part of the troop to turn back with her. As it was, a fury for which she had no explanation made her foolishly act as if what she had done was normal, and, of course, knowing that what she was doing was foolish only made her more furious.

Sybelle's diatribe finally penetrated Walter's bemusement. Suddenly realizing how ridiculous he must look, Walter growled, "See to it, Dai, that the goods are returned, and round up the men and bring them before me." After which he stalked away, stiff with rage.

It was fortunate for Walter's men that their master had a fine sense of humor and that the youngest of three brothers does not long retain an exaggerated sense of his own importance in the world. By the time Dai had determined which of the men had been on the patrol that went astray, wrested their loot from them, and returned the items to a few of Sybelle's men who had waited for that purpose, Walter had passed from a fury of embarrassment to an impersonal appreciation of the ridiculousness of the situation. Thus, he did not have the erring men tortured to death or hanged, as he might have done in his first rage. Each man was punished with fifty lashes, the leader of the troop with one hundred, and everyone was satisfied with the justice done.

Still later, Walter found himself roaring with laughter when he reviewed the picture of himself standing like a stick of wood and gaping as Sybelle told him his duty. It was funny, Walter realized, even if the joke was at his expense. Simultaneously, however, he was shocked—not at Sybelle's language, although that was far beyond what a well-bred maiden should know, let alone use—but by the fact that she had accompanied the men, seemed quite ready to see battle joined, and had told him his duty with all the assurance of his old master. It was unwomanly, that boldness and assurance. But most shocking of all was that Walter realized at least half of his inability to reply to Sybelle had been caused by the intensity of his joy and desire upon seeing her so unexpectedly.

Walter began to suspect that marriage to Sybelle would not be as simple as he had assumed. He could not believe her merely a shrew. He had spent enough time in her company and seen her demeanor toward servants and serfs in her grandparents' keep. She was loved and respected, not feared. And she had been very angry when she lashed out at him. However, it was not the temper that disturbed Walter. It was the air of command and the fact that he had found himself desiring her just as hotly as ever—hotly enough so that he did not dare relax his grip on his bedrobe—when he should have been disgusted by her behavior.

The personal contretemps had been swiftly submerged in the total breakdown of any hope of a quick solution to the rebellion when the king broke his oath concerning the return of Usk to the Earl of Pembroke. In the tense anxiety that followed, with the specter of a bloody and interminable civil war hanging over their heads, Sybelle and Walter's quarrel was thrust into the background. For Sybelle, the quarrel itself was easily forgotten—all except the woman who had fled Walter's tent. He, too, could have put the matter out of his mind completely, except that Sybelle's masterful contributions to all political discussions in her father's house continued to remind him of the incident.

CHAPTER 4

Had Walter gone one step further in his talks with Geoffrey so that he felt himself committed, he would have suffered much less. Once oath-bound to do so, Walter would have taken a serpent to his bosom and tried to make the best of it. For that matter, had Sybelle shown the smallest sign that she expected him to make an offer for her, he would have been equally committed, accepted her for whatever she was, and blamed himself for carelessness if he were not content. But neither of these obligations bound him. He knew he was perfectly free to advance or retreat.

Needless to say, every moment that military duty did not occupy his mind, Walter debated the question. His desire for Sybelle grew no less because of separation. He had never before come across a woman who both excited and contented him in the same way; however, he did not dare allow himself to ignore the aspects of her personality that disturbed him.

Nor could there be any question of breaking Sybelle to his will—not without contemplating war with the Roselynde clan. One blow on that pretty face that Sybelle herself did not accept as just correction would bring Simon roaring out of Wales, Adam thundering up from Sussex, Geoffrey flashing down from Hemel, and even Ian riding forth with all of Roselynde's strength in his tail. Not that Walter wished to beat and torture his wife into total submission, but he felt it dangerous not to consider the catastrophe that could ensue from any misunderstanding between himself and Sybelle. Unfortunately, thinking about how unwise it would be to marry her only made him want her more.

Under the circumstances, Walter was delighted with Richard's commission to fetch his wife and sister-by-marriage from Pembroke keep and bring them to Brecon. Naturally, ever since Walter had heard of Simon's wedding, utter turmoil had raged behind his quiet face. A series of impractical notions that seemed to offer a hope of seeing Sybelle sooner continually invaded his thoughts. By removing the possibility, some of Walter's unrest was soothed, and the need to devise a polite way of telling Lady Gervase she must not insult Prince Llewelyn or his clansmen completed the calming process. It was an interesting challenge, and Walter was feeling quite cheerful when he arrived at Pembroke keep.

Set in rather low-lying lands, the great round tower, some seventy-five feet high, could be seen for leagues. It served as a warning from afar, and the remainder of the castle fulfilled that threat. A stone wall strengthened by large semicircular towers had been thrown completely across a narrow spit of rock that protruded between the two small rivers that emptied into the harbor.

The town crouched at the foot of these walls. From a distance through the gray pall of rain, it looked a poor, muddy place, but as Walter rode through, he saw that the houses were better built and more commodious than one would have expected so far to the west. In fact, near at hand, Pembroke town had a smug look to it, almost like a fat, insolent steward who knows himself to be essential to his master and thus protected.

Owing to normal Welsh weather, Walter arrived wet and muddy; and owing to the fact that the servants in Pembroke were devoted to their master and not given to great formality, Walter had been brought to Gervase without a moment's delay when he identified himself as Richard's messenger. The combination made the challenge Walter faced even greater, since he appeared dirty and bedraggled before the ladies, scarcely the image of an elegant courtier. The initial meeting also gave Walter considerable sympathy with Richard's attitude toward his wife.

There was nothing charming about Lady Pembroke's manner, although the picture she made, seated at the exact distance from the fireplace to obtain the best warmth, playing a board game with her sister, was most attractive. Gervase was dark, plump, and pretty. Walter was able to identify her immediately because her gown, gold on rose with a trim of ermine, and her wimple, embroidered and bejeweled headdress, and ring-laden hands were finer than her sister's. Moreover, Gervase's manner was higher. She waved Walter to a halt and bade a decently dressed maidservant bring her the letters, as if closer contact with Walter would somehow contaminate her.

Walter hardly noticed the rudeness. His eyes had passed naturally from the elder sister to the younger, had settled for a moment, and then politely moved away—but Marie's image remained. She was—Walter's mind hesitated and then chose the word—delicious. Marie, too, was dark, but a rosy rather than an olive brunette, with a heart-shaped face, large black eyes, a delicate nose, and very small, very red, pouting lips that somehow seemed appropriate for her lush body. She had flashed Walter one provocative sidelong glance from under long, lowered lashes before looking at the letter her sister held.

Having examined both her husband's letter and Llewelyn's invitation without asking Walter to sit down or offering him dry clothing or refreshment, Gervase turned to her sister. "We are to be let out of prison for a few days," she announced caustically. "Apparently we are summoned to some kind of primitive rite among the natives. Not invited, mind you, *summoned.*"

But Marie had been examining the invitation Gervase still held in her hand. She could not read the words from where she sat, but she could see the quality of the parchment, the elegant lines of the scribe's handwriting, and the fact that the broken pieces of seal, which still dangled from the cord, were flecked with gold. Gervase was furious and spiteful, but Marie was quite sure that the invitation her sister held did not come from any primitive.

Marie smiled at Walter, turning her head so that Gervase would not see. Until she was safely out of Pembroke keep, Marie was not going to take the risk of annoying her sister. Gervase would not be above leaving her behind for spite; however, neither was Marie going to miss the chance of ingratiating herself with Richard's messenger, who might be a mine of information.

"And who are you?" Gervase asked of the patiently waiting Walter.

"My name is Walter de Clare, madame," Walter replied quietly, concealing his amusement. Spiteful court ladies were part of his experience; he knew what to do about them—and he had seen Marie's smile.

"Are you an escort or a warden?" Gervase queried nastily.

"An escort, I assure you, Lady Pembroke. My purpose is to see to your safety and comfort."

"And if I do not choose to go?"

Gervase's challenge was clear, but Walter would not respond with pleas or explanations of why it was necessary to her husband's purpose, nor did he offer threats. He recognized the pettish challenge as worthless, an attempt to make him fearful or uncomfortable to ease Gervase's own helpless frustration. It was clear enough to Walter that Gervase would have attended a dung-throwing contest so long as it would take her out of Pembroke keep.

"I have neither instructions nor authority to enforce your coming to Brecon and Builth," Walter said calmly. "If you do not choose to go, you need not. I will be sorry for it because you will miss an interesting spectacle. Any celebration conducted under Prince Llewelyn's auspices is bound to be most entertaining."

"Prince!" Gervase exclaimed contemptuously. "Prince of what? Five scabby sheep, barren mountains, and a few naked savages?"

Walter dropped his eyes to conceal their expression. His branch of the de Clare family had lived with and fought against the Welsh of the Marches for nearly two hundred years. Other Englishmen might think the same as Gervase did, but Walter knew better. The Welsh were a poor people, that was true, and many lived in the old way by hunting and gathering, their wealth concentrated in the herds of cattle and sheep that grazed nomadically over certain areas; however, the upper classes were no more savages than those of England or France. Still, Walter's expression did not change, despite his growing irritation.

"You will find some of the guests have different manners and customs, I daresay," Walter remarked, "but others will be English. It is possible that King Henry's cousin Lord Geoffrey FitzWilliam will come, since the groom is his brother-by-marriage."

The bait was just what should draw such a woman as Gervase, Walter knew, but he felt a warm stirring within him that had nothing to do with the interest she could not hide. Sybelle, he realized, would come with her family. And then he felt vaguely guilty about how attractive he was finding Marie. Distracted by this thought, it took Walter a moment to feel surprise because there were no exclamations of amazement or disbelief. Marie, who had been examining the letters Gervase had laid down, suddenly jumped to her feet and began to whisper into Gervase's ear.

The interlude gave Walter time to realize that these women knew nothing of the political situation; possibly they had no idea that there was a war in progress. He wondered whether to tell them, then decided he had better not do so, at least, not immediately. In her present mood, Gervase was likely to refuse out of hand to go if she hoped her refusal would do her husband political damage. And Walter did not know her well enough to be able to guess whether she would later reconsider, knowing that whatever damaged Richard must damage her, or whether she were so foolish or stubborn that she would cut off her nose to spite her face.

Walter was prepared to answer more questions, but did not expect the one that came next. After picking up Richard's letter and studying it again, Gervase laid it down once more and stared at him with knitted brows. At last she asked, "Are you uncle to the Earl of Gloucester?"

"Yes," Walter said, wondering what relevance his relationship to poor little Richard of Gloucester could have.

"My dear man," Gervase cried, getting up and coming toward him while Marie rang a little handbell to summon more servants, "why did you not say so? And why are you running Richard's errands?"

Walter could think of no sensible answer to the first question at all. Did the woman expect him to march into the hall, crying, *I am Richard of Gloucester's uncle?* And of what value was his relationship with a helpless boy, whose estates were in the king's hands? Later, Walter realized that it was his birth in a titled family that had made the difference to Gervase, but at the time his attention was fixed on her second question, which he knew well how to answer so as best to forward his purposes.

He smiled, lifted his brows, and said, "Surely you must know why I came? Is it not plain that I greatly desired to meet you? Perhaps England is the end of the world, but we are not so far from the center as to be ignorant of your reputation, Lady Gervase."

This gross flattery went down very well. Although she did not reply to it directly, Gervase immediately busied herself with giving orders for Walter's comfort, scolding the maids as if it was by their failure that his cloak had not been removed, nor a bath and dry clothing prepared for him. Walter had a bad moment wondering whether he had gone too far in his admiring looks so that the lady would offer herself to him. It would not be the first time it had happened, but to Walter, the wife of a friend, no matter how immoral herself, was sacred. However, there was no need for anxiety. To his delight, it was Marie who accompanied him to the prepared chamber. Unfortunately she did not stay. Despite a smile as provocative as her earlier glance, she only gave instructions to the elderly—and very ugly—maidservant who bathed him and helped him to dress.

When Walter rejoined the ladies—clean, dry, shaved, and with his hair neatly combed—he found a supper laid beside the fire. He was invited most graciously to join his hostess and her sister, and he gave them his most graceful bow as he accepted with thanks. It was very clear that he was approved, and nothing could have been pleasanter than Gervase's demeanor. Walter had to remind himself sharply of her discourtesy only a few hours earlier.

After the meaningless compliments and stock phrases of greeting and thanks had been exchanged, Walter was prepared to satisfy the curiosity he was sure his hostesses felt concerning the wedding. However, he was wrong again. All the questions were about himself—whether he was married and what property he held. Walter was astonished, but he felt the ladies might think it polite to flatter him by showing interest in him.

Also, it was his duty to keep Lady Gervase in a good humor so he could convince her to be polite at the Welsh court. Therefore, he answered their questions fully except on one subject. He did not mention his hopes of obtaining Sybelle as his wife because he had no right to do so; however, he told them the whole tale of his inheritance, forgetting until after he mentioned the war that he had not meant to speak of it. Then he braced himself for cries of horror and fearful questions about the conflict with the king in which Richard was engaged, but no anxiety appeared on Gervase's face, and Marie looked at him as if she found his face more interesting than his words.

"You mean that although you do not now control the

lands, they *are* yours," Gervase said. "There is no question of contested ownership, for instance, from the Earl of Gloucester?"

"Richard is only a boy," Walter replied automatically, wondering if perhaps Gervase and Marie had somehow not heard what he said about the war. "Gloucester has no power to contest my ownership, and, besides, he never would. He loves me and is of a singularly sweet nature. Yes, the lands are mine, but one does not, in such times as these, simply ride up to a keep and say one is its overlord. No, that is not true. There are many castellans who would honor their oaths, but not, I fear, my brother's men. At least . . . perhaps I missay them. In any case, my affairs can wait."

"Why?" Marie asked.

"The whole realm is in turmoil," Walter pointed out patiently. "I do not wish to add to that."

"But if you came with a strong army," Gervase persisted, ignoring what Walter had just said, "and took the keeps, they would be yours. Am I correct?"

"Yes," Walter agreed, again mechanically.

It had by now occurred to him that Gervase and Marie *had* known about the war; it was simply of no interest to them—so they ignored it! Walter was stunned by this attitude, since if Richard were defeated, their situation would surely be very difficult. And then he realized that to Gervase, anyway, it might not seem that way. Nothing that happened to Richard would affect her property in France. She probably believed she could simply go back there. Perhaps she even wished for it.

That thought ran into another. There could be no doubt that Richard did not desire Gervase's company. Then why had he brought her to England? Because he could not trust her alone in France? Walter told himself it was not his business. His business was to pacify Gervase so that she would not offend Llewelyn. That was the duty Richard had laid upon him, and he must perform it without regard to his feelings about the woman.

Walter smiled. "Well," he continued, "the lands would be mine if the leader of the army does not decide to keep for himself what he had won for me."

"Richard would not do that," Gervase said. "You may

trust him, I assure you. Was that why you did not ask his help? Because you did not trust him?"

Walter just stared. He could not believe his ears. Twice he had said a war was in progress and that his affairs were relatively unimportant. Did this silly goose believe that it would ever have crossed his mind to ask Richard to divert his army—or any part of it—from his own defense to overawing castellans? Even setting aside the catastrophic political effect of bringing a rebel army into parts of England that were at peace, the notion was ridiculous.

As if she believed that Walter was unconvinced about Richard's trustworthiness, Marie put a hand on his arm—but the impression Walter received was that she wished to touch him. "Really, Richard is most honest," she urged. "We are not truly prisoners here. That was just Gervase's way of speaking because we are bored. If we had any place to go, we would not be restricted, I am sure."

"You misunderstand me," Walter said, finally regaining his voice. "I have no lack of faith in the Earl of Pembroke. I knew him in childhood and was a member of his brother's household. Indeed, I love and honor Richard. Because I believe in his cause, of my own free will I have joined Pembroke in opposing the king. One does not do such a thing lightly."

"Why, then, there can be no trouble." Gervase smiled at him. "Richard is a great one for doing favors for childhood friends or dependents of his brother. You have only to ask him."

With enormous effort, Walter restrained himself from bellowing, *You silly nit, there is a war going on!* In fact, it was the final words he spoke aloud, his voice rather choked in his attempt not to shout.

Gervase lifted her brows. "Oh, yes, the war. I had forgot about that. It is so odd that there is always a war whenever Richard does not want to do something. The war must come first, of course." There was a bitter bite to her voice.

"This war, at least, must come before my small problems," Walter said soothingly. "My troubles will be solved just as easily next year as this."

"You mean that you believe the war will soon be over and that then you will ask Richard's help?" Marie asked.

"As to the war, I do not know," Walter replied. "I hope

the king will soon yield to reason. As to troubling the Earl of Pembroke about my property, I believe there will be no need to do so when there is peace in the land."

In fact, Walter hoped he would be betrothed to Sybelle, and the backing of Roselynde would obviate any need for anyone else's help. However, he was not such a conceited coxcomb as to talk definitely of his acceptance by Lord Geoffrey until he truly was accepted. The vague statement was true, and hopefully, it would divert Gervase and Marie from urging him to ask for Richard's help or, worse yet, from urging Richard to offer assistance to him.

Marie's eyes brightened. Richard owed her restitution for what his selfish fixation on his own affairs had caused her to lose. For a while she had feared he intended to forget that debt or to cancel it altogether by immuring her in this isolated keep. However, it was now clear that he had other intentions, and these were most satisfactory to Marie.

Of course, she would have preferred if Walter himself had a respectable title, but her widow's portion was not large and the uncle of the Earl of Gloucester was not to be scorned. A title might be arranged later if Richard won this war that Sir Walter kept harping on. More important was the fact that Sir Walter was rich and not only was not now married but had not ever been married. That meant that there were no sons who were in line to inherit his lands. Considering all these facts, Marie had immediately leapt to the conclusion that Richard had sent the man to see and be seen preparatory to suggesting an alliance that would end her widowhood.

Walter had unintentionally encouraged this notion by being slightly more attentive to Marie than to Gervase in handing dishes and pouring wine. A sharp comment from Gervase made him aware that he was bestowing noticeable attention on the sister he found more attractive, and after that he made sure not to favor either lady—but it was too late. He had fixed into Marie's mind the notion that he was hers to take or leave.

After saying that he expected to be able to take hold of his lands once the war was over, Walter was able at last to lead the discussion away from his private affairs. Marie had asked why he expected King Henry to yield to reason now when he had not done so for two years—proving to Walter that he had been right and that she did know about the war but chose to ignore it.

"Because more and more men have flocked to Richard," Walter replied, "and, to speak the truth, because Prince Llewelyn has actively entered the fray."

"Are you implying that a Welsh savage can win a war when half the nobility of England could not?" Gervase asked distastefully.

"Prince Llewelyn is not a savage," Walter replied with a slightly condescending smile, as if he knew something she did not. "Indeed, he may act the barbarian from time to time to trap an enemy, or in society to make fools of those stupid enough to fall into the assumption that he is less than he really is. It is a sport with him to expose silly people ignorant enough to look down on him as crude and uncivilized before they have met him. His court is only waiting to laugh at those who behave contemptuously."

"That does not seem to me to be polite and civilized behavior—to make fun of your guests," Gervase remarked, but her expression was wary.

"Oh, Prince Llewelyn himself is always polite," Walter said innocently, rather stretching a point, for Llewelyn could be both crude and vicious when it was expedient. "His speech is fine and gentle, but he sometimes asks questions that might seem simpleminded or makes remarks that could be taken as naive. When an unwise person replies contemptuously or with a sneer, then the jaws of the trap close. To anyone who is civil, Prince Llewelyn is most gracious. But this is silly talk. So elegant a lady as yourself could not be other than gentle and forbearing in speech, even to those whose manners are a trifle rough. Neither you nor Lady Marie, I am sure, have anything to fear from Prince Llewelyn."

Walter was relieved to see that this combination of veiled threat and gross and false flattery, which his own experience contradicted, had made Gervase thoughtful. Marie, on the other hand, seemed unaffected, but this was not because she intended to be rude. She had dismissed that idea when she conceived the notion that Richard had presented Walter as a possible second husband and that the wedding at Builth would permit her to examine other available men. Marie was no longer interested in spiting Richard; she was quite pleased with him. Although she did not find Walter physically attractive, he had good manners, good birth, and wealth. Marie was satisfied. Unless she could find someone with similar qualifications who happened to be more appealing physically, she would take Walter.

Accordingly, Marie began to discuss what would be necessary to take to Builth. Since Gervase did not cut off her sister's questions, it was clear that she no longer intended even a pretense of reluctance. Walter was sure there would be a separate chamber and bed for Richard, no matter how crowded the keep, but he was not equally sure that Gervase would share that bed with her husband. It was not the sort of question a man could ask; Walter compromised by suggesting that Marie's bed should be carried—thinking privately that the sisters could sleep together if necessary—as well as chairs and cushions, which might be in short supply. Gervase nodded, but Marie laughed at him.

"I do not know whether that answer satisfies my sister," Marie said, "but *I* wish to know what clothes to bring. Will the ladies be dressed in the latest fashions? Are they so poor that they wear no jewelry? I do not wish to offend by my dress anymore than by my manners."

"I am not too knowledgeable in such matters," Walter began defensively, "but you need have no fear of much outshining the other ladies in jewels."

He remembered the rivers of pearls and emeralds and diamonds that Lady Alinor's husbands had won for her and with which she was bedecked at court functions. Nor was Lady Joanna less well endowed. It almost seemed as if her devoted husband wished to drown her in seas of moonstones and sapphires. Adam's favorites were rubies, and they well befitted his dark rose, Gilliane. Simon had not had much of a chance yet to bestow precious gifts on Rhiannon, but Walter knew she hardly needed his contributions. He recalled to mind the way she glowed like a rainbow with the jewels her grandfather had left.

"Nor," Walter continued thoughtfully, "do you need to fear that your style of dress will be thought too advanced. Roselynde is a great port, and Lady Joanna, at least, is always dressed in the highest style."

"We certainly need not fear being too advanced," Gervase snapped, "since we have seen nothing new for near two years. I said we were not prisoners, but we might as well have been, for all we have seen of the outside world."

"Then I am sure we will fit well with most of the ladies," Marie put in quickly. "After all, Sister, a grand affair in Wales will still not rival a modest one in the court of France."

Walter was grateful for being saved from needing to comment on Richard's behavior in leaving his womenfolk in Pembroke keep. Actually, Walter did *not* disapprove and quite agreed with the platitudes he would have had to offer about the necessity of being sure the women were safe and that great fondness sometimes might breed an overprotective attitude. Nonetheless, he knew those platitudes would irritate Gervase, who wanted sympathy with her own viewpoint and to hear her husband blamed for carrying on a war that inconvenienced her. Thus, Walter's eyes rested on Marie with sincere approval.

Gervase sniffed and tossed her head, but she made no further embarrassing remarks. She was aware of Marie's notion with regard to Walter. Although she did not agree that Richard had sent Walter deliberately because he was suitable for Marie, knowing better than her sister her husband's single-minded concentration on war and politics when he was engaged in those pursuits, Gervase was very willing for Marie to marry Walter if she could get him.

Walter's lack of titled status pleased Gervase. The last thing she wanted was for Marie to be her equal in rank, and Walter's putative wealth pleased her, also. Gervase could not deny her sister fine clothing and comforts, but she was tired of having to find the money to supply these from her own purse.

Boredom supplied a better spur than Walter could, and he was clever enough to know it. Without any urging on his part, Gervase and Marie were ready to leave within two days. Nor was Walter as exasperated as Richard would have been by the slow pace mandated by the baggage wain and the large, luxurious traveling cart. After her father's death, Walter had often escorted his mother on various journeys; thus, he was accustomed. Moreover, unless it rained particularly hard, Marie would often ride beside him.

Walter enjoyed her company, although there was none of the easy rapport he had had with Sybelle. Marie wanted compliments first and gossip next. She wanted character sketches of everyone they were likely to meet and a précis of relationships. Although Walter obliged her, insofar as he knew the people, what he said soon brought Marie's tinkling laugh and a coquettish flick of her eyelids.

"Either men and women in England are all saints," she trilled, "or you are very innocent. Do you know nothing but good of anyone?"

Walter felt a qualm of distaste, but he did not express it. He merely shrugged. "I am no priest. I am not interested in other men's sins. My own are enough to concern me."

"And women's sins?" Marie persisted. "Are you equally uninterested in them?"

"I am not interested in *talking* about them," Walter replied, hoping to discourage the line of conversation and yet not be openly rude by the use of a suggestive remark from which any woman not looking for trouble would withdraw.

"Then you cannot worry overmuch about your own sins," Marie retorted merrily.

A corner of Walter's wide mouth curved upward, and the lids came halfway down over his bright blue eyes, giving them a sleepy, sensual look. All he said, however, was, "No, not overmuch."

Walter felt a surge of physical excitement. A response like that could not be mistaken. Marie de les Maures wished to play. He had thought her a delicious piece from the first seeing, but all the questions about his estate and marital status had made him cautious. He had feared to suggest a special interest, for Marie was not the kind of woman he wished to marry. That word brought Sybelle to mind, and Walter felt a pang of guilt, which was succeeded by a sensation of resentment. There was no need for him to feel guilty, he told himself. He was not promised to Sybelle. Lord Geoffrey had not even been willing to listen to his proposal. And marriage had nothing to do with the game of love he wished to play with Marie anyway.

Marie had been babbling prettily, and Walter let his eyes rest on her. She would make a sweet, soft armful abed, and since Richard played with moderate freedom himself, Walter did not expect any moral objection. But there was another problem: Richard might have a political purpose for his sister-by-marriage—to make some alliance, in which case he would not want Marie's attention occupied. However, it would be easy enough to determine Richard's attitude when they met him at Brecon. Until then, he would have to walk a tightrope between too great and too little encouragement of the lady. However, conditions on the road in November were not conducive to illicit romance, so there was little danger of a too-quick ripening of the verbal dalliance.

Neither rain nor baggage wagons impeded the progress of the party from Hemel. Having decided to go to the wedding, Geoffrey and Joanna set out the very next morning just at dawn and arrived at Roselynde keep late that same night, a day before Ian and Alinor had indicated they would leave for Wales. The keep was safe in Sir Guy's hands, and Adam and Gilliane had agreed to remain in England to guard against the unlikely chance that there would be a major attack on any of the family's property that would necessitate forming an army. From Roselynde the whole party rode nearly due north toward Oxford, much of the time cross-country, ignoring roads and fording streams and rivers.

Joanna kept an anxious eye on her stepfather and her mother, but Alinor's vigor seemed little less than her own, despite the fact that she groaned and complained most comically at every rest period of the rheum in her bones. Really Joanna's primary concern was Ian, who had long suffered an affliction of the lungs that shortened his breath and, if he was chilled, came near to choking him to death. It was therefore necessary to keep Ian dry and warm—no easy thing in an English November, and in particular when the object of her concern was frequently impatient with his weakness.

However, Alinor and Joanna had their devices for protecting Ian. There were endless changes of clothing for him, and the women took it in turns to find some excuse to caress him so that they could thrust their hands beneath his cloak and outer garments to be sure he was dry. One thing Ian could never resist—even when he guessed the purpose—was a display of affection from his wife and stepdaughter. There was also a clever garment of thin, oiled parchment, which could be worn over his cloak to shed water when the rain was heavy.

The party stayed at the abbey at Abingdon that night, and the next morning, at Oxford, they gathered up Geoffrey and

Joanna's sons, William and Ian, who were wild with joy at their deliverance from a dull routine of lessons and practice combat. William was particularly indignant at having been left behind in safety when the king went off to war, and he complained vociferously as they traveled west that he would never learn to fight if he had no experience.

Although he gave William no encouragement in Joanna's presence, Geoffrey looked thoughtful. At fourteen, William's age, Geoffrey had been actively supporting Ian, his master, on the walls of a besieged keep and had gone with him and guarded his lord's left shoulder in full-scale combat when he was sixteen, after Owain, the senior squire, had been knighted.

On the one hand, Geoffrey's heart failed him when he thought of the dangers to which his elder son would be exposed if he were permitted to go to war. On the other, he was seriously disturbed by the truth of William's complaint—that the king was too fond and therefore too timorous for the safety of his cousin's sons. Geoffrey feared there was real substance to William's argument that he was ready, not merely a boyish desire for an adventure about which he knew nothing. Henry was too emotional and had too little personal battlefield experience to judge William's readiness for action.

One of the purposes of fostering was to strike a balance between the too-great love and, therefore, too-great fear of a natural parent and the indifference of a stranger. A boy fostered from the age of eight or ten engaged the affection of his master, who would not carelessly expose his fosterling to unnecessary danger; however, neither was the boy's foster father blinded to the growing prowess and capabilities of a developing young man by memories of infant gurgles and kisses or toddling, uncertain footsteps with a chubby hand clinging to a father's fingers for support.

In truth, Geoffrey knew that Henry should have taken William with him and assigned to him such duties around camp and keep as were commensurate with the boy's tutor's judgment of his abilities. At the least, William could carry messages and suchlike, even if he were not permitted on the battlefield. This would give him experience of the life in camp, would provide him with examples of men who cared for and neglected their soldiers, and generally would broaden his outlook. Moreover, Geoffrey knew it was time for his son to be blooded, to see death dealt out and the broken wreckage of bodies that war leaves behind. Eleven-year-old Ian was too young, but William should be ready.

To William, Geoffrey recommended patience, but the matter was serious enough to make him wish to discuss it with Ian. The women could not interfere, since they were accommodated in a guesthouse in a separate walled enclosure. Even so, it was not easy to find a private moment. First, Geoffrey had to wait until the simple evening meal of bread and milk had been served and the good brothers had gone off to bed, and no talking was possible during the meal. Courtesy required that guests maintain the same silence as their hosts and give at least the appearance of attention to the religious work being read aloud.

Then William and Ian demanded the attention of their doting grandfather so they could boast of the increase in their prowess and attainments since they had last seen him. Finally Geoffrey shooed them off to bed, sending William also, ostensibly to be sure that little Ian did not get into mischief. Rid of the boys at last, he raised the question of William's further training and the problem of removing the boy from King Henry's too-careful hands.

Finally Geoffrey said, "I have just bethought me of an excellent person to give William experience. Did Walter de Clare tell you of his problem in taking hold of the property he inherited from his brother?"

Ian began to laugh. "Walter said very little to me beyond 'Eh? What?' He never heard what I said because he was too busy looking at Sybelle. I would have thought him deaf, except that he heard every word Sybelle said to him perfectly well—and her voice is softer than mine, I warrant."

Geoffrey laughed also. "He was sore stricken. I suppose you know that he came rushing to Oxford after me when he left Roselynde."

"Yes, Joanna wrote, but we would have known anyway. You should have seen his face when Alinor by chance made a jest that Sybelle was somewhat overripe on the vine. I nearly choked, keeping from laughing. He was both terrified and furious, believing that at that very moment you might have been selling his pearl of price into slavery."

"Oh, he meant to have her," Geoffrey agreed. "It was all I could do to stop him from making the offer—but you know, Ian, it was not the time for it. Walter would not compromise his loyalty to Pembroke, even for a wife, and we are black enough already in Henry's mind without a son-by-marriage who is an open rebel.''

''Well, he has not yet been proscribed,'' Ian said, ''and I do not think it is now likely unless he cries defiance on his own. I am sure Pembroke is trying to avoid that. From what Simon has written to me, Walter has not been involved in any of the attacks on the king's men or property. I would lay odds that Richard is arranging to keep Walter out of the way. Richard is very much like his father, a good, kind man as well as an honorable one.''

''Yes, but we are wandering rather far afield,'' Geoffrey commented. ''The only reason I brought Walter into the conversation is that preparatory to asking for Sybelle, he detailed his property to me, with every lack and fault most clearly underlined.''

''That is only honest,'' Ian said, but he was grinning.

''Yes,'' Geoffrey retorted sardonically, ''only there really is a lack. The property is legally Walter's; he has been invested with it by the king. But he has not the strength to force the castellans to yield to him, and he does not trust them.'' Geoffrey detailed the situation as he had heard it from Walter.

Ian listened, nodding now and again. ''I see. Do you think he courted Sybelle so that we would support him?'' Ian asked. But before Geoffrey could reply, he had recalled Walter's besotted state and begun to laugh. ''No. I take back the question.''

''Yet there is good reason to ask it,'' Geoffrey pointed out. ''I will tell you what I think. He is fond of Simon and knew we were strong; therefore, he came to Roselynde to see if what Simon said of us were true and to ask, perhaps, if there were a girl available for him. Then he saw Sybelle.''

''Very likely you are right,'' Ian agreed. ''But it does Walter no disservice in my eyes. It is a reasonable way to look for a wife.''

''Yes, it is and shows considerable common sense, but we have lost the thread again. Naturally, if Walter makes an offer and Sybelle is willing, I will support Walter's effort to subdue his brother's castellans—''

''And so will I,'' Ian interrupted with enthusiasm, pleasure lighting his eyes at the thought of a small, private war that could have no large, catastrophic repercussions. "And Adam will come, too. Poor Adam, he is furious that all the action in this war is so far away and no one has insulted him or even raided his lands. Moreover, the more furious he gets, the meeker are his neighbors."

Geoffrey began to laugh again. "And so would I be meek if I lived close by Tarring and Adam were roaring around looking for trouble. But, Ian, the point of all this talk is that I can send William with Walter when he takes action against the castellans."

Ian did not answer immediately. He was very tenderhearted and had a sudden vision of his dearly loved eldest grandson climbing a scaling ladder to storm the walls of a keep and finding death there instead of adventure, as so many did. Then he called himself a fool. William would go up a ladder only behind Walter de Clare, as Geoffrey had gone up behind him, and Walter de Clare was a strong bulwark. Besides, it was most unlikely that Walter would permit so untried a youth to take part in an attack on the walls.

Slowly, Ian nodded approval. "Yes, if a contract is made, or even if Walter only makes a proposal—for there can be no doubt he will keep any commitment he makes—William would do well with him. In place of the fondness of fostering, there will be the care for his betrothed's brother. You need fear no carelessness toward William on Walter's part, and no over-protectiveness, either. Walter has, as we agreed, a great deal of common sense."

Geoffrey grinned. "He has, even if it does not show when Sybelle is in the room." He rose and stretched. "I am for bed, Ian. Thank you. I am easier in my mind now. In fact, if we can get Walter and Sybelle married before he takes over the lands, we will have an ideal excuse for William to go with him. I will ask that William be given leave from the king's service to accompany his sister, who is shy and timid and needs the support of a member of her family in her new home."

Ian had started to swing his leg over the bench on which he was sitting before rising, but his head snapped up and he let out a whoop of laughter at hearing such a description of Sybelle.

"But how is the king to know it is not true?" Geoffrey asked reasonably. "In Henry's presence, she is as meek and silent as the most proper maiden alive. And if that clever mischief-maker Winchester is gone from Henry's side and can no longer whisper in the king's ear that the women of Roselynde are not customarily timid and shy—just to arouse Henry's suspicions against us—Henry will accept such an excuse easily."

There was no use in Ian's defending Winchester to Geoffrey, who now had a personal grudge against the bishop—a most unusual thing, for ordinarily Geoffrey was exceptionally, even uncomfortably, clear-sighted—so Ian finished rising and, when Geoffrey was also standing, kissed his son-by-marriage and patted his shoulder. Then both left the refectory, where the last few tallow candles were guttering out. Ian turned into the first tiny cell in the men's guesthouse, bare except for a narrow cot, a three-legged stool, and an earthenware pot for night soil. Geoffrey continued down the hall, presumably to look in on his sons to be sure they were abed, and then to go to his own small cubicle.

When he was alone, Ian began to undress himself, laughing occasionally as he fumbled with ties and bent into uncomfortable positions to undo his shoes and crossgarters. Fortunately he had unarmed when they first arrived, or he would have needed to ask for help. Geoffrey had forgotten that Ian no longer had squires. Some years back Ian had refused to take any new boys because he felt he could not do full justice to their training and, worse, might die before they were finished knights. Before he had sent his last young protégé into the world, there had always been a squire or a maid to help him undress—or Alinor.

Ian felt a surge of loneliness for her even though she was only a few hundred yards away, and then a rush of heat; that made him laugh again. He was an old man. It was ridiculous that passion should still stir him so strongly, but it did. And Alinor's response was as lively as ever. Shrugging, he bent and got the pot. It was a far less pleasant solution, but sometimes relieving one's bladder solved the problem.

He lay down on the hard monk's cot and pulled the thin blanket over him. Then, with a grunt of displeasure, he got up again to wrap his furred cloak around him; he did not wish to have another attack of being unable to breathe in the middle of Simon's wedding. Ian hated those attacks more because of the terror they engendered in every member of his family than because of the pain he suffered or any fear of death. Then his expression grew very tender and happy; they feared because they loved him, and he fought to live, no matter how tired he was, because he loved them. Ian needed love. There could never be too much, no matter how much was poured out on him, and he could never do too much to win and hold that love.

Naturally, the thought of love brought Sybelle and Walter back to Ian's mind. Would Alinor and Joanna urge Sybelle too strongly? Mother and grandmother were growing impatient over Sybelle's reluctance to settle on a man. They wanted somebody ready to pick up the burden and hold the clan together if he and Geoffrey should die. Adam would, of course, do what he could, but he was not the official head of the Roselynde family. And Simon was useless for such a purpose. He would fight to defend Roselynde, but he would not govern the estates.

Then Ian chuckled. Neither Alinor nor Joanna would ever allow such a thought to enter her mind. Alinor loved him and Joanna loved Geoffrey, and to the best of their abilities both women pushed all thought of their husbands' deaths out of their minds. But deeper than love of any man lay the love of the land. Either Alinor or Joanna would lay down her life for her husband—without a murmur or a hesitation—but both would sell their husbands' lives and their very souls for the land. Sybelle, too. It was bred into her bones.

Ian sighed. He had labored under the whip of Alinor's love for her estate for nearly thirty years. Then he smiled again. They had been good years, full of battle and love and laughter. And Geoffrey and the two women were right; Walter was ideal for the purpose—clever, capable, strong, and honest. If Sybelle wanted him, it would be good.

CHAPTER 5

Sybelle did not know, of course, what her grandfather was thinking as she lay staring up toward the ceiling of her cell. She could not make out the ceiling clearly in the dim light of the small oil lamp, but she would not have seen it anyway, for her mind was busy with the same subject that had preoccupied Ian just before he fell asleep. Sybelle had become aware of a subtle pressure urging her toward acceptance of Walter de Clare.

At first her mother had seemed totally neutral, but now she, too, seemed quietly to favor Sir Walter. Sybelle was not annoyed by the pressure. She knew if she said definitely that she did not want Walter, the pressure would cease, and there would be no punishment, not even nagging or nasty looks. Furthermore, Sybelle acknowledged that it was just that Sir Walter should have an answer and not be kept dangling. Her father had explained about the estates and that Walter would need a family that could help him enforce his rights. Clearly, then, he could not afford to waste time over a girl who might withdraw and leave him without the necessary alliance.

The need for alliance was good, Sybelle thought. That Sir Walter had sought it at Roselynde showed he knew the strength of the family. She was not at all hurt that Sir Walter should look at the family before he chose a girl. Then she smiled. Perhaps he had come to look at the family, but he had stopped looking for a girl when he saw her. Or had he? There was that woman in his tent? . . . *Do not be ridiculous,* Sybelle told herself. *Such a thing has nothing to do with you or with marriage. Grandmama and Mama have told you more than once that such couplings are as meaningless as pissing.*

In the abstract, Sybelle was willing to accept the fact that men took whores to relieve a need wholly analogous to the need to eat and void. Simon had often told her of his escapades, and Sybelle knew that Sir Walter had been in his company more than once on such adventures. That had not disturbed her nor made her less willing to talk and laugh with Sir Walter. If Cedric, the master-at-arms, had come back to Kingsclere and told her the story, Sybelle knew she would have laughed her head off. It was ridiculous that seeing the woman should have made such a difference. Then why had it?

In an effort to understand her unreasonable reaction to so common a sin, Sybelle thought back to the scene. It leapt into her mind with startling clarity: the smell of her overheated mare; the hard-trodden earth of the camp; the coarse hide and wool shelters of the men; Sir Walter's tent, with its red and yellow panels, the de Clare colors; and his shield leaning nearby the tent opening—its red chevrons on a silver, rather than gold, ground to show he was a younger son. Then Sir Walter himself, bursting out of the tent, sword in hand, with his bedrobe hanging open to expose a body covered with light red-brown hair.

When she recalled the scene, a chuckle shook Sybelle, but the low laughter was followed by a sensation of warmth and a slight prickling of her skin. Sybelle found herself wondering what it would be like to touch a man so covered with hair. The only male bodies with which she was familiar were those of her father, grandfather, and Simon, and none of them was hirsute. Yet there was, for some reason, a feeling of desirability and familiarity about Sir Walter's thickly haired body. Someone had been described to her? . . . Grandfather Simon!

Unexpectedly, Sybelle saw a picture of herself running her fingers through and making curls in the hair on Sir Walter's body. The image caused a very odd sensation in her belly, and the unusual warmth of her body flowed and centered in her loins. The feeling was pleasant but made her restless. Sybelle opened her legs. In the next moment she drew them forcibly together again, and most of the heat of her body had flown to her face in a blush. Simultaneously, the image of Sir Walter's camp flashed back into her mind, but this time she saw the woman creeping out of the tent and running away.

Momentarily a cold fury replaced Sybelle's blush, but then she flushed red-hot again. Sybelle had found her answer. She had been infuriated by seeing the woman because she knew the whore had coupled with Sir Walter—and she had desired him for herself, not in any vague way as a husband but then and there. The sight of him half-naked . . . no, all naked, for he had only clutched the bedrobe about himself when he saw her. Sybelle giggled. That was why he had not picked up his shield! He had been reaching for it, had seen her, and had hastily pulled his robe together.

Well, then, Sybelle thought, *the question is settled. I suppose I do want him, and Papa can propose a marriage between us as soon as it is politically safe*. She snuggled down more comfortably, aware of relief and pleasure, but then she frowned again. Once, when Rhiannon had spoken of her fear that Simon would be unfaithful to her after marriage, Sybelle had assured her he would not. The men of Roselynde, Sybelle had said proudly, did not do such things. They chose a wife when they were sure of what they wanted and clove only to her thereafter. But Walter—Sybelle's mind checked for a moment, aware that she had dropped the Sir from Walter's name—Walter was not bred to Roselynde either by blood or by custom.

Not all men, Sybelle knew, believed that conjugal fidelity was a matter of great importance. Then a slow smile curved her full lips. She was remembering another part of that conversation she had had with Rhiannon about Simon's fidelity. She had pointed out to Rhiannon that it was a wife's duty to make a marriage satisfying and interesting. Men, Sybelle remembered saying, were essentially simple creatures in matters of love, and it would be no burden to keep a husband anxious and eager. Yes . . . that was what she had said, but she had been mouthing what she had been told by her mother and grandmother. Now that she was facing the problem on her own account, did she believe her own words? And what if she did not?

Her mother had hinted that her one reservation was Walter's age and the possibility that he had fixed the pattern of his life. If so, there was bound to be conflict because Sybelle had been trained to independence and to ruling what was her own—a pattern not only foreign but offensive to most men. Would that drive Walter to seek other, more docile women? What then was she to do? Sybelle asked herself. Was she to marry one of those callow youths who dogged her footsteps each time she appeared in public? Doubtless one of those young sprigs could be molded into meek acceptance of Roselynde ways.

Something inside Sybelle shuddered away from that thought, trembled at the idea of being everything—tutor to her husband, judge and defender of Roselynde and its vassals, centerpoint of the whole clan. No! Even Grandmama did not carry so heavy a burden. Grandpapa was not only a fighting machine, docilely obeying his wife. He was the counterpoise on the wheel—and for all his soft and loving ways, he had a will and a temper of his own. Sybelle could remember eruptions between her grandparents that she thought would bring the roof of the keep down on them all.

Mama and Papa were also equal. They did not boil over and shoot sparks as easily as Grandpapa and Grandmama, but there were hot disagreements argued out no less violently, despite the level tones of the opponents. Arguments or no arguments, Mama and Papa supported each other, each gaining strength from the other. *I cannot do it alone,* Sybelle thought, and felt tears sting her eyes. *I need a man, a real man. Surely I will be able to hold him.*

Then two comforting thoughts came to her at once. Aunt Gilliane never, never quarreled with Uncle Adam—but most of the time things went the way *she* wanted them to go. And, Sybelle knew, she had said quite shameful things to Walter over that stupid mistake his men had made. But he had got over it. He had looked at her much the same after that meeting as before it happened.

Sybelle slept easily after her decision was made and in the morning calmly told her mother that she was willing to accept Walter if he offered marriage. Joanna nodded without surprise. She had noticed that Sybelle had been much quieter than usual since they had met at Roselynde and assumed she had been thinking over what was undoubtedly the most important decision of her life.

"Very well," Joanna said with equal calm, although her heart swelled with tenderness and anxiety at the thought of Sybelle's embarkation on the stormy sea of womanhood. "However, leave it to me to tell your father and your grandfather. It will be better for them to think the issue is still in doubt." Then she smiled, and her eyes twinkled. "Men," Joanna went on, "have altogether too much sympathy for the moans of others of their kind. Before we know where we are, Geoffrey and Ian will be assuring Walter you are his devoted slave."

"I will swiftly disabuse his mind of that notion," Sybelle replied tartly.

"No doubt you could," Joanna replied, "but that would leave a very sour taste in his mouth. Better for him to think his courtship has won him a difficult prize. Then, if he still offends, you may withdraw with seemingly renewed doubts. Thus, he will consider any difficulties of his own making."

Sybelle's bronze-gold brows drew together in a thoughtful frown. She was a very direct and honest person, and such deviousness troubled her.

"There are times," Joanna warned, understanding her daughter's expression, "when too much honesty is cruel. Men have their pride, and it must not be broken, for honor washes away with the crumbs of pride. A woman must walk warily between what is best and what will destroy her husband's pride."

"Yes," Sybelle responded, "yes, I see that. But between a husband and a wife there should be no pride and no deceit."

Joanna smiled. "That is true—and not true—my love. It is not deceitful to bring about the same result in a way that makes a man feel happy and pleased with himself rather than leaving him with the ugly fear that he is a slave to his lust."

"But seeing reason is not the same as bowing to lust," Sybelle protested.

"Do not talk like a fool," Joanna said, shaking her head. "When a woman disagrees with a man, it is always his conviction that *she* is the unreasonable one. And if he yields, then he does not trust his judgment and believes himself to have been deceived by his desire for her. However, if instead of saying, 'Do not be an idiot,' a woman says, 'Dear love, do *you* believe this to be true? How can it be? Explain it to me again, for I am only a woman and do not understand.' Then, often, reason prevails."

Sybelle laughed. "I have seen Aunt Gilliane doing that, and for matters of the realm, or even of our own lands, I can see that it is right." Then her eyes darkened, and the frown returned. "But what if he does not speak to me at all? And . . . and there are things that are not a matter of reason. . . ."

"Yes. That brings us back to why I do not wish that Walter be too sure of you at first. In the wooing, you can easily show him what it is that wakens your interest and also make it habitual for him to tell you those things you desire to hear.

Very likely he will wish to tell you that your eyes are like stars and your lips like cherries—or some such nonsense. Do not too sharply check him, but lead him gently to talk of more sensible matters.''

That brought another laugh from Sybelle. ''I do not think it nonsense for him to tell me my eyes are like stars.''

''Perhaps not once or twice,'' Joanna agreed, laughing in turn, ''but you will soon find conversation very dull if that is all Walter has to say.''

''I imagine he will find a few other parts of me to praise,'' Sybelle remarked with mock seriousness.

''Piffle!'' Joanna exclaimed. ''We must hurry or we will be late on the road. Just remember what I said to you. If your father or Ian raises the question of Walter to you, say only that you have no objections to him but need to know him better. I am serious, Sybelle. You must determine how Walter will behave to you once he has your father's permission and knows there can be no rivals. Moreover, since no marriage contract can be written without your grandmother's approval, you will be able to withdraw if you find you have mistaken your heart or Walter's character.''

Sybelle made no answer to her mother's last statement, merely nodding and then turning away to pack the few things that the maids had left out of the traveling baskets for last-minute use. However, Joanna had noticed that her daughter was not indifferent to the notion of rejecting Walter. Her expression, although quickly masked, had betrayed Sybelle's feelings.

Joanna sighed softly, undecided whether she was glad or sorry. Apparently her daughter was far more interested in de Clare than her calm manner had at first implied. If Walter were clever in his handling, Sybelle *would* be his devoted slave. Joanna walked to the first small chamber to see whether she could help her mother make ready, but her talk with Sybelle had delayed her too long. Alinor was out before her, and Geoffrey's voice, making some light remark to her in the courtyard, came in to Joanna through the little high window. Suddenly Joanna smiled, her heart lifting. To be enslaved by love—with the right man—was not so bad.

When Walter delivered his charges to Brecon keep, he found a message from Richard requesting him to send word of his arrival to Abergavenny. If he could, Richard's letter said, he would come at once, but there were signs of renewed activity from two of Henry's men, Baldwin de Guisnes, who held Monmouth keep, and John of Monmouth, who was at Grosmont. Walter considered and decided to go to Abergavenny himself. Things had progressed to such a point between Marie and himself that he would need to make a definite move in one direction or the other now that they were in a keep of substantial size where privacy might be found if assiduously sought.

Walter could not deny his strong physical desire for Marie nor that she encouraged him, and he could not bring himself to reject her out of hand; however, if Richard had plans to use his sister-by-marriage to make a political alliance, Walter knew he could discipline himself. The safest move, then, was to commend the ladies to the care of the castellan, soothe them by assuring them he was going personally to bring Richard to Brecon as swiftly as possible, and remove himself to a safe distance.

Arriving at Abergavenny not long after the prayers at None, Walter found that Richard had gone south to Usk that morning. Since it was only about ten miles farther, Walter continued on and finally came into the Earl of Pembroke's presence as the early dusk of the end of November was darkening the sky. Walter was greeted affectionately, but with a certain amount of regret—which amused him. Although the regret was somewhat mitigated by his report that he felt sure the ladies would behave with the utmost propriety at Builth, Richard still seemed relieved that Walter had arrived too late for them to leave for Brecon that day.

Also, since it was impossible for Richard to dismiss the subject of his wife and sister-by-marriage without at least decent inquiries as to their health and well-being, Walter had adequate opportunity to discover what he wanted to know. It was soon clear that Richard was totally indifferent to what Marie did and that he felt union with her would make enemies rather than allies for him.

"In God's name," he said to Walter, perceiving both more and less than Walter had anticipated, "*you* are not thinking of marrying her, are you? Believe me, for all her grand airs, her dower is not worth it—and if it were ten times as much, it still would not be worth it."

Walter thought that Richard was going too far. He assumed that the earl's bitterness was owing to his problems with his wife, which washed over onto Marie. Walter believed there was no harm in Marie, barring a bit of foolish pride and an overgreat love of scandal—but that was common in women. And then Walter thought, *But not in all women*. Sybelle might amuse herself with a wicked jest now and again, but she spread no evil nor wished to hear of it. The thought of her slipped out into speech.

"No, I am all but sworn to—" Walter stopped short, remembering that he had no direct approval from Lord Geoffrey and had no right to any claim on Sybelle.

Indeed, to make such a claim could have very serious consequences if for some reason Lord Geoffrey decided to make a contract for Sybelle elsewhere. A claim of prior betrothal could be used to invalidate a marriage. Walter was suddenly aware of a shocking desire to make his claim and, thereby, have a lever with which to force Sybelle's father to accept him. He flushed slightly with shame at the thought and shook his head.

"That is an exaggeration," he went on hastily, his voice uneven. "I have an alliance in mind, but it is in my mind only. I have made no offer as yet, and I have no . . . no assurance that the offer will be accepted when I make it."

"If there is something I can do," Richard suggested, "you have only to tell me."

Walter made a poor attempt at a smile. The fact that so dishonorable a notion had entered his mind, together with the sick sensation that had churned his vitals at the thought of Sybelle being given to someone else, had made painfully clear how much he wanted her.

"You may be sure," he said, "that I will call on your good offices if necessary. I hope . . ." He left that unfinished.

Richard nodded. "You mean I might do more harm than good—"

"God in heaven, no!" Walter exclaimed. "That was not what I meant at all. I—"

"Well, just do not take Marie as second best," Richard interrupted, smiling at Walter's vehemence, although he was not sure it was justified. "Believe me, she would not make a suitable wife for you. If I ever have the time, I will find her a court toady. No, do not look at me that way. They would both be happy. I do not hate Marie, but she is what she is."

Although he still felt that Richard was blackening Marie with Gervase's tar, Walter was not going to argue about it. He asked instead whether Richard wanted him to take the ladies on to Builth and was again amused when an expression of relief appeared on Richard's face. However, the expression was replaced almost immediately by a firm, if unhappy, resolve.

"No," Richard said. "Gervase has the right to expect me to escort her. To send her to Llewelyn alone would do harm to her dignity." He sighed. "I wish they had not been so prompt—but I should have expected it."

"I can return and say you will be delayed a day or two," Walter offered.

"God, no!" Richard exclaimed. "I would never hear the end of it." He smiled wryly. "It was only that Bassett has planned a raid on the town of Monmouth tomorrow, and I wanted to look at the keep while the garrison came out—if it came out—to protect the town. Monmouth is one of the places I am thinking of attacking."

"There is no reason why we cannot go by way of Monmouth as well as by any other road," Walter said.

"Go by way of Monmouth!" Richard looked startled. "But Monmouth is to the east and Brecon to the west."

"Monmouth is also to the north," Walter pointed out with spurious gravity. "Brecon is to the north. Moreover there is a fair passage from Monmouth to Abergavenny along the Trothy River."

Richard burst out laughing. "You are right, there is," he agreed. "And Gervase will never know there is a much better way along the Usk from this place to Abergavenny. Very well, we will go with the army to Monmouth—but I warn you, I will cry craven and say you led me astray if we are blamed for being tardy or if my wife learns from someone that we went the long way around. After all, I have lived so many years in France I would not know, and south Wales is your home, Walter."

They talked lightly of the next day's venture after that. Monmouth was an obvious target for Richard's forces, being the most southern and westerly of the castles still held by the king or his supporters. The major problems were two: First,

Monmouth was not isolated. There were major strong points held by Poitevin adherents of the king close by: Grosmont, less than sixteen miles up the river Monmow; Goodrich, about eight miles across the Wye Valley; and less than twenty-five miles to the west, Gloucester, where the king himself remained, boiling and fuming over the injuries done him. If Monmouth could be taken swiftly by assault, it would be a heavy blow against Henry; however, a siege would probably result in the besiegers themselves being surrounded by the king's forces.

The second problem, which neither Walter nor Richard mentioned but was certainly at the back of each of their minds, was that it was very doubtful that Prince Llewelyn could be induced to aid in any attack on Monmouth. Llewelyn's lands lay in north Wales. Doubtless the Lord of Gwynedd wished to strike a blow that would further embarrass Henry's ministers and aid Richard, but he was less eager to rid south Wales of royal influence than to make a profit out of the enterprise. The probability was that if Richard wished to take Monmouth, he would have to do it with the forces at his disposal and with such aid from the Welsh in raiding and harassing the king's forces as had previously been accorded him. If he wanted full cooperation, like that at Grosmont, an objective more suitable to Prince Llewelyn's purpose would have to be chosen.

CHAPTER 6

To Walter's way of thinking, Richard's desire to inspect Monmouth was very reasonable. However, the earl did not intend to join the action against the town and surrounding countryside himself, so Walter was disappointed when he was asked to join Richard's group rather than Bassett's after they left Usk the next day. Walter was not particularly interested in the foraging expedition on which Bassett was engaged, but he had looked forward to the attack by the garrison. He had not seen any action since a very minor skirmish with a rogue knight and his band of cutthroats near Upavon. Still, he was pledged to Richard and obeyed him without grumbling, never for a moment thinking that this was another ploy of the earl's to keep him out of any direct conflict with Henry's forces.

They were a troop of about one hundred altogether, not large enough to offer any threat to Monmouth keep but too large, particularly as a full thirty of them were belted knights, to encourage any small part of the garrison to attack them. It was Richard's assumption that the purpose of the garrison would be to protect the town, and it was an assumption with which everyone agreed. No English landholder would permit a rich town that owed dues to him to burn in order to attack a nonaggressive group too small to damage his keep. Thus, Richard and his escort watched the gates of Monmouth open without any concern, more interested in examining the mechanism and catching sight of the inner portions than attending to the emerging force.

Walter was close by the earl, well in the forefront because he was particularly interested in a personal way in the problem of taking castles. He asked several eager questions, which Richard answered good-naturedly and with the authority of considerable experience. Suddenly, in the middle of an explanation, the earl's voice stopped abruptly. Startled, Walter followed the direction of Richard's staring eyes. Then Walter stared, too, unmoving for just a moment because he did not believe what he saw.

The garrison of Monmouth was not streaming out toward the town, from which smoke was already rising as Bassett's troops accidentally or deliberately set on fire the houses and shops they were invading. Instead, the men of Monmouth were forming up for a charge—at them!

Behind Richard, one of the men cried, "In God's name, my lord, let us go. There are two or three thousand of them."

"Do not be a fool," Richard roared. "If we flee, they will pick us off in small groups that can make no defense. Philip, Martin, Giles, ride for the town. Tell Gilbert we are beset. Bid him come back, but tell him first to break that bridge we saw between the town and the castle."

Galvanized by Richard's voice, Walter pulled on his helmet and lifted his shield to his arm. He had no lance—no one had, because they had had no intention or expectation of fighting, except perhaps to defend themselves against groups of stragglers from the main force. Richard was calling the crossbowmen forward—probably a useless gesture since there were not more than twenty of them—but if they could bring down the front riders, confusion would make wider gaps in the phalanx of lances directed at them.

Pembroke moved slightly forward, his sword in his hand ready to strike aside any lance. Instinctively, Walter drew his horse to Richard's left, to the place vacated by Richard's senior squire, who had been sent off to warn Bassett. Quietly but firmly, Walter ordered the younger boys to fall back, and they did so—not for lack of courage but with the understanding that Walter's greater strength would be a better protection for their master.

The crossbowmen bobbed up and down as they wound or pulled the bowstrings back and loaded the bows with quarrels. Walter heard the earl ordering them to hold their fire until the oncoming army crossed the little stream at the foot of the rise on which they stood. Walter judged that the distance would permit no more than two, or for the quickest loaders, three volleys, but it was useless to expend arrows earlier. There would be little chance of doing much damage at a greater distance, and with a nearly solid block of targets rushing forward, little use in worrying about accuracy and testing for wind drift.

Oddly, although the distance was not great and Walter could plainly hear the thunder of the oncoming hooves, there seemed to be plenty of time to think. The first idea that went through his head was that if he came out of this alive and was taken prisoner, he would ask Lord Geoffrey to pay his ransom rather than Richard of Cornwall. The thought made him ridiculously cheerful despite the fact that, in view of the forest of lances coming toward him, he was likely to be spitted like a pig in the next few minutes.

Then the first group was across the stream. Walter laughed aloud and pulled his sword, while beside and behind him he could hear men cursing, muttering, laughing, or drawing deep, gasping breaths as was characteristic of their unconscious preparation for battle, but no one tried to back out or edge away. Pembroke's reason for standing his ground was valid; each man knew his chances were better fighting hard than attempting to run.

Amid the other sounds the *twang* and *hum* of twenty bowstrings was almost inaudible, but hard on the heels of that deadly music came the screams of horses and men. The center of the oncoming army was hardest hit, since twenty bowmen cannot cover a wide range and Pembroke had sensibly ordered the men to concentrate their fire. Walter laughed again. Likely he would live through the first impact, anyway.

The forest of lances was becoming more like individual trees as some horses fell and others tripped over them. At the same time, others leapt sideways and tried to bolt or began to buck in reaction to pain, causing those behind or alongside to collide with them. Walter did not doubt his ability to protect himself so long as he was not spitted by a second or third lance while he warded off the immediate attack.

Then Richard shouted, and the whole group charged forward, bellowing at the top of their lungs. They had not far to go, but screaming, opening their ranks suddenly, and moving forward at what speed they could generate, further startled the already nervous horses of the enemy and confused the aim of the lance wielders. Walter saw Pembroke beat aside a lance so fiercely that the holder turned sideways in his saddle and lost a stirrup. Then his own sword made contact, and, almost simultaneously, there was an impact on his shield. He slatted that off nearly without effort and certainly without thought, reacting by the conditioning of many tourney jousts where the lances were better aimed. Walter was more concerned with his third opponent, who had seen that his sword was extended right and his shield left.

There was no time for Walter to bring his sword across to thrust the lance away to the right or to cover his breast with his shield. And if his horse reared, the animal would take the lance blow in the chest and be killed. Walter had been given Beau when he was a gangly-legged colt. He had trained the destrier himself, and the animal, fierce as a wild boar in battle, would follow him, begging for caresses like a lap dog. Walter would not sacrifice Beau while there was any chance, no matter how slender.

Walter prodded his stallion forward sharply, dropped his shield as far as he could, and swung his sword hard down and inward. The lance point scraped across his mail, catching irregularly, but he had hit it hard enough and it skittered past his ribs. As the point cleared, Walter raised his left arm outward, and leaned his body forward and into an enormous backhand blow with the sword. The edge bit through the mail hood of the lance wielder, blood spurted, the lance dropped, its haft bruising Walter's thigh—and then Beau was past his opponent, and Walter was free.

There were a few seconds in which Walter had time to look around. Richard was still slightly ahead of him and did not seem to have suffered any hurt. Just then Walter saw still another lance fly out of an opponent's hand as Richard struck. Then someone, veering away from the earl's too-great strength, came at Walter. He disposed of the lance easily and moved in to strike the man, whose destrier rose and took the blow.

Walter shouted a curse; he hated to hurt horses and hated men who used them as shields. Worse yet, the stallion had fallen almost under Beau's feet, but that sagacious animal leapt ponderously over the dying horse—destriers not being built for jumping lightly. The rider had cleared his fallen mount and ran forward, sword raised, to pull Walter from Beau and mount Beau himself. Walter had been watching for that and beat outward with his shield, knocking his enemy aside. He was sorry the man had not approached from his sword side, for he would have liked to kill him, but he was out of reach.

The next attack came from the left. Having avoided the lance aimed at him, Walter did not pursue the meeting, instead prodding Beau with his left knee to turn him right. He had been driven too far from Richard, Walter feared. One great danger of being so few against so many was that each man could be isolated, then surrounded by five or ten opponents. The initial charge had been necessary to save them from being too compact a target for the lancers. Now, however, the movement was working against them, permitting them to be spread out too widely. Walter began to shout, *"À Marshal! À Marshal!"*

As the call burst from Walter's mouth, a whole group turned toward him. Walter gasped with surprise and checked Beau's movement toward Richard. He had meant to rally support and bring their party together, not to endanger the earl by attracting attention. Then, as he readied himself for an onslaught he could not withstand, it flashed through Walter's mind that the purpose of bringing the army at their small group rather than using it to protect the town was to take prisoner or to kill the Earl of Pembroke. Someone must have been longsighted enough to recognize Richard's arms, even at the distance they were from the keep. Apparently de Guisnes felt the loss of the town was less important than the death or capture of Pembroke.

He was right, of course. With Pembroke dead, there would be no focal point to rally around, and the disorganized rebellion would have little chance of forcing the king to dismiss the Bishop of Winchester. Walter tried to turn Beau even farther away, still calling *"À Marhsal,"* hoping they would think he was Richard. Sometimes a leader in extremity would take a vassal's shield to escape capture. It was not a dishonorable thing to do—although it was not very well thought of, either—because the leader would then pay his vassal's ransom and all would be well. Of course, if the vassal was killed, it was unfortunate.

However, Walter's effort to get clear of Richard was useless. He was hemmed in. Fortunately, by now nearly all the lances had been expended. With the desperate excess of strength that extremity gives, Walter struck one and then another lance out of the hands that held them while managing to absorb several sword blows with his shield. Beau struck down a horse with a sidelong lunge, which simultaneously gave Walter a clear strike at the rider and exposed his left side to an oncoming lance.

He just managed to catch the lance on his shield, but he knew he had caught it too low. If the tip slid off his shield now, it would catch him in the throat. Desperately, Walter tried to move the shield both upward and away from his body, but just as he was straining his uttermost, all resistance gave way. His shield flew outward, catching the shaft of the lance as it fell and flinging it away to the left.

Walter heard a cry of consternation, but he had no time to see what that freak accident had accomplished. He had barely managed to beat away a blow launched not at him but at Beau's neck. Because the man's arm was down, Walter's sword caught that, rather than the blade of his weapon. He shouted with satisfaction as the blade bit true, and his voice was almost drowned in the shriek of his victim. Walter knew he had not severed the arm, but he had felt the crack of bone. That man would not strike at horses again.

The best of defenses, however, was not adequate against too many opponents. Walter saw a sword angled to thrust in front of his shield, which he had not yet been able to bring back into position on his left, while another was coming down to strike at his sword arm on his right. He kneed Beau urgently to the left, knowing the horse could not get around in time, but neither blow fell. The man thrusting at his breast pitched forward and sideward, falling right across Walter's lap and Beau's neck while his horse collided violently with Walter's left leg.

Walter shrieked with pain as his knee was crushed against the saddle, and his shield, caught against the destrier's head, hit him on the shoulder and then wrenched his left arm up and back. But the force of the collision pushed Beau so far to the right that the sword blow aimed at Walter's arm struck the back of the man lying across him. Then the destrier on his left was gone, and the one on the right had veered off, too, leaving Walter still gasping with pain but with no serious injury. He managed to push the man off, although he felt as if he were moving a mountain. And now, all over the field, men were calling "*A Marshal, à Marshal,*" as Pembroke's party recognized the danger of being scattered and tried to draw together.

A form loomed up directly ahead. His eyes still misted

with tears of pain, Walter braced for another onslaught, bringing up his sword. However, *Marshal* was roared at him, and he realized it was the earl himself. Desperately, Walter caught at the reins tied to the saddle pommel with the fingers of his shield arm to check Beau. There was a dreadful pang in his shoulder, but Richard's horse crossed in front of him, avoiding a collision by inches, and charged off to the right.

Instinctively, Walter tried to press his left knee into Beau's side to turn and follow Pembroke, but the effort hurt horribly, and he could not exert much force. Beau did turn, but so slowly that Walter was some distance behind when he saw a compact party of thirteen riding directly at the earl. Walter dug his spurs into Beau, and the horse leapt forward, but the damage to his knee was still taking its toll.

Prodded harder on the right than on the left, the destrier edged away in the direction of least pressure, bringing Walter off to the side of the group attacking Richard rather than right into them. And again Walter was on the wrong side, the side that required him to use his left knee or left hand to turn his horse. Before he could communicate his need to Beau, they were well past the group attacking the earl and Walter himself was engaged again. He was so frustrated and furious, however, that he made quick work of his opponents, screaming imprecations as he strove to turn.

Finally, Walter managed to seize the right rein in his shield hand and pull. Beau came around smartly, just in time for Walter to see Richard's horse run through by a lance. Walter bellowed with rage and terror and drove spurs into Beau with desperate energy, so distraught this time that he did not even feel the pang in his knee and succeeded in getting the horse to charge in a straight line. Unfortunately, the effort was utterly useless. Walter knew he was too far away to be of any help, although he was close enough to see Pembroke save himself.

As the horse went down, Richard slipped his feet from the stirrups and jumped, landing crouched with his shield over his head. He did not come upright, but scuttled forward a few feet, dodging the milling horses, to thrust upward from behind a man and pierce his thigh. Walter did not see the next move because it was blocked by the sidling horse, but he did hear the cry of the man Richard had attacked choke off and then rise to a startled shriek as he pitched off his horse. A moment later, Richard was in the saddle and had struck down two more of his opponents.

By then Walter had reached the group and slashed one man from the rear. Another turned to drive him away but found that task more than he could handle alone and called for help, which drew still another man from the attack on Pembroke. There were now only four left of the thirteen who had originally ridden to the attack, and the leader of the group was growing desperate.

The man was shouting orders, but Walter could not really understand because his French had so strange an accent, and, together with the noise and the fact that he could spare little attention to listen, the orders were incomprehensible. Fortunately, Walter rid himself of one of his opponents just then and caught a glimpse of Richard engaged with three men in the front while the leader worked his way around to the left rear—where Walter should have been.

Walter roared a warning, but it was too late. The man behind Pembroke launched a blow at his head. It struck only glancingly and at so odd an angle that the sword twisted in its owner's hand and fell. Either the earl had heard Walter's warning or some sidelong glance had warned him so that he ducked. Nonetheless, he must have been partially stunned, for his sword arm dropped and his head bent forward. Seizing his opportunity, the leader leaned forward, grasped Richard's helmet from the back, and wrenched it off with such violence that the metal tore the earl's lips and nose and the helmet struck his forehead a brutal blow. Between the pain and the blood, Richard was effectively blinded. Walter bellowed and surged forward, regardless of the threat of his remaining opponent, but it was not possible to ride through a horse.

Beau reared on command and flourished with his hooves, neighing and snapping, while the other destrier, caught down and too close, backed away. Walter leaned out so far he almost toppled from the saddle, but he did manage to get in a blow made extra powerful by the tilt of his body, and, in thrusting out his right leg to save himself from falling, he kicked the backing horse in the shoulder. Prodded, the beast obediently turned away, still backing, carrying his reeling rider out of harm's way, but Walter had no intention of pressing his attack. He was only interested in reaching the man who had now seized the rein of Richard's horse and was leading it rapidly away in the direction of Monmouth keep.

The three men who had attacked the earl from the front had now fallen in behind him and were prodding him forward. Half-stunned and blinded by his own blood, Richard turned in the saddle and swept his sword around behind him so swiftly that he caught one man on the forward sweep and the other on the backstroke. Still, he was helpless to prevent himself from being drawn forward because he could neither control his horse nor reach the man who was leading it. Walter was coming up from the rear, but others in the opposing force were closing in on the pair more quickly. Walter knew he would never reach them in time. Glancing wildly around, Walter saw three men on foot, wearing tabards striped green and yellow, bearing a rampant red lion.

"Shoot! Shoot!" he screamed. "The earl is taken prisoner."

The bows came up. Instantly, Walter bitterly regretted what he had done. Crossbows are not the most accurate of weapons. If any of the men happened to be an unusually bad shot, Richard instead of his captor might be skewered. Walter shut his eyes in terror.

The desire to shut out the sight of a disaster one has caused is natural, but under the circumstances it was also stupid. Walter opened his eyes at once and saw his action vindicated. Richard's captor had dropped the reins of the earl's horse and was falling sideways off his own mount. Walter barely caught a glimpse of a dark shaft protruding from the man's chest. The instant the reins were released, Pembroke kneed the horse he rode sharply away from the falling man. The enemies who had been closing on captor and captive to escort them abandoned the earl in favor of succoring their master, and Walter was able to overtake Richard's stumbling mount, retrieve the reins, and thrust them into the earl's fingers.

The crossbowmen were running toward them, and Walter felt an enormous relief that he would not need to try to protect Richard without help. He ached all over and felt so tired that he wondered whether he would be able to remain astride of Beau, let alone fight. To make matters worse, somewhere to the left Walter was aware of a considerable increase in the noise of battle, but he had no time to wonder what new disaster had befallen them.

They were assailed again. Although he had not believed he

could lift his arm, Walter found himself so angry because he would not be allowed to rest that new strength flowed through him. There was a grinding pain in his left shoulder and a sharp agony in his knee, but that only made him angrier, and he struck and struck again at those who denied him rest and freedom.

When Walter woke, he felt the softness of a real bed under him. This left him very puzzled, and he considered the matter before he opened his eyes. He had not slept in a real bed since he had joined Richard, a natural result of being one of the earl's less important adherents. Then he must be a prisoner, Walter thought. But before he realized how unlikely it was that a prisoner should be provided with such luxury, he groaned and opened his eyes.

"Did the earl escape?" Walter asked of the face hanging over him. And then he recognized the face and cried, "Dai! What do you do here?"

"Attend you, my lord. Yes, of course the earl escaped. Escaped? Was he in danger of being taken?"

By this time it had occurred to Walter that Dai had not followed him into captivity. Indeed, Dai could not have known Walter had been captured, because the master-at-arms had been sent with Walter's troop into the town of Monmouth. Walter had not wanted to deprive the men of whatever chance of loot was available.

Now he tried to sit up and groaned again, every bone and muscle crying out with pain. Walter could not remember aching so excruciatingly since his early years as a squire, when his big body, combined with great swiftness, had made him overconfident and boastful—a condition his master had cured by using him as a fencing partner.

Dai then lent a hand, and Walter found himself sitting upright, the sharper pangs of discomfort subsiding to a dull overall malaise. Walter stared dazedly around, still not certain where he was. Dai began to look concerned.

"Are you hurt, lord?" he asked.

Walter gaped at him. There was no part of him that did not hurt—except his head. Then he understood what Dai meant. "No, but I feel as if I had been soundly beaten from neck to toe." He glanced round the chamber again. "Where am I?"

"In Abergavenny keep," Dai replied, looking more worried still. "Your head does not hurt? You were not struck there?"

"There is nothing wrong with my head," Walter replied, "but I have no idea how I came here or what I am doing in this chamber."

"You rode in with Lord Pembroke, he crying aloud to all that you had saved him. The chamber is Sir Ralph's. The earl bade you lie here."

"Bade me?" Walter started to lift his left hand to his head, gasped, and desisted. He used his right hand instead to feel around, but there were no soft spots in his skull, not even tender ones. It was, apparently, not a blow on the head that had wiped out his memory of the latter part of the battle.

He began to shrug away the problem, and another pang in his left shoulder made him crane his neck to look at it. What he could see of the flesh was a beautiful medley of dark blue and purple, splotched with maroon. The rest of his body was patched with similar bruises, and here and there a cut that had been sewn, but the only spot that rivaled the depth and variety of the color on his shoulder was his left knee. That, Walter remembered. Gingerly, he stretched and bent it; he needed to set his teeth over a howl of pain, but the knee moved as ordered. And when he got out of bed, it supported him, although under violent protest.

With Dai's help, Walter got dressed and limped out into the hall. The first person he saw was Richard, and he gasped with shock. The earl's face was a horror, nose and mouth swollen out of all proportion, scabbed, and even more fancifully colored than his own shoulder and knee. Walter rushed forward and would have fallen flat on his face when his knee gave way if Dai had not kept pace and caught him.

"Are you all right, my lord?" Walter cried, and then bit his lips when Richard glared at him. It would be cruel to laugh, Walter knew, because Richard would be tempted to laugh, too, and that would wreak further havoc on his torn lips. "Sorry," Walter said. "A stupid question. I could have killed Dai when he asked me if I were hurt. I hurt all over. But it is the strangest thing. I do not remember anything after that captain who was leading your horse was shot."

"De Guisnes," said Gilbert Bassett, who was sitting beside Richard at the table. "It was Baldwin de Guisnes himself. King Henry left him in charge of Monmouth. We were fools not to consider that more carefully. De Guisnes, who is Poitevin, would not care if the town of Monmouth were burnt—it is not *his* land—and Henry would not care, either."

Richard grasped Bassett's arm and shook it.

"Oh, well," Bassett temporized, "he would not care in comparison with taking prisoner or killing you, Pembroke, and you know it. We laid that trap ourselves, for ourselves, and then fell into it. I swear, God must favor our cause. After all our stupidity and carelessness, we have succeeded in decimating the garrison of Monmouth. Oh, sit down, Walter, sit down."

Dai brought up a stool, and Walter sank down on it gratefully. "If we have done them so much harm," Walter asked, "could we take the keep before new troops are brought in to replace those killed and wounded?"

"That is just what Richard and I have been talking about," Bassett said, and, then smiled. "At least, I have been talking, and Richard has been writing his replies. At first I was of your mind, Walter, but even undermanned it would take more men than we have to break Monmouth. That means Lord Llewelyn's help, and even if he were willing to give it, nearly a week would pass before we could try an assault."

"No!" Walter exclaimed. "That is too long. The assault must be launched at once—tonight. Men can come from Goodrich in only a few hours. . . ." He stopped to consider, began to shrug, winced, and remarked, "But likely it is already too late, unless de Guisnes is dead or unconscious and his captains all such fools that they did not send out word of what befell them."

"That is what Richard said—wrote," Bassett remarked, and Richard nodded approvingly. "And we cannot stop them," Bassett continued. "If we set up a siege, they can surround us. We had losses, too, in that battle."

Walter did not reply directly. While he had been dressing, Dai had told him that two of his fifty men were dead and another seven injured, two seriously and the others lightly. Since Walter knew his men to be as well trained as any of the others, the damage to the remainder of the force must be at least proportional. That meant that eight out of every hundred of Richard's army were useless, either dead or too badly hurt to fight, while another ten out of every hundred would be sore and inefficient. He himself would be nearly useless for an assault, which meant climbing and fighting afoot.

Walter frowned. "If you still wish to take Monmouth, my lord," he said slowly, "you will need to leave men in concealment to watch. A trap could be set against us. The keep could be filled with double or triple the men it held this time on the chance that you would think it undermanned. I do not think so many could have moved in yet, but—"

"Yes," Bassett interrupted, "we have thought of it, but it is not so easy to do as to say. The country is open there, nothing but small woods anywhere near enough to watch the place, and if they are bringing up extra men, they will have patrols."

"Prince Llewelyn has men who can hide beside a blade of grass," Walter pointed out. "You look straight at them and do not see them. I have seen—or, rather, not seen—Simon de Vipont's men disappear before my eyes."

"Good God," Bassett cried, "so have I. And Sir Simon will lend his men, surely. As he will be marrying, he will not have any use for the troop for a while."

Richard had been scribbling and now pushed what he had written over for Walter to read: *Idea good but no attack. Warned and on guard.*

Bassett, who had leaned over to read the note also, shrugged. "Yes, I think so, too, but we should do something, and quickly."

Walter agreed emphatically, and Richard also nodded and reached for the parchment. Walter pushed it to him, and Richard wrote a few words and pushed it back. Walter read: *Brecon tomorrow. Can you ride? Llewelyn soon as possible.*

"I can ride, my lord," Walter replied, as the question was obviously meant for him.

In fact, Walter would have preferred to rest a day or two and meet Richard and his womenfolk at Builth, but he realized that someone was going to have to talk for Richard to Gervase and Marie. Walter had also heard from Dai the tale of hurt and missing among Richard's small party. The earl's senior squire had been less fortunate than his master and had been captured on his way back from the town where he had been sent to summon Bassett to their aid. Both of the younger squires had been hurt. It was believed they would live, but Richard would take no chances with their well-being. They were to remain in Abergavenny to be cared for until they had recovered completely.

Then, Walter thought, it had better be he who accompanied Richard to Brecon. He had already established a relationship with Gervase and Marie. Besides, Walter remembered that Bassett was not coming to the wedding. There was not much choice; he would have to ride to Brecon with Richard.

Meanwhile, Bassett had approved Richard's decision to make future plans immediately in conjunction with their Welsh ally but was urging the earl to have Llewelyn's men also watch Monmouth. Richard was clearly doubtful of the efficacy of this move. He had heard of the skill of the Welsh woodsmen and he knew that Bassett felt the attack on Grosmont would not have been half as successful or a tenth as profitable if the Welsh had not spied out the way and removed the guards and sentries. However, Richard had not taken part in the expedition against Grosmont and had never seen these men at their work. He was trained and experienced in traditional methods of war and found it difficult to believe such unorthodox procedures had great value.

After several exchanges, through which Walter sat silent, he realized that Bassett would not be able to convince the earl. This was something, he supposed, one must experience.

"My lord," Walter said, "there is no need for you to be involved in this matter at all. It is true that Lord Llewelyn may not consider the problems of south Wales to be important to him. However, they are important to me. Goldcliff will fall if Usk or Chepstow be taken or even if they are passed by so that the king's men may sup off easier meat. Let me write to Simon. Sir Gilbert is quite right that Simon will not need his men for a week or two, and he will be very willing to do me the favor of having them watch Monmouth."

"Excellent. Excellent," Bassett said, before Richard could begin to wonder whether it was right for Walter to ask as a personal favor what Richard himself did not wish to ask as help from an ally. "Go and write to Sir Simon at once," Bassett urged. "Do you need a messenger? If so, bring me the letter when it is finished, and I will have it sent out."

Taking the hint to remove himself before the earl began to worry about fine points of honor, Walter went off out of sight, found a place to sit down, and sent Dai to find a clerk to write the letter for him. Walter could write; it was no longer acceptable for an earl's son to be illiterate, but at the moment he felt that even writing was too strenuous an exercise for him. When the letter was off, he staggered back to bed, able to think of little beyond the horrible fact that the next day he would need to ride about forty miles to Brecon.

CHAPTER 7

Actually, the ride was not nearly as bad as Walter expected. Richard had been battered almost as much as Walter, and they seldom went faster than a walk, which permitted Walter to allow his left leg to hang loose with a rolled shirt thrust under his thigh so that the knee did not come in contact with the saddle. The ride was also dull because Richard could not speak without pain—and it was useless anyway, for when he did speak it was almost impossible to understand him. Thus, Walter was left to his own thoughts, all of which were unsettling.

He was not sure what he wanted to do about Marie. What Richard had said about her made it clear that his sister-by-marriage's behavior was of no importance in his political plans. Thus an affair was possible, and Walter was hungry for a woman of his own class. Still, even if Marie did not wish to marry, she might be offended if he bedded her while he was negotiating for Sybelle.

Walter uttered an oath. He was perfectly sure of what he wanted to do about Sybelle. He shifted uneasily in the saddle; the folded shirt slipped, Walter tightened his thigh to catch it, twisted his knee, and cursed again—but not because of the pang in his knee. It was ridiculous that a girl's name should have such an effect on him. Yes, he knew what he wanted to do about Sybelle, but that was not in his power. Walter wished it were his own wedding toward which he was riding. Knee or no knee, he would have been progressing a good deal faster.

At this moment the only doubt in Walter's mind with regard to Sybelle was whether he should approach Lord Geoffrey again. Had the victories at Grosmont and Monmouth changed the situation enough? Walter did not wish to seem to importune Lord Geoffrey, who might think his hunger for help in obtaining his inheritance was greater than his hunger for Sybelle. But if he did not approach Lord Geoffrey, would Sybelle's father think he had lost interest in her? And what did Sybelle think? Walter was startled at the mental question. What did it matter what Sybelle thought? She would obey her father, and he would be a good and tender husband so that she would very soon come to care for him. But even as the ideas ran through his mind, Walter knew there was something very wrong with this classical formula for marital bliss when associated with Sybelle.

Unbidden, various images of Sybelle came into Walter's mind: Sybelle flaying him for carelessness with regard to his control of his men; Sybelle brightly adding clever and all-too-accurate guesses to an all-male conversation concerning the king's doings; Sybelle flatly contradicting her father and grandfather and boldly offering theories of her own, which the men considered with grave thoughtfulness. No, although Walter still knew what to do about Sybelle, he had a feeling his task would be more complicated than simply gaining her father's approval for the marriage.

That feeling, oddly enough, increased rather than diminished Walter's ardor. He then hastily removed his mind from the question of marriage with Sybelle, since he was well aware that it was uncomfortable to ride a horse in a state of sexual arousal while wearing armor. Thought of his armor recalled to his consciousness the ache in his left shoulder. Something more than bruising was wrong there, Walter feared. The pain when he raised his arm to put on the hauberk had been killing—which led to the unpleasant thought of getting the hauberk off again, and that took his mind to the arrival at Brecon.

No matter what the relationship was between Richard and Gervase, she must ask what had befallen her husband. Walter would have to explain. As the miles passed, Walter worked out what he believed to be an acceptably brief history of the events. Actually, owing to the slow pace their injuries made necessary, they arrived too late for any conversation with Gervase and Marie. But even the next day Walter found, to his amazement, that his carefully prepared tale was not needed. No curiosity or concern was shown by either Richard's wife or his sister-by-marriage about his and Walter's battered state. In fact, Marie acted toward Walter as if they had hardly exchanged so much as a civil greeting. Walter was not offended, however; he was grateful to Marie for her discretion and complimented her for it when they were briefly out of the hearing of others in the great hall.

She glanced up at him under her lashes and said, "Oh, you will find me a model of propriety when it is necessary."

"And a model of impropriety at other times?" Walter teased suggestively.

"If I am provoked," she rejoined, and quick as a flash reached out to draw a finger down Walter's cheek and along his neck.

"I am very desirous of knowing what will provoke you," Walter urged, his voice somewhat thickened.

She did not reply to that other than by a glance because Gervase came up to them and said that she believed Richard wanted Walter. This was true, and Walter was busy giving orders and, in general, being Richard's voice for the rest of the day. Nonetheless, he found odd moments to wonder about Marie's behavior. He could not understand how she could be so openly inviting and yet not take the first chance that would not betray her interest to ask him why he was limping and moving his left arm as little as possible.

Walter did not want Marie to love him; that would be both dangerous and undesirable. However, considering her display of sexual attraction, a friendly interest in his physical well-being would seem natural. Had he loved her himself, he would have been crushed, but since his feeling for Marie was all in his loins, it was not important to him, only slightly puzzling. And the next day, which was spent in traveling from Brecon to Builth, he became so disgusted with both women that his desire for Marie was much abated.

Unlike the journey from Pembroke, Marie did not come out of the traveling cart to ride with him and talk—for that Walter was at first grateful. The distance was only about twenty miles, but it took all day. Part of the way was very hilly, and it was necessary to unhitch the team from the baggage wagon and combine it with the team drawing the traveling cart in order to get the heavy vehicle up the steep slope. Then, of course, both teams had to be unhitched from the traveling cart, allowed a period of rest, and brought down to pull the baggage wain up the hill.

Several repetitions of this process, which was also necessary for fording streams with steep or muddy banks, did no one's temper any good. By the afternoon, Richard's patience was exhausted, and, when carts and men found themselves in particular difficulty in a deep and dangerous ford, he forgot himself and tried to shout orders. This split his lips anew, and Walter had considerable ado stanching the bleeding.

At this point Walter felt that he would like to murder Gervase and Marie both—although he blamed Marie less because she was only Richard's sister-by-marriage. The baggage wain was stuck in the middle of the ford; it was impossible for the men, thigh-deep in water and straining to keep the oxen from panicking and to prevent the wain from overturning, to see the way out for themselves. It was Gervase's duty, no matter what her feelings about him, to come and attend to her husband while Walter tried to help the men save the baggage.

Under the circumstances, Walter "did not see" Richard's negative shake of the head when he said he would summon Gervase. But Walter discovered that Richard had not been trying to avoid his wife's attentions, only to save Walter's time. When Walter told Gervase for what she was needed, she simply covered her face with her hands, shuddered, and said that she fainted at the sight of blood. This made Walter stare with surprise and wonder what she did about her fluxes. Did she remain in a faint all week?

Angrily, he turned back toward Richard but was waved urgently away toward the stream, where he arrived just in time to prevent a disaster. This was accomplished, however, only at the cost of getting soaking wet, since amid the sound of the water, the bellowing of the frightened oxen, and the shouting of the men, he could only make himself heard and seen by going back into the stream himself. There, despite being astride Beau, he was liberally splashed by the struggles to extricate the cart.

Wet or not, Walter had no desire to remove his armor and underclothing in the open on a cold, late November afternoon. A dry blanket was found to replace his soaked cloak, and they continued at the best speed the tired carriage teams could make. The swelling of Richard's face, which had diminished, was now almost as bad as it had been in the beginning, and Walter could have wept for his friend. Not only did he grieve for Richard's current discomfort, but he knew the earl was nearly starving, as the condition of his face prevented him from opening his mouth more than a sliver and made chewing equally impossible. Now it would be several days more before Richard could eat properly. Nor was the wetting, chill, and exertion doing his own injuries any good, Walter thought.

It was no very happy party that arrived in Builth just as dusk was shading into full dark, and they were led directly into the great hall, where Prince Llewelyn was sitting, by a gentleman who recognized the Earl of Pembroke's colors and was eager to do him honor. By then, Walter would gladly have forgone the honor of being Richard's companion, dropped out of the group, and found a place to rest—but someone had to answer questions for Richard. Half-blind with pain and fatigue, Walter hardly saw the members of the group seated around the hearth, but he was startled into alertness by Lady Alinor's voice.

"Merciful Mary, what has happened to your face?" Alinor cried, and in the next breath, before Walter could take the few necessary steps forward to answer, she rose to her feet and took Richard's hand. "No, never mind. Come with me to your chamber at once. Rhiannon, have you a poultice that will take down this swelling?"

"Yes, I will go prepare it at once," Rhiannon replied, jumping to her feet and rushing off down the hall.

Alinor had been examining the hurt and now said, "This is not new, even if the blood is fresh. You silly boy, did you try to speak? Joanna, go tell the cooks to prepare something for Richard to eat that he can get into his mouth and will fill his stomach. He must be starving." At which point Richard squeezed her hand, and Alinor continued sharply, "Yes, I thought that would be what you would need most, but there is no need to break my fingers. Is there no one with a grain of sense in your company? Where are your squires?"

Looking around for them, Alinor missed the expression of pain and anxiety on Richard's face at the reminder of the young man in prison and the two boys lying hurt, but she did see Walter. "Walter!" she exclaimed. "Why did you not—" And then, as he limped forward and his face came out of the shadows into the light of fire and candles, her voice checked. "Good God," she cried, "You are in no better case than Richard. Sybelle, take Walter to my chamber and see what is wrong with him. If you need my help, send a maid for me."

Walter knew quite well that he should draw forward Gervase

and Marie, who had been completely overlooked in the general anxiety over Pembroke's condition, but his voice stuck in his throat. As Sybelle rose from the stool on which she had been sitting, desire, anxiety, embarrassment, and relief all boiled together in the stew of Walter's exhausted and aching body, and he reeled. Lord Geoffrey, who was closest, jumped up to support him, and Lord Ian and Simon also rose, temporarily blocking Walter's sight of Sybelle.

"I am only tired," he said, "and here are Gervase, Lady Pembroke, and her sister, Lady Marie de les Maures."

Every head turned toward the ladies. Walter had a brief glimpse of Lady Alinor's face, her eyes flashing and lips thinned with fury as she realized that Richard's wife had been with him and had not attended to his very apparent needs. But it was only a single glance. Then Lady Alinor turned and drew Richard swiftly away. Lord Geoffrey and Lord Ian looked surprised, as if trying to fit together the presence of Lady Pembroke and her husband's untended condition. However, Prince Llewelyn got up from his chair and came smoothly forward.

"My ladies," he said, his voice warm and resonant, "let me make you welcome, very welcome. Will you not sit down here by the fire and rest until Lord Pembroke is made comfortable and we can take you to your chamber?"

Walter heard no more, although he was aware that Llewelyn was still speaking, because Sybelle had come near and said softly, "Can you walk, Sir Walter?"

He nodded mutely, disengaged himself from Geoffrey's supporting hand, then found his voice and said, "Yes, of course," completely unaware that Geoffrey and Ian were both smiling with kindly amusement.

Having passed tactfully behind her father and grandfather so that her movement would not attract attention, Sybelle took a few steps more and came to Walter's left side. "If you will come this way," she urged.

But for the moment Walter could not move. He had remembered Sybelle as beautiful and desirable, of course, but the perfection of her face struck him like a physical blow. He had not seen her since the very beginning of October, and over that time he had forgotten the way her bronze brows arched over her golden eyes, the mat perfection of her creamy skin, the exquisite bow of her rosy lips with the very full, sensual lower lip protruding just a bit beyond the upper. And there was in her expression sufficient worry to send his pulse leaping with the thought that she was concerned for him. The wrong words rose to his lips, not proper, civil words of greeting, but hot and passionate words most unfit for this time and place.

Sybelle had seen Walter long before he had seen her. Somewhat bored by the relation and discussion of news that was not news to her, she had allowed her eyes to wander over the hall now and again while she listened. Thus, she had seen the party advancing toward the hearth where Prince Llewelyn's chair of state was set. She had not recognized the Earl of Pembroke, not having seen him since she was a child—although she might not have recognized him anyway owing to his injuries. However, she had recognized Walter, despite the dim light, with an ease that surprised her and made her feel self-conscious.

The early scrutiny, which noted his bad limp, had told her of one of his injuries before her grandmother had noticed them. The fact that he was walking without support had quelled her first impulse to rush to his assistance. She remembered her proud words when her mother had said her father and grandfather would assure Walter she was already his devoted slave: *I will swifty disabuse his mind of that notion,* she had said.

It would hardly be possible to convince Walter that she was not totally committed to him if she ran to him weeping and asking breathlessly how he was hurt. It was necessary and proper to maintain a reserve. As proof that her reasoning and actions had been correct, she had been rewarded by her grandmother's order to take Walter into her care.

Concentrated as she was upon his injuries, Sybelle misunderstood Walter's slowness to respond when she asked him to accompany her. She believed pride had made him deny a need for assistance. It was silly, but Sybelle was accustomed to the idea that a man's pride must always be protected. She came even closer and said, even more softly, "I am very strong. You can lean on me. No one will notice."

Walter thought of saying that there was no need, but he was afraid his voice would come out as a squeak, or nothing would come out at all when he opened his mouth. Besides, the thought of putting his arm around Sybelle and leaning on her—ever so lightly because, of course, he never believed she could really support him—was very attractive. He had never yet touched any part of her but her hand. She was at his left side because she had noticed it was his left leg that was lame. Forgetting completely the injury to his shoulder, Walter raised that arm to lay it across Sybelle's shoulders and barely bit back a howl.

Although Walter actually uttered no more than a low grunt, Sybelle was instantly aware. She slipped swiftly to his other side, slid herself under his good shoulder, and put her arm around his waist. Surprise and a wave of vertigo made Walter sag against her, but she steadied him and began to move slowly away from the group at the hearth. By the time they came to the exit from the hall, Walter was supporting himself and Sybelle was able to dismiss the fear that despite his objections she would have to call for help to get him up the stairs to her grandmother's room. Nonetheless, he did not withdraw his arm from Sybelle's shoulders, nor did she suggest that he do so.

Inside the chamber, she steered him toward a stool and gently released herself. Sybelle had been frightened when Walter first leaned on her so heavily but soon recognized that it was only a momentary weakness. She knew she could have left him to walk by himself, only she found it very pleasant to be cuddled against his side. Perhaps if he had not been so damp, had not been wearing armor, and there had been a discreet way to prolong the embrace, Sybelle would have done so; however, under the circumstances, it was not practical.

"Stand a moment," Sybelle said, leaving him near the stool while she rapidly made up the low-burning fire and then thrust a long splinter of wood into the flames with which to light candles. Having done so, she came back to Walter and bent to catch the hem of his hauberk. "Now sit," she ordered, as she lifted the mail shirt. She had it up chest high when she remembered that he could not raise his left arm without pain and paused.

"Take it off," Walter said, understanding her hesitation. "I do not know why my shoulder is so sore, but I have had the mail on and off several times."

"I can summon the armorer to cut it off," Sybelle suggested. "Just the sleeve, which could be easily mended."

"He will likely hurt me ten times as much. Just take it off."

In a moment, Sybelle decided he was right and pulled off the hauberk as quickly as she could. Walter's face was white when it came into sight, but he had been prepared for the pain and showed no sign of faintness. Satisfied, Sybelle went to lay the armor carefully away as she had been taught.

"I will tell one of my father's squires to dry and clean it," she assured him, "but let me get those wet clothes off you first. I hope you have not already taken a chill. However did you get so wet? It has been fine all day. Is it now raining?"

"No. It was in fording a stream. The baggage wain was mired, and Lord Pembroke had just broken open his mouth again, and . . ." He laughed ruefully. "I would rather not remember it. Hoy! What do you do with that knife?"

"I will cut off your tunic and shirt. There is no need for you to be hurt again, and to move that arm when it gives you so much pain may be doing it harm."

"There is no need to ruin a shirt and tunic over a small pain," Walter protested. "My shoulder will mend."

"So will your shirt and tunic," Sybelle said, laughing. "Did you think I planned to rip them to shreds? I need only cut the threads of the seam, which can be resewn in a few minutes—but preferably after the garments are washed." Then she added, wrinkling her nose, "You need a wife, Sir Walter."

The words had come out without thought, just a light remark such as she had made hundreds of times to Simon before he had met Rhiannon. If she had continued to speak lightly, the words would have had little significance in the context in which they had been spoken. However, at that moment Sybelle recalled to whom she was speaking. Her voice faltered, a deep blush suffused her face, and the hand that held the knife dropped it and came up to cover her lips.

"Yes," Walter said, with such intensity and meaning that Sybelle blushed even harder. There was a breath-held pause, and then he said, "Sybelle?"

"You will catch your death of cold," she gabbled hastily, bending to pick up the knife. "I did not mean anything, you know. It is only a proof of the old maxim that every woman goes about to arrange the marriage of every man. . . ."

"Yes," he repeated, and then added, "please."

That did not make much sense, except that Sybelle understood quite well, and the look on Walter's face was such that she backed away a step. The movement recalled him to reality, and he dropped his eyes. He was appalled at what he had done. It was not honorable to court a girl before receiving her father's permission to do so. Hardly realizing what he was doing, Walter stood up and turned toward the door.

"Where are you going?" Sybelle cried.

"I must speak to your father," Walter said. "I—"

"Not soaking wet and dressed in an arming tunic," Sybelle protested, restraining laughter. Her embarrassment had dissipated, and she was amused by Walter's confusion. "You may not have noticed," she added dryly, "but the hall is full of guests. Come and sit down again. When I have looked to your hurts and you are warm and dressed, you will find Papa easily enough. They will be talking politics for hours."

Walter looked down at himself, stood irresolutely for another moment, and then reseated himself on the stool. Sybelle knelt down beside him and began to cut, then tear out, the stitches of the seam of his tunic. For a while Walter stared straight ahead, then cautiously shifted his eyes to look down at Sybelle. When it was clear that she was attending only to what she was doing, he allowed himself to gaze at her.

Surely, he thought, she must be aware that he intended to ask for her in marriage and surely she must be willing. If she had not been willing, she would have told him not to speak to her father or discouraged him by saying her father was too busy to talk to him. But she had not said that. She had said Lord Geoffrey would be easy to find. Did that mean she knew her father would accept his offer? The strong hope generated by that idea made Walter's muscles twitch as an impulse to go out and make his proposal at once swept over him.

"Did I prick you?" Sybelle asked, pulling the knife away and looking up.

"No," Walter replied shortly.

He shifted his eyes from her, then felt foolish because she must already know he had been staring at her and looked at her again. She was back at work, but her complexion was somewhat rosier than it had been. Walter smiled. He was behaving like an idiot, but plainly that was doing him no harm with Sybelle. It never did harm for a woman to think she had bemused a man. Then the smile turned a little wry as Walter considered the fact that in this case it was perfectly true. There was nothing he was not prepared to offer to obtain her as his wife.

Again he shifted restlessly, and this time the knife did prick him. Sybelle exclaimed apologetically, and Walter said it was his fault.

"Are you sitting on something uncomfortable?" Sybelle then asked with spurious innocence.

"Yes," Walter replied, recognizing the teasing and now prepared to give back as good as he got.

Surprised, Sybelle looked up again. "What is it?" This time her question was sincere. She did not remember anything on the stool that could make him uncomfortable.

"It is the question I wish to ask your father," Walter rejoined. "I wish you would hurry with what you are doing."

Sybelle turned red once more. "I can only go faster if I cut the cloth," she said.

"By all means," Walter agreed promptly. "This is a cause good enough for me to sacrifice an old shirt and tunic."

For one moment Sybelle stared at him, then she burst into laughter. She was not accustomed to men outside her family who could parry her wit and land a hit on her, but it was much better fun, she decided, than poking holes in strawmen who either looked hurt or did not understand.

"It is not," she assured him. "For you will get the same answer whether you go now or later, so there will be no profit in ruining your clothing."

The reply made Walter stiffen slightly, but, although Sybelle had lowered her head to her work again, he could see the curve of her cheek and noted that she was smiling. There was nothing cruel in Sybelle, Walter was sure. Nor was she a flirt. That must mean he was acceptable to Lord Geoffrey, that she knew it, and that she was willing.

Walter relaxed. The last few stitches of the tunic gave way, and Sybelle rose to her feet to remove it, giving Walter a clear view of her face. She was smiling, but her look was mischievous rather than grateful or even pleased, and Walter's unease returned. He still believed that Sybelle thought her father was willing to make contract with him and that Sybelle herself was not opposed to the marriage, but obviously there was a jumping jack in the package.

Whatever Walter felt, the preceding conversation had removed any awkwardness Sybelle had felt. As she started work on his shirt, she asked how he came to be so battered. Walter obliged with the narrative he had prepared for Gervase and Marie, but he got no further than the attack by Monmouth garrison on their small force when Sybelle interrupted.

"Heavens! Are you all idiots? One hundred men against thousands! I can just hear Lord Pembroke pronouncing with high chivalry, 'I have never yet turned my back upon an enemy in battle, and I do not propose to do so now. Let all those who wish to flee—' "

"He did not say anything of the kind," Walter snapped. "What he said was that if we fled in disorder, we would be taken from behind and destroyed, whereas if we turned our faces toward the enemy and fought bravely, the army, which was no great distance from us, would have time to come to our rescue. And that is what happened."

Sybelle's busy hands had stopped during Walter's reply, and now she looked up at him. "I am very sorry. I should have known better than to make a stupid criticism when I did not know the full circumstances. Do not be angry." Her eyes were large and very serious.

Before he thought what he was doing, Walter's hand touched her cheek. "I am not angry," he murmured. "I do not think I am capable of being angry with you."

He started to lean forward. Sybelle's face lifted toward his, and then she uttered a small gasp and turned sharply away. Walter straightened.

"You had better finish with me and let me go before I do something inexcusable," he muttered.

"Please go on. Tell me the rest," Sybelle urged, as if he had not spoken.

"There is nothing more, really, to tell, unless you want a blow-by-blow description of the fighting—and I do not imagine that would interest you. Richard has a cool head. He remembered to tell his senior squire and the two knights he sent off to warn Gilbert Bassett that we were trapped and to tell Bassett also to break down the bridge between the army and the keep. I understand that it was a great slaughter."

There was a slight pause. A few hours earlier, Sybelle would have commented with enthusiasm on the blow delivered against the king's cause. Her father would not break his oath of allegiance to Henry, but Sybelle had given none and could see no reason why she should not speak her mind—in safe company, of course. However, as the shirt fell away and exposed Walter's body, displaying several suppurating slashes and the horrible bruise on his shoulder, Sybelle suddenly thought that it was only by a miracle that the slaughter had not gone the other way. What if it were Walter who lay dead on the field before Monmouth keep? Did not the other men have wives, sisters, mothers? She could not find it in her to rejoice in their dying. She shuddered suddenly, remembering her mother's and grandmother's haunted eyes when their men went off to battle.

"What is it?" Walter asked, feeling the quiver that had run through her.

"Nothing," she answered. "Just the wet sleeve touched me. I am warm with work and with kneeling in front of the fire." And then, because he was looking at her doubtfully, not quite satisfied, she cast about in her mind for something to distract him and remembered an odd phrase in what he had said. "You understand that it was a great slaughter?" she repeated questioningly. "What do you mean? Were you not there?"

"I was," Walter replied, laughing ruefully. "I have been assured that I did my duty, but to speak the truth, I do not well remember the coming of the army or what took place after they came. When I first woke in Abergavenny the day after the battle, I thought I had been taken prisoner."

"You were struck on the head?" Sybelle asked anxiously, getting hastily to her feet and staring into Walter's eyes. "Have you had other lapses of memory?"

"No, and I was not struck on the head. That is the odd part. I thought as you did, but my head was the only part of me that did not hurt. Also, Dai thought I must have been stunned because it seems I rode into the keep, fell onto my cot, and did not wake all the time they moved me to a chamber, unarmed me, and sewed me up. He told the leech to look carefully at my head, and he did and said there was no sign of a blow on it. I felt it myself, also, and all seemed well."

"I cannot say I think much of that leech's knowledge," Sybelle remarked, looking down now at the bruise she had uncovered. She snipped another few threads and drew off the shirt, looked at the other bruises on Walter's body—not that she could see them all because of the thick mat of hair that covered his skin, but some on his ribs were exposed—and she shook her head. ''There is something amiss,'' she murmured, more to herself than to him. ''The others are fading to green and yellow, and there is no swelling.''

Gently she felt around, unconsciously coming closer. After a moment Walter turned his head away very sharply. ''I am sorry,'' Sybelle said. ''Did I hurt you? Is that where it is most tender?''

''No,'' Walter replied in a stifled voice.

''This is no time to be a great hero,'' Sybelle retorted sharply. ''I will think better of you if you cry out and let me discover what is wrong.''

''I am not being a hero. I tell you I am no more tender where your hand is than any other place.''

''Then why do you look away?'' she asked, for Walter's head was turned as far from her as possible.

He began to shake with laughter. ''Because if I turn my head and then open my mouth to speak, I will end up taking suck.''

Sybelle gasped and stepped back hurriedly, realizing that her well-developed breast was just about where Walter's mouth would be if he looked straight ahead. ''Why did you not say I was too close?'' she asked querulously.

She was not annoyed with Walter, of course, but with herself. She had resolved after that first embarrassing exchange about Walter needing a wife to watch what she said and did and to remember that he was not her father, brother, or uncle, but she had forgotten again. For safety's sake she moved around behind him, where she could see just as well and not create a problem.

There was a brief pause. Walter knew the question was rhetorical and that Sybelle neither expected nor wanted an answer. He also knew that he probably *should* not answer, but it was irresistible.

''Why should I complain over what gave me pleasure?'' he asked.

''Do not be crude,'' Sybelle snapped, but she spoiled the stricture with a smothered giggle.

She was not, she thought ruefully, following her mother's advice very well about keeping Walter in doubt, but it was very difficult when he was so comical. The first comment about needing a wife had been an honest mistake, and after that the conversation had got out of hand. If he had said anything loverlike, she could have been repressive and severe. But how could one be severe with such remarks as he made? She giggled again, thinking of the "uncomfortable thing on the stool" being the question Walter wanted to ask her father.

All the while her fingers had been pursuing their quest, and Walter stiffened suddenly and said, "There."

Sybelle raised her hand at once, moved it farther along, and touched him cautiously. "Better? Worse?"

"I do not know," he replied between set teeth.

She felt the knob of the shoulder, top, back, and front, but did not need to question because she could feel the slight relaxation of Walter's body. "Not too bad," she said with satisfaction. "You have broken your collarbone just before it joins the shoulder. That will mend easily. I had feared you had damaged the joint, which is a very bad thing, for even when it heals, sometimes it will be stiff and painful always. But that leech was a fool."

"More likely he had many others to attend to," Walter pointed out.

"That is true," Sybelle agreed, but abstractedly.

She was not absolutely certain how to deal with the injury she had found. She could set the bone, but how to keep it in place was a problem. Better ask before she meddled. She would need salves for the cuts, also. They were not healing cleanly. And it would be simplest if Walter just got into a bath so she could wash everything at once. The only other thing of importance was the injury to his left leg that made him limp. Sybelle came around in front of him and said briskly, "Stand up and take off your chausses."

Walter jumped slightly. He had been both relieved and irritated by Sybelle's discovery. He, too, had feared an injury to the joint, which might cripple him permanently. The broken collarbone was better than that by far, but it was a nuisance since it would keep him out of action for some time. He had been contemplating what to do about it so that Sybelle's order took him by surprise.

"No!" he exclaimed.

Sybelle stared at him, astonished. "But I must look at your leg," she said. "I cannot see the hurt through the cloth."

"You are like to see a good deal more than my bruised knee," Walter retorted dryly.

A frown of puzzlement creased Sybelle's brow. "I know men are made differently than women. You are not the first man I will have seen naked."

"I am the first you will have seen in *this* condition," Walter snapped. "For merciful Mary's sake, Sybelle, find me some clothes, and let me ask your father for you. When you are mine, you may do with me what you please."

CHAPTER 8

Actually, Walter did not get to speak to Lord Geoffrey until the following day. Confronted by a flat statement of the situation, Sybelle had fled to obtain authoritative assistance, and had found her mother already coming to join her. Since Rhiannon and Alinor were attending to the Earl of Pembroke, Joanna felt free to see what her daughter was doing. Moreover, she felt that Sybelle and Walter had been alone long enough. Joanna was somewhat annoyed by her mother's mischievously thrusting them together, because she felt that Walter's condition might induce too much tenderness in Sybelle.

Thus, Joanna sent Sybelle to see that a more private place was found for Walter to sleep than the great hall and that at least a cot would be provided for him. This was no easy task in the crowded conditions at Builth. In the end, Sybelle was reduced to ousting her brother William from his cot, demoting him to a pallet beside young Ian's, and giving his place in the antechamber of her parent's apartment to Walter. This made the small chamber almost too crowded to walk in, unless one minded one's steps very carefully.

Walter was delighted. The placement seemed to make him already part of the family he wished very much to join and was another tacit confirmation that his offer for Sybelle was expected and welcome. The peace of mind this gave him permitted him to acquiesce with little argument when Joanna said firmly that he was to go to bed at once, after he was bathed, salved, and the broken bone set.

What Joanna did not expect was that Walter's eagerness would follow him into his dreams. True, no dreams troubled the first part of his night; he slept too deeply for that. However, Walter was young and very strong. Images of Sybelle—of her bosom pressed against his cheek, of her sweet breath gently tickling his ear, of her beautiful face—came to make his sleep uneasy. Walter woke, then slept again, only to slide into far more intimate fantasies. He woke again with an urgent need.

For a time he lay quiet, expecting wakefulness to calm him, but his waking mind was almost as unruly as his sleeping one. Finally, groaning softly with stiffness and frustration, Walter sat up and slid carefully out of his cot to go to the garderobe. Perhaps if he relieved his bladder, this other urgency would also dissipate. The cot creaked, and Walter paused to look at Sybelle's brothers. There was no sense in waking the boys. Neither of them stirred, which drew a smile from Walter in memory of his own sound sleep at that age. He rose, pulled his nightrobe awkwardly over his shoulders, and began to pick his way carefully to the door. Just as he reached it, there was a gentle touch on his arm.

"Do you need something, Sir Walter?" Joanna asked. softly.

"Only to piss. I am very sorry if I wakened you," he replied in a whisper.

"It does not matter," she said, gesturing toward the hall where a gray light could be seen. "It is almost dawn. You do not feel ill? You are sure?"

"Not at all," he assured her earnestly, and then added, "I am only restless."

Joanna arranged the night robe more securely around him, then, suddenly, smiled. "You are very eager to be put out of your misery—or into it?"

"Yes," Walter replied, frowning. "But I do not understand. I thought—" He glanced back toward the place he had slept beside her sons, as if he were one of them.

"I am sorry," she said hastily. "I did not mean to imply you would be refused, but it is possible that you . . . Go. I hear Geoffrey stirring. He will be ready to speak to you when you return. It will be better this way, for there will be no need to explain your going apart with him if there is an unexpected problem."

Walter made his way to the waste shaft in a very thoughtful frame of mind. Even if he had not desired Sybelle for herself, it was hard to imagine any conditions in which a man in his position would refuse a marriage alliance with the Roselynde clan. Unless . . . Walter stopped abruptly and set his jaw. Unless the condition was that he abandon Pembroke's cause. Suddenly he remembered the way Sybelle had been silent and then shuddered after he mentioned the slaughter of the garrison of Monmouth keep. Those men were her father's allies, possibly there were even friends of his among them. Lord Geoffrey was the king's cousin, and Sybelle herself was related to Henry. Naturally, she would be appalled to hear of the king's losses.

What could he do? Walter asked himself. He could not abandon Richard, even though Richard would certainly give him leave. Still, he could not do it. The question was not only one of personal loyalty but of right and wrong. The king and his ministers were breaking the law and flouting established custom. If they were not checked, every man in the realm would be a slave to Henry's will. That was wrong. Every free man had his rights. Even the serf had his small rights. Moreover, Richard was not a rebel for his own profit. He was the upholder of right and good custom. No matter what the personal sacrifice, Walter knew he could not abandon Pembroke's cause.

Then he would have to refuse to make contract. Walter had been walking slowly back toward Lord Geoffrey's chamber while he reasoned out his attachment to Pembroke. Now he stopped again and drew breath sharply. Perhaps there could be some compromise. Walter started forward again. Lord Geoffrey was an honorable man. Surely he would not have held out hope that Walter would be acceptable as Sybelle's husband only to trap him into abandoning the rebel cause.

At an accelerated pace, Walter went directly to the entrance to the bedchamber and called, "My lord?"

"Come in," Geoffrey replied promptly, and when Walter did so, Geoffrey gestured to a chair opposite his beside the newly made up fire.

"Lord Geoffrey," Walter said, still standing, "you must know that I am very eager to take your daughter, Sybelle, to wife, but—"

"I was aware," Geoffrey interrupted, unable to control a slight twitching of the lips. "I will set your mind to rest and tell you at once that I have no objections. However, the situation is not so simple. Do sit down. This will be a long conversation, and your knee will be the better for a chair and a footstool."

"I understand that your loyalty to the king and mine to the

Earl of Pembroke makes a difficulty, but surely we can come to some arrangement—''

''That is not the situation to which I was referring,'' Geoffrey interrupted again. ''What I have heard from some of the men who came with you and Pembroke about this fiasco at Monmouth gives me reason to believe that a peace—or at least a truce—will soon be patched together. Perhaps it will not be possible to have a formal betrothal until that time, but I do not think that you and I need to worry about formal, legal bindings. I think you believe I will keep any promise I make, and I am sure you will keep any promise you make. The trouble is that the decision does not rest with either you or me.''

Walter stood stock-still, staring at Geoffrey. The dismissal of the fear that he was going to be asked to turn his coat had momentarily blocked all feelings but relief, which was followed by amusement at his own self-importance. How could he have thought for a moment that he and his few men-at-arms would be considered valuable enough to Richard's cause to make Lord Geoffrey propose a dishonorable act as the price for his daughter? But in the wake of relief and amusement came astonishment.

''What do you mean the decision concerning your daughter's marriage does not rest with you? I can see how it would not rest with me, but—''

''Will you sit down!'' Geoffrey exclaimed. ''I am getting a twist in my neck from staring up at you. I have told you already that this will be a long explanation.''

''I beg your pardon,'' Walter said hastily, and sat.

''Put your foot up,'' Geoffrey suggested, pushing a footstool into position. Having seen Walter meekly accept this gesture, Geoffrey steepled his fingers and looked at him over them. ''I will deliver the heaviest blow first,'' he said, grinning. ''Roselynde and all the honors attached are held in the female line.''

''What?'' Walter gasped.

''I repeat: Roselynde, Mersea, Kingsclere, Iford, Clyro, and about half a dozen smaller keeps, plus I do not know how many farms and manors, are heritable only in the female line. Lady Alinor is holder now. My Joanna will inherit when Alinor dies—and may that be never or, at least, not until after *I* am dead—and after Joanna, they go to Sybelle.''

"What?" Walter repeated.

Geoffrey laughed. "Just think about it for a while. The shock will pass."

"But there is Sir Adam and Simon. . . ."

"Adam has his father's lands, which I assure you are not nothing, and atop them, Tarring and all its dependencies. Simon . . . Simon has the Welsh property and will inherit Lord Ian's northern keeps. Simon would not take Roselynde, anyway. He does not wish to support that burden. And Lady Rhiannon . . . she cannot be long away from the hills of Gwynedd. In any case, none of this matters. It is Lady Alinor's will that the property be so disposed, and each of her husbands agreed. The marriage contracts are ironbound. This is what you must understand. The lands will be *Sybelle's*. She will rule them as she sees fit. She will leave them as she sees fit—almost certainly to her eldest daughter. Of course, if no female child is born or survives . . . But even then, she might decide to will the lands to a niece or a cousin. You must accept this."

Walter opened his mouth, then closed it. Finally, he said, "I am not a greedy man. I greatly desire to have Sybelle to wife. If you will help me take hold of my own lands, I will settle a good property on her and take her without dowry."

Geoffrey smiled at him, but his eyes were sad. "You are *not* greedy—and I cannot help but be glad of it and of the fact that your wish to marry Sybelle is for herself alone. I love my daughter, and I desire for her the joy in marriage I myself have had in my union with her mother. But you cannot have Sybelle without the promise—or, should I say the threat?—of the burden of Roselynde. Sybelle would never agree."

"If you bade her . . . I do not mean that you should force her. I hope I do not sound like a coxcomb, but I believe her to be willing. . . ."

His voice faded as Geoffrey shook his head. "I do not know my daughter's exact state of mind, although her mother assures me that she is not *opposed* to the match. You understand, I would not force her on any account. I love her. I have encouraged you because I think you could make her happy. What influence I have with Sybelle, and it is not negligible, will be applied in your favor. However, I could starve her and beat her and not make her take you if it meant the loss of Roselynde. Nor would it matter if she were mad for love of you. She would break her heart, but she would not give up Roselynde."

"I do not believe it!" Walter exclaimed. "Sybelle is not greedy nor is she proud. I have seen her life day by day, and she goes about among the maidservants as simply as any chatelaine of a single, small holding. I will have more than enough to assure her comfort. She will be denied no pleasure, no luxury. . . ." Again Walter let his sentence drift unfinished as Geoffrey shook his head.

"Sybelle does not desire pleasure or luxury." Geoffrey paused and frowned. "I was about to say that she desired power, but that is not true—at least, not in the sense that she wishes to rule the lives of others. She wishes to care for Roselynde and the lands that are hers. No, that is not right, either. The *need* to care for Roselynde is bred into her blood and bone. Perhaps she took it with the milk from her mother's breast. Someday you will hear her say 'mine, to me!' Perhaps then you will understand. I can tell you tales. . . . But tales are not to the point. Take it from me, who am husband to Joanna of Roselynde, that you may obtain Sybelle *and* Roselynde, but not one without the other. Do you wish to withdraw your offer? None will know we spoke of this, and I will not be less your friend. In fact, I will pledge myself to help you take your lands for your friendship's sake."

"You say you will assist me to curb or replace my brother's castellans whether or not I marry your daughter?"

"Yes, because it will serve me well to have your friendship, and I do not think more than your word is necessary," Geoffrey assured him.

"But I would not have Sybelle!" Walter burst out.

Geoffrey began to laugh. "I was not any happier when Joanna was proposed to me. Of course, the way the property was held was no shock, because I had been Ian's squire. Hoo-haa! You should have heard the pitch barrels bursting when my lord and his lady had some difference of opinion. But when the argument was on a matter of the land, there was nothing womanish in what Alinor said. She was never too angry to listen to reason about the estate. Neither is Joanna. And Sybelle, like Joanna, has been trained from birth. You need not fear that Sybelle will mismanage her property and that you will be helpless to restore order."

"I did not think that," Walter answered truthfully. He had,

in fact, already heard Sybelle say the equivalent of *mine, to me*. Geoffrey had recalled to his mind the scene in his camp when Sybelle and her men had driven off his foraging party. He had been hearing her voice as she said, *I have been protecting my property,* and *Are you going to return my property?* "Indeed," Walter went on, "I have been wondering how I would support the role of a gilded popinjay."

Geoffrey made a wry face and pulled an earlobe. "You should wonder instead when you will have time to eat and sleep. The ladies of Roselynde do not allow a tittle or a jot to be wasted, nor certainly the labor of an able-bodied man. You will not lack for employment. On the other hand, you will not lack for pleasure or laughter, either. If I am in bondage to my wife—as it has been said now and again by one man or another—I have no desire to throw off that bondage. I am repaid a thousand, thousand times for my labor in comfort and joy."

Walter stared at Geoffrey in silence, then he looked away into the fire for a time. At last, he looked back, smiling with twisted lips. "I want Sybelle. I will take her any way I can get her."

"Ah, yes," Geoffrey said. "Well, here comes the second blow. *You* must get Sybelle. I cannot give her to you. Let me state the problem plainly. I can pledge myself not to accept any other offer for her. I can turn away any other proposal that is made. However, I cannot make a contract for marriage for her. Because Roselynde is Sybelle's inheritance, only Lady Alinor can make a contract for marriage, and my wife must approve it. After all, whatever dower goes with Sybelle comes out of Joanna's inheritance."

"I said I would take her without a dowry," Walter snapped.

"But Sybelle would never agree to marriage under those terms," Geoffrey reminded him gently, "and I have said already that I will not command her against her will."

"This is insane," Walter fumed. "To get Sybelle, I must court her mother and grandmother!"

"No, no," Geoffrey laughed. "Knowing the conditions, I would never have allowed matters to go so far if Alinor and Joanna were not satisfied. It is Sybelle you must convince."

Walter closed his eyes and scrunched up his face. "I think there is something wrong with my ears or my head today. Accepting that Sybelle is the ward of her grandmother and her mother, if they are content with me why cannot we come to contract? What has Sybelle to say? I will disclose the state of my affairs to Lady Alinor and Lady Joanna and tell them what I can offer in settlement. I know that it will be paltry compared with Sybelle's own property, but—"

"No settlement will be necessary," Geoffrey interrupted. "It would be ridiculous. Your lands must go entirely to your son. The contracts are always thus: Yours to you; the woman's to her. Usually any lands acquired during the marriage are kept as portions for a second or third son or added to the inheritance of the eldest if the younger ones are married richly enough. But you are missing the point. Sybelle's marriage is for Sybelle to decide."

"What?" Walter was back to angry amazement. "Sybelle is only a girl. God knows what silly popinjay, who will flatter her out of eagerness for her wealth, she might choose. I am willing to accept the decision of her mother and grandmother, but a silly girl—"

"Sybelle is not a silly girl," Geoffrey interrupted again, this time sharply. "Why do you think she is unmarried at sixteen? For lack of offers? I have been besieged with offers for her since she was born, and for the last four years the problem has become acute. You are not the first Alinor and Joanna were willing to consider. It is Sybelle who has rejected out of hand every man who has been proposed to her."

"Then perhaps," Walter retorted, "she is a silly girl. Who knows what dream is in her mind. No man may be a match for it."

Geoffrey shrugged. "You will find that Sybelle is not overgiven to dreaming. And I have this encouragement to offer you, although my wife would be angry if she knew. Sybelle is not a flirt. She has never encouraged any man. If she gave you reason to think she might be willing, there is real hope she is considering you seriously. Now attend to what I say. It does not matter whether you approve the fact that she may make her own choice. That is the reality. If you want to marry Sybelle, you must make her want to marry you."

Walter heard the finality in that. Again he stared in silence at Geoffrey.

"There is a great deal to be gained by such an arrangement," Geoffrey urged gently. "You say you desire Sybelle. Say also that she married you upon my order or her mother's or grandmother's, even though she was indifferent to you. It is possible she might come to love you; it is also possible that she might not, that she might never have more to offer you than a dull and grudging obedience. Would you like that, Walter?"

"No!" The word burst out before he thought, a result of a medley of images of Sybelle's bright and mischievous ways. To have those dulled into weary resignation . . . Walter shuddered.

"This way, if she agrees, you will know she desires you. You will never need to doubt her love. It is a very unpleasant thing to doubt your wife's love."

There was a note of deep sincerity in Geoffrey's voice. Walter was startled, for Geoffrey had spoken with equal depth of feeling of his satisfaction in his marriage. There were two questions on Walter's tongue—one concerning Geoffrey's last remark and the other an exasperated *What am I to do?* But neither was asked. At that moment Joanna came in and said she was sorry to interrupt but that Richard was coming to break his fast and needed Walter to explain to Prince Llewelyn what had happened at Monmouth.

Since Walter was not yet dressed, there was no time for further talk. All he said was, "Do not accept any other suitor for Sybelle. On any terms, I am willing."

That was perfectly true, but Walter was also totally at a loss as to how to proceed. He was well practiced in the techniques used to seduce a woman he did not want to marry, but it seemed ridiculous to use such blandishments on a wife. A wife was a man's property; one did not need to woo her. Walter also knew how one behaves to a woman betrothed, but he and Sybelle were not betrothed. At least, Walter thought sourly while he dressed, he was but she was not.

At that point in his thoughts, he entered the great hall. The high table was set, Prince Llewelyn and the Earl of Pembroke seated side by side, but Walter's eyes did not linger on that objective. Without particular volition they ranged, found Sybelle where she was standing and talking to Simon and Rhiannon, and somehow his legs started off in that direction.

He did not reach them, however. As he came to the midpoint of the hall, Prince Llewelyn called out, and Walter saw Richard gesturing for him to join them. Duty was duty, and Walter turned that way at once, but his eyes lingered on Sybelle for just a moment. She looked up when she heard his name; their glances met—and the sourness went out of the notion that he was betrothed while she was not.

Oddly, Walter did not feel frustrated at the postponement of his meeting with Sybelle, nor did he, as he would have expected only a few minutes past when he entered the hall, feel relief. He was filled with a sense of well-being, of pleasant anticipation. Mostly, he told himself severely, that must be owing to a marked increase in his physical comfort. Although he was somewhat irked by having his left arm bound to his body so that he could not move it, the resulting lessening of the pain in his shoulder was more than compensation. Also, his knee was nearly back to normal. Lady Joanna had bound some poultice over it that had seemed to suck out the ache during the night. It was still stiff and protested if he bent it too far, but it was no longer a nagging misery.

Walter looked at Pembroke and smiled broadly. Apparently the Roselynde women had worked their magic on him, also. True, Richard's mouth and nose were still horribly scabbed and discolored, but the swelling was down almost to normal, and the earl was spooning some dark-colored mush into his mouth with relative ease and considerable avidity.

"Good," Richard mumbled, seeing Walter's eyes on the uninviting-looking slop.

The word was slurred, but it was at least intelligible. Walter thought it must still be uncomfortable for Pembroke to talk and probably he had been warned not to do it, but at least the earl could direct the conversation more quickly and easily than by writing—and that must be a great relief. Meanwhile, Llewelyn had invited Walter to sit beside him and eat while he told the tale of the battle. By now, Walter had that down pat and spun it off quickly, although Llewelyn did ask a number of sharp questions. Some Walter was able to answer from his own observations; others he could only satisfy with information obtained from Gilbert Bassett. The last few questions concerned Walter's own part in the battle, and when those were answered, Prince Llewelyn laughed and shook his head.

"That is not quite the way I heard it," he said. "I was given to understand that you were the hero of the day."

"Who? I?" Walter asked with honest astonishment. "Who told you that, my lord?"

"I never reveal my sources," Llewelyn teased.

But Richard banged his spoon on the table, nodded his head enthusiastically, and mumbled, "Saved me," holding up three fingers.

"Yes, and I nearly killed you at least once," Walter protested, laughing, "by shouting your name and calling attention to you. Also, my lord, you saved me at least as often, so we are quits."

Richard waved his spoon about energetically, but what he wanted to say was obviously too complex for his ability, and he gave up and pointed at Llewelyn, who smiled.

"There are major advantages," the Lord of Gwynedd said, "to having a conference with an ally who can barely speak. I get to do all the talking, a thing that suits me well. Now, I understand that Lord Pembroke originally desired to take Monmouth keep—"

"With respect," Walter interrupted, not wishing to leave any chance that Llewelyn would think the earl rash, "rather to see whether Monmouth could be taken."

"Very well, but either way that is out of the question now." Llewelyn glanced toward Richard, who shrugged and then, more slowly, nodded. It was apparent that he was not going to attempt to argue. "I would never have liked the idea," Llewelyn went on. "I can see why it would be attractive to you, Lord Pembroke, but with the king's keeps of Goodrich, Grosmont, and even Gloucester so close, so much effort would have to go into defending Monmouth once it was ours that little else could be accomplished."

To that, the earl made no reply even by gesture or glance, stolidly spooning food into his mouth with his eyes on his plate. Walter guessed that the "disadvantage" Llewelyn mentioned might have been one of the attractions Richard felt for the project. Pembroke was not interested in loot nor in gaining more property. What he wanted was to make King Henry feel that he was losing the war without actually attacking him, so that the king would desire to make peace. Taking Monmouth and beating off attacks against it would have served that purpose very well while, on the whole, reducing the casualties to Pembroke's army and keeping the war off Pembroke's land.

Prince Llewelyn's aims, however, were different. He certainly wished to see Henry dismiss ministers who had so strong a taste for absolute power. Such men were insatiable. Having reduced England to submission, they would at once turn their eyes to any land that was not already in their control. However, there were any number of roads that would lead to that point, and Llewelyn wished to take the road that would lead to the enrichment of his eternally impoverished people and treasury.

"Nonetheless," Prince Llewelyn continued, "had it been possible to attack Monmouth while the garrison was still reduced, I assure you I would have lent what aid I could."

Richard looked up at him, plainly surprised, and Llewelyn nodded.

"One must support one's allies," he went on in response to Pembroke's expression.

Walter was certain the impression of sincerity that came across with Llewelyn's statement was false, but he gave no sign. He was not even sure that he would tell Richard later what he felt. Walter was positive that, at this time, Prince Llewelyn's purposes would forward Richard's cause better than Richard's own plans. It would be stupid, then, to arouse any doubt in Pembroke's mind about his ally. And then Llewelyn's next statement wiped away the twinge of guilt Walter felt at concealing anything from the earl.

"Of course," Llewelyn was saying blandly, "what help I could have given would not have been much. My people are not trained or armed for the taking of keeps. We can only make up in lost lives the lack of armor and weapons. Thus, I must admit that I am not sorry the question of taking Monmouth keep can no longer arise."

"Why?" Richard asked.

"Because the garrison has been replaced and more than replaced. Baldwin de Guisnes is still hanging between life and death, I understand, but John of Monmouth himself is now in the keep. He brought many men with him, and more are coming each day. I believe something is brewing there, but we will know in good time."

"How?"

Llewelyn looked at the earl with surprise at that question. "Was it not by your order that Sir Walter here wrote to Simon and asked him to have Monmouth watched?"

"It was I who wrote," Walter answered quickly, "but not by Lord Pembroke's order. I thought if revenge were contemplated, the king's men might avoid the great keeps and ravage the land, which might affect my own keep of Goldcliff. But I do not think that was the meaning of Lord Pembroke's question. I believe that was owing to surprise at how much you know and how soon."

That brought a smile. Walter could not guess whether it was owing to pleasure at having astonished the earl or amusement at Walter's pandering to Richard's delicate conscience. It was not a question Walter particularly wanted answered, but he was not concerned; he trusted Llewelyn's tact.

This faith was rewarded, since Llewelyn only said, "You will have to ask Simon exactly what his men have done—although I am not sure you will get any very sensible answer. Simon is a trifle preoccupied these days. Still, I am sure the reports are reliable."

Richard nodded acceptance. He trusted Simon and had found his information gathering to have been accurate in the past, but now the earl frowned, a little troubled at Walter's acceptance of the responsibility, which he felt he should not have abandoned to him. However, there was a more important problem than that. The garrison at Monmouth had already been large, certainly large enough to discourage any attack. When Richard had gone to look over the keep, he had not known how many were within it; that was one of the things he had been hoping to discover. Having learned how many men were in the keep, he probably would have given up any intention of an assault unless someone had come up with an unusually hopeful stratagem or device. Thus, it was very peculiar that Monmouth should bring in still more men.

"Why more?" Richard asked, hoping that Llewelyn would understand the simplistic question.

"I cannot answer that yet," Llewelyn replied, "unless John of Monmouth takes you to be a fool. Can that be possible?"

"I do not believe so," Walter put in. "Sir John knows Lord Pembroke well enough, and I do not think Monmouth to be a fool, either, which he would need to be to deceive himself about Lord Pembroke's capacity or ability."

Llewelyn looked at Richard, who nodded and shrugged. "Very well," the prince said, "I do not think John of Monmouth is a fool, either. Therefore, as I said, something is brewing. However, it is necessary to allow him to make the first moves. Unfortunately, whatever that move is will be against you on your land. Thereby, win or lose—you lose. Now, I would like to suggest that we divert the attention of the king's men from offense to defense and that we take this war onto soil other than our own."

Richard stopped eating. A silence fell. Without a word being said, Walter felt that he had seldom been aware of so eloquent an argument. He wondered why he was being kept at the table when it was clear that Richard was perfectly capable of making his points with a single word or, as in this case, without speaking at all. The earl's reluctance to initiate an attack in an area not already armed and engaged in the war against him was expressed in every line of his face and body. Equally clear, however, was Prince Llewelyn's conviction that this must be done. At last Llewelyn spoke again—one word.

"Shrewsbury."

Had Walter been capable of it, he would have pricked up his ears with interest. If Richard agreed to attack Shrewsbury, there were two routes he could use to take his army north. As far as travel went, the easier route lay to the east. The land was less hilly along that route, and the roads were better. However, the road passed by Grosmont, Hereford, Leominster, and Ludlow. Whether any of the towns or keeps would attack Pembroke's army if they were not themselves attacked first was questionable; however, warnings would certainly fly north ahead of the army to Shrewsbury and south to the king in Gloucester.

The other route ran up along the Usk through Talgarth and then along the valley of the Wye. It was a harder road, but mainly settled by Welsh, who had little interest in the war as long as it did not burn them out. And if Richard did choose the westerly route, he would likely pass by Knight's Tower—a keep that Walter owned by law but did not control. Would Sir Heribert, the castellan of Knight's Tower, dare hold out against Richard's army? Walter would not ask that Richard pause to take the keep if the castellan resisted, but he thought the threat to do so would be enough.

For the sake of the supplies that Walter would be glad to offer, it might even be worth a feint. And once Knight's

Tower was in Walter's hands, it would be an advantage to Richard. It was only some thirty miles from Shrewsbury, or a little more. Then Walter felt ashamed. It was not right for him to permit personal considerations to influence him. As Pembroke's man, he should be thinking of his lord's advantage, not his own. And it was quite plain that Richard was not at all happy with Llewelyn's suggestion.

"Why?" the earl had asked, after allowing the silence that followed Llewelyn's naming of Shrewsbury to last just a trifle too long. But Pembroke had met his match.

"Why not?" Llewelyn countered. "Do you desire that this war continue forever?"

The look of horror on Richard's face was sufficient answer for that question.

"It will continue as long as Henry's ministers can convince him that he has a chance of crushing you," Llewelyn stated flatly. "And they will be able to convince him of that as long as the fighting goes back and forth in the same place. Henry will not ask how many men are lost or what is the cost—as long as he does not see the men die or feel the pinch of the price. And, I assure you, both will be hidden from him as much as possible now. Moreover, Lord Pembroke, it is true enough that time is on the side of the king and his ministers. He has all of England to drain for men and gold, and he can summon more and more mercenaries from the Continent. You and I have no such resources."

"God," Richard mumbled.

"You mean that God will help us?" Llewelyn's lips twisted. "Lady Alinor attended you last night," he said. "Do you know her favorite maxim? It is that God helps those who help themselves."

Walter saw the muscles in Richard's cheeks tighten and quiver as he strove not to laugh. The mention of Alinor's oft-quoted maxim had brought a wealth of memories flooding back on Richard, most of them happy. The tie between the Marshals and those of Roselynde had been very close all through Richard's youth. Although the families had never intermarried—perhaps because the bond was so close that no additional ties seemed necessary—Richard regarded Alinor as an aunt. Not only was he familiar with Alinor's maxim, but he recognized that some of that lady's devices for helping herself smacked more of the devil than of any heavenly power. Moreover, Richard feared that Prince Llewelyn was one who would have applauded even the least savory of her devices with enthusiasm.

Knowing that the discussion was causing Richard considerable mental anguish, Walter was puzzled by the signs of repressed laughter. Yet somehow there was a cast to Richard's expression that implied a certain trepidation as well as mirth. Combined with what Walter had heard that morning from Geoffrey, the reference to Lady Alinor gave him food for serious thought. However, he was distracted from these faintly ominous implications by the need to attend to what Llewelyn was saying.

"You will want to know, of course, why I chose Shrewsbury rather than another place," Llewelyn said, having seen the effect of his challenge about the support of God for the righteous and being too wise to wait for a response. "I will admit that some of my reasons are selfish. These I will give at once: Shrewsbury is rich, and Shrewsbury is convenient for my forces, most of whom are afoot. But these are not my only reasons. Shrewsbury is ill-prepared for attack, so it will fall with less cost to us. In addition, it is far enough from King Henry, who lies at Gloucester, to serve two further purposes: It will make it more difficult for him to bring an army to Shrewsbury's aid—and it cannot be considered any direct personal threat by our combined forces against the king himself."

Walter barely prevented himself from whistling with admiration at that particular thrust. He doubted strongly that Llewelyn cared a pin whether or not Henry felt personally threatened, but he was equally sure that Richard did care. Walter looked at the earl's face. Richard's eyes were fixed on Llewelyn, and there was in them both calculation and understanding. Pembroke's expression relieved Walter of the doubts that had been raised in his mind earlier in the discussion about warning the earl of Prince Llewelyn's deviousness.

It was reasonably apparent to Walter that Richard did not believe in Llewelyn's sudden concern for Henry's feelings any more than Walter himself did; still, Richard was ready to acknowledge the truth of the reasoning and the fact that it was compelling to him. Llewelyn's face was impassive; he knew, Walter thought, that Richard did not believe he cared, but the point had been made, and that was what was important.

Suddenly, Walter wanted no more part of this silent fencing. "If you do not need me any longer, my lord," he said, "may I have leave to go?"

Richard nodded absently, his mind still busy with Llewelyn's proposal. The prince spared Walter a smile, glad of the opportunity to look away from his ally/opponent for a moment. When he was free of the bench, a delicate operation to spare his knee, Walter bowed mechanically to both men, quite unaware of whether or not they had noticed. His eyes were already seeking Sybelle, and although she had moved from the position in which he had last seen her, they seemed to know of themselves where she was and found her at once.

CHAPTER 9

When Walter saw to where Sybelle and her companions had moved, he felt a strong sense of satisfaction. They had left the vicinity of the tables, where an abundance of bread, cheese, small pasties containing spiced chopped meat, and tall flagons of wine were available, and had taken possession of a quiet corner produced by the protruding stones of the great hearth, where an enormous fire burned. Since it burned, to a greater or lesser extent, day and night all year, the stones gave out a steady heat.

It was not as warm as a position in front of the hearth, but it was more private, and Walter wondered whether Sybelle had steered them to that place. He set out to join them, but as he moved down the hall, Walter realized that the quiet corner was also half-hidden from the table where he had been sitting. That made him wonder, with a flicker of embarrassment, whether he had been unconsciously watching Sybelle all the time he was at the table with Pembroke and Llewelyn. He told himself it did not matter. The earl and prince were too busy with their own affairs to have noticed, and he was already aware of the strong fascination Sybelle held for him. Perhaps that should have worried him, but the nearer he came to her, the lighter and more cheerful he felt.

"I have spoken to your father," Walter said as soon as he was close enough to Sybelle to be heard without raising his voice. "I have his permission to marry you."

This was no surprise to Sybelle, who had been told by Joanna of Walter's conference with her father. Nor had she been surprised by his voice, although her back had been toward him as he approached. She had been somehow aware of him all the time that he was involved with Richard and Prince Llewelyn. Knowing that Walter was there, in close conference with the two most important men in Wales, had given her a strong feeling of satisfaction. Sybelle was accustomed to her father's being high in the councils of the king. It was right and proper that her future husband should be equally respected. It was all she could do not to smile brilliantly on Walter and claim him as husband at once.

Perhaps because he saw her difficulty or perhaps out of sheer mischief, Simon saved her. "Good morning, Walter," he said gravely.

Walter's eyes flicked to his longtime friend, and if looks could kill, Simon would have dropped where he stood. His eyes returned to Sybelle. "Well, what have you to say to me, Sybelle?" he asked sharply.

A beautiful bell tone of laughter cascaded from Walter's right. "I think we are *de trop,* Simon," Rhiannon exclaimed.

"Oh, no," Simon replied. "He does not even know we are here. Walter, will you not say good morning to Rhiannon? She is the bride, you know, and must be treated with extra courtesy."

This time when Walter looked at Simon, there was resigned exasperation on his face. "I beg your pardon, Lady Rhiannon." He smiled. "To you I will say good morning with all my heart. But to you, Simon, I will say farewell. Go away, you nuisance. I never saw a more mischievous devil. Do you want your niece to remain unwed forever?"

Simon laughed. "Let me tell you something, Walter. It is a little out of the usual way to begin a courtship with 'What have you to say to me?' Mostly men say their chosen one's beauty has drawn them to her, or—"

"Sybelle knows she is beautiful," Walter said.

"She would be an idiot if she did not," Simon agreed, "but nonetheless, women like to be told."

"Simon, if you do not go away, I will murder you." Walter sighed exasperatedly. "Let me manage my own affairs in my own way."

Rhiannon began to tug at Simon's arm, and he laughed and allowed himself to be drawn away. Walter called thanks after her and then turned to Sybelle again.

"I am very ready to tell you how beautiful you are," he said, "but I do not wish to be a fool. Last night you gave me reason to believe I was not distasteful to you—but was this only as a friend?"

Having subdued her first impulse to throw herself into

Walter's arms without delay or consideration, Sybelle was frightened by her desire to do so. She had spent an uneasy night, trying to reconcile her mother's warning with the powerful attraction Walter held for her. While she had examined his injuries the previous evening, Sybelle had honestly concentrated on that problem. Nonetheless, below the level of her concern for his physical condition, she had been aware of a strong sensual pleasure generated by seeing and handling Walter's body.

Sybelle was aware, too, that no other male body she had touched had stimulated her in the same way, and this, of course, made Walter seem even more desirable. It did not occur to her that every other man she had dressed or bathed was a close relative, known to her since birth and surrounded by the taboo of incest. All she recognized clearly was her desire to touch and be touched, and it frightened her.

"You ask a clear question, Sir Walter," Sybelle said, "but I have no clear answer to give you. I have only this to say," she added slowly, almost with reluctance, "that I have refused outright every other offer made to me, and I have not refused yours—so you cannot be a fool whatever you choose to say. You are pleasing to me as a man, but as a person I do not know you."

Walter felt puzzled and looked it. "I have a good name among men," he said. "Your father would not have listened to me for a minute if I did not." He smiled at her. "I am kind to my horses and dogs, even to my serfs. The Earl of Pembroke will vouch for my courage, I believe."

Sybelle laughed shakily. "You know that is not what I mean." Then she grew serious. "There is a special relationship between a man and wife. So much closeness can breed great love—or great hate. I . . . my father must have told you something of my special case. It is important to me to . . . to know my man. Sir Walter, I am not bred to meekness as most women are."

"I have seen that."

"You have not lived with it," Sybelle countered. "It is not always easy, even for a man like my father, who was raised in my mother's household, to be obliged to give heed to a woman's bidding."

"That was not what your father said."

Although he had had no direct answer—and Walter's original abrupt question had been an attempt to surprise Sybelle into an immediate affirmation of their relationship—Walter was content. It was not only Sybelle's manner and, indeed, what she said that gave him confidence. But it intrigued Walter that he felt so much at ease talking to her in as much as the subject was unusual. A man did not ordinarily discuss marriage with a girl. Parents arranged marriages, and boys and girls did as they were told. Or a man like Walter might ask a girl's father for her, but it was her place meekly to accept. Nor was it quite proper to question the results of marriage. Being made in heaven—in the priests' words—all marriages were assumed to be happy and fruitful. Thus the subject might have bred awkwardness between them, but Walter did not feel awkward.

"What your father spoke of," he continued, "was his long joy in his wedded life. That is what I seek, Sybelle."

"I, too," Sybelle murmured, staring up at him.

"We share the desire, let us also share the joy," he urged.

Sybelle lowered her eyes and her head. Walter could see she had clasped her hands together because they had begun to tremble. He took the clasped hands in his, and she did not pull them away, but she whispered, "I am afraid."

"Of me?" Walter asked incredulously. "But you of all women have nothing to fear from any man. You know your menfolk will rise to your defense, and I have been told the lands will remain in your hands. There is nothing to fear, and least from me. I love you."

"That is what I fear."

Her voice was so low that Walter had to lean close to hear her. He was bewildered but felt no irritation as he did when women were artfully coy or he believed they were trying to wrap a simple thing in a veil of emotion to seem mysterious. There was nothing coquettish in Sybelle's manner. He accepted that there was a real problem, even if she had not stated it clearly. He did not understand what was troubling her, but all he felt was a surge of protectiveness. He dropped her hands and put his one available arm around her shoulders. It was a gesture of comfort rather than an embrace, and Sybelle leaned against him almost as if she were tired out by some struggle.

"I do not understand," Walter said gently, "but if you try to tell me, I will listen."

Sybelle looked up. "People who love each other hurt each other."

It was a startling statement. Walter began to protest, to utter soothing platitudes, and then recognized the profound truth in what Sybelle had said. A murmur of sweet nothings would be an insult to the seriousness and honesty she was offering him.

"Yes, but people who love each other also help and support each other."

"But which will we do?" Sybelle whispered.

"Both," Walter replied honestly. "Dearling, it is impossible in a long life together, which I pray we will have, that we should not differ." He smiled down at her. "I have sampled your sharp tongue already. I was then too much surprised to answer—and there was some truth in your complaint, although not much—but another time I fear I will also say what comes first to my lips, and so we will quarrel."

She sighed. "It is not the quarrels I fear but what comes after."

The only women with whom Walter had ever quarreled had been his mistresses, some of whom used that device to extract an extra trinket before yielding their bodies or occasionally out of jealousy or even to add spice to the affair. In any event, every quarrel Walter had ever had with a woman had been reconciled between the sheets of a bed.

Before he realized that Sybelle's experience must be different, he said, "Making love? You fear coupling?"

Now Sybelle looked startled. "I do not think so," she replied. "From what I have heard it is a joyous thing—but what has that to do with quarreling?"

Walter flushed, hesitated over the impulse to say he had misunderstood her, and instead answered truthfully, "It is the way most quarrels between men and women are settled."

"But how can that settle the disposition of a case of justice, or—or who should be appointed as castellan, for example?"

"What—" Walter began, and stopped abruptly. He had been about to ask what Sybelle had to do with justice or the appointment of castellans when he remembered that she would, indeed, make such decisions. "Do you think we are likely to quarrel about such things?" he asked instead. "Your father assured me that your mother and grandmother were always ready to listen to reason with regard to the property. Are you less amenable?"

"It would depend on whether what you suggested as reasonable seemed reasonable to me," she retorted with a flash of her normal sauciness. But then she continued seriously, "The ways of Roselynde are long set, and they may not fit with those to which you are accustomed. So it might be that we would differ."

"But not quarrel," Walter said, with the first hint of impatience he had shown. "I do not wonder you have doubts about accepting me as a husband if you think me such a fool as to quarrel with you over long-established custom on lands with which I am not familiar."

Sybelle's eyes dropped again. "I do not think you such a fool or a fool at all. I think you are a man—truly a man. That is why I fear."

"I am lost again," Walter confessed, but the irritation was gone from his voice. The subtle flattery had soothed him.

But it was not flattery, and Sybelle, who had been aware of the flicker of impatience, did not perceive why his mood had changed. "Will you not grow tired of a wife always intruding into what you think of as a man's affairs?" she asked nervously.

"Why should I?" He smiled at her. "I might grow angry if your intrusions were silly or womanish, but your father assures me that will not be the case. I cannot see that Lord Geoffrey has grown in the least tired of your mother. And I should say, from what I saw in the weeks I spent in Roselynde, that Lord Ian is perfectly besotted on Lady Alinor. They have been married well over twenty years. Why should you hold me less firmly?"

"Perhaps I am not as beautiful or clever—"

Walter's arm, which had relaxed its grip during the conversation, tightened suddenly. "Shame!" he cried, laughing and interrupting her. "Oh, shame, to throw out so plain a lure for a compliment. You know quite well that you are the most beautiful woman I have ever seen. As to clever—of that I am less certain. Surely a clever girl could have found a more subtle way to induce me to tell her what she wished to hear."

Sybelle could not help laughing, too, but amid her amusement there was a treacherous warmth, an insistent desire to return Walter's embrace, to taste the mouth smiling down at her. And his grip was no longer simply comforting. There was a disquieting light in his blue eyes and an eager tension in the hand that held her. Sybelle's breath quickened. Where his fingers touched, her skin felt odd, and she could sense heat, although she knew quite well that it was impossible for warmth from the hand to penetrate her woolen overdress, tunic, and shift.

"I am cleverer than that, Sir Walter," she said, twisting out of his hold. "You mistook honesty for a lack of subtlety. But I must admit that if I had desired a compliment, I might have been clumsy in fishing for it. I have never needed to do so, you see."

"And so you have proved my point," Walter retorted, still laughing. He had noticed Sybelle's response to his own sexual urge. The fact that she had freed herself from his embrace only underlined her awareness that its character had changed. "You have just shown that there is no reason for any man ever to tire of you. You know yourself beautiful. I will take your word for it that you are clever, merely inexperienced in flinging out lures for men—"

"You must stop teasing me," Sybelle interrupted, sensing that his humor was as much a danger to her as his desire. "We are supposed to be engaged in a serious discussion. Do you not consider marriage a serious subject, Sir Walter?"

"Of course I do, but there is no sense in pursuing the path you wish to take, Sybelle. You are not being reasonable. No matter what I say, I cannot convince you of what my future feelings will be. It is not in saying but in doing that proof comes. I am more than willing to prove myself in the test of time." He held out his hand to her.

Involuntarily, she not only laid her hand in his but gripped his fingers. "I am afraid," she repeated. "Is there no way for us to gain a better knowledge of each other? I will not lie to you, Sir Walter. I am not indifferent. I . . . I think I would like to be your wife, but . . . but I am afraid."

Walter looked at her helplessly. There was no way to ascertain the future. He understood better now what Sybelle meant. Unlike most women, she was not physically afraid. He knew she understood that she could separate herself from him physically, that her father and uncles would defend her and her property, drive him away or even kill him if he were cruel to her or dishonest in his dealings with her. Obviously she did not fear that. What she feared was that the differences in their outlooks, his the natural one and hers developed in response to God-only-knew what special circumstances, would cause such friction between them that their marriage would be ruined, that their initial love would be changed to indifference or even hatred.

"How can I ensure the future?" he asked. "How can I make you sure? I can only say I *feel* that nothing, no quarrel, no matter how long extended or how often renewed, could change the love and desire I have for you. Dearling, I cannot even assure you that I will live beyond the next attack on Pembroke or the next offensive he launches—"

He stopped speaking abruptly because Sybelle's nails had dug painfully into his hand when he mentioned the possibility of his being killed. Walter bit his lip. That was a stupid thing to have said, he realized, and began to talk soothingly of how unlikely it was, really, that any harm should come to him, to explain that ordinarily he was only one among many, no great leader to ride in the forefront. The battle at Monmouth, he pointed out, was an exception.

Even as he said the words he realized that they would cease to be true when he married Sybelle. Between his own greatly expanded property, her dower lands, and whatever added force or responsibility Lord Geoffrey or Lord Ian wished to give him, he would be a great leader, very much to the forefront. However, Walter felt no need to amend what he had said. From Sybelle's expression it was plain that she was not listening in any real sense of the word. This, he knew, was not because she was uninterested in his well-being but because she had heard such soothing phrases many times before.

"I have thought of something, Sir Walter," she said calmly when he ran out of words, just as if the subject of war had not been raised. "Perhaps it would not be fair to you, but still I will ask because I can think of nothing else."

"If it will lead to our union, I will agree no matter how harsh the test," Walter replied recklessly, the clear evidence of Sybelle's concern for him a spur to his desire.

"I would like to pretend we are betrothed, that you already have a right to be involved in all of my business, and I have a right to be involved in all of yours."

Walter burst out laughing. "That will be no harsh test."

"I hope it will not," Sybelle replied, not responding to his laughter. "I hope we will find that we agree or that if we do not, our differences can be reconciled—outside of a bed—without leaving any bitterness between us. But . . . you must know that . . . that if I . . . if I feel the marriage would prove unhappy I . . . I will withdraw. This is why I said it might be unfair, not only a waste of your time when you are looking for a wife but perhaps . . . perhaps it will leave you open to . . . to jests. . . ."

Oh, the dear little bird, Walter thought. *How can she be so innocent, so honest? Does she not realize that any man faced with such a proposition would be smooth as goose grease until she agreed and the contract was signed?* Sybelle's eyes were clear as golden glass, open and trusting. Walter lifted her hand to his lips and kissed it. He resolved that he would not take advantage of her guileless heart. He would behave as honestly as he could. Except . . .

"There is one thing, Sybelle," he said. "Do you mean that we are to behave as betrothed only for matters of business? That would not be a fair test of how our life will be. And I do not think I could . . . er . . . refrain from displaying marks of my affection when we talk over our affairs in private."

"Oh." Sybelle blushed. "I will not couple with you," she said frankly. "At least, not until contract is made. . . ."

"Nor until we are well and truly married by a priest," Walter said firmly, somewhat shocked. "I never meant any such thing."

"Well, then, I suppose you must act in every way as you would if we were betrothed," Sybelle murmured, her blush hotter than ever. "And I must accept or deny as is my honest feeling, also."

"I am content," Walter agreed. Then, as she began to take her hand out of his, he said gravely, "A betrothed couple may hold hands." And when her hand relaxed in his, he continued, "Only I must point out one thing more, my love. If we were betrothed, it would be your duty to accept my wooing; it would be wrong for you to deny me. A kindly father, having made contract for his daughter, provides a period of betrothal so that the girl may be weaned from too-great modesty by courtship. But if, out of modesty, she constantly rejects her suitor's attempts to teach her love, then she would never learn; thus, it is her duty to accept even such advances as may shock—''

''You are making a May-game of me again,'' Sybelle said, laughing and pulling her hand away. ''You know I am not likely to be shocked by being wooed.''

Walter grinned at her. ''Perhaps, but you must see it is to my advantage that you should feel it your duty to endure a kiss or two. After a time you might become accustomed, even find pleasure in it.''

Sybelle opened her eyes wide. ''I could endure the kisses with fortitude, I think. They will not be the first forced upon me—although I promise not to strike you as I struck the others, since we are pretending betrothal. However, I am puzzled by your assurance they would be to my taste. Would it not be safer to bind me by contract first—''

''Oh ho, little wasp, you have unsheathed your sting, have you?'' Walter's eyes had again lost their mildness and glinted brightly blue, but only for a moment. Then he drew his face into a caricature of injured innocence. ''Do you know that the best way to remove a sting is with the lips? Now that you have wounded me, will you not suck out the venom?'' The questions were asked with sighs as spurious as they were pathetic.

Sybelle bit her lips, partly because if she dared open them, she would laugh, but also a trifle in chagrin. Walter was easily as clever as her father, she thought, and there was pride in the thought, but there was also the recognition that he would not be easy to deal with. She could not run circles around him in talk as she could with most other men.

Meanwhile, Walter's expression had brightened, as if a very good idea had just come to him. ''Come,'' he said, all eager innocence, ''we can accomplish two purposes at once. You can cure me and discover whether my lips are distasteful.''

''You are bold to fling a challenge here in the hall where you know propriety must prevent me from accepting,'' Sybelle countered, but her cheeks were red as fire again.

Walter clicked his tongue in disapproval. ''No, my love, that was a bad move. I hope you are better at chess. I must teach you tactics. Now I have only to say 'Come away to a private place,' and where will you be?''

''Right here,'' Sybelle snapped. ''It is only a man who is afraid to back down on an unwise word.''

''Women,'' Walter sighed, ''have no sense of honor.''

''And it is just as well,'' a cool, new voice interposed, ''or the world would be in an even worse state than it now is—if you mean by honor what I think you mean.''

Both heads turned. Walter bowed. ''Lady Joanna, I regret to say that you are probably quite correct.'' Then he laughed. ''I must also apologize to you for not thanking you earlier for the efficacy of your treatment. I feel a new man this morning.''

''So I see,'' Joanna remarked, her lips quirking, ''but you will soon feel much older if you do not sit down and put up your leg. And I assure you it is not yet in such condition as to permit too active a pursuit of game.''

''Not even if the game does not run away too fast?'' Walter asked innocently.

Sybelle uttered a small, outraged gasp, but her mother did not look at her. ''Not even if the game runs at you,'' Joanna said dryly, ''which, if Lord Llewelyn's huntsmen are not mistaken in what they have marked—two fine boars—is likely to happen. I have come to tell Sybelle that her father is waiting for her.''

''Oh, gracious,'' Sybelle cried, ''I had forgot. Excuse me, Sir Walter.''

She dipped a curtsy at him and ran off, feeling annoyed and relieved at the same time. Walter's remark to her mother was the outside of enough, yet she had deserved it. She had thought herself very clever, laying that trap of a pretense betrothal. It was an invitation for Walter to act like a milksop, agree with everything she said, and behave in all ways like a pattern piece in a romance. Such behavior, Sybelle had thought, would be a warning of a basic dishonesty with regard to women, which many men who were in other ways the soul of honor did not think mattered. It was clear that Walter was not going to fall into that trap. Far from it. But his lighthearted lovemaking—appealing though it was—was no guarantee of his future sincerity, either.

Walter watched Sybelle run off, holding up the skirt of what he realized for the first time was a riding gown. He had not looked at what she was wearing, only at her. Then he had been so startled by her rapid retreat that he had just watched her go. When she was out of sight, he turned to Joanna.

''Boars? Do you think it wise for Sybelle to go boar hunting?''

"Why not?" Joanna asked. "She will not dismount—at least . . . No, Geoffrey and Ian would never permit that, nor even William, young as he is. Only that Simon . . . Oh, well, she will be well guarded. She will not come to any hurt."

"It seems that in some things Sybelle is more daring than in others," Walter remarked. He was not accustomed to women hunting boar.

Joanna looked at him with a touch of surprise. "I hope so," she said, raising her brows. "You would be ill-suited as a husband if she were as venturesome in love as on the hunting field."

The bluntness was startling, but Walter accepted it without a blink. "As to that, yes, but I am not sure I am so well pleased with her being on a hunting field at all."

"We all hunt," Joanna stated flatly. "My mother, old as she is, is out today, and the only reason I am not is that I must see what I can do to amend the menu of these Welsh cooks. I like leeks, but not in everything, and they will put them in the sweets if they are not restrained. I must also tell you plainly that Sybelle will laugh in your face if you bid her not to hunt. Sir Walter, think well. Think whether you wish to take to your bosom such women as we. We are not to hold nor to bind where our lands are concerned. On other matters, if you win her love, Sybelle will try to please you—but she is not the kind to sit by the fire sewing a fine seam."

"I suppose I should have known." Walter smiled wryly. "After all, she did not hesitate to ride out with her men to drive off what she thought were reivers. And you may rest assured that I will deny Sybelle *nothing* that gives her pleasure. I was only concerned for her safety."

"You will have sufficient to concern you." Joanna sighed and then shook her head. "Come, sit with me by the fire for a few minutes, and I will try to explain."

She led the way around the bulge of the fireplace to some chairs set to one side by the hearth. Most everyone had gone to take part in the hunt, so the hall was nearly empty except for a few servants clearing the last of the food and wine from the tables. Walter winced as he followed Joanna. His knee had stiffened with standing, and he smiled gratefully when she drew over a footstool and lifted his leg to it. He thanked her and then waited while she seated herself also.

"It is all that madcap Simon's fault," Joanna said. "While

Sybelle was a little girl, I spent most of my time at Roselynde because my mother was with Ian all over the country. And then, when Geoffrey was so much at court, Sybelle still remained mostly at Roselynde because I do not think a royal court is a healthy place to raise a girl. Besides, she had to learn to know the lands and people that would be hers. And she adored Simon—well, who does not? But Simon, as you must know, has very little common sense."

Walter burst out laughing. "Indeed, I know it. It was my sad duty all too often to chastise him for his lunacies. I do not know whether I beat him harder for fear I would not beat him at all, or whether he got away with half his punishment because I was laughing so much."

"Yes, that would be the way of it. But you see, Simon adores Sybelle, and between being unable to deny her anything she asked of him and the fact that he never saw the danger or lack of propriety in his pranks, when he was at home he led her to do the most astonishing things. And I am very much afraid Sybelle has never got over the notion that climbing cliffs, breaking horses, shooting with the longbow, and suchlike are ordinary, everyday things. I have told her, of course, that those activities were not ladylike, but all she said was that she was not likely to engage in any of them in fine company. This is true, but she is quite likely to engage in them in the presence of her husband. I thought you should be warned."

This time it was Walter who sighed. "Yes, I am very glad you told me. I will do my best not to forbid what Sybelle will think me a fool for forbidding—or what I cannot enforce. But none of this matters. We will learn each other's ways. I want her to wife, and, to speak the truth, I believe she wants me." He paused and looked steadily at Joanna, his eyes demanding an answer.

"She told me that you were attractive to her," Joanna answered truthfully, if somewhat reluctantly. "She has never said that about any other man. However, she said to my mother that she was not sure you would make a good husband."

"In God's name, why should she doubt it?" Walter cried.

"I suppose she fears what other women fear, that once you have her and she is yours by right, you will find the hunt for a doe that flees more interesting than the docile cow in the byre."

For a moment Walter sat with his mouth inelegantly open. Then he closed it and swallowed. It was true enough that the women of Roselynde were different. They trod without flinching, it seemed, on every ground that a man might consider by right to be his own. Then he found his voice and said, "Surely Sybelle cannot believe that I could be so unkind or, indeed, indecent, as to bring a mistress into her household."

"It is far more than that," Joanna pointed out coldly. "I do not believe my daughter would suffer her husband to keep a mistress at all—anywhere."

Then, while Walter was too stunned to say anything, Joanna rose, nodded farewell, and walked away toward the doorway that led out to the bailey where were the cook sheds. Deprived of a riposte, Walter fumed. Wise or unwise, he could not have refrained from saying plainly that his moral state was a matter between God and himself or his confessor and himself and not a subject with which his wife should be concerned. What Sybelle did not know could not hurt her, and why the devil should she even think of such a thing anyway?

The answer came on the heels of the question, and Walter barely bit back a roar of rage. Simon! That thoughtless idiot Simon had always talked to Sybelle about his women and his troubles with them. Walter ground his teeth. Naturally, Simon did not care if he gave Sybelle the impression that all men were satyrs. All that lunatic wanted—he had told Walter so—was a woman's point of view from a woman who would not be jealous.

Was that what Sybelle had been skirting around when she was talking about the differences in their ways of looking at things? It must have been. The management of lands could not be so very different in Roselynde from elsewhere. Well, at least Sybelle had the delicacy not to state flatly that she wished to make a eunuch of her husband. Yet Lady Joanna had made it abundantly clear that Sybelle would not take it kindly if *her* little amusements, totally unfitting for a woman, should be curbed. Regardless, his life was to be regulated according to Sybelle's fancies. They would see about that!

Walter was furious, but it did not, even fleetingly, pass through his mind that the simplest solution to the problem was not to marry Sybelle. Nor was his determination to have her owing in the least to the fact that he considered himself bound to her morally. It was perfectly true, but he never thought of it. He wanted Sybelle, and every check and difficulty only made her more desirable and him more determined to have her on terms with which he could live.

As Sybelle fled out to the hunting party that was gathering in the bailey, she considered the interruption of her conversation with Walter. She had not desired any interruption, despite her confusion, yet she knew her mother's coming had been timely. If she had not been off balance, she would have offered to remain with Walter, since it was obvious he could not join the hunt. That would have been a mistake, however, implying that he could expect her always to put aside her pleasure to suit him. She would do so when she was his wife because it would be her duty. But he should not *expect* it, nor suspect, Sybelle thought, smiling, that it was a greater pleasure to remain with him than to do anything else.

Her eyes danced as she thanked her father for lifting her to her saddle, and Geoffrey asked, "What has put you into so high a good humor, mistress? Lusting after blood, are you?"

The question made Sybelle laugh aloud. "Yes, Papa," she replied merrily, "but not the kind of which you are thinking."

She remembered, then, her mother's warning about not confiding her willingness to accept Walter too soon to her father, but the sounding of the horns and the excited yelping of the hounds saved her from having her answer investigated. Geoffrey uttered a warning that Sybelle not allow herself to be carried away into trouble, then set spurs to his horse and cantered out in the forefront of the hunt.

Sybelle had loosened her rein, and her lively mare, Damas, went ahead at her own speed. Her mistress's whip, which was usually busy at the beginning of a hunt to assure Sybelle of a good place to see the kill, hung untouched from the wrist. This time Damas was allowed to canter along with the other ladies who had come and were generally less eager than Sybelle both for the thrill of the ride and the thrill of the boar's charge. Sybelle had discovered that the management of a man could be more thrilling and dangerous than any hunt.

There was, however, the ever-present danger of yielding too soon and making what was offered seem cheap. Sybelle knew she had been very near doing that. All her natural instincts were toward total openness and honesty. It was, thus, very exciting even to think of hiding what she felt. Sybelle had never had any need to conceal her love from anyone. To refrain from responding to Walter's embrace with an equally warm one, then, took on a kind of glamour of wrongdoing—mischievous wrongdoing, not evil—Sybelle only wished to tease, not to wound.

There was a serious side to the necessary resistance. She must talk over with him the subject of his lands and those which were to be her dower. Sybelle felt an odd sinking of the heart. Obviously her father had told Walter how matters would be arranged, but it was one thing to hear it from a man he respected. It might be quite another matter entirely when a girl he thought of as his chattel began to make conditions. When they came in from the hunt, Sybelle thought, she must ask which lands Walter felt would march best with his own and offer to suggest those to her grandmother for her dowry. If he fired up at her interference . . . Again Sybelle felt that odd sinking of the heart. Perhaps she should not tempt fate?

Was it not too soon to begin Walter's next test? He had passed the first with flying colors. Then Sybelle admitted to herself, she dared not wait, dared no longer play with words and looks. That would only give her desire for him time to grow . . . and it was great enough already. Was it even now too great? Walter had said he would love her even if they quarreled, that he would not tire of his conflicts with her and seek a more complaisant woman. And it was true that her father and grandfather were faithful. Sybelle's heart lifted.

Suddenly there was a great belling from the hounds and the hunting horns blew wildly. The first boar had been scented. Sybelle caught up her whip and laid it sharply across Dama's haunches. The mare sprang forward, leaving the other women behind, and Sybelle cried out with the thrill of the chase. Yes, perhaps it was already too late for her, but only in the sense that she had taken the first steps into a new life.

CHAPTER 10

Walter had not sat long alone brooding over Joanna's remarks when his attention was drawn to Prince Llewelyn, who, to his amazement, had not gone to hunt and was standing before him in the company of Gervase and Marie. Instinctively, Walter began to rise, but the prince waved at him to remain seated for the sake of his knee.

"I saw you looking black as thunder," Llewelyn said lightly, "and I do not blame you—being tied by the leg and missing a hunt. To speak the truth, I feel much the same, for I have business that keeps me here when I had much rather be riding behind the hounds. However, I have been reconciled to the loss of the hunt by only a few words with these charming ladies. Little as I wish to yield them to anyone, I must."

"Then I am doubly a gainer," Walter said, "to have my tedium so delightfully relieved and to win so easy a victory over the Lord of Gwynedd, for had I earlier seen Lady Pembroke and Lady Marie in your company, I would have tried to draw them away from you."

As he spoke, Walter's eyes met Prince Llewelyn's. Both men were smiling pleasantly, but each read in the other's expression a politely restrained desire to laugh. Walter knew that the pressing business Llewelyn had was getting rid of Pembroke's ladies without offending them. Walter had no doubt that Llewelyn had discovered, between last night and this morning, that they were utterly useless for any political purpose. Not only did they know nothing and were not particularly interested in finding out, but they had no influence with the earl. Moreover, Walter was sure that Llewelyn knew he understood.

More civilities were exchanged; chairs were set for the ladies, and, at last, Prince Llewelyn bowed formally and took his leave, casting one glance over his shoulder that spoke volumes to Walter when he was sure neither Gervase nor Marie could see him. Walter could not help smiling a trifle more broadly. He had been both thanked and offered commiseration in that glance; however, he did not feel he needed any sympathy. True, he considered Gervase selfish, stupid, and self-important, but that was what he expected of most women anyway. And as his memory of the horrible journey from Brecon to Builth faded, he felt he had judged Marie too harshly. Richard was not her responsibility.

In any case, he did not mind pandering to their weaknesses if it suited Prince Llewelyn, for despite their faults they were as pretty and amusing as caged birds. In his opinion, wits, particularly in the resentful mood that still seethed under Walter's smiling exterior, were not necessary for women.

"You are amused, my lord?" Marie asked.

"Not at all," Walter replied hastily and somewhat guiltily. "I am pleased. I hope you found the prince enjoyable company. He was sorry to part with you."

"So it seemed. His manners are very good," Gervase admitted. "I would not have expected it in this godforsaken corner of the world. I quite enjoyed talking to him."

She sounded as surprised as if a dog or a horse had been the other party in the conversation. Walter struggled with himself, striving to keep his desire to laugh under control, and became suffused with a longing for Sybelle to have been present to share his amusement. Except that he knew Sybelle would have led Gervase on, and then, most likely, he would have disgraced himself. But the sudden desire for Sybelle brought back his feeling of resentment, too. Walter became aware that Marie was staring at him with raised brows, and he realized that his reply had been delayed too long. He wished he could stop thinking about Sybelle.

"I have been considering those you would find equally good company," he said. "Have you yet been introduced to Lord Geoffrey FitzWilliam?"

"He was at the table last night, but he said little," Gervase replied.

"He is reserved," Walter commented, with a mischievous sense of satisfaction at involving Sybelle's father. "Owing to the fact that he is the king's cousin and dear to Henry, he must be careful where he extends friendship. Too many wish to use him as a bridge to the king. But if you show him that is not the case and make an effort to charm him, you will find him a rewarding companion.''

That seemed perfectly reasonable to Gervase, who nodded and then rose to her feet suddenly, saying, ''Why, there is Lady Joanna. I will go and greet her and ask how she does. No, Marie, you stay here. We do not wish to overwhelm poor Lady Joanna.''

Walter was striken mute, first by amusement at the thought that being accosted by two women could overwhelm Joanna, second with alarm at the notion that Gervase might repeat what he had said about Geoffrey. There was nothing wrong with it, of course; it was even true, but Joanna might be rightly annoyed at having Gervase foisted off on her poor husband. It was not until both of these ideas had passed through Walter's head that it occurred to him that Gervase's move might have less to do with her desire to talk to Joanna than with her desire to leave him alone with Marie. If so, was this Gervase's idea or Marie's? Marie was very lovely; desire rose in Walter again, dimming her faults.

''You are very quiet, Lady Marie,'' he remarked, watching her face.

''There was no need for me to speak when all my questions were being answered,'' she replied, ''but I am less in need of safe companions than Gervase. Have you no one to suggest to *me* as interesting?''

The look openly and blatantly invited Walter to name himself, and he was just about to do so when he remembered that his situation had changed since the last time they had engaged in flirtation. Then he had been free, although he had wished to make an offer for Sybelle. Now he was bound because he had made his offer and been accepted—if Sybelle were willing. Resentment surged up in Walter again, and he smiled meaningfully at Marie. His lips parted to say ''Will I not do?'' but the words would not come. It was not fair to Marie. He did not think she wished to marry again. With as strong, kind, and indifferent a protector as Richard, and having her sister for company, she might well prefer the relative freedom of widowhood.

Still, there was a chance that Marie's attentions were owing to her consideration of him as a suitable prospect for a second husband. Walter felt he must make it clear that he was no longer available. Certainly there had been an excessive interest in his property and the chance that Richard would help him take control of it. It seemed, in retrospect, that Gervase had done most of the questioning and urging. Perhaps Gervase wished to get her sister remarried and off her hands. In any case, a definite statement regarding his offer for Sybelle would clarify the situation beyond doubt. If Marie wanted a husband, she would turn cold.

"I would suggest myself," Walter said, "except that I will very soon be encumbered with a wife—and that makes some men very dull company."

"A wife!" Marie was plainly shocked, but she made a strong and rapid recovery and laughed. "This is very sudden," she said archly. "You were not promised when you came to Pembroke keep, and you were gone from us only a few days. Did you win your maiden on the battlefield like a savage? Or did Richard suggest the girl to you?" The last words came out in a bitter snap.

"No!" Walter exclaimed, and then he remembered how Richard had warned him against marrying Marie.

Walter and Richard had not been alone during that conversation. Could Marie have heard of it? Walter was appalled. Whatever Richard thought of his sister-by-marriage, Walter did not want her to be hurt. He was sick at heart, also, at the idea that he had misunderstood Marie and thought her flirting merely playful rather than serious. The least he could do was to take the blame on himself and remove any stigma from Richard. Also, he must not hurt Marie further by admitting he had been in love with Sybelle all along and had only been playing with her.

"No," Walter repeated. "I have long wished to ally myself with this girl's family, but I could not offer for her earlier because of the political situation. It was only this morning that I was able to speak to Lord Geoffrey and suggest myself as a husband for his daughter."

"You came to terms quickly," Marie said. "Perhaps you will make it a double wedding."

"Oh, no." Walter barely prevented himself from adding *I wish it could be*. Instead he said, "It was only the most preliminary discussion. I had to know whether I was acceptable at all. However, there is no written contract. We did not even discuss terms."

That was not completely true, but Walter was certainly not going to confess to Marie that the decision was Sybelle's to make. Actually, the written contract was irrelevant. Once words of honor were exchanged, the thing would be certain and settled. The only purpose of the written contract, in Walter's opinion, was for a case at law—if, in future years, someone outside the families should challenge the ownership of property of children or grandchildren. Then the naming and disposition of the lands could be proven from the written contract, which would be deposited in the strong rooms of Roselynde, Goldcliff, and the Church. Between himself and Lord Geoffrey, or himself and Sybelle, Walter was sure no more than the exchange of kisses of peace was necessary.

"But I do not understand." Marie sounded puzzled. "How has the political situation changed? Is the war over?"

"You know it is not," Walter answered, smiling uneasily.

It had occurred to him suddenly, shockingly, that the first time he had approached Lord Geoffrey, the king had had the upper hand in the struggle; it had not even been known whether Lord Pembroke would escape the traps laid for him. Now, however, the opposite was true. Soon Richard and Llewelyn would move on the offensive.

"But you cannot marry until the war is over," Marie said, "unless you plan to shift your allegiance."

"Shift my allegiance!" Walter echoed. "Of course not. The matter was never mentioned."

His voice was a little louder than necessary, as if to stress his certainty. He remembered that he himself had suspected that might be a condition of acceptance of his suit, but Geoffrey had waved the subject away. Then common sense reminded him that he was of small significance on either side, a single knight with a small troop of men-at-arms. Of course, once he took hold of the other lands, Walter would have far greater power. Could that be Lord Geoffrey's purpose? Could he wish to secure the lands, arrange the marriage, and then urge his son-by-marriage into the king's party? Nonsense. Lord Geoffrey was a man of honor, and Walter had already stated his unalterable attachment to Pembroke.

"Then your marriage may be long delayed."

Walter knew there had been a longish pause between his rejection of the notion that he would change sides and Marie's comment. He must have been looking at her steadily all the while, he thought, without taking in what he saw. Now he realized that she was smiling, a slow, thoughtful smile of satisfaction rather than amusement, and suddenly she leaned forward and touched the back of his hand with one finger, drawing it from wrist to nail slowly and suggestively.

It never occurred to Walter for one moment that saying only preliminary talks had taken place could be misunderstood to mean his intention to marry Sybelle was not irrevocably fixed. Thus, he felt Marie's gesture to be an open declaration that she wished to play at love, not marry. Still, he did not believe her to be very clever, so instead of implying—untruthfully but romantically—that her company could make years of waiting seem short, he said, "The delay may not be very long. It will depend on what action Prince Llewelyn and Richard plan, and, of course, on the king's response."

"Oh, does Lord Geoffrey intend to remain in Wales long after the wedding?" Marie asked.

"No, he cannot do that," Walter replied, somewhat puzzled, and then he realized that if Geoffrey and Joanna went back to England, Sybelle would go also.

Conflicting emotions swept through him: first, a sense of loss because he did not want Sybelle to go where he could not see her and talk to her, and simultaneously a recognition that Marie was indicating to him the period in which it would be safe to play their games. Walter relaxed and allowed his eyes to caress her smooth skin and cherry lips, to wander down her lush body. What a delicious partner she would be, and he would not even have to feel guilty about offending a cuckolded husband. He uttered an artificial sigh and remarked that it would be very lonely for him after his family-by-marriage had departed.

"But you will have Richard and your war." Marie pouted delightfully.

"No war for me, at least not for a few weeks while this bone heals," Walter pointed out. "Until then, I am useless. Will you not have pity on me and give me your company? No one else will have time for me. I will be like an old dog left in the kennel because he is too lame to hunt."

"It must make everything difficult for you, losing the use of one arm," Marie cooed sympathetically.

"Not everything," Walter smiled suggestively. "For some

enterprises, it only provides an interesting challenge and invites one to think of new ways of using old . . . er . . . skills."

Marie smiled at him seductively. She had not been wrong, she thought; he was most certainly attracted to her, and he had shown no great interest in the girl he was to marry, nor any special eagerness for the marriage to take place. He had not even said the girl's name. Obviously what was important about her was that she was Lord Geoffrey's daughter. No doubt she would be richly dowered. Lord Geoffrey was cousin to the king, and he must be very rich. There were two sons, Marie had heard, but there would still be enough for a lavish daughter's portion.

Smiling and fluttering her lashes, Marie made some ambiguous remark that invited further advances while expressing doubts of Walter's sincerity. Although he launched at once into compliments and assurances, Marie hardly listened. What could have happened between the time he had brought them to Brecon and his return there with Richard? His eagerness to go to Abergavenny himself to fetch Richard, Marie had been sure, was owing to his intention to secure her. Why then had he not made a proposal to Richard? Then it came to her. Walter must have asked Richard about her dower property and learned that the lands were held by her first husband's brother. And Richard had either offered nothing or offered too little.

"Have I offended you, Lady Marie?" Walter asked, a brow quizzically cocked.

"Not offended, Sir Walter," Marie murmured, lowering her eyes. She realized she must have flushed with rage or showed some other sign of the emotion when she thought that Walter had slipped out of her grasp because of her brother-by-marriage's selfishness and niggardliness. "Perhaps you go too fast," she added coyly.

"Alas, your loveliness spurs me on," Walter declared.

His voice had a tinge of flatness, but Marie did not notice. She fluttered her lashes a little more, held up the edge of her sleeve to shield her face as if a spurt of modesty had overtaken her, and made another remark that would draw more compliments and pleas. Walter responded as he should, but only a very small part of Marie's mind carried on the conversation. The rest of her thoughts were running over the men she had seen and met the previous night. Most likely Prince Llewelyn had introduced the most important guests and members of his entourage. Perhaps a few more would arrive today and tomorrow, but from what Marie had seen and the hints she had gathered, Walter was the best catch.

She need not commit herself totally until after the wedding, so she would have nothing to lose. If a better prospect appeared, she could cut Walter off sharply with the excuse that she feared for his happiness since he was all but betrothed to another. More important was the question of whether his greed for the dower Lord Geoffrey was offering was greater than his desire for her. Marie gave a little more attention to the conversation, so that Walter's interest, which had been lagging under the need to find more and more compliments, sparked.

Marie was again assured of his eagerness for her, but whether it was intense enough to substitute for good land was still in doubt. She would have to see the girl, Marie thought. If she were ugly or ill-tempered, it might be possible to make Walter understand that a wife he desired was more important than an extra estate, particularly since he already was, or would be, rich.

And surely the bond with Richard would be as important as the bond with Lord Geoffrey. Of course, she was not Richard's sister or daughter, so the bond would not be as strong. Still, a fool like Walter could probably be so bemused by lust that he would not think at all. Or, if he could not be bemused, he could be trapped. . . .

Suddenly Marie realized she was letting matters get out of hand. She must have agreed to more than she intended while her mind had been elsewhere. Walter was leaning forward, his lips a trifle fuller than normal, pointing out that so many were out hunting that the keep was unusually empty. Marie drew back, tittered, and hid her face in her sleeve, crying out faintly that she had not understood, that he was trying to trap her into an immodesty. Then she allowed her eyes to show over her arm as she whispered that he must not tempt her, that it was unkind to offer what would be immoral to accept, that she must run away from what she desired but knew was wrong to take.

Walter was thoroughly puzzled when Marie actually did run away, but he was also somewhat relieved. True, he would have been glad if she had agreed to go off with him somewhere so that he could bed her, but her on-again, off-again attitude irritated him, and he was finding the conversation, the need to flatter and plead, very dull. In the past Walter had enjoyed his pursuits, prided himself on the fact that although he had neither wealth or particular beauty, nearly every woman he approached had yielded to him.

This time, however, every time Walter uttered a fulsome compliment, a vision of Sybelle's astonished and amused face would flash across his mind. He could envision her response, too, very like Marie's—except that Sybelle would make a caricature of it so that he would burst out laughing. It had happened to him in Roselynde, soon after he first met her. Not knowing any better, he had tried to woo Sybelle as he wooed other women. Both he and Sybelle had enjoyed themselves very much, but Walter knew that path was no way to Sybelle's heart.

Bored and frustrated, Walter blamed both women: Marie for being dull and coy at the wrong time, and Sybelle for being beautiful, desirable, fascinating, and at the moment unattainable. Then he cursed the injured knee that had kept him from going on the hunt and thus not only condemned him to boredom and frustration but deprived him of watching over Sybelle's safety. Fortunately he did not have much time for these thoughts because Prince Llewelyn's pleasant voice broke into them.

"Am I forever in your black book for dropping those two silly women on you?" he asked.

"No, my lord," Walter replied. "They are silly, perhaps, but I do not see much harm in them. I find them pleasant company."

"You do not look it." Llewelyn laughed. "Or are you angry because they left you?"

"I am angry at myself, my lord," Walter replied, and, induced by some charm Prince Llewelyn seemed to exude that often made people confide in him—even when it would be wiser not to do so—told him about Sybelle having gone boar hunting.

"God! Those women are enough to drive a man mad—though I should not say it when my own daughter is as bad or worse." Llewelyn laughed heartily as he dropped into the chair Marie had vacated. "I am fortunate that Simon was willing to have her. He is accustomed to madwomen. So, you plan to take the golden goddess to your bosom. I wish you good fortune."

"If she will have me," Walter said, knowing somehow that Prince Llewelyn would be neither incredulous nor amused that Sybelle, a mere girl, was to be allowed to make her own choice.

"You need not fear she will not," Llewelyn responded, as if what Walter had said was the most ordinary thing in the world rather than a most peculiar exception. He gave Walter a broad smile. "I have quick eyes. I saw her face when you first came into the hall. It was all she could do to stop herself from running to you. She will have you—but are you sure you know what you are doing? Those women . . ." Llewelyn allowed his voice to drift off and then shook his head. "Some years ago . . . good God, it is more than twenty, although it seems only like yesterday—I found Lady Alinor leading an army into Wales. I admit she asked me to take them into battle, but had I refused, I know she would have done it herself."

Walter burst out laughing. "The blood in them has not grown any thinner with time," he began, and then told of Sybelle leading her troop right into his camp in pursuit of his erring men. Walter's feelings had shifted uncertainly from irritation and embarrassment to amusement whenever the incident came to mind, but retelling it to Llewelyn in the wake of the prince's disclosure now gave Walter an odd feeling of pride.

"There are few like unto them," Llewelyn agreed, chuckling at Walter's revelation. "And I will say this," he added, becoming serious. "If you can endure their boldness, you have a treasure that can have no price. They cleave like welded iron to their men. Neither their eyes nor their hearts wander—and that, with women so beautiful, is a miracle. However," he grinned again, slyly, "I have heard it said that they expect that courtesy to be returned. Oh, well, with such a wife it can be no great burden. But I did not come here to talk of those engaging witches of Roselynde. Since you are tied by the leg anyway, I cannot spoil your day by asking you to do a small task for me."

"Most gladly, my lord," Walter replied, moving to rise.

"No, no. Sit where you are. It is a matter of movement of

men and the supplies needed for it, to be worked on parchment. I will have a table brought."

The table appeared with some swiftness, and Walter was left to play with the question of how long it would take to move an army from one point to another along a variety of routes, plus what supplies would be needed to feed them, considering on the one hand that they were allowed to loot freely and on the other that looting was forbidden. It was an interesting exercise for Walter, who had not had such problems set for him since he left the household of William of Pembroke. Walter was responsible for his own men, of course, but that was a much smaller group, and time and quantities were never simply proportional.

As he worked, Walter realized that if he married Sybelle and if she did succeed to her grandmother's estates, he would have almost as many men to plan for as his own levy. It was a most sobering thought, even though Walter knew the results he was working out were not crucial. Each master-at-arms or captain of mercenary troops requested what he felt would be necessary from his lord, and each lord was supposed to obtain supplies for his men out of his own resources. However, in the case of the rebellion, many had been stripped of their lands and incomes so that Richard had to find food and arms for them also.

Walter's estimates would be used only to check on whether anyone was asking for more than he really needed. Some, Walter was sure, would do so. He remembered how Richard listened with sympathy to certain men and with considerable coolness to others. How did one know? Walter wondered, and then smiled at himself. One knew by doing what he was doing now and by talking and listening to the men, by visiting their keeps and looking over their lands. He knew it would be a heavy burden and remembered that Lord Geoffrey had told him he would be fortunate to find time enough to eat and sleep. Suddenly Walter chuckled. He would forgo the eating and sleeping, just so long as there was time enough for love.

CHAPTER 11

Because he was busy, the morning passed away more quickly than Walter expected. From time to time he had heard feminine voices and laughter and assumed that the ladies who had not gone to hunt were amusing themselves somewhere in the hall. He had no inclination to look that way. Somewhat later, Prince Llewelyn appeared, and they talked about the estimates Walter had made. During the conversation, Walter found an appropriate time and place to mention Knight's Tower. He was pleased when Prince Llewelyn showed a definite interest in placing that stronghold in Walter's hands. Soon after that, however, Llewelyn cocked his head to the side and remarked that he heard the hunt returning.

Walter was surprised. He did not think himself deaf, but he heard nothing. Surely enough, though, only a few minutes after Prince Llewelyn had made the remark and excused himself, Walter heard voices and laughter as men and women trooped into the hall still talking out the excitement. Walter's eyes flew to Sybelle as she came through the entryway. She was arguing some point with her brother, but as she came in, her glance went to where she had last left Walter. Since he had not moved far, their eyes met. She hesitated, and before Walter could push away the small table at which he had been working, get his leg off the footstool, and rise, she had pushed William on his way and come across to where Walter sat.

"I am sorry you were not with us, Sir Walter," Sybelle said. "It was a lovely hunt."

Walter looked at Sybelle and swallowed. He had seen from across the room that her dress was disordered, but at close range the impact of her loveliness in wild disarray was stunning. She had lost her wimple and headdress, and her bronze mane was full of twigs and leaves, loose tendrils curling around her face and making her eyes look like molten gold. Her color was still high with cold and excitement, her lips very red, and, adorably, the tip of her pretty nose was as pink as her cheeks.

"Missing the hunt is the least of my regrets," he replied, forgetting all about how annoyed he had been.

Sybelle batted her eyes at him exaggeratedly and tittered. "Oh, how you flatter me, my lord."

Walter stared at her in surprise, barely touched by guilt. Her manner was a caricature of Marie's. Could she know? he wondered. Uttering a theatrical groan, Walter shook his head. "Worse and worse!" he exclaimed. "How can I court you when your response to a compliment is so unnatural?"

Sybelle burst out laughing. "The polite thing to say," she choked, "is exceptional. How do you expect to win me if you insult me by calling me unnatural?"

"I will now call you unreasonable also," Walter retorted. "Did you not just by your manner chide me for desiring to flatter you? Then when I speak unpolished truth you object to that. Which do you desire?"

Sybelle's eyes glinted, and Walter waited eagerly for the clever rejoinder, but it was never made, for Joanna arrived to sweep away her daughter with exclamations of disgust at her condition and a sharp reminder that the servants were already preparing the hall for the serving of dinner.

Neither Walter nor Sybelle found anything of interest in the meal or the entertainment, since they were not seated together. Partners of both found them somewhat absent of mind, although Walter came off better in this respect than Sybelle. Most of the conversation addressed to him concerned the battle at Monmouth, and he was able to answer nearly all of the questions by rote, having answered similar questions several times already. Sybelle was unusually quiet, and her eyes had a disconcerting way of wandering off to where Walter was sitting. When their glances met, both lost track of what they or their dinner partners were saying.

As soon as the tables were cleared, they gravitated together as if some irresistible force drew them. Joanna sighed as she saw them again in the sheltered corner by the hearth. Sybelle loved to dance, yet she did not seem to have heard the musicians. She had simply shaken her head at several young men who had accosted her, doubtless with requests to dance, and continued on her way to Walter.

Joanna rose when Geoffrey held out his hand to her. His lameness made Geoffrey an awkward dancer, but he enjoyed it nonetheless, and it was a considerable pleasure to know that lame as he was, Joanna preferred him as a partner to anyone else. This time, however, she looked distressed, and Geoffrey asked what was wrong. She pointed to Sybelle and Walter as Geoffrey led her out onto the floor.

"I have pulled them apart twice today already. I suppose it is useless to separate them again," she said.

"But why did you try?" Geoffrey asked, considerably surprised. "I am gladder and gladder of this opportunity for them to be together in this festal atmosphere. If Walter is given to drink or wild behavior, it will show and Sybelle will withdraw. What is more, although I am certain Walter would not use her dishonorably, even if he wished to do so, it is too crowded. What do you fear, my love?"

They were then parted by the steps of the dance and Joanna had time to consider before she replied. Truly, she did not know what she feared, although it was certainly not that Walter would physically seduce her daughter. Nor had she ever thought him more prone to drink or wildness than any normal man. What she feared, actually, was Walter's clever handling of Sybelle.

Joanna felt that Walter was playing Sybelle like a fish, and she did not like it. He had seen very quickly that lugubrious sighs of love only tickled Sybelle's funny bone, but deliberately making her laugh, while gazing at her with the eyes of a lovesick calf, was turning the silly girl's head. Also, Joanna had seen Walter with Marie de les Maures. She had not tried to hear what had passed between them, but it was clear that a flirtation was in progress. Very possibly it meant nothing; Walter was bored and alone and could well have been whiling away the time, but Joanna did not like it.

Although there was some justice in Joanna's concern with Walter's interest in Marie, she was investing him with far greater astuteness than he was capable of bringing to bear in his relationship with Sybelle. It was true that, finding him physically attractive and having been urged in his direction by everyone she loved, trusted, and respected, Sybelle was allowing herself to fall deeper and deeper in love, as her mother feared, but so was Walter. It was also true that he was making all the right moves in his wooing, but that was more a result of his extreme responsiveness to Sybelle than to his previous cleverness in handling women.

The intent conversation that Joanna had noted between Sybelle and Walter had begun prosaically enough with Walter's questions about the hunt and Sybelle's animated description of the chase and kill. Then, naturally, she had asked what he had been doing all morning.

"I missed you," he replied.

Sybelle laughed at him. "You have paid your dues. Now tell me what you really did all morning."

Walter was a trifle nonplussed, wondering again if Sybelle had heard of his conversation with Marie. In defense he decided to abandon compliments and actually tell her about the task Prince Llewelyn had set him.

"Now that is odd," Sybelle responded, immediately thoughtful. "I believed it was characteristic of the Welsh to live off the land during a war."

Walter blinked. He had expected a moue of distaste and a remark about the dullness of his occupation. Sybelle's answer produced the need to reorient his thinking that he always experienced at the beginning of their conversations and concurrently a strong sense of comfort and pleasure. There was no need to hunt for pretty words. It was possible with Sybelle to talk about what really interested *him*. He brought his mind to focus on what she had said.

"That is true," he agreed. "I had not thought of it. Perhaps it is something Richard wanted done. No, that cannot be. Richard can do that kind of thing in his head." And before he thought, he asked, "Could your father or grandfather have suggested it as a test for me?" He was appalled as soon as the words came out, but Sybelle did not look offended.

"I suppose it is possible," she replied, "but Grandpapa is not at all devious, and, truly, I think in your case Papa would just have asked you himself. I know he likes you very much. No, I will tell you what *I* think. Lord Pembroke will object to the Welsh raiding promiscuously, of course, and I will lay you odds Prince Llewelyn wished to know how much he can ask to prohibit them from doing so."

"The old fox!" Walter exclaimed, for Sybelle's analysis

rang true to him. "Damn him. I hope I was not too generous in my estimates."

"I do not think it matters," Sybelle pointed out. "I would imagine whatever you suggested would be used as a low point. Prince Llewelyn, I would guess, *intends* to ask for too much. I am sure he prefers to allow raiding. After all, a great deal more is picked up than food."

"To speak the truth," Walter said, "some raiding is better for my purposes. If the Welsh lay waste the land as they approach Knight's Tower, Sir Heribert, my late brother's castellan, will be more likely to yield it."

Sybelle frowned. "But will that be best? If this Heribert yields at once, what excuse will you have to put him out? You have not previously demanded your dues, I believe. Do you know that he deserves to be dismissed? And, say he does, will he not return and perhaps make trouble as soon as you must leave? The people must be accustomed to obeying Heribert. What of the men-at-arms who are now in Knight's Tower? They must be Heribert's men. Have you replacements for them?"

"I have been thinking about just those questions," Walter said, although he was startled by Sybelle's grip of the knottier aspects of his problem. "I think my next move must be to demand my dues."

"I think so, too," Sybelle agreed approvingly. "Would you like me to write the letter for you? It is very hard to write when one has only one hand."

Walter was surprised again, although this time the sensation was mild and brief. The ability to read and write was not common in women, whose business in the nursery, weaving room, stillroom, and kitchen hardly seemed to require Latin, or even French, prose. Even as that idea passed through Walter's mind, he remembered Geoffrey's remarks. Sybelle would spend little of her time in nursery or stillroom if she managed her own lands.

"I do not think I will write," he said slowly. "Since I will be useless for any military action for some weeks, the best I could do to forward Richard's plans would be to obtain the use of Knight's Tower for him. I think I will go in person."

"No!" Sybelle cried. "Oh, no. That would be very foolish. It would be . . ."

She did not permit herself to finish the sentence. She had

been well schooled never to say to a man that an action was dangerous, at least not that it would be dangerous to him personally. However, it was too late. Although she had not said the words, what she meant was clear enough. But Walter was far more interested in the evidence her distress gave of her concern for him than with any challenge to his competence in protecting himself.

Her loveliness filled his eyes, the rich orange tawny of her velvet overdress seeming to raise a reflection in her netted mass of hair, the gold silk of her underdress, and the topazes that circled her throat, matching the gold of her eyes. Her lips and cheeks were still reddened by her morning's exercise in the cold, but her elegant nose was now properly a match for her mat cream skin. Walter took a small step closer to her and seized the hand she had half raised in protest.

"Sybelle, why do you tease me with a denial of my right to love you?" he asked softly. "I see you care for me, and you know I want you for my wife. I do not wish to pretend we are betrothed. I wish to be so in truth and to set an early date for our wedding. Will you not say you will have me and allow me to settle the business?"

"Will you stay with me if I say yes?" Sybelle whispered, forgetting everything she had ever been told about men because of her fear for him and her desire to keep him safe.

He pulled her even closer and bent his head above hers. "You know I cannot," he murmured. "My dear love, even if I were to write to Knight's Tower instead of going, as you desire, I would soon have to go with Richard. You would not have me be an oath-breaker, would you?"

Sybelle lifted her head, and their faces were now so close that no more than an inch or two was between their lips. The temptation was irresistible. Walter lowered his head a little farther and kissed her. Almost immediately both realized that they were not yet betrothed and were in public—and they stiffened. Still, their lips did not part instantaneously; there was a lingering. But then the music stopped. Sybelle turned her head a trifle. Walter lifted his and stepped back.

"I would rather have you an oath-breaker than dead," Sybelle said rebelliously, but then she laughed and shook her head. "No, I know it is not right to ask such things. You must do what you think is best. I do not like it. I confess that. I think it foolish, as there is so little chance of a happy outcome and so great a chance that ill will befall. Will you not speak to Papa before you decide finally?''

''I will certainly speak to your father if you wish me to do so, but I feel he will agree with me that this is the best thing to do.''

During the final bow of the dance, Marie de les Maures had caught sight of Walter and Sybelle. She could not see Sybelle's face and did not recognize her, but she guessed from the glimpse she had of Walter's expression that this was not a casual conversation. As she moved away from her partner, Marie saw what seemed to be an attempt on Walter's part to kiss the girl beside whom he stood and the turn of her head that frustrated his purpose. Whether this was a new flirtation or the beginning of a courtship, Marie decided she had better find out just what was going on.

Knowing that Walter could not dance, Marie had not sought his company at the end of the meal. There were so many fewer women than men at Builth that Marie had been certain Lord Geoffrey's daughter would also find a partner. It hardly seemed worthwhile to give up the pleasure of dancing to keep Walter company.

Now, however, she thanked her partner hastily, over her shoulder, as she excused herself and made her way toward the couple. She arrived in time to hear Sybelle say, ''I do not like it. I confess that,'' and several other sentences, all of which made it certain that she was Geoffrey's daughter and might imply that she was pleading with Walter to free her from the prospective contract. And Walter's reply was scarcely that of a passionate lover nor even of a man *very* determined to make the contract.

It seemed to Marie to be a good time for her to step in and show that she was not indifferent to Walter. Whether or not a man desires a woman, the knowledge that she does not desire him rankles. Marie thought Walter a dreadful fool to be moved by a girl's plea to release her when he wanted her dowry, but that was exactly the kind of fool who probably would also prefer a woman who ''loved'' him and who could be convinced to give up a larger dowry to obtain such a wife.

Marie arrived beside Walter and Sybelle just as she said, ''Thank you,'' and smiled at him. Sybelle had infinite trust in her father's caution and good sense. Possibly Geoffrey would agree that Walter should go to Knight's Tower in person, but if he did, he would doubtless suggest safeguards so that the castellan could not do Walter any harm.

The relief she felt brought higher color into Sybelle's face and made her eyes glow even brighter than usual. This glowing countenance was the first close view that Marie had of Lord Geoffrey's daughter, and her immediate reaction was fury. How was it possible that Walter should be interested only in the girl's dowry? Walter had deliberately been making a fool of her, Marie thought. Nonetheless, the words she had planned to say came automatically from her mouth.

"Good afternoon, Sir Walter. I have come to relieve your companion so that she, too, may have the pleasure of dancing."

"Lady Marie!"

The exclamation seemed more of surprise than of welcome, which did nothing to improve Marie's temper, but the smile she had from Sybelle was warm. *She does not wish to be alone with him,* Marie thought. *She will go away and seek a dancing partner*. Marie felt a spiteful satisfaction from intruding and spoiling whatever plans Walter had had for winning the girl and her lands. However, Sybelle did not move away.

"You must be Lord Pembroke's sister-by-marriage," Sybelle said. "I am glad to meet you. I am very sorry that you should have come to this country in such troubled times. It must be lonely for you, pent up in a place where you can see few people."

"True," Marie replied, "but you have the advantage over me. I do not know who you are."

"I beg your pardon." Walter bowed an apology. He had been watching Sybelle too closely to pick up his cue, but he was still not certain whether she had heard anything of his flirtation. "Lady Marie de les Maures, let me present you to Lady Sybelle Alinor Ela FitzWilliam, daughter to Lord Geoffrey FitzWilliam, who is the king's cousin."

Sybelle burst out laughing. "How silly you are, Sir Walter. Why do you not now name all Papa's properties and honors? This is not a formal court presentation."

"I was only making up for my previous rudeness in not presenting you to each other at all," Walter said easily, but it was not true.

Remembering Gervase's supercilious attitude, he had wished to make sure that Marie did not underestimate Sybelle's rank.

It was true that Walter had not seen quite the same haughtiness in Marie as in Gervase, but he was taking no chances on Sybelle's being offended. He had glanced at Sybelle when he answered, but his eyes went back to Marie, wondering whether she had noticed that he had presented her to Sybelle—thereby indicating Sybelle was the lady of higher rank. However, he had been careful to phrase the introduction backward, so that unless one listened closely it sounded as if he were presenting Sybelle to Marie. In this way he hoped to avoid hurting Marie, while indicating that Sybelle was more important.

Concern brought a slight rigidity to Walter's expression, a downturn to one corner of his mouth. Marie was aware only that his eyes had returned to her even while he spoke to his almost-betrothed. Perhaps, Marie thought, Walter did not like Sybelle's type of beauty. Marie knew she was equally attractive, although in a different way. Walter's attention soothed her anger. It would be better, she decided, not to irritate him by overt interference in his plans—yet. For now, if Sybelle did not accept as a dancing partner one of the several men converging on them, it would be enough to show her up for the dull English clod she must be.

Sybelle, in the meantime, saw more than the fact that Walter's eyes had moved quickly from her to Marie. She was, in fact, startled by her awareness of his thoughts, by her ability to read them from the small muscular reactions of his face and body. She had never, except in the one or two instances when she had faced real physical danger, been as perceptive of the intentions of any other creature. To Sybelle it was apparent that Walter was not pleased by Marie's intrusion, that the formal introduction, the presentation of Marie to herself—an unmarried and younger woman—were meant as a subtle curb for Marie's tongue or manner.

From this and from a few exasperated remarks her mother had made about Lady Pembroke and her sister, Sybelle concluded that Walter found Marie haughty and boring and did not like her. On the other hand, it was clear to Sybelle that Marie liked Walter. Mistakenly, Sybelle decided she had better act as a buffer between them. Thus, when the men Marie had noticed approaching began to request both ladies to dance and offered various inducements, Sybelle refused with a series of lighthearted excuses, among which was that none of them could offer such thrilling conversation as the hero of the battle of Monmouth.

"And where is he?" Walter asked caustically. "You silly chit, that was no battle. It was a rout—first one way and then the other. And I am going to murder you if you go about implying that it is my one subject of conversation."

Sybelle only giggled in response, but the younger men clamored for Walter to tell them of the event. This was what Sybelle intended because it provided a group and diluted the chance that Marie would flirt with Walter and that he be cold in response. Not only did Sybelle achieve her purpose, but she discovered that Marie's caressing manner was turned on each man to whom she spoke. The manner, in Sybelle's opinion, was even sillier than that of most other women. She twittered and gasped and fluttered her eyelashes, expressing her horror and repugnance for any discussion of war. Sybelle thought her pathetic and ridiculous.

Although Sybelle herself was not particularly interested in any blow-by-blow description of a battle, having seen far too much of the result of those blows, she knew such talk was a mark of a man's pride in himself and must be listened to with attention. In fact, between Marie's interruptions and Walter's genuine reluctance to discuss the battle anymore, the talk soon wandered to other subjects and then, when it became clear that neither lady was going to leave Walter to dance, the young men drifted away to find other partners.

Sybelle was rather surprised when Marie did not accept any of the invitations. Of course, *she* found Walter far better company than any of those young cockerels. . . . And with that thought she realized that Marie might also find Walter better company. Sybelle was not jealous; she was moved by pity for the silly woman. Perhaps Marie's manner meant nothing, but her lingering did imply she favored Walter. It was wrong, Sybelle felt, to allow her to believe Walter was available.

"You should not forgo your pleasure to stand here and talk with me," Walter said.

The remark was not specifically addressed to either woman, but Sybelle was certain it was not meant for her. Still, Marie repeated her first statement that she had come to relieve Sybelle so that Sybelle could dance and enjoy herself. It made Sybelle feel very guilty, reminding her of her grandmother's point that it was unfair to leave the matter of her betrothal hanging midair. Of course, Lady Alinor had been speaking about Walter, but Sybelle now saw it was unfair to others also.

Glancing sidelong at Walter and noting the slightly thinned line of his lips, which marked his distaste for the situation, Sybelle felt even guiltier. Poor Walter, he had done everything he could within the bounds of politeness to rid them of Marie. There was no way, Sybelle knew, in which he could clarify matters without claiming more than Sybelle had given him a right to claim. He could not say he was betrothed, for example, without seeming to force her into an agreement she had not made.

The slight pause after Marie spoke was growing noticeable. Walter turned a little more toward Sybelle; she felt there was a helpless perplexity in his eyes. The urge to help him was irresistible. "But it is my duty not to enjoy myself if Sir Walter cannot," Sybelle confessed, laughing to show she was jesting. She put out her hand to him. "Sir Walter has asked for me in marriage, and my father has given his consent. When the contracts are written, we will be betrothed. Thus, if Sir Walter is lame, Sybelle cannot dance."

The look of stunned amazement on Walter's face gave Marie considerable food for thought. First, it confirmed her original idea that Sybelle had been resisting the betrothal. Second, it confirmed the notion that although Walter had made an offer for Sybelle, he was not really very eager to have her, despite her dowry. It seemed that he had been considering her plea that he should not make contract, since she was unwilling, as a good reason to back out of his offer. Third, Marie assumed that Sybelle had suddenly, owing to jealousy, changed her mind, dumbfounding Walter.

Marie was annoyed with herself. Perhaps if she had not intruded, Walter *would* have told Lord Geoffrey that his daughter was not willing and not made contract.

To gain time to think, Marie made vague comments of surprise. She was wondering whether she should give up. There were many other men, but spite rose in her. If she could not win Walter, she could give Sybelle good reason for her distaste for him—but first she would try to take him from under the girl's nose. She could pursue Walter whenever Sybelle was absent, telling him in plain words that he was irresistible to her but that she avoided him when he was with Sybelle to prevent making trouble between him and his betrothed. That would show a tender consideration for his welfare that should surely make the fool believe she loved him.

They would be in Builth at least another week, Marie believed. That would give her a day or two to see how such treatment worked and still leave her time to use other tactics if necessary. What Marie wanted to avoid now was a more public statement of the planned betrothal. Once it was general knowledge, Sybelle would feel obliged to stand by it, no matter how much she disliked Walter. For the moment, however, Marie was aware that her murmurs of "happy" surprise had gone virtually unnoticed by the other two. Nor did they seem to have noticed that there had been another marked pause in the conversation. They were staring at each other, and Marie noted with satisfaction that Sybelle looked somewhat frightened and Walter looked decidedly worried.

"I see I have teased you into a declaration earlier than it should have been made," Marie said archly. "Please do not be concerned. I swear I will tell no one, not even my sister. If something should cause a slip between the cup and the lip, there will be no rumor of this from me."

That clear statement penetrated, and Sybelle turned her head. "Thank you. It is true I have been somewhat free with news that is yet to be confirmed. I will be grateful if you keep it private."

"And now I see I am *de trop,*" Marie murmured. "I shall leave you to yourselves."

No one said her nay, and she slipped away just as the musicians started to tune up for another dance measure. She was noticed by a young man who had not found a partner and swept into the dance before she could see the immediate reaction to her departure, but the next time she had a chance to look at the corner alongside the hearth, both Sybelle and Walter were gone.

Marie was particularly charming to the young man who partnered her after that, and to several other partners, for she had seen, when the third dance started, that Sybelle was also dancing. It was not significant to Marie that Sybelle was partnered by her uncle Simon, and later in turn by her father, grandfather, and brother. All that Marie cared about was that

Sybelle seemed to have fled from Walter. Marie could not know that Sybelle was performing her first act of obedience to her future husband.

As soon as she had left them, Walter had released Sybelle's hand and smiled at her. "I am not going to let you back out this time," he said. "I will speak to Lady Alinor at once and ask her to settle a time for us to talk of contract, since I understand from your father that it is to your grandmother I must apply."

Sybelle looked at him with wide eyes and shook her head slowly, not knowing what it was about Walter that drew her so strongly. In comparison with her uncles he was not at all handsome: a typically square, ruddy, Norman face; sandy hair; blue eyes that could look sharp or mild; a wide mouth that, soft and full, looked sensual but could be thinned to cruelty. His face would never produce the delight one obtained from looking at Simon or Adam, but it gave Sybelle a sense of confidence and security. Walter would not suddenly disappear in a moment of crisis as Simon did, nor would he burst into roaring rages as did Adam. Sybelle did not look downward from his face to his body, but she was strongly aware of it. That held a different appeal, more dangerous because the appeal did not respond to reason.

Having thought of it was enough. "I will not go back on those words unless you force it on me," Sybelle said softly.

It was Walter's turn to shake his head, but he made no direct answer, saying only, "Find a partner with whom to dance, Sybelle. Yes, I wish it. I must put my thoughts in order, and I cannot think"—he smiled at her—"at least, not of anything practical, when you are near."

So Sybelle danced with "safe" men, and Walter talked war and politics with those who could not find partners or did not care to dance, but both their minds were busy. Sybelle was worried that her mother would be angry because she had yielded so quickly. It had been that concern that made her look frightened a moment after she had committed herself. Not that Sybelle was afraid Jo-anna would beat her or scold her, only that her mother would think she lacked good sense and strength of purpose. Aside from that, Sybelle was very happy. A great burden seemed to have fallen away from her. She enjoyed her evening's entertainment, particularly as every glimpse she had of Walter showed him blamelessly occupied and seemingly at ease.

This last impression was mistaken, although Walter had suffered no rebuff from Lady Alinor. He had found her quickly enough, sitting between her husband and Prince Llewelyn, who were happily reminiscing about events that stretched over thirty years. Lady Alinor's eyes had brightened with laughter when she saw Walter's purposeful advance toward them.

"Here comes our future grandson-by-marriage," she said. "Perhaps the middle of a dance is not the time to discuss a marriage contract, but I could scarcely object after I agreed to attend a wedding in the middle of a war."

"It was a most felicitous moment," Llewelyn said, perfectly straight-faced, although his eyes twinkled. "Simon wished to be married on the first of December. All the soothsayers were agreed that the aspects were extraordinarily favorable—and I wanted to speak to Ian and Geoffrey."

"You have this in common with the young man about to join us," Alinor remarked with a lifted brow, "that it would take a blow from a war ax to let out of your head any notion that came into it."

"Lady Alinor," Walter said as he bowed, having reached them at that moment, "Sybelle has given her consent to our marriage. I would like to know when the terms of the contract can be discussed and decided."

He was somewhat startled when all three burst into laughter, but smiled himself when Alinor explained—in more tactful terms than she had used to Llewelyn and her husband—what they had been saying just before he arrived. He pointed out, however, in the most guileless fashion, that he was not asking to discuss terms then and there, only requesting that a time and place be set. "Thereby," he finished, "proving myself more reasonable than your prediction."

Ian chuckled. "Touché," he murmured, as if he were adjudicating a sparring match and Walter had landed a hit.

"But no less determined," Alinor pointed out, a slow smile curving her lips.

"Did you expect me to confound myself in apologies and back away?" Walter asked, also smiling.

"Some would have done so," Alinor replied.

"Not one worthy of taking Sybelle to wife," Walter riposted.

"Oh, good hit!" Llewelyn cried.

Simultaneously, Ian laughed aloud, saying, "He has you hard against the wall, my love. I think you should yield this match."

Alinor laughed also, and her eyes were contented. *Here,* she thought, *Sybelle will find the strength she needs while she is young.* "Very well," she agreed, "but it is not so easy to decide on a time. Tomorrow will be the wedding, the next day the joustings, and the day after that the melee."

She watched the conflict in Walter's face. Quite obviously he was very eager to have the details settled and get a marriage contract written. He knew it would be impossible to do this on the day of the wedding, but the thought of being penned up doing business while a tournament was taking place was also close to sacrilege. Then, a flash of uneasiness passed over his face.

"Let it be the day after tomorrow," he said quickly. "I cannot joust, and it is more important to me to make sure of Sybelle than—"

"But not to me," Ian interrupted, smiling. "Geoffrey and I cannot do business that day. William is to be matched against his peers in the joust, and we must be there. I would like you to look at his skill also, Walter. You have some claim to be a jouster, I have heard." Ian stood up and put a hand on Walter's shoulder. "You will not lose by this, I can assure you. A few days cannot matter. We were all agreed some months ago that if Sybelle could accept you, you would be welcome to us. Is this not true, Alinor?"

"In truth a few days cannot matter," Alinor agreed soothingly, although she was puzzled by Walter's uneasiness. "If Geoffrey made clear to you that what will be Sybelle's is to be *hers* and not under your direction except by her will, then you need not worry about coming to terms. We will have no demands to make upon you. Let us set the day after the melee, after the breaking of our fast, for a formal sealing—at least by kiss of peace. Will that content you?"

"Yes, of course," Walter said, but rather flatly.

"You may have my own chamber for privacy," Llewelyn offered, "and I will stand witness if you desire." He smiled also. "I do not think I will be long discommoded or kept from my own affairs. I foresee a quick agreement."

That was a form of dismissal, and Walter bowed and withdrew, leaving the old friends alone to talk of the past. He should have been content with what he had accomplished, having virtually received assurances that the contract was already as good as made. However, he kept seeing the concern in Sybelle's expression, as if something she had no intention of saying had been forced out of her. By jealousy? Could Sybelle be jealous of Marie?

If so, Walter thought, she was a fool. He had passed his word to her father. She must know that he would consider no other woman for wife unless and until he was formally rejected. A wife could not be jealous of a passing bed partner—or, at least, should not be. But Walter had not forgotten what Joanna had said . . . and then Prince Llewelyn had virtually repeated it. He had said the women of Roselynde clove like welded iron to their men *but demanded the same courtesy*.

Although Walter did not lack for company, being handed from one group of young men to another like a refreshment, the conversation did not hold much interest for him. Mostly he was required to discuss what he was beginning to think of as "that accursed battle." Thus his eyes wandered frequently, and nearly every time they did they found Sybelle, *and* each time he saw her, she was with one of her own menfolk. Certainly she did not dance with any man who was not a member of her family, and even when he saw her in conversation, one of the group was a relative.

Walter grew more and more uneasy. If Sybelle's sudden acceptance of him had been to warn away Marie, was this studied avoidance of all men except those blood-bound to her another signal? And, if so, was he to yield tamely? Was his life to be no longer under his own direction?

CHAPTER 12

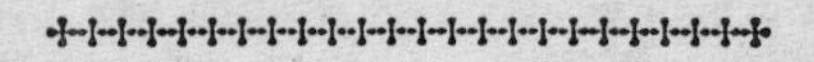

The wedding was a merry one. Rhiannon was no frightened maiden, and Simon's reputation was such that the precoital jests were more than usually bawdy. Some of the guests were a trifle startled by the fact that the nuptial bed was presided over by an overlarge gray-striped cat, but since the bridal couple themselves greeted the beast's presence with cheers and laughter, those who did not know Math soon forgot about him.

One of the few who did not go to bed perfectly happy was Walter. He had a very bad night. He had done nothing for two days except sit and walk about gently, so his body craved exercise. Because he was not physically tired, he was aware of the ache of his shoulder and knee and that the usual, comfortable positions in which he ordinarily slept were denied to him. Worst of all, his body craved more than exercise. He had been continent far longer than was usual for him, so he craved a woman. This craving was considerably increased by the jests and innuendos of the bedding ceremony and by his constant contact with Sybelle throughout the day, since his desire for her had honed his appetite to a fine edge.

To seek out a woman was impossible in his present situation. It would have been different had he been lying in the hall. The overcrowding of Builth had thrust maidservants out of their usual quarters and made them available. Also, those who sold their favors had naturally flocked to the celebration from every town and village within several days' walk. But Walter could not bring a woman into the chamber he shared with two young boys. Young Ian was certainly innocent, even if William was not—and both were Sybelle's brothers.

Nor could Walter leave the room. William's excitement about the following day's joust was making him restless, if he was asleep at all. For Walter to be away for any length of time would certainly raise questions in the bright mind of that youth. Walter closed his eyes and tried to think of other things, like the problem of the castellan of Knight's Tower. But that only brought Sybelle back into his mind, her care for him and her cleverness reinforcing his craving rather than reducing it.

Eventually, most sinfully and unsatisfactorily, Walter eased himself. Then he slept, but not deeply or dreamlessly, and he was restless enough to wake completely when William began to stir. An instant later, the boy was up, throwing off his blankets and jumping up from his pallet, regardless of the cold, already wildly excited. Walter watched William shiver his way into shirt and arming tunic and then sat up himself.

By quiet demands for service, he checked William's impulse to rush off and get his horse ready long before the lists would be open, although he agreed that William should arm himself and helped as much as he could one-handed. While they dressed, Walter also tried to channel the boy's enthusiasm with some suggestions on how to achieve control and avoid the useless waste of strength that excitement breeds. In this he was soon seconded by Lord Geoffrey, who came from the inner chamber, also armed. Now Walter could see why Lord Ian had been eager for his presence at the joust. William listened to his father and said yes most politely, but it was clear that Geoffrey's suggestions had far less weight than Walter's.

The hall was a scene of chaos at this early hour—servants being routed out with kicks and blows; those already awake trying to pick their ways between the lesser gentry, who were still asleep on their pallets, to revive the fires; other servants of a better class glancing fearfully at the knights and minor lords, men who had no ladies or had not brought them, who were grouped on cots nearest to the great hearths. Those people had to be roused before the sleeping arrangements could be cleared away and replaced with tables that would carry the pasties, cheeses, bread, and wines with which all would break their fast. Unfortunately, the dancing and drinking had continued late into the previous night, and the task of waking the sleepers to hear Mass and eat would not be easy or painless—either to the sleepers or the servants, who would likely be beaten for doing their duty.

Walter, William, and Geoffrey wrapped their cloaks tighter

around them and left the confusion behind for the peace of the chapel. Here they stood quietly, waiting for the priest, as pale light and sharp cold filtered through the stone fretwork of the windows. About twenty others were also waiting, the better sort of folk in the front and center of the room, where their brilliant cloaks made a summer garden patch in the midst of the cold, dim chamber. The servants were back against the gray stone walls or hunched in corners.

Sometimes Walter wondered at the arrangement. One would think the crude serfs would be more in need of God's blessing than the ladies and gentlemen. This thought passed through his mind again, and his lips twitched. Perhaps not. If he were going to joust, he would have needed to confess his evil desires and his evil deed of the preceding night to cleanse his soul. Mayhap the serfs, who worked hard all day, had less energy for such desires—and then again, mayhap not; they certainly bred fast enough.

A gentle tug on his cloak wakened Walter to the facts that the priest was already singing the Mass and the congregation was kneeling. Walter went down, grimacing with pain, and then had to be helped to his feet by his companions when it was time to stand. When they left the chapel, he realized he had not heard a word of the Mass. Had he made the responses? He must have done so without even realizing it. For a moment this troubled him, but then the feeling dissipated into the usual confident warmth that followed hearing Mass. He had been there. God would have seen his body, heard his voice, and blessed him with the others.

From their expressions, Walter doubted that any of his companions had heard the Mass, either. They had been the first group, but others were pushing past them to enter the chapel. There would be many Masses sung this morning.

Walter's thoughts were interrupted by William saying he would go down to the stables to ready his horse.

"For what purpose?" Walter asked. "Surely you will not allow your destrier to stand out in the cold until the last moment. Have some wine first, then run down and see if the heralds have made up the order of jousting. Come back here then to tell us whether or not they are ready. If you then choose to stand outside and let your muscles stiffen, that is your affair, but I do not advise it."

Geoffrey's mouth had opened just as Walter spoke, but he

had closed it again and said nothing until William was gone. Then he remarked, "That was masterly."

"I beg your pardon," Walter said, abashed. "It is your place to order your son, but—"

"But I am his father, and he would resent it from me. Yes, I know that. Why are all boys such fools? I love my father well and always did, but I can remember feeling the same way."

"I, too," Walter admitted, "but many men are fools, also. They have forgotten what they felt and blame their sons."

Geoffrey smiled wryly. "I am not immune from that, either. If you were not by, we would have come to angry looks."

Walter smiled back with warm understanding, and then he remembered his promise to Sybelle that he would speak to Geoffrey about his intention of going to Knight's Tower. This was a good time for it. He explained the circumstances and outlined his plan to demand his dues so that he would have cause to dismiss Sir Heribert from his post.

"There is no point in going there," Geoffrey said slowly. "If Sir Heribert invites you in, you must either refuse, thereby giving him just cause for complaint against you, or take the chance of walking half-crippled into a trap. Your purpose will be better served by summoning him out to meet you. If he comes and you still feel you cannot trust him, keep him with you. Thus, you will come to know the man better."

"It would be best indeed," Walter agreed, "and I can use this silly shoulder and knee as an excuse. But summon him where? Goldcliff is far enough that he could make easy excuses to delay, and truly I would not wish to be out of Richard's reach in case I should be needed. And to summon him here or to Usk or Abergavenny would only give him an excuse to ask the king to invest *him* with the lands because I tried to draw him into the rebel cause."

"True," Geoffrey concurred, "and Henry is furious enough just now to do anything, no matter how foolish. Then, to make him undo it later will be near impossible, even if he regrets it. But you could safely ask your castellan to come to Clyro, which is a keep held by your betrothed wife's family, a place neutral in these troubles, and no more than a day's ride from Knight's Tower."

Walter did not have a chance to reply because William

returned just then, flushed with pride, to tell them that he had been accorded a place near the end of the boys' jousting. Although this meant he had to wait some time to try his skill, it was an honor. Those who were thought to be the nearest to men in performance had been placed closest to the time of the men's jousting, when more of the spectators would have finished breaking their fasts and have come down to the lists to watch.

By the time Geoffrey and Walter had finished expressing their satisfaction and approval, Ian, Simon, and the women had joined them, Ian also armed for jousting. Geoffrey frowned and glanced at Alinor and Joanna. Ian had been one of the great jousters of his day and was still a formidable opponent for a single set or two. It was Ian's endurance that was failing, not his style, knowledge, or ability.

Ian noticed Geoffrey's frown and laughed. "I have already promised that I would run no more than two sets of three," he said. "Richard asked for a friendly meeting, and seeing my advantage with his face so bruised, I agreed. Now who else? Geoffrey?"

"Absolutely not!" Geoffrey exclaimed, laughing, "I have no mind to be lifted off my horse and dumped on the ground—which is what happens every time I joust with you. I will gratefully allow someone else to have that honor. You need not fear there will be any lack of aspirants. Just remember your promise—two sets only."

Walter said, "I—" and then stopped, remembering his broken collarbone.

"Some other time," Ian said, smiling at him. "You will be often at Roselynde. We will have opportunities enough to try each other. I cannot think why we did not do so when you visited us last."

"Because he was too busy following Sybelle around to bother with you, Papa," Simon teased.

"I must say I approve his taste," Ian said. "If I had a choice between my company and Sybelle's, I would choose hers, too."

"I cannot say *I* agree," Rhiannon put in with a false air of serious thoughtfulness. "I think I would prefer you, Ian. Sybelle is all very well, but . . ."

Everyone laughed, but attention shifted back to William as

Ian examined his grandson's accouterments with some care. Walter glanced at Sybelle and caught her looking at him. She smiled sunnily, seemingly not at all put out by the family teasing, and Walter immediately forgot both the mild embarrassment Simon had caused him and his previous night's frustration and sleeplessness. All that remained to disturb him was a regret that he could not take part in the tournament so that Sybelle could see how good he was.

Walter thought he might have taken the prize. Richard might be as good a jouster as he was or even better, but Walter did not think that Richard really intended to compete. Simon was out of the tourney, too; the groom did not take part in wedding tourneys. There was too much chance that if he did, he would not be able to perform satisfactorily in the principal act of the celebration. Of the remaining men who might compete, Walter thought he himself probably was the most skilled. He moved his shoulder experimentally.

"No," Sybelle said softly into his ear, having come unnoticed to his side. "No, it is not healed. You cannot hold a shield against the buffet of a lance."

Walter looked down at her. "It is going to be a very uncomfortable marriage for me if you are able to read my thoughts," he said reproachfully.

"A blind idiot could have read your thoughts just then," Sybelle rejoined, smiling. Then she put a hand on his arm and said more seriously, "I am not sorry you cannot fight, my lord. I know it is very silly of me, but I would fear for you."

"Do you think me such a looby that I cannot hold my own in a joust?" Walter asked, but there was no anger or sharpness in his voice. The question was only posed to draw from Sybelle the declaration he wished to hear.

"You know that is not so," she replied on cue. "But when something one desires very much is almost within reach, does not everyone fear that thing will be snatched away by some unexpected circumstance? Or am I more foolish than most?"

"Not if I am, to you, that desirable thing," Walter assured her softly.

"Perhaps it is wrong to admit it, but I would not wish to lose you now." Suddenly mischief crept into Sybelle's expression. "It would be too much, after all the trouble I have had to make up my mind, to have to begin again."

"Little adder, if we were alone, I would make you regret those last words," Walter whispered.

"First a wasp and then an adder. No wonder you feel you must threaten me," Sybelle murmured, pushing her smiling lips into an adorable pout.

"Threat? What threat? That was a promise!" Walter exclaimed softly, and then laughed as Sybelle blushed.

He had the last word in that exchange because young Ian came up to them at the moment with goblets of hot, spiced wine, and another boy offered a tray of cheese, pasties, and bread. Sybelle and Walter were forced a trifle apart by the business of choosing what to eat and were then drawn into the general conversation. Soon after, there was a concerted move to leave the hall. Walter was relatively certain that it was initiated by William's urging of his indulgent grandfather and that it was still too early, but he had noticed Simon gesturing at him furtively, so he made no attempt to divert the group from their purpose.

As they walked toward the doorway and out, Simon and Walter both fell back so that they were the last to leave. "Efan came last night," Simon said. "I have some news for you. It is not urgent, but, I think, interesting. Not only are men still coming into Monmouth, but patrols have been out along the roads between that keep and both Usk and Abergavenny."

"Has Richard been told?" Walter asked.

"I will leave that to you," Simon replied. "Llewelyn knows, of course. If you can get free of Geoffrey and my father, you can talk to Efan yourself. There is no point in adding to the uneasiness they suffer by making our differences more plain. In any case, I do not believe you will learn any more from him than what I have already told you and what you already know. All signs in Monmouth still point to expectation of another attack on them."

"And if it does not come?"

Simon shrugged in answer. Whether he would have said more, Walter did not know, because both of them saw Geoffrey looking back toward them, and they moved forward more quickly, unwilling to give the appearance of wishing to be private. It was very awkward, Walter thought, to have political differences within a blood bond, particularly where there was love to cement the bond.

Eager William had run ahead, so by the time they reached the stables, they found that his horse and Geoffrey's and Ian's were already being saddled. The tourney ground was no great distance. Walter, Simon, and the ladies elected to walk. They arrived before the mounted members of their party and looked about. However, they were very early, and there was little enough to see. The lodges were set up: bare benches somewhat sheltered from the wind by a three-sided pavilion in gold and red and barely warmed by braziers of charcoal. The cushions to make the benches comfortable, the footstools and foot warmers, all the bright appurtenances that would give an air of festivity would be brought down by servants when the spectators came.

A decent distance from the lodges and back from the jousting field, a troop of men-at-arms with their master-at-arms watching keenly were already busy keeping the commons in order. At the moment it was no difficult task. Many of the people had walked all night to see the jousts and partake of the largess that would be distributed. Most of them sat or lay around the large bonfires they had been permitted to make, resting, eating, and drinking. Later, under the influence of free beer and brawn and excitement, they might become rowdy and the men-at-arms might be forced to break a few heads to calm them, but now all was quiet merriment.

The highborn group gave them a glance and a smile, but there was nothing to hold their interest. They passed around the empty lodges, Simon walking between his mother and Rhiannon, Walter between Joanna and Sybelle, both groups talking animatedly. When they had cleared the end of the pavilion, they could see the lists. And here there was activity, with William not the only eager boy. Around the marshals of the joust there was a milling crowd of younglings kept only minimally in order by the few more indulgent, or more sober, masters who had come down to the field. Simon and Walter both smiled and advanced on the crowd. The women exchanged glances.

"My dears," Lady Alinor said, glancing from Rhiannon to Sybelle with a wry smile and a little sigh, "bride and bride-to-be, and both I believe, truly beloved, you have just seen the limit of your powers. When the trumpets sound, you will have lost your men. Remember it. Have patience and courage."

She had been speaking lightly, although she meant what she said, but her expression changed as the mounted members of their party came onto the field. "A woman," Alinor added, her voice no longer steady, "must know when to open her hand and let her man go."

Sybelle, Joanna, and Rhiannon all knew Alinor was speaking of Ian and of her struggle with herself to allow him to lead a normal life in spite of the danger to his health. Thinking of this, Joanna shuddered, and for a moment, her teeth clenched. That time had not come to *her* yet; she prayed it never would. It was hard enough to let Geoffrey go off to war. She did not know if she would have the strength to stand by passively and let Geoffrey kill himself because it would make him unhappy to be nursed and cosseted.

Rhiannon's heart was wrung for both Alinor and Ian. She loved them both and feared for both—but she could not even think of those words with respect to herself and Simon. Where he went she would follow fleet-footed, even into the land of Annwn, for if he were dead, she would not be alive, no matter if her heart still beat.

Sybelle was least affected by these grim thoughts. Young as she was, she had seen death often and had been truly saddened by the losses of old servants, children, women in childbirth, and men-at-arms in war. Still, she did not really believe anyone *she* loved could die. And yet her grandmother's words seemed strangely significant. They rang in her head: ". . . open her hand and let her man go."

Now servants were hurrying across the ground with cushions and furs for the ladies of the party. Sybelle turned toward the lodges, dismissed all foreboding from her mind, and prepared to enjoy herself heartily. Other ladies and gentlemen, whose sons or fosterlings were to joust, were coming out also. Gay greetings and laughing comments were exchanged. Most of the gentlemen soon gravitated to the lists to offer wise counsel or stern admonition to their charges.

A few of the younger women were nervous, fearing harm for the younglings. Wiser ladies, like Alinor, who had seen many boys tried, offered what comfort they could. The lance points would be blunted, and the lances themselves would be made of brittle wood or even deliberately weakened. There might be some broken bones, but nothing worse, and hopefully none of the young contestants would be more than bruised.

The confusion around the marshals was now diminishing. Tutors and masters led the boys away for last-minute examinations of their armor, horse, and harness, and sergeants-at-arms led men carrying bundles of lances to each end of the tilting field. Then a single trumpet called—there would be ten or fifteen to make a joyous noise for the men's jousting—and two contestants rode into position at each end.

All watched with absorbed interest, even the women, although each contest was, in a sense, identical. The boys settled their lances between arm and body, holding them as steadily as possible with the right hand. The left arm was passed through a loop on the inner side of the shield while the hand gripped a handle fastened near the edge. The reins of the horse were fastened to the pommel of the saddle, the animal being guided by pressure of feet and knees. It was a complex and difficult task to guide the lance, hold and move the shield, and manage the horse all at the same time.

Since the boys had been matched as well as possible by size and weight, it was a combination of skill and eagerness that determined their success. However, too-great eagerness could also undo a jouster by making him thrust forward a trifle before the actual moment of impact so that he delivered less than the full blow of which he was capable. This was the most common fault of the young riders, although there were a few who should not have been allowed on the field at all. These were not yet able to coordinate lance, shield, and horse, and missed their opponents totally, either by not being able to aim their lances or by allowing their mounts to wander from the straight line.

William ran his courses fairly without any embarrassing inefficiencies; in fact, he overthrew his opponent. However, if he thought he would find praise, he was sadly mistaken. Father, grandfather, uncle, and future brother-by-marriage fell upon him with loud objections to almost everything he had done: His timing was off, he had held his shield wrong, he had steered his horse too wide and started him too slowly, his lance was not at the perfect angle, and he had been thinking too much of his own attack and not enough of positioning himself to avoid or slat off his opponent's lance. If William was a little disappointed, he was not crushed. First of all, he was accustomed to criticism. Second, the vociferous objections proved that his male relatives had high hopes for him. Had he failed miserably, he knew they would have offered consolation.

"You watch your grandfather," Geoffrey ended. "He is a jouster who knows what he is doing. You will not see his horses wandering all over the field or his shield inviting a lance point to slide off into his belly."

Still, a slight curve of the lips and the brightness of his eyes betrayed that Geoffrey knew this was a little unfair. After all, Ian had almost fifty years of experience beyond William.

By the time the boys' jousts were finished, the lodges were crowded to capacity. Now the full panoply of chivalry was displayed. First came the blare of trumpets, then came the heralds, gorgeously arrayed, and following them, the contestants armed and mounted. The knights rode two by two, down the field and around, parading before the lodges, dipping lance tips in salute—upon which the excited ladies hung favors. Laughing like girls, Alinor and Joanna bestowed bright-colored and specially embroidered stockings upon their husbands' lances, to be carried for their honor.

In the interests of preventing what was meant as a joyous occasion from turning into a bloodbath, pursuivants who would boast of their patrons' skills and insult their opponents' had been forbidden. Although there were hard feelings between some of the guests, who were long-standing opponents in the never-ending minor wars of the Welsh Marches, all had been urged to put away old animosities for this time, and most came with the intention of doing so. However, Llewelyn was taking no chances that were not intrinsic in simply mixing Welsh and English. Only his own heralds called the challenges, and only good words were said of each man.

When the cavalcade had gone round, the knights divided into two groups, each of which moved toward one end of the field. Most of the men dismounted; there was no sense in tiring their horses when they would have to wait a considerable time for their turns to joust. Richard and Ian, however, made ready, testing shield straps, helmets, and stirrups for security and coming to the head of the lists when they were satisfied. There, each was handed a lance, specially blunted but not weakened or of brittle wood as the boys' lances had been.

"In God's name, do your battle," the herald cried.

The meeting between Ian and Richard, which opened the serious jousting of the day, was a display of near-perfection in one of the arts of war. It was also a fine demonstration of two immovable objects meeting two irresistible forces.

Before the herald's voice had died away, both destriers leapt forward, reins having been dropped from the fingers of the left hand and spurs having been raked hard. Even so, the first pass was a mere gentle testing, Richard being concerned for his "uncle" Ian's age and Ian not wishing to jar Richard too hard for the sake of his bruised and tender face. Since neither man had exerted his full power and each had deliberately aimed his lance just a trifle awry, the lances did not splinter, sliding harmlessly off firmly held and cleverly tilted shields.

Despite the gentle consideration of each man, the shock delivered was strong enough to inform the other that he was not dealing with frail age or delicate discomfort. The used lances were cast down, the snorting destriers were wheeled into position, and new lances were seized and fewtered. On the call, both riders thundered forward again. This time, there was no holding back. Each man threw himself forward with all his strength and all his skill.

Each lance hit fair. Each destrier was thrown back on his haunches. Each man rose two inches in his saddle, impelled upward by the enormous shock. Two loud cracks, nearly simultaneous, signaled the shattering of both lances. Each man dropped the two inches he had risen, the destriers recovered, thundered on past each other to the end of the lists to be wheeled into position again. The third pass was a near-perfect repetition of the second, except that Richard's lance broke first. For five interminable seconds, Ian's held; for five interminable seconds, Ian pressed forward, but not an inch farther could he move Richard out of the saddle, and at last the sharp report of cracking wood released them both.

The crowd roared its approval. Usually they were rather bloodthirsty and preferred the stronger excitements of falls and injuries, but so excellent an exhibition of strength and skill drew appreciation. Besides, it was only the beginning of the day. There was plenty of time for blood and screaming. Meanwhile, Richard and Ian had brought their horses back to the center of the field and both had dismounted and embraced, each more delighted that the other had withstood the match without shame—although every man mouthed the words that there was no shame in being unhorsed by a stronger opponent—than that he himself had escaped.

Yet in a way it was true that shame did not necessarily follow defeat in a jousting. Now that Richard and Ian had proved each other "invincible," the marshals were besieged by appeals to joust against each of them. No man who offered his name as an opponent had any hope of unhorsing either, but to withstand a shock against one of them would be high honor, and even to be put down would win a man notice for his courage. All offers, however, were refused, the marshals explaining that each man would run only three more passes and that these had been prearranged.

In fact, these six passes provided considerable amusement for the audience. Ian and Richard ran alternately, and on each pass they unhorsed an opponent with such skill that none was hurt beyond the bruising of the fall. And with each fall, the men and women in the lodges cheered and shouted louder. It was as good as a play, and when it was over, everyone, including those men who had been overthrown, were in high good humor.

It was a most auspicious beginning and fortunately an accurate prediction for the remainder of the contest. Through a long day's jousting, no one was seriously hurt and, owing to Richard and Ian's good example and Prince Llewelyn's careful preparations, no one lost his temper and cried for a duel *à outrance*. And when at last the trumpets blew for an end, all were able to walk back to the keep to warm themselves and fall like ravening beasts on the lavish dinner provided, for the ladies had expended almost as much energy as the men, jumping up and down and cheering on their favorites.

Nor was it only the gentlefolk who fed well. Out on the field, whole oxen and hogs were roasting, hogsheads of bread were being emptied, and barrels of beer broached. The fires leapt man-high, and the coarser type of minstrels twanged their instruments, juggled, and danced. It was a night that would be long remembered at Builth, the beginning of a two-day halcyon period of aching heads and full stomachs that would be the foundation of a definite increase in the population of little bastards in the area as well as of tall tales—and a near deification of Prince Llewelyn.

CHAPTER 13

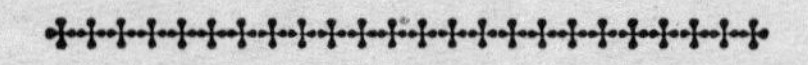

Sybelle was enjoying herself completely. For the first time in her life she was totally at ease with men other than those of her family. Previously, owing to her beauty and the presumption that her dowry would be munificent, the smallest sign of friendliness had encouraged advances she did not desire. Now she had only to say she was promised already, and she was free to talk, to jest, and laugh, and dance—Walter having told her not to be a fool and take whom she would for partners. But the reason she was happy was that she found, even with this new freedom, she still enjoyed Walter's company most of all.

Their conversations were no more loverlike than those she had with other men. They ranged over much the same subjects, except for that which, to Sybelle, was the most absorbing: Which property should come with her as dowry. When the topic was first broached, Walter looked much taken aback.

"That is not for me to decide," he said. "I will take whatever Lady Alinor offers." Then he smiled. "My main object, after all, is to have you, Sybelle. And after that I desire union with your family."

Sybelle blushed faintly with pleasure, but now that Walter was hers, she found no difficulty in keeping to the point, which was to discover how he reacted to female interference in male affairs. She no longer felt reluctant to examine the subject, buoyantly sure that if one route were blocked, she would find another path. For the first pass, she chose the most direct.

"But you will not need to say anything," she assured Walter. "I will discuss the matter with Grandmama. Nor do you need to feel she will be offended. If she has decided already, she will tell me. But if she has not, she will be glad to listen to me, for you know best the disposition of your lands and what will be easiest for you to defend and administer.''

Walter looked taken aback again, but he made a quick recovery and enthusiastically accepted Sybelle's suggestion. The question of what lands would come with her had troubled him. Since he was not being asked to contribute to the bride's share—to provide her with a more comfortable widow's portion—and therefore could not say he wished what he gave to march well with what her family provided, he felt he had no right to do other than accept whatever was offered. However, if the dower properties were far to the east or north, it would add to his difficulties.

He should have known better than to doubt Lady Alinor's good sense and goodwill. In one way he did not, but he was unaccustomed to dealing with women in business terms, and the things the priests preached, men said by rote, and Walter himself had sometimes found to be true in dealing with his mistresses and casual whores, colored his instinctive responses. Although he *knew* better, he still subconsciously expected Lady Alinor to take some sly advantage of him.

Thus, much time was spent in describing—to the best of Walter's knowledge—the whereabouts and extent of his putative holdings. Sybelle was able to match properties to some of these. Clyro keep, on the border of Wales, was very nearly midway between Foy, south of Hereford, and Knight's Tower. It was not on a direct line between them, being well to the west of Foy, but it would make a comfortable day's travel from either Foy or Knight's Tower.

Then there were the rich farms at Braydon. There was no true keep there, only a strongly fortified manor house on the shore of a small lake. Braydon was no great distance from Barbury keep, about ten miles, and would be easy to oversee and protect. Other, somewhat less attractive alternatives were also discussed, and the more they talked, the more comfortable Walter became. More and more it seemed only natural that his chosen wife should know as much and care as much about the essentials of defense and administration as he did. He rejoiced in the knowledge that he need never agonize over the choice of a man or men to manage his lands when he was absent. He would leave behind Sybelle as a deputy who was almost part of himself when he was called away to war—and it was impossible, times being what they were, that this should not happen.

The unromantic quality of their conversation gave Sybelle neither doubts nor regrets. Actually, she did not regard it as unromantic. Although Walter spoke of lands and whether it was better to have an extra stronghold rather than rich farms and a lake plentiful in fish, his expression and the occasional touch he allowed himself on her arm or shoulder or face were a constant proclamation of his desire. Sybelle found that the subtle caresses, which probably were entirely unrecognizable to anyone except herself, were far more to her taste and far more exciting than overt words of love. She was, in fact, growing very eager for the marriage and the consummation that would come with it.

Walter was no less eager for that marriage, but he was more clear-sighted about the probability of its taking place in the immediate future. He was aware that Richard and Prince Llewelyn were more often than not absent from events devised to amuse and occupy the wedding guests. Not long after Richard had run his courses against Ian in the jousts, the earl had disappeared. And although both Richard and Llewelyn were present at the opening of the melee and were there when the trumpets sounded the close of the action, Walter had not been so taken up with the battle that he did not notice that both men had slipped away for a substantial span of time.

He and Simon had taken advantage of the event in the same way to requestion Efan and go over together his description of what was taking place at Monmouth. Although Simon had been correct in saying Efan had no more to tell than he had already transmitted to Walter, Walter's greater familiarity with the area had indicated that the patrols Efan reported were not only defensive. It seemed very likely to Walter that if Richard did not soon move to assault Monmouth again, John of Monmouth would make some move of his own. He might plan to attack Usk or Abergavenny, but Walter thought it more likely that he would try to pass around or between those formidable strongholds and attack some easier target.

Thus, despite Geoffrey's assurances that the king would soon be persuaded to come to terms with Richard, Walter had little hope of an early marriage. This conviction did nothing to assuage his physical frustration, nor did the family understanding of his betrothal help because this, though unspoken, continually thrust him into Sybelle's company. Not that Walter would not have sought her company on his own. She drew him as a flame draws a moth, and like the moth, he found what he sought a very painful pleasure. He strangled words and gestures of love, not because he was more interested in the lands that would come to him with Sybelle or because he wished to test the capability her father had claimed for her, but because he could not bear her eager response.

This restraint was of little help, either. Sybelle seemed to know what he was feeling while he spoke soberly of practical affairs. She, too, confined herself to the most impersonal conversation possible, but she could not completely control her complexion or the way her eyes caressed him. Never in Walter's life, not even when scarcely more than a boy pursuing his first highborn mistress, had his feelings been such a turmoil of joy and misery. He chided himself for being a fool, telling himself that when Sybelle returned to England with her family he would be free to enjoy whatsoever other woman or women he chose. It was cold comfort. Walter wanted Sybelle.

The day after the melee, the family met in council in Prince Llewelyn's chambers. In spite of all assurances that they would come to quick and easy agreement, Walter found himself nervous, oppressed by the feeling that he was one against many. At last he asked Richard to accompany him, to which the earl readily agreed. Although Pembroke's support was pleasant, Walter realized in minutes that it was totally unnecessary.

Hardly were they all seated when Lady Alinor said, "Sybelle tells me that you believe Clyro and the manor and farms of Braydon would be most suitable to match with your own lands."

Walter flushed slightly. "I did believe so, but, of course—"

"That will suit us very well," Alinor interrupted kindly, aware of Walter's embarrassment and eager to assuage it. "I had thought to give somewhat more with her. All of Mersea went with Joanna. Is there not some other manor or keep you would like to take in charge?"

Although he had never previously partaken in any discussion of a marriage contract, Walter had the feeling that it was most unusual for the bride's family to press more on the groom when there was no question of matching the dowry.

His bewilderment must have shown on his face, for Ian smiled.

"I am getting old," he said. "Alinor and I have sufficient for our needs, more than sufficient. Poor Geoffrey is already run ragged between his lands, Joanna's, and doing what he can for his father."

"That last statement is too true," Geoffrey muttered fervently.

Ian smiled sympathetically at him and continued, "It is better for you to ride like a madman from one place to another, Walter, than for me to do so. These days I have a great desire to bide quietly with Alinor."

"But you do not need to give the land with Sybelle," Walter protested. "I will gladly do whatever you ask of me. I swear I will take no less care whether the property is Sybelle's or yours."

At which point Richard made a noise that would have been laughter if he could have opened his mouth freely. "This is the maddest marriage council I have ever heard," he said. "Usually the bride's family fights like cats to give least and the groom's to grab what they can. Here everything is upside-down. If you wish to give Walter more, then give it. Why do you ask him?"

Lady Alinor looked at the second most powerful man in England with the tolerant patience of a mother for a squalling infant. "Because, for some years, until he can bring the people on his late brother's estates to respect and obey him, Walter will have troubles enough of his own without adding any of ours. I do not yet know how he likes to manage the question of men-at-arms. If he prefers to choose men from the land and train them up and keep them, then an estate with loyal serfs will be of great benefit. If he prefers to hire blank shields, to use them, and then to dismiss them, gold would be of more use to him."

"I prefer my own men," Walter replied instantly, and even as he noticed the satisfaction in the faces of the Roselynde contingent, he recognized how cleverly Alinor had phrased the choice. There was no way he could have determined which procedure she favored from her words. It was not, he thought, a trap but an attempt to learn how his mind worked, and he continued honestly, "I have never hired blank shields because I had no need, but in this case I might do so. I would not have to dismiss them, you see. Those who served well and wished for a permanent place, I could keep, since I fear it may be necessary to turn out some or all of the men who have served my brother's castellans."

"That is true," Geoffrey remarked, "and it would be a boon for the realm. When this fighting is over, there will be hundreds, perhaps thousands, of masterless men roaming the countryside. I have often found that once trained as soldiers, serfs are not willing to go back to tilling the soil—and even if they do, they become far from docile. If you can find place for a few hundred in your keeps, it would be a good thing."

Richard nodded. "That is very true, and you need not set loose those you replace. There will be reason enough, I suppose, to hang them."

There was a general murmur of approval, which Alinor ignored, her brows knitted in thought. But when she spoke, it was to Ian. "You know, my love, I do not think there *is* anything else we have in the west. Our weakness there was one of the reasons Geoffrey so strongly favored Walter's suit, and it would not be practical to drag Walter down to the southeast for one keep."

"What about the farms near Oxenwood?" Ian asked.

"Walter may have them, and welcome, if he likes," Alinor replied, "but they are only about fourteen miles from Kingsclere, and Sir Harold can oversee those without trouble. I think five thousand silver marks would do Walter more good. And when his affairs are settled, he and Sybelle can buy land with it." Suddenly her face was old and sad. "There will be masterless estates in plenty when this war is over." She sighed.

The most interesting thing Alinor had said, in Walter's opinion—until she mentioned the huge sum of five thousand marks—was "we have." Walter knew the lands were Lady Alinor's and that, by contract, Lord Ian had no rights in them at all, yet that "we" had a well-used sound, as if it were natural for her to think of her husband as a full partner in everything she owned. It was a happy prognostication for the future. If Sybelle were accustomed to thinking in the same terms, his position as her husband would be much easier.

Of course, the mention of so much money put every other thought out of Walter's head. He gasped, and even Richard blinked. "It is too much," Walter cried, before he thought.

Naturally that produced another chorus of laughter, and Geoffrey said reprovingly, "What? Do you not think Sybelle worth so much?"

Walter flushed but said doggedly, "I think her worth so much that I had rather have her dowerless than be overwhelmed by obligation."

"But there can be no obligation," Joanna pointed out dryly. "We are not offering *you* anything. Do not forget that everything will be Sybelle's, at *her* will, not at yours."

"What?" Richard cried.

"It is a family custom," Alinor said soothingly, "and between myself and both my husbands, it has caused no trouble." She stared down Geoffrey's groans and Ian's laughter with mock severity. "When there is love and each partner's desires are reasonable, there can be no difference of opinion, no matter to whom the lands belong."

"What woman's desires are reasonable?" Richard asked bitterly.

Alinor looked concerned and leaned close to him. "Dear Richard," she said very softly, "when these troubles are over, I wish you would come to Roselynde and bring Gervase. Her mother, I understand, has been long dead, and she never met your mother." Alinor's voice quavered slightly. Isobel of Clare, Richard's mother, had been her dearest friend, her only real woman-friend aside from Geoffrey's stepmother, Ela. Isobel's death had been a hard blow to Alinor, one she had not yet absorbed completely despite the length of time. She steadied her voice and went on. "Perhaps Gervase would be interested to hear of your early life and family."

Richard stiffened a trifle, then dropped his eyes. "We will come. I thank you," he said equally softly.

The others waited with varying degrees of understanding through this private exchange. Absorbed by his own affairs, Walter hardly noticed it. Having originally been as shocked as Richard, Walter now surprisingly found himself impatient with the earl's protest about the way his marriage contract would be written. Several days' familiarity with the terms and his serious discussions with Sybelle had reconciled him completely.

"Indeed, I understand, Lady Joanna," Walter said, "but the good must come to me in the end, even if it passes through my wife's hands first. If you believed me likely to wish to play at ducks and drakes with Sybelle's dowry, you would not have accepted my offer in the first place. Thus, what you give my wife does obligate me."

"Nonsense," Lady Alinor said sharply. "What Ian said was true. He and I do not need what we offer. It is better for you, who will have uses for it, to have it. From what you have said of your brother's governance, your lands may yield little for some years. It would be stupid for you to be in straitened circumstances, unable perhaps to put improvements into effect, while useless silver sat in my strongboxes."

Walter looked at the faces around him. All the Roselynde contingent smiled kindly; Richard laughed and said, "Do not be a fool. Lady Alinor is perfectly right." Thus adjured, he, too, smiled and nodded.

"Then we are all agreed," Lady Alinor said. "Clyro, the property at Braydon, and five thousand marks will be Sybelle's dowry. She will retain all rights; that is, Sir Roland, castellan of Clyro, will do her homage; she will give justice there and at Braydon; she will have absolute right of refusal on any use of the silver; and all these she may leave by will to whomsoever she chooses, not constrained by primogeniture or even by ties of blood. Do you so swear, Sir Walter?"

"I do so swear, provided that my honors of Foy, Thornbury, Barbury, Knight's Tower, and Goldcliff be mine alone, free of any claim by my wife. I do also swear that these my lands and honors will be heritable in male tail by sons legitimately conceived upon my wife, Sybelle of Roselynde, or, failing sons of my blood, heritable by daughters, legitimately conceived, and failing any living issue of our marriage that said lands and honors be heritable by my nephew, Richard, Earl of Gloucester."

Both Walter and Lady Alinor rose and exchanged the kiss of peace, and then each of the other members of the family repeated the process. The witnesses then took oath that they had heard and understood what was sworn, and everyone relaxed, smiling. The scribe at a small table to the side scribbled away, busily making copies of the rough agreement so that each of the parties might have one to be rewritten in fuller terms with the necessary legalities, but no one paid him any mind. As far as Walter and the others were concerned, they were finally committed and no legal document could bind them more firmly.

"So, that is done," Geoffrey said, "and we are agreed, but there remains a problem. All of us are direct vassals of the king and therefore must have his permission to marry or give in marriage."

A blank silence followed this statement. Richard sighed heavily. "I have no desire that my troubles flow over onto Walter," he said. "For my part, I gladly free him from all obligations, and I sincerely pray that he will not hesitate to make contract on my account."

"I will make no contract on those terms," Walter snapped.

"Gently, gently," Geoffrey soothed, "the question does not yet arise. You did not give me time to finish. All I meant to say was that the terms I now stand on with my cousin Henry are so bad that I do not wish to approach him with this proposal. In fact," he smiled wryly, "I do not wish to approach him at all. Thus, while we may consider ourselves sworn, I think it would be unwise to write a formal contract or to give official confirmation of our arrangement."

It was smoothly said and sounded sincere, but Walter felt uncomfortable. He wondered whether, if he had not been so quick to speak and had been less vehement, Geoffrey would have said the same words. Then, once again he told himself that his participation on either side of the quarrel could not be significant. Still, he resolved to watch what he said and did lest he find himself, all unaware, abandoning Richard. These rather unpleasant ideas were scattered by Lady Joanna's laugh.

"I fear it is too late," she pointed out. "Sybelle has already told half the men in Builth."

"That may be so," Geoffrey agreed, "but aside from our own party, my love, I do not think any of the guests here are likely to have direct contact with King Henry." As he spoke he looked at Prince Llewelyn, who, except for speaking his part as witness, had been uncharacteristically silent.

"I do not think so, either," Llewelyn said blandly, "but even if it should be so, there would be no mention of a contract being made. If the king should hear anything at all, it would be merely a vague rumor."

Since all knew it would be useless to press Llewelyn further, no more was said on that subject and the formal conference broke up. Richard rose, and Walter did also. Because of the vague suspicions that had been aroused in him, he felt a need to associate himself as strongly as possible with the earl. Although he knew it was ridiculous, it seemed like a form of betrayal to remain with his new blood-bonded family and let Richard go out alone. However, Geoffrey had risen almost as quickly as Walter and came forward to join them.

"Lord Pembroke," Geoffrey said as they came out into the antechamber, "do you have any duties for Walter until his shoulder heals?"

Walter opened his mouth to protest, but before he could find words that would not be offensive, Richard had shaken his head. "To speak the truth," he admitted, smiling, "I have little to do myself but watch and wait—at least, for a few weeks. If you need him, I will yield him to you."

"No, no," Geoffrey hastened to say, seeing the outrage on Walter's face. "It is nothing to do with me at all but with one of Walter's keeps. He was speaking to me the other day about wishing to summon the castellan of Knight's Tower to a . . . ah . . . neutral place to test his loyalty."

Richard's brows drew together, and he looked at Walter with an expression of doubt. "Does Lord Geoffrey know—" he began, but Geoffrey held up a hand.

"I do not wish to know anything," Geoffrey said quickly. "The keep is Walter's by right, and it is my purpose to forward his taking it into his hands with the least destruction as soon as possible." His face was hard at first, but the distress on Richard's countenance made his expression soften into sympathy. "It cannot really make any difference who holds Knight's Tower, can it, Pembroke?" he asked.

"No, it cannot," Walter put in before the earl could speak. "It is my belief that my brother's castellan does not care a fig for anything but his own well-being. Thus, if he has any purpose, it will be to rob me of my right. If I am wrong in this belief and he is an honest man with strong feelings one way or the other in this conflict, then the sooner I know, the sooner it may be possible to come to some fair accommodation."

"Yes," Richard agreed, "but I would not wish to take any advantage—"

"It is nothing to do with you," Geoffrey said. "Walter is betrothed to my daughter, and Clyro will be part of her dowry—you heard it sworn. Thus, he may be as free with that keep as if it were his own. My question was asked only because we will leave here tomorrow and pass by Clyro keep. I wished to give Sir Roland warning if Walter intended to go there in the next week or two. On the other hand, I would not want him to expect the visit if there is no chance that it will be made." He smiled. "You know that no matter how well-managed a property, a castellan must be in some unease when a new master takes hold."

"But there will be no new master," Richard pointed out.

"No." Now Walter was smiling. "But this Sir Roland, whom I do not know, might believe that a new husband would have some influence on his bride."

Richard shrugged. His experience of marriage had not given him similar expectations. However, he assured both Walter and Geoffrey that there was no way Walter could be of use to him and that Walter would be free to pursue his private affairs. It was interesting to Geoffrey that the assurances were given with considerable warmth and that Richard looked relieved rather than resigned to the loss of Walter's service. He abandoned the topic for the moment, talking easily for a time on subjects of general interest, until they came into the main hall and Walter, seeing Sybelle, hastily excused himself and went to her.

Then Geoffrey said, "I am well pleased with my future son-by-marriage. He is a man of high honor. It is unfortunate that he is being made so uncomfortable by my kinship to the king. I have tried to assure him that aside from delaying the formal betrothal and marriage, it will make no difference, but—"

"For my part," Richard interrupted, "I could wish he would make no delay of either. I cannot say that I would not care if he took up arms in the king's party, for he is able and would be a dangerous enemy, but if he would go east and attend to winning a hold on his own estates, I would be glad of it. So far I have held him back from crying defiance, but if he goes with us to attack—" The earl stopped abruptly, remembering that he was speaking to one of King Henry's men.

"I agree from the bottom of my heart," Geoffrey said, acting as if Richard had finished his statement, "but I dare not say a word to him. The first condition he made when he offered for Sybelle was that he would not withdraw from your party. If I suggest he look to taking his keeps, will he not think it is a subtle way of reducing your power?'' Geoffrey paused and looked Richard full in the face. ''I do not wish you harm, Pembroke, I swear it.''

''You need not swear. I have better proof than oaths from you. Do you think I have forgotten how you came to warn me of the trap laid for me in August?'' Richard hesitated a moment, his face thoughtful. Finally he nodded, having come to a decision. ''Very well, I can make this betrothal plus his injury an excuse to send him about his own business. God knows I do not want Walter's outlawry on my soul. But I wish to make clear to you, Lord Geoffrey, that if I need him, I will recall him to service and, more, if the property he controls will be useful to me, I will make use of it.''

With that Geoffrey was well content, and he and Richard parted soon afterward, each satisfied with what had been decided. Walter had not noticed that Pembroke and his father-by-marriage had lingered in each other's company. As soon as he laid eyes on Sybelle, all he could think of was that Geoffrey had said they would leave the next day. Having separated her from her companions without much effort, he first told her the contract had been sealed and the terms. She was not much surprised by the large sum of money and seemed inclined to begin a discussion of how best it should be used.

''Never mind that now,'' Walter said. ''Did you know your parents intended to leave tomorrow?''

''Yes. I think Papa does not wish to try King Henry's patience too far. It would be foolish to linger after other guests have left.''

''Do you not care?'' Walter asked softly. ''It may be long, many months, before we see each other again.''

''I . . . I have thought about it,'' Sybelle said, and then asked hesitantly, ''Do you wish that I remain behind?''

The question was serious, even anxious, and Walter suddenly realized that he had spoken with such enthusiasm about obtaining the properties that he had most desired and five thousand marks besides that he might have raised doubts in Sybelle's mind as to what was most important to him. He was eager to make clear to her that having contract sealed had not abated his desire for her in the least, but the group with which she had been talking was close by and love words are better spoken in private.

Just at that moment one of the more important Welsh guests, armed and cloaked for riding, came out of a chamber behind them. He paused to speak a word or two to Walter and Sybelle while servants carried out the last of his baggage. Then, with a jovial hope that Walter's shoulder would be healed in good time for their next enterprise, he strode away. Never slow to recognize a good thing, Walter seized Sybelle's hand and drew her quickly into the chamber, which he hoped was empty. Not only was this hope gratified, but, in addition, a fire was still burning brightly in the small hearth and the room was pleasantly warm.

With battle-trained swiftness and a dexterous twist, Walter released Sybelle's hand and got his arm around her waist, pulling her close to his side. "How can I not wish that you remain with me?" he asked. "But if your parents go . . ."

Sybelle made not the slightest attempt to free herself. In fact, she rested her head confidingly against his shoulder. "Simon and Rhiannon will be here—or somewhere in Wales, but I think not far from Prince Llewelyn, and he, I suppose, must have affairs to discuss with Lord Pembroke. . . ." She let that trail away, and lifted her eyes to watch Walter's face, where eagerness strove with doubt.

"Will they permit you to stay with Simon?" Walter asked. "Your mother spoke somewhat sharply of his heedlessness."

Sybelle smiled. "That is Mama's way. Simon is her 'little brother,' but she knows that he would protect me with his life. And he is steadier now, for he thinks Rhiannon is too wild and that he must be sober for both. I would have asked sooner but I did not know. . . . If you have duties that will keep you away . . ."

Instead of answering that in words, Walter dropped his head and kissed her, at the same time changing his grip so that her body was turned and pressed front to front against his. For a moment she was passive, her mouth unresisting but not answering to his, either. Then, just as doubt and disappointment were rising in Walter, her lips fulled under his, one arm went around his waist and the other around his neck, and she pressed forward.

Sybelle had been taken by surprise. Until that moment, Walter had given none but the subtlest signs of his desire. She had found those restrained touches and glances quite exciting, far more stimulating, in fact, than words, but she had, oddly enough, not thought beyond them. Her previous experience with kisses had been limited—excepting, of course, formal kisses of peace—to those one or two experiments several years before with young men of the court and a few more taken from her by force or by surprise more recently by swains carried away by her beauty or by their own cupidity.

After the initial blank moment, however, Sybelle found that either she had changed or that Walter's kiss, as he had once teasingly implied, was different from others. This was right, Sybelle knew at the core of her being. This was sanctioned by her family, by the Church, by God. The warmth of Walter's lips generated an answering warmth in her own. The pressure of his arm around her was a pleasure that made her feel a desire for even greater closeness. But just as these desires became clear, there was an infinitesimal slackening in Walter's grip and in the strength of his kiss. Instinctively, Sybelle put an arm around his neck to keep his mouth fixed to hers and her other arm around his waist to keep them close.

The immediate response she received surprised her again. Walter's lips parted, and his tongue, gently touching her closed mouth, made Sybelle shiver slightly. As her lips parted, Walter's tongue touched hers and ran across it and around the inside of her mouth. Sybelle shivered again. Although the feeling tickled, it produced no desire to laugh. In some strange way the sensation connected itself with her nether mouth. There, too, the lips seemed full and hard, and moisture gathered. There, too, was a tickling that required soothing, but there was no tongue to soothe it as Walter's tongue moving in and out soothed her mouth.

She pressed still closer, dropping her arm from Walter's waist to his hips to draw him tighter against her throbbing lower body. Simultaneously, his arm rose from her waist to the middle of her back, his hand curled around, then his fingers extended, caressed the side of her breast. An inarticulate murmur of protest rose in Sybelle's throat, for the touch on her breast increased the sensation in her loins. She thrust her hips forward against him and became aware of the hard bulge of his swollen shaft.

That set Sybelle to shuddering with excitement again, but in a strange way it was also calming. Whereas previously her desire had been formless, as frightening as it was thrilling because she had not been capable of thinking about how to satisfy her craving, the physical contact with the means of satisfaction answered her doubts and questions before they truly developed. As instinct had answered, so it also drove Sybelle to shift her position, and she strained upward against her lover.

Walter had been taken by surprise, also. His first flicker of disappointment when Sybelle had not immediately responded to his kiss had put him a little off balance so that her rapid change of attitude and her obvious growing sexual arousal induced him to go further than he had intended. When she began to rub herself against him, however, Walter made an effort to collect his scattered wits. He realized that in another few minutes they would be down on the cold floor trying to content each other in an ugly huddle of half-undone clothing. At any time, Walter found such a coupling distasteful, fit only for the commonest whore or a serf girl seized in a field. For a high-bred maiden's first experience, it was unthinkable.

He dropped his arm from Sybelle's back to her buttocks and held her still. He withdrew his tongue; Sybelle's promptly followed it. In the furor that caused inside him, Walter almost lost sight of the fact that he intended to break their embrace. It had been many, many years since Walter had been so far out of control during the foreplay of lovemaking. He was trembling himself, and his legs were unsteady. With a desperate wrench he freed his mouth.

"Stop, beloved," he whispered hoarsely. "Heartling, my soul, we are going too far."

Sybelle had been blindly lifting her face toward his to renew their kiss. Now her eyes opened, and she drew back her head so she could see him. Walter's eyes looked somewhat glazed, more heavy-lidded than usual, and his normally ruddy complexion was rather pale. Sybelle sighed as, with the abrupt termination of nearly all sexual stimulation, her mind became capable of meshing with her body. Walter was right, she thought. This was not the time or the place. Her acute craving faded. Still, it was delightful to see that he was as aroused as she was. She could feel the quivering tension in his body as he held her, and the hard bulge along his thigh had not diminished.

Although her hips were held immobile, Sybelle's upper body was now free. Playfully, she rubbed her breasts lightly against Walter's left arm, which was still bound firmly across his chest. He drew in his breath sharply, but he could see there was more mischief than passion in her expression, and he let go of her abruptly and administered a slap on the buttocks he had been holding. Sybelle's arms dropped from around him, and she sighed again, far more dramatically.

"I see it is with you as with all men. No sooner is a woman irrevocably in your power than you become cruel."

"It is not cruelty but regard for your health and your good name that forced me to put a stop to our play," Walter said with perfect gravity, although there was laughter in his eyes now, too. He knew quite well that was not what Sybelle had meant. "You would surely have taken a chill had we lain down on the floor here, in spite of the fire, and what would you have said when you had no proof of maidenhead on our wedding night?"

"Coxcomb!" Sybelle cried, half outraged and half laughing. "First you beat me, and then you accuse me of lusting after you."

"Do you not?" Walter asked, and the laughter was gone from his face and voice.

Thrown off balance again, Sybelle raised troubled eyes. "Do you think it wrong?" she asked in return, her voice uncertain. "My mother has told me that to take joy in love with one's husband and to give him joy is good."

For answer Walter swept her into his embrace and kissed her hard again, but he did not sustain the kiss and he stepped back away from her when he let her go. "I think so well of your mother's advice, my love, that I dare not stay too near lest I put it to the proof too soon for your honor and mine."

Sybelle came no closer, and her expression grew even more troubled. "Then what shall I do? Do you now desire that I go back to England with my parents?"

"No!" Walter exclaimed, then raised his hand to his head and scratched it. "I do not know," he admitted. "It might be safer. . . . In God's name, Sybelle, I swear that I have not felt this way about a woman in fifteen years. I am gone back to being a green boy, so eaten with desire that I cannot think straight."

Extending a hand toward him, Sybelle said softly, "Yet I know you will do me no harm. Let me stay, Husband, as it is greatly my desire to do so."

CHAPTER 14

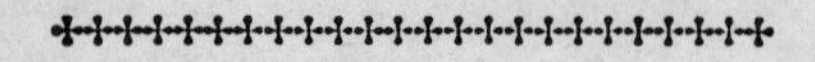

The keep emptied of guests rapidly all through that day. Once the excitements and entertainments Llewelyn had offered were over, men with property in southern or eastern Wales remembered that a war was in progress and that the king's party had not been celebrating. Their lands might have suffered damage or might be threatened by an invading force at that very moment. Those from northern or western Wales might have been inclined to linger, since there was no danger to their property from the war; however, there were other dangers in war than attack by King Henry's forces.

Prince Llewelyn might demand help or support from them, and it would be nearly impossible to refuse if the request were made directly. Letters could be ignored, for a little while at least, with the excuse that one was not at the place where the letter was delivered; and one could write back asking questions or offering excuses. Thus, those uncertain of the outcome or less eager for war departed swiftly. Some, of course, were both willing and eager to join in whatever action Pembroke and Llewelyn were planning, and those remained, but Builth was now almost empty compared with the crowded conditions during the wedding.

Walter moved into one of the vacated chambers, ostensibly so that William could spend at least one night more comfortably than on a pallet on the floor. However, he had personal reasons for desiring privacy, the primary one being that he felt if he did not soon take a woman to his bed, he would forget all about anyone's honor the next time he was alone with Sybelle. Although he knew he should not, he had agreed at once that she should stay if she could obtain permission. She had asked him so sweetly, and then she had run swiftly away before he could have second, more rational, thoughts.

For a little while Walter had remained alone, staring into

the fire and telling himself that he must go and tell one of Sybelle's parents it was not safe to allow her to remain where he could get at her, but he could not make himself do it. Instead, he promised himself that he would under no circumstances be alone with her. If he were careful, he could have the warmth and joy her company brought him without skirting disaster again. He had been a fool to draw her into that side chamber. If there had been others present, they would not have gone so far. Even if he had not been able to resist tasting her lips, the touch would have been brief, and little could have followed.

When, some little while later, Walter realized he was lingering in the empty room in the expectation that Sybelle would return to tell him her parents' decision—and had not permitted himself to think about what he was doing—he left the place at once. However, he still did not seek out Geoffrey or Joanna. In fact, he made himself inconspicuous in a chair beside the hearth in the great hall. This was not the same, he told himself, although the place was far from crowded and it was the very spot he had held several conversations with Sybelle. If she guessed where he was and came to find him, it would be safe.

However, he saw no more of Sybelle that day. It was Marie who found him. She stopped as if surprised when she saw him and exclaimed at discovering him alone. Walter rose from his chair with alacrity and greeted her with genuine warmth. He was very pleased with Marie, believing she had behaved with the utmost delicacy. He thought she had perceived the jealousy that had precipitated Sybelle into accepting his offer and had avoided him to prevent any increase in that jealousy.

To a limited extent Walter was right, although Marie thought that Sybelle's attitude had more of a dog-in-the-manger quality than jealousy over love. Both of them had failed to recognize the combination of innocence, self-confidence, and a feeling of superiority to Marie that armored Sybelle. This simple error caused Walter to prefer that Sybelle not find him in Marie's company. Thus he soon suggested that they move to a more "comfortable" place.

Marie gave a single, brief glance at the chair from which Walter had risen but she did not smile, although she was aware that it was as comfortable as any other he was likely to find and that the corner by the hearth was private enough for any except the most intimate purposes. She had been well occupied during the three days encompassing the wedding and the tournament. Women were scarce, and Marie was pretty and an expert flirt. At no time had she lacked for attentive male company, so she had not missed Walter's in the least.

In addition, she had been much preoccupied with convincing her sister to try to establish a better relationship with her husband. This was less philanthropic than practical. Marie realized that if Gervase annoyed Richard, she would be sent back to Pembroke keep without delay, and Marie, although she might be guiltless, would have to go with her. It was true, Marie admitted, that the knights of Richard's entourage and the Welsh clan leaders who were attached to Prince Llewelyn were not the equal of the men of the French court. Nonetheless, Marie pointed out, they were better than no company at all.

Gervase agreed, perhaps reluctantly, but she did agree. Two years of virtual isolation had taught her something. She moderated her manner sufficiently so that Richard was not rubbed raw by continual fault-finding and complaining. Moreover, the time he had spent in company with Alinor, Joanna, and their husbands had reminded him that marriage could be more than a nagging burden at the back of one's mind. This, combined with a vague feeling of guilt about his treatment of his wife, made Gervase's effort to be agreeable fall on fertile soil. Richard said nothing about sending his wife or her sister back to Pembroke, nor did he move to a separate chamber when one became available.

It was Marie who moved, and her sister did not oppose the separation as she had in the past. For one thing, Gervase did not at this time wish to use Marie as a weapon against her husband; for another, both agreed that Walter was the most suitable man they had seen. From what they had heard, it did not seem that the war would end soon, and even after it did, it seemed hardly likely that Richard would be in favor or seek the court. Nor, whatever the outcome, did it seem likely that Richard would return to Normandy or allow them to return without him. In fact, he was already talking of going to Ireland, an even more barbarous and primitive country than England or Wales. Thus, there would be no wider choice.

Moreover, Gervase had her own row to hoe, which made

her more amenable than usual to listening to Marie's advice. Gervase did not wish to go to Ireland. She did not like Wales and did not think she would like Ireland any better; however, if Marie married a man Richard liked and trusted, it was very likely that Gervase would be allowed to stay with Marie in her brother-by-marriage's care. This, Gervase decided, would be better than being dragged along in her husband's tail from one war to another. Walter it must be, and Gervase and Marie had discussed at considerable length the problem of separating Walter from Sybelle.

Marie contended that Walter showed a strong personal preference for her and had offered for Sybelle only because Richard refused to provide any dowry or suggested too insignificant a marriage portion. Gervase did not contest this opinion, but pointed out that there was no way to induce Richard to increase his offer to Walter. War cost high; perhaps when it was over, Richard would consider a higher bride price—but it might be too late by then or, still worse, Richard might be defeated and then fined so that he would have less to give Marie. Even if Richard won, the situation might not improve. It would be just like him to rush off to Ireland, dragging Gervase and Marie with him.

Something would have to be done and done quickly, before the informal agreement, of which all the men seemed to be aware, became a written contract. Gervase pointed out there was no evidence that Walter felt any active distaste for Sybelle whether or not he might prefer Marie. And Gervase was not so sure that Sybelle did feel distaste for Walter. After all, it was Sybelle who had told nearly every man in Builth that she was betrothed.

Under the circumstances, Gervase and Marie agreed, drastic action would have to be taken. It would be necessary for Marie to allow Walter to seduce her. Then, depending upon the amount of time they had, she could hope he would get her with child. If that were not possible, they could set a trap in which Gervase would "discover" them in the act of coupling. Either circumstance should bring him to abrogate what they believed was a casual agreement with Lord Geoffrey and marry Marie instead. And if he did not offer to do so voluntarily, Gervase would carry the information to Richard, who would force his liegeman to fulfill his responsibilities.

At first Gervase counseled caution, fearing that forcing

Walter's hand might generate a dislike for Marie that would make him misuse her. However, Marie pointed out that he would not blame her; Gervase, not she, would be the one to carry the tale to Richard, and Marie herself could be tearfully apologetic about it, vowing she had had no such intention. She could even claim she begged her sister not to betray her, but Gervase would not listen. It would do Gervase no harm if Walter was angry at her, since he had no power over her. And if Marie played her game well, he would soon come to terms with a situation that was irrevocable.

So, when Walter suggested a more "comfortable" situation where they could talk at ease, Marie did not teasingly comment on the comparative quality of comfort in different chairs or giggle archly. Instead she cast a blatantly admiring glance at him and said softly that she had moved to an apartment separate from her sister and her husband's.

"And owing to your foresight in suggesting that I bring my own furniture, we can indeed be comfortable," she finished.

Although Walter had been considerably surprised by this unusually frank invitation, he concealed all but a single blink. When he made the suggestion that they leave their present location, he had been thinking no further, actually, than removing to a place less familiar to Sybelle and where she was not likely to seek him. Owing to the excitements of the tournament and his deepening relationship with Sybelle, he had all but forgotten his flirtation with Marie. It had recurred to his mind from time to time, when his physical frustration rose to uncomfortable levels, but all such occasions in the past had come at moments when taking action on the thought had been impossible.

Now, however, everything conspired to make him regard Marie's suggestion as manna from heaven. A swift glance around the hall indicated that no one he knew well was present to carry tales. Moreover, although his acute readiness for sex had, of course, dissipated, an ache of general need pervaded his entire body. He took fire at once, leaning forward to murmur caressingly that Marie was as kind as she was lovely.

Walter did not scruple to leap at the offer or think of restating the fact that he was as good as married. Richard had been present at the sealing of the contract for Sybelle; it never occurred to Walter that Richard would not pass on so interesting and harmless a piece of information despite Geoffrey's remarks about not spreading the news. Neither Gervase nor Marie was likely to be talking to King Henry before peace or a truce was declared, and all women were interested in news of a marriage.

Neither did Walter consider that Richard might not have had time to speak to his womenfolk. To Walter it seemed as if hours and hours had passed since the morning conference, whereas it was less than one hour. In addition, Walter was already growing accustomed to the pleasure of hurrying to Sybelle with any bit of news and discussing it with her. If he had really thought about it, he would have remembered that Richard was not on the same terms with his wife as he was with Sybelle. But Walter was not thinking clearly at all.

Thus, he was sure that Marie, like himself, felt the need for a physical pleasure that had no significance beyond the pleasure itself. He was eager for that, yet was aware also of a vague discomfort, half his mind manufacturing excuses to offer should he come across any member of his new family. Guilt was not new to Walter, but in the past it had been associated with the husbands he had cuckolded. Then, the guilt was not difficult to assuage. The ladies who had betrayed husbands had good reason to do so—or had told him they had good reason. Now it was Sybelle who was being betrayed, and that was not so easy to excuse.

But there was no betrayal, Walter told himself, while murmuring compliments and suggestive phrases to Marie. What he was doing had nothing to do with Sybelle; in fact, it was in a way for her that he wished to relieve his need for a woman. If she remained in Wales, he would be less a danger to her honor if he were drained out. It would be easier to refrain from tempting her and himself. Although these rationalizations did not satisfy him completely, the unease that remained made him irritable, reminding him of his resentment at Joanna's and Sybelle's assumption that he was no longer a free agent, no longer the only judge, under God, of his own behavior.

Among rationalizations, resentments, and lust, guilt could make little headway. Walter simply pushed away all considerations beyond his physical need as he walked into Marie's chamber, which was a single one with a hearth but no antechamber. She had chosen with care, her purpose in mind, a room not far from Richard's apartment but one that had no place for a maid except the floor of her own bedchamber. It was an act of kindness, then, to suggest that her womanservant share quarters with Gervase's—and it ensured the privacy she needed. The maid was not stupid; sharp lessons with a whip had made her very perceptive, and a bare hint was sufficient. The room was prepared for company at any moment, with wine and a covered platter of cakes ready and a warm fire, which was tended as long as the door was open.

Marie had gestured for Walter to enter and followed him, quietly closing the door behind her. He sensed what she had done and turned when he was only a few steps into the room. She hesitated, her hand still on the door.

"Do you think me shameless to invite you here?" she asked.

"I think you are beautiful and generous," Walter replied immediately and most sincerely.

He did not wish to hear of shame. Marie was hurting no one; if one of them should feel shame, that one was he. But the idea flitting through his head made him angry, and he held out his hand to Marie. However, she did not put her own into it as Sybelle would have done. She turned half away, simpering.

"You go too fast, sir," she cried coyly.

Mentally Walter shook himself. Could he have forgotten all his skill in so few days, just because Sybelle was so perfectly attuned to him that she responded to his every mood like a fine harp? When he was in a light humor, Sybelle could be teasing enough, but when he was moved by a desire to give and receive affection, she was direct and loving. Naturally, the persistent thoughts of Sybelle increased Walter's guilt and resentment. He felt like one possessed, as if the golden girl he loved had taken his soul into bondage; he could not be rid of her for a moment. This was nothing to do with Sybelle, he told himself again, angrily.

Meanwhile, he had smiled at Marie and chidden her gently for having so great charms as to make a man forget his manners. And while she was bridling up at this unusual way of giving a compliment, he had confessed himself at fault for being too much smitten. This was a fault easily forgiven by any woman.

Marie giggled more naturally and said, "You are excused

for that,'' and when Walter put out his hand again, she touched her fingers to it.

To her surprise, Marie found she was enjoying herself. Although Walter was not paying her the extravagant compliments common in the circles to which she was accustomed, he was producing in her the feeling that she was truly valued. She nearly dropped her flirtatious manner and responded naturally, but as Walter's fingers began to close over hers and move upward so that he could take her whole hand into his and draw her closer to him, she remembered that she must not make herself cheap. Thus, she twitched her fingers about and played with his, teasingly preventing a handclasp.

Walter was sufficiently familiar with this technique to know what it meant. Many, many times he had set himself to convince a woman—or to let her convince herself—that violation of the rules of chastity would not reduce her value to him. It was something Walter did not understand. His mistresses never seemed to worry about the violation of God's law. Oh, they acknowledged the sin and would confess it and do penance for it, no doubt, but it was not the sin or God's anger they feared; it was that they would be diminished in Walter's own mortal and very unimportant eyes.

He set himself to soothe Marie, combining praise of her features and form with more especial praise of her kindness and generosity. ''One does not forget, cannot forget, the free giving of such a prize. We cannot know the future—'' He had captured her hand by this time and had pulled her nearer, but not quite against him. ''It may be that circumstances will not permit us to meet this way again. I hope it will not be so. I wish . . .'' He let that trail away artistically, not stating but implying the lie that his desire was for a permanent relationship.

The implication did not worry Walter. No mistress of his had suffered a broken heart. Usually it was the lady who broke off the connection, either because she saw something that appealed more to her or because she discovered Walter was no chick to be plucked at will. A few had parted from him with real regret because circumstances had changed and it was no longer safe to have a lover; one or two had severed the relationship because they felt themselves in danger of caring too much. Whatever the cause, every woman to whom Walter had made love in the past had understood the hint for what it was—a declaration of respect, an assurance that Walter did not regard her as a whore, to be used and cast aside.

Perhaps Walter should have been warned that Marie's interpretation of that soft "I wish . . ." was different by the way her hand relaxed in his, and she came closer without being drawn. But the reaction was not very different from others he had experienced, and his sexual need was such that he might have ignored an even clearer warning.

"Will you not give me this gift to hold in my heart?" he continued. They were nearly breast to breast now. "Do not think I will misjudge you for offering this treasure," he murmured. "If circumstances were otherwise . . ."

It was the same unfinished implication designed to soothe away fears of contempt, but the repetition convinced Marie of the accuracy of her belief that Walter wanted her and had taken Sybelle for the dowry that came with her. If that were the case, in Marie's opinion there was far less danger in forcing Walter into a marriage. However angry he might be at the loss of Sybelle's property, coddling and sexual compliance for a few weeks or months would pacify him. She put an arm around his neck and raised her face to be kissed.

"I should not," she sighed, and then allowed the meeting of their lips.

Walter found it pleasant. His body responded in a normal fashion, but he was aware of an underlying sensation of impatience with the need for giving reassurance and the somewhat dampening knowledge that this was not the end of it. Once they had coupled it would be worse. He would need to find a hundred ways to say—without actually saying the words—that as far as he was concerned Marie was still a woman of virtue. He was also aware that the violent uprush of desire he had felt for Sybelle was lacking.

This did not really displease Walter. It was one thing to be transported with passion for one's wife; that was a delicious pleasure. It was quite another thing to lose control with a mistress; that was dangerous. There was no chance of it in this case, Walter thought, as he fumbled one-handed to remove Marie's headdress. He had no inclination to linger over undressing or foreplay. The kisses he gave, the murmurs and sweet words were a duty, the payment he owed to a woman who could not be paid in coin. What Walter wanted was relief.

By the time he got it, it had passed through his mind several times that it was unfortunate Marie had come upon him before he had thought of seeking out a compliant maidservant. If he had not been aching with need, he would not have leapt so quickly on her suggestion. In fact, if it had not been that Walter was too kind to hurt a woman by rejection after they had gone so far, he would have left Marie's chamber and gone out to look for a whore on whom to ease himself.

Marie, as it turned out, was a dreadful disappointment to Walter. In general, a woman who sought a lover did so for one of two reasons: She had a strong appetite for coupling or she wished to spite her husband. Walter had always avoided the latter, not only because there was more than ordinary danger that the husband was the jealous kind but because such women were often hard to satisfy—if not totally frigid. Because Marie had no husband to spite and he had told her he was betrothed, Walter had assumed that she desired to couple because she felt a need for it. He expected her to be as eager as he was himself.

But when they came to it, he did not find her eager at all. It took twice as long as Walter expected to get Marie into the bed in the first place, and she interrupted him half a dozen times, both while he was trying to ready her and while they were actually coupled, with awkward questions about the permanence of his affection for her. Although Walter found answers the first few times that seemed to satisfy her without actually lying or compromising himself, he was ready to murder his bedmate long before he came to his twice-aborted climax.

For all his patience and restraint, Walter did not even obtain the satisfaction of knowing he had contented Marie. She was not cold to him; she was all compliance—when she was not talking about eternal love. Her body moved with his, and she even seemed mildly to enjoy what was taking place. But she never clung to him with the desperation of a woman on the border of unbearable joy, he felt no tension building in her, and her voice was steady, not tremulous with passion, when she asked him whether he would be willing to live in poverty with her as she would be to live with him so long as they could be always together.

Walter did not answer that question at all. He himself was

at the edge of the last extremity when she posed it, and he could not have spoken at that moment in any case. Still, the question shocked him so much that the rising flood was stemmed. Only the fury caused by his aborted pleasure, for which it seemed to Walter that he had already waited far too long, kept him from withdrawing altogether. By now Walter was grimly determined to relieve himself, even if he had to gag Marie to accomplish it.

When he finally was finished, he was utterly exhausted, not with languorous pleasure in the usual way but simply physically exhausted. Because of his broken collarbone, Walter had first asked Marie to mount him. Although she had seemed surprised, she made no protest, but her movements had been irregular and she was apparently more puzzled than delighted with her freedom. Walter had given her some time to find a rhythm that would please her, but although he had kissed and sucked her breasts and, indeed, done everything else he could think of to stimulate her passion, she had showed no signs of increasing pleasure. The only result of his efforts had been to excite him until he had to stop Marie's movements to hold back his orgasm.

Thinking Marie might be distressed by an unaccustomed position, Walter then reversed them, straining to support himself on one arm so that he would not crush her and confining his efforts at stimulation to simple kisses. That served no better except that Marie did not talk quite so much. It was then that Walter gave up and determined to content himself and end a passage at arms that had continued far too long. He dropped his defenses and concentrated on the basic physical sensation created by friction and, at last, came near to climax a second time, only to be frustrated by Marie's question about living together in poverty.

Third time lucky, Walter thought, desperately concentrating on his own need. This time he concealed his increasing tension as much as he could and finally brought himself to climax. He then rolled himself off Marie immediately, and as soon as he could gather breath apologized for failing her.

"But you are content, are you not?" she asked. "That is all that is important. I did it for you."

There was a brief pause while Walter sought for words that would explain without offense that he was a man who wished to give as much pleasure as he received. Before his tired mind could find suitable phrases, Marie spoke again.

"I wished to please you. Did I not do so?"

The anxiety in her voice wrung Walter's heart. How could he say she had nearly driven him from her bed despite the need that had pushed him into it in the first place? "You are all that is lovely and gracious, and kindness itself," he murmured, stroking her arm. "It is not in my power to say more. You know that."

"Here in private you may say anything," she urged.

Walter was in a quandary. It seemed crude to him to remind Marie again and in more specific words of his betrothal at this moment. He had intended that oblique mention of it as a delicate hint that Marie should not expect a repetition of this meeting. However, she had not taken the hint. Moreover, Walter was determined not to offer further assurances that he desired an infinite continuation of their relationship. It was no longer true. If it were in his power, Walter never intended to expose himself to a second such experience.

He was altogether greatly puzzled by Marie's actions. Until she had brought him into her chamber, he could have sworn that she had no deep feeling for him. Then it occurred to him that this might be Marie's first experience with an extramarital relationship. If that were true, it was no wonder that she was pressing him so frantically to reaffirm his devotion or, for that matter, that she had been impossible to satisfy. The poor woman must be consumed with guilt and with the fear that she had soiled herself and was now worthless.

Walter turned and tenderly took her into the crook of his arm. "Marie, if there is any fault in what we have done, that fault is mine. It is a man's curse that he desires beauty when he sees it. I should not have yielded to that desire, my situation being what it is. I have taken base advantage of the sweetness of your nature and, I fear, of your innocence. My dear, no great harm is done. You have betrayed no oaths, hurt no living person, and you have given me a gift I will remember always."

If Marie had not been totally fixed on her end purpose, she would have slapped Walter's face. Her hopes had been sky-high when he came with her so eagerly and hinted so clearly that she was what he really wanted. Nonetheless, no matter how she pressed him or how carefully she timed her pleading—not even when he was nearly in the throes of his culmination—would he say outright that he loved her or imply in any way that he would be willing to—or even wished to—abandon the proposed contract with Sybelle.

She was utterly and absolutely furious. Never had she endured so long and devious a coupling. Did the man think she had nothing else to do than be mauled about? Was no part of her body to be private to herself, but his plaything? And after all her patience and compliance to his whims, all he had to say was that *she* had done no great harm. He confessed he was at fault. How generous! No doubt he felt that to be so great a concession as to repay her for everything. Marie knew that if she did not get rid of Walter immediately, she would say something that might make it impossible to carry out her plan to marry him.

Now she pushed him away gently, exerting all her willpower to resist the temptation to shove him right out of the bed. "So you say," she muttered, her voice shaking with her effort not to scream at him, "but others will not be so generous. It is always the woman who is blamed and shamed. I beg you, go now."

It was exactly what Walter most desired to do, and his eagerness made him feel even guiltier. Her words seemed to confirm the conclusions he had drawn about the cause of her behavior. He drew her close again and kissed her gently on the forehead.

"There is nothing to fear," he soothed. "I am certain none saw us enter here, and I will swear on my honor, on the souls of my mother and father, if you will, that none will ever hear of this from me."

Since this was exactly the opposite of what Marie wanted, Walter's attempt to pacify her was, to say the least, ineffectual. Marie had hoped that they would be noticed entering her chamber together, and she had assumed that Walter would be unable to resist boasting of his conquest. She had counted on those boasts to back her claims that he had seduced her. Marie was not one to believe overmuch in honor, but she could not mistake the sincerity of Walter's promise not to betray her and no man, no matter how light-minded, swore on the souls of the dead close in blood to him.

Moreover, Marie's cry that it was the woman who would

be blamed and shamed had been designed to draw from Walter a statement that he would not permit it, that he would shield her by giving her his name. Thus, his declaration of secrecy, plus the implication that he was not prepared to shield her in any other way, infuriated Marie so much that she shook with rage. Feeling her tremble, Walter tried to clasp her closer. "There is nothing to fear," he insisted. At which reiteration of the statement that had enraged her in the first place, Marie shoved him so hard that, taking him by surprise, she loosened his grip on her and he nearly did fall off the bed.

"Go! Go!" she cried, not trusting herself to say another word.

Since his attempts to comfort her seemed only to make Marie more frantic, Walter rose and began to dress, watching her with troubled eyes. She had turned and buried her face in the pillows, pulling the blankets high over her as if she wished to hide from him. Walter felt like weeping, but he had no idea what to do or say to give her ease. The one thing that he knew would make her happy, he could not offer.

Never again, Walter vowed, would he so casually trust his judgment of a woman's reactions. As the vow passed through his mind, he realized he would never need to play at such games again. Soon there would be Sybelle. A flood of relief and joy washed over him that changed to shame with another glimpse of the sad huddle in the bed that was Marie. He longed to flee without another word, but when he was dressed, which was no easy task one-handed, he forced himself to the bedside and gently touched Marie's shoulder.

"I am going, as you bid me," he whispered only loud enough for her to hear. "I am sorry, Marie. So sorry."

CHAPTER 15

Walter did not know what to do with himself when he came out of Marie's chamber. Sensitized by what he thought was her fear, he made very sure that not even a servant saw him, and he left the area completely. In all his life he could not remember feeling so sick of himself and so miserable. All he could think of was finding Sybelle and pouring the whole thing out to her. She would comfort him, for it had all been a horrible mistake caused by his unsatisfied lust.

However, he had given his oath to Marie that he would tell no one, and as the visual impact of Marie's misery dimmed and his pain and shame diminished a little, he recognized that the last person to tell was Sybelle. Not only had he been warned that she was of a jealous nature, but he knew it from his own observation. Had she not agreed to their betrothal in a spate of jealousy of . . . oh, God . . . of Marie? And must he not, for Marie's sake also, keep this incident from Sybelle? The bitterest gall of all to the failed aspirant is the fact that the successful contender knows of the failure.

The moment he realized that he could not confess to Sybelle, Walter became utterly terrified of meeting her. There was no way he could act normally until he shed his burden, but he had sworn he would tell no one, and if he could not speak of it, he could find no one to share or lift the load from him. Among all the sins he had committed, there were several regarded as far more heinous by priests. . . . Then Walter's thoughts were checked suddenly by a comforting realization. There was God.

As carefully as if he were on a secret night raid, Walter made his way to his chamber and found his cloak. Then he stole out of the keep altogether, not even stopping at the stables for Beau, so he had to walk to the village. He would not confess to the priest of the castle chapel. That was too nearby. Walter knew that to betray the secrets of the confessional was anathema and sure damnation for the priest who did it, but priests were men, and some of them feared damnation less than they should.

The village church was poor and mean, its stone walls without ornamentation, its windows mere slits in the fabric so that only narrow bars of light fell on the floor. Near the entry, when Walter had closed the door behind him, it was almost pitch-black, but diagonally across, just a few feet from the altar table, there was a lighter patch, which Walter realized was an open door into some outer building. Knowing Wales, Walter assumed it was the shedlike structure in which the priest lived.

"Father," he called.

Almost immediately the patch of light was blocked, and a voice replied. Although Walter did not understand the word, he assumed, since it was a single syllable, that it was a general question, such as: *Yes?* He was relieved. It was quite likely that this priest did not understand French. Thus, aside from the formal confiteor, what Walter said would be incomprehensible to him. Walter would, indeed, be speaking to God.

Walter drew his hood forward until his face was masked, although the corner in which he stood was so dark that it was unlikely the priest could make out his features. The voice of the priest was thin, uncertain, the voice of an old man. Walter knelt down on the cold stone floor and bowed his head.

"Father," he said, "I confess I have sinned." The words brought back so vivid an image of Marie huddled on the bed that his voice broke and he began to weep. "I have sinned most foully, and there is no help in me. . . ." He choked his way through the formal Latin phrases and then began to pour out the story of his lust, his lack of understanding, and his inability to comfort the woman he had hurt.

The priest stood above him shrouded in a cloak or blanket, a black pillar visible only in outline against the somewhat lighter interior of the church. That he did not understand a word Walter said, beyond the Latin opening, was irrelevant. He could recognize true contrition in the broken voice and bowed body. And it did not matter what sin was being confessed since, however dreadful, it could go no further. In a way, the old man was glad he could not understand. He knew from voice and language that this penitent was of the nobility. He was too old, he thought, to have on his heart whatever sin could drive such a man into his poor church and wring such bitter tears from him.

Walter's confession finally came to an end, and he heaved a huge sigh. In his thin, uncertain voice, the priest asked the formal questions, and Walter gave the formal answers. Then, there was a pause. The priest knew he could ask for payment of what would be a fortune to him in penance and that the man would pay gladly—only he did not speak the penitent's language and the penitent did not speak his. Would the man know Latin? And then in the dark the old man smiled bitterly; he did not know enough Latin himself to make clear what he wanted to say. Sighing, he named the prayers, the Aves, the Paters, that Walter must say and tried to make clear how many repetitions of each how many times each day and how many days. Then he said the words of absolution and turned away.

Walter remained crouched on his knees until the rectangle of light that was the doorway was blocked again by the priest's body. He was not suspicious of being seen; he was not really conscious of the old man's retreat. He was only savoring the relief of having exposed his sin to God and having it lifted from him. Walter was still sorry for the misunderstanding that had upset Marie, but the wrenching guilt was gone.

He rose to his feet, grunting as his knee reminded him that it was not yet completely healed and did not favor kneeling for long periods on cold stone. As he trudged back up the hill toward Builth keep, Walter conscientiously said the Aves and Paters, hoping that he had understood the priest correctly. To be sure, he said a few extra of each, but he was not worried about that. God would know he had no intention of cheating and would not blame him if he was mistaken.

Although his conscience was easier, Walter still felt awkward about meeting either Sybelle or Marie, and instead of reentering Builth, he went to the stables. Just as he was walking up the row of horses to Beau, Simon's voice hailed him.

"Where the devil have you been?" Simon asked.

"Not with the devil," Walter replied, "at least, not for the past half hour. Why?"

"Everyone is either packing to leave or having conferences to which I am not invited." Simon grinned impishly. "I thought it would be a good day to ride down to Cwm-du or Llwyncrwn. In one village or the other there will be a man sent by Siorl, and we can hear the latest news from Monmouth keep."

Walter smiled so broadly that he thought his face would split. His spirits lifted mercurially. To his mind, this was a clear sign that he was forgiven. He was sure that the Holy Mother herself must have listened to his contrition, for only she was so merciful and kind as to provide him with this respite.

"Done," he agreed, but then doubt assailed him. He was no longer completely free to do as he chose. Surely it was his duty to leave word for Sybelle, and there was another problem. "But I am not armed," he said, "and Sybelle—"

"I told Rhiannon I would go and that I intended to have your company if I could," Simon assured him. "Rhiannon will tell Sybelle. As to being armed, how could you be with your arm strapped that way? I do not think we will find trouble. I intend to go by safe ways."

Flicked for a moment by past guilt, Walter felt it was too easy. "Will Sybelle not be offended if I do not leave word myself?" he asked.

"Not Sybelle," Simon said confidently, laughing. "She is no *grande dame sans merci*. Do you think you are living in the pages of a romance?"

At that moment, William came trotting down the aisle, calling somewhat breathlessly, "I could not find— Oh, there you are, sir. Shall I see to the saddling of the horses, Simon?"

"We will see to it," Walter said. "As soon as you catch your breath, run back and tell your sister that I am going with Simon and will not be at dinner."

Simon burst out laughing. "You will make a model husband, Walter. I see Sybelle already has you well trained."

"It is not Sybelle," Walter said defensively. "My mother used to worry so. . . ."

Simon clapped him merrily on his good shoulder. "So much the better for both of you, and you are quite right. It is a fool's trick to ride out without telling your wife when you expect to be back. How could she come to your assistance if she did not know you were missing and needed aid?"

If Walter was somewhat startled at Simon's confident assumption that a wife should ride out to rescue her husband, he was growing sufficiently familiar with the ways and thinking patterns of Roselynde not to comment. He called to the grooms and watched with interest their trepidation at approaching Simon's Ymlladd, who, indeed, greeted their invasion of his territory with slashing hooves and snapping teeth. Nor did he completely spare his own master, and Simon cuffed the horse a blow with a balled fist that might have shattered the skull of a lesser animal.

It was not surprising that Walter was mounted before Simon. Beau, too, was very lively, prancing and cavorting because he had not been exercised for several days, but he certainly did not try to buck Walter off his back, which Ymlladd seemed determined to do to Simon. Simon sat out the antics with accustomed skill, smiling and patting the destrier when he quieted and consented to go forward.

"Now that you are betrothed to Sybelle, you will have your pick of the young stallions at Roselynde," Simon said cheerfully. "There are two that are of especial spirit and strength."

"By spirit, I suppose you mean a temper like that fiend of yours," Walter retorted. "Is this a device to rid the family of me? And so soon? Do I deserve it?"

"Oh, you will have little trouble with them." Simon shrugged casually. "You are a good two or three stone heavier than I. Mama says they were docile as lambs under Simon—her first husband, I mean. It has something to do with the weight, she thinks."

Walter cocked an eye at Ymlladd, who was now cantering along in a way that suggested he could continue to do so indefinitely. Although he could not believe that any rider or circumstance could make one of those destriers docile as a lamb, Walter was not indifferent to the beauty and stamina of the beast. And by the end of their thirty-mile ride, when Beau was beginning to show signs of tiring, Ymlladd took exception to one of Simon's men crossing his vision and put on an exhibition of attacking as if he were fresh from the stable. Really, the animal seemed tireless, and Walter determined to accept a stallion if one were offered. At worst, he could dilute the line with a more common mare, hoping to retain strength and some of the spirit while eradicating the devil's temper.

They found one of Simon's men waiting in Cwm-du, but his news was two days old, not much more recent than what Efan had brought. Still, he had one new item to add. There had been a great cutting of trees in the forests near Monmouth, great trees, and the sound of the forges in the keep could be heard right through the nights.

"A great cutting of trees sounds more like attack than defense," Walter said.

"True enough," Simon agreed, shaking his head. "I do not like it."

"Nor I." Walter's statement was emphatic. "You know that Llewelyn has been urging Richard to attack Shrewsbury, do you not? I cannot guess how word of their plans could have come to Monmouth, but it is by no means impossible. So if Richard draws off his men from Abergavenny and Usk to join Llewelyn and go north, John of Monmouth might break the undermanned keeps before Richard could come back."

"Yes," Simon agreed, but he did not look happy. "I think we need to know more. What do you say we ride on to Abergavenny and stay the night? That will give time for Siorl himself to come from Monmouth and speak with us."

"I say we must do it," Walter said, sounding both approving and sympathetic; after all, Simon had only been married for three days.

However, Walter was delighted for himself. The longer he was away from Builth, the longer Marie would have to compose herself. Then he realized he might miss saying farewell to Sybelle if her parents refused her permission to stay, an idea that pleased him much less. But in a moment he had a solution to the problem. If she were gone from Builth when he returned, he would borrow a horse and ride on to Clyro, which was not more than twenty miles away. Lord Geoffrey had said they would stop there.

Simon sent two men back to tell Llewelyn what they had heard and what they planned to do, with specific instructions to be sure Rhiannon also got the message and, if Sybelle was still in Builth, that she was told Walter would return as soon as he could. At Abergavenny they discussed the matter with Gilbert Bassett, who was not inclined to scoff at their concern. He had had messages from Richard, and thus knew all but the latest news. This he liked as little as Simon and Walter.

"They will catch us in a cleft stick," he snarled. "If we must stay pent within waiting for them, the king will have time to gather money and still more men. Moreover, if Richard refuses to fall in with Lord Llewelyn's plans, he is like to . . ." Bassett left the words "turn traitor" unsaid, remembering that Simon, although tied by the bond of fostering to Pembroke, was Llewelyn's man by fealty. "And we cannot attack them," he went on bitterly. "Manned as Monmouth is now, we could more easily break ourselves against its walls than break them."

"Let us see what Siorl has to say," Simon offered soothingly.

Neither he nor Walter was much disturbed by Bassett's seeming despair. Gilbert had a habit of describing the worst view of the situation and trying to convince himself and others that there was no other possible course of events. For him, this had the happy effect of making *anything* that happened no worse than expected and, usually, a great deal better. Those who knew him either ignored his gloomy prognostications or had similar natures and reactions so that they did not suffer from his peculiarity. Occasionally, of course, someone who did not know his ways was exposed and badly shaken.

This time, however, the gloom did seem to have some basis. Siorl's report confirmed the worst assumptions. Two of Simon's men had actually been inside Monmouth, having taken the place of a couple of Welsh serfs. There could no longer be any doubt that John of Monmouth was preparing to attack, and preparing carefully. War towers and machines were being built in sections so that they could be transported and set up quickly at their destination. Cattle were being collected, no doubt to be driven along with the army for the double purpose of having green hides to shield the towers and rams, and feeding the men. In addition, men and supplies were still coming into Monmouth, and this time they were coming by the safest roads, well protected by armed escorts.

Since he had already predicted this, Bassett seemed almost grimly pleased. "Well, well," he said, as Simon and Walter mounted up the next day to bring the unwelcome tidings to the party at Builth, "I suppose we will have to do something, perhaps make a feint at Gloucester itself."

To this, neither Simon nor Walter made any reply. Bassett was an honorable man, but he regarded his outlawry in a no-holds-barred way. He felt a real grudge against the king, unmitigated by any of the qualms of conscience that made Richard so unhappy. It was not likely that Richard would choose the method Bassett had suggested as a way out of the trap John of Monmouth was setting. Richard felt a real horror at the thought of any direct attack on Henry. Nor was it likely that Llewelyn, whose heart was set on the loot to be gathered from an assault on Shrewsbury, would agree to the delay and losses that would be incurred.

Therefore, in the discussions between Simon and Walter on the way home, Bassett's suggestion was virtually ignored. They rode hard, stopping only once to rest the horses while the light lasted and then to wait for the moon to rise after dark fell. By the time they came to Builth, Simon's men had fallen miles behind and Beau's head was hanging with exhaustion. Only Ymlladd still had strength to shy at shadows and whinny with irritation because Simon held him back to Beau's pace. Walter stroked Beau's neck with affection to encourage him. He loved his destrier and he would ride him often enough so that he would not feel neglected, but he was reconsidering the notion of mixing a softer strain into the Roselynde line of great grays.

The different sound of the hooves on the harder-packed road of the village drew Walter's attention from the horses. They were passing the church when he looked up, and he suddenly remembered the events of the previous morning, a shadow of the burden he had carried into that church passing over him; he bit his lip. He had forgotten his penance. He pulled Beau's rein and the tired beast stopped.

"Simon," Walter called softly, "have you a purse?"

Simon had to back Ymlladd, who had gone ahead. "Yes," he replied.

Walter dismounted and walked a few steps toward Simon, eyeing Ymlladd cautiously. He held out his hand. "Give it me. Do you know what is in it?"

"Nothing much, twenty or thirty shillings," Simon said, unfastening the purse from his belt and dropping it into Walter's hand. His eyes were bright with curiosity, but he knew Walter could not see that in the dark, and he asked no questions.

"Ride on," Walter bid him. "Tell the gatekeeper that I will be but a few minutes behind you."

He fastened Beau's rein to the door-pull and went in, again pulling his hood up over his face. Because of the dark outside, the light of the tiny eternal flame seemed to illuminate the whole small interior. Walter made his way to the far wall and to the door of the priest's room, which he opened.

"Father," he called, and as soon as he heard the priest's frightened gasp, he added, "do not rise, Father. I have only come to say that I have sinned again, not in the same way but in the press of events I did forget the penance you laid upon me."

He heard the creak of the bed and remembered that the priest could not understand him, but he knew the old man was no longer frightened because he was coming toward him. Walter put Simon's purse into his hand. He knew that what was nothing much to Simon might be half a year's revenue to this poor priest.

"Mea culpa," Walter said. *"Mea culpa,"* knowing the priest would understand that.

The old man clutched at the purse. *"Te absolvo,"* he replied, and something in the way he said it told Walter that his voice had been recognized.

"Benigne dicis." Walter hoped that meant thank you. He had heard it in situations that implied thanks. *"Benigne dicis,"* he repeated, as he backed away.

The priest did not follow, but when Walter had gone out and closed the door, he came forward into the church and opened the purse to examine its contents in the wavering light near the altar table. Then he fell to his knees and thanked God with great fervor. He would not have dared to ask so much, yet God had provided, forgiving the greed that had racked him with regret for the past two days.

Walter let Beau take his own slow pace up the hill, feeling a warm sense of satisfaction as he found the opportunity to recite the prayers he had forgotten earlier. The repetition of the well-known, blessed words was soothing, and he himself was half-asleep by the time he reached the keep. It had been a long ride, and the previous night they had talked so long with Bassett that he had had little time abed. However, he was startled into alertness by a retainer who was waiting at the door to lead him to Prince Llewelyn's chamber. Here he found Simon warming himself at the fire beside which the Lord of Gwynedd and the Earl of Pembroke sat. Both wore bedrobes and had the heavy eyes that result from being awakened from the first deep sleep.

"Do you agree with this hothead's conclusions about what his men report?" Pembroke asked Walter, squeezing Simon's arm fondly.

From the question, Walter understood that Simon had already managed to relate the information. "Yes, and so does Gilbert Bassett," Walter replied.

"Oh, Gilbert would see the worst in a gift of ten pounds of gold." Pembroke shrugged. "I do not doubt that they are preparing for war, but I cannot see how they could have heard that I intend to move my forces north." He looked at Llewelyn. "We were private when we spoke except for that one time at the breaking of our fast, and I do not think Walter spread the news. So how . . ."

"Why should it be needful for John of Monmouth to know our plans?" Llewelyn asked. "The very fact that we have made alliance—and all the king's party must know that—would imply that future action might take place nearer my lands. Also," he pointed out, "since you did not press the attack on Monmouth within the first week, while you might have been supposed to think the garrison was in disarray, John could believe you to have been more weakened by the battle than you were."

"I did not think of that," Pembroke admitted, his brows knitting into a frown. "*Merde!*" he exclaimed, rising to his feet suddenly. "They might be planning to attack now, while I am here."

"Sit, Pembroke, sit," Llewelyn said. "No one could march an army from Monmouth to Abergavenny or to Usk before you could ride there from here."

"They are not ready to march yet," Simon assured him. "My men were in the keep only a day or two ago, and at that time the preparations were less than half-complete."

"Yes, but it is more than that," Walter put in. "Something was said, I am sure, that made us believe John of Monmouth *did* know you were planning to go north." He turned to Simon. "Was it the man at Cwm-du or was it Siorl? I cannot now remember exactly what, but all of us, Bassett, too, were convinced that—"

"It does not matter," Llewelyn put in smoothly. "As I mentioned at first, it would be a natural assumption by any man who knows me—and John of Monmouth has been both friend and enemy for some time. Let us, like Bassett, assume the worst, that somehow Monmouth is privy to our plan to attack Shrewsbury."

"I suppose we must change the plans, then," Richard remarked, without notable reluctance.

"Not at all," Llewelyn said, shaking his head. "Far from it. Monmouth expects you to draw your forces out of Abergavenny and Usk and go north. Do not disappoint him. You must certainly march the men out of the keeps." He laughed at the expression of outrage that was growing on Pembroke's face. "Now, now, Pembroke, I am said to be a sly fox by many, but no one has yet called me a fool. I said the men should leave the keeps. I never said they should go far."

"By God!" Richard exclaimed. "I must still be half-asleep not to have seen that myself."

He was bright eyed now, holding back a smile, not because he wished to conceal his pleasure but for the sake of his scabbed lips. Richard still could not feel easy about initiating an attack on the king's men or property, but he had no qualms at all about defending himself. If John of Monmouth came out of his keep with an army and weapons designed to take Richard's castles, it was right and just, to Richard's way of thinking, to use any means to protect himself and his lands. Obviously, Llewelyn was suggesting an ambush.

Walter had understood a minute or two sooner than Richard because his close acquaintance with Simon had given him a better notion of how Llewelyn's mind worked. That notion, however, was making Walter very uneasy. It seemed to him that Prince Llewelyn had been too eager to abandon the question of how the news of Richard's intention to take his men north had got to John of Monmouth.

Walter could not help wondering if, perhaps, the wily lord of Gwynedd had sent out the little bird that sang the tale into Monmouth's ear. But why? At first Walter felt that would be insane, a senseless act of treachery. Then he saw that it was not insane at all. It was a device to produce exactly what seemed about to take place.

John of Monmouth believed he could attack and take Usk and Abergavenny while Richard was too far away to defend his property. Thus, he would bring a sizable army out into the open where Richard's army, hopefully, could destroy it. Then, provided Richard's forces had not been too badly mauled, they would rush northward, join with Llewelyn's men, who would make up, at least in numbers, for those lost fighting Monmouth's army, and attack Shrewsbury. Doubtless, Llewelyn hoped that the king's forces would be so shocked and discouraged from the beating they had taken that they would not come to Shrewsbury's aid.

There was nothing treacherous about the plan, Walter thought—except the devious way it was arranged. It would provide Richard with an opportunity to strike a telling blow, and it would save Llewelyn from any risk at all. Few or none of his forces would be involved in the battle with Monmouth's army. Walter's attention came back in the middle of a sentence.

Llewelyn was saying, ". . . need near-perfect timing. You must take your men out within a day or two of when Monmouth is ready to move. You cannot lie too long in ambush, for there is too much chance Monmouth's patrols will happen upon some sign that would warn him."

"Yes, indeed," Richard agreed cheerfully, "but that should be possible with Simon's men on the watch. I suppose I may count on them?"

"Of course," Simon said.

Llewelyn nodded, but he was frowning. "I do not think it would be helpful, however, to offer you more than a few hundred archers. My men, as you know, are ill-prepared to fight a standing battle. At the moment of surprise the archers would be of use to you, but the common men-at-arms would be cut down like chaff. Worse yet, they would likely run away and thus do you more harm than good."

Richard accepted that with a curt yes. He was not much concerned, Walter could see, with what help Llewelyn would give. He was too satisfied, also, with the result of John of Monmouth's knowledge or guess about his plans to question the cause. To Walter it almost seemed as if Llewelyn could lead Richard to dance to any piping he chose. Involuntarily, Walter shuddered. Simon put out his hand and drew him nearer the fire. The movement caused both Richard and Llewelyn to look at the pair.

"By God's teeth," Richard exclaimed, "I had forgot that you two have ridden nearly sixty miles today. Go to bed, both of you. You have heard the meat of the matter already."

"In fact," Llewelyn said, smiling, "I think they have heard all of the matter. There is little more we can do tonight. My lord of Pembroke, we will do ourselves more good in bed than devising plans on no basis but expectation."

Walter hesitated a bare heartbeat, then bowed and moved toward the door. Simon was already in the outer chamber. There was no doubt in Walter's mind that when he was gone Llewelyn would find some pretext to keep the earl, and plans would go forward. Walter was not offended. There was neither animosity nor contempt behind Llewelyn's action. It was natural for that devious man to trust no one he could not control.

There was nothing he could do about it, Walter realized. Nonetheless he quickened his step, wanting to catch up with Simon and discuss the matter with him. Simon was faithful to his lord, who was also his father-by-marriage, and he loved Llewelyn, too, but he would be willing to speak his mind to Walter. It was not only a matter of trust, although Simon did trust Walter. Simon was amused by Llewelyn's devices. He was, Walter thought, growing more and more Welsh.

CHAPTER 16

Despite Walter's rapid pace, Simon was nowhere to be seen when Walter came from Prince Llewelyn's chambers. At first Walter suffered a sickening sinking of the heart as the suspicion crossed his mind that Simon was deliberately avoiding him. The next instant he had to struggle to hold back a guffaw. How stupid he was! If Sybelle were waiting in his bed, Walter thought, as Rhiannon was waiting in Simon's, he would not have lingered, either. Then his impulse to laugh disappeared. He had forgotten to ask whether Sybelle was still in Builth.

One thing was sure, he could not go back and ask now. Llewelyn would never believe he intended, if she were gone, to borrow a horse and ride out again in the hopes of getting to Clyro before the family left in the morning. The prince would think such a question was merely an excuse to come back and catch another portion of the discussion or simply to see whether Richard was still with him.

Walter stood irresolute, suddenly aware of how tired he was and that his knee was aching unmercifully. He wanted to go to bed, but he could not bear the thought of not seeing Sybelle, even for a few moments, to say farewell.

Still, it was ridiculous to ride all the way to Clyro only to discover that Sybelle had obtained permission to remain with Simon and Rhiannon. Rhiannon. Rhiannon would know. Walter made half a turn in the direction of the nuptial bedchamber, stopped, and blushed. Interrupting Simon and Rhiannon would be worse than intruding on Prince Llewelyn and Richard. Then how the devil was he going to find out whether Sybelle was still in Builth? Whom could he ask at this time of night?

Walter's hand came up suddenly and struck his forehead. *Idiot,* he thought, *you are so tired your brain is in bed even if your body is still standing.* Would Sybelle leave without farewell? Naturally not. If her parents had insisted that she go home with them, she would have left a letter. She might have given it to Lord Llewelyn, who in concentrating on the news had forgotten it, but it was really more likely that she would simply leave it in some obvious place in his room. Walter set off for his chamber as quickly as his knee would allow. Now that he realized it hurt, he was limping again.

At the door of the chamber, he stopped and stiffened. Candles were alight on a small table beside a tall chair, neither of which had been in his room when he left it the day before. Again his heart took a sickening drop. Was Marie lying in wait for him . . . possibly in his bed? There was movement in the shadowy corner of the room where Walter's cot stood. A dreadful impulse to take to his heels and run seized him. He had actually backed a single step from the doorway when a pang in his knee warned him he could not run.

Walter's halting half step brought the shadowy figure swiftly forward with hands outstretched, crying softly, "My lord, let me help you."

The voice brought everything instantly into place. Now Walter recognized the chair and table as those he had seen in Lord Geoffrey's chamber. Beyond that, he knew quite well that Marie was not one to give up her furniture to another's comfort.

"My God, Sybelle," he said, "have you been waiting here for me all night?"

She laughed softly. "No, of course not. How could I know you would come tonight? I now sleep in the chamber that adjoins Rhiannon's, so I heard when word was brought to her that Simon had returned. Then I came here to be sure your chamber was readied for you."

The light of the candles was behind and to the right of her now. At this hour of the night, she wore only a bedrobe. The voluminous garment concealed her figure; her hair, not confined by a headdress, glowed like molten bronze, and the edge of her cheek and the tips of her nose and chin were highlighted. Walter drew in a long breath, realizing that his passage with Marie the day before had done not the slightest good. It was not relief he needed; it was Sybelle. He knew she was not immune to desire, either. Why had she come to his room? Was it an invitation to slake both their thirsts?

Walter did not take Sybelle's hands but came forward into the room. As he drew level with her, she turned and the candlelight fell more fully on her face. He felt ashamed of the questions that had crossed his mind. The golden eyes were faintly anxious; one hand was still slightly raised to catch him should he stumble—but there was not the smallest sign of passion in Sybelle's expression. She had come, just as she said, to be sure his comfort had been provided for. Yet he was certain that if he took her in his arms she would take fire at once.

Their eyes met, and it was immediately apparent to Walter that he would not have to go so far as to touch her. "No," he said softly, backing away a step. "Your parents left you here believing in my good faith."

Sybelle dropped her eyes and bent her head. It was a charming gesture that Walter took to be a mark of gentle embarrassment. And he was half-right, in that Sybelle had been surprised by the surge of eagerness that rose in her in response to the hunger in his eyes. She had not expected to react quite that way to so subtle a stimulus. Walter's unspoken passion had always excited her, but in a formless, general way that quickened her breathing and made her feel as if her skin was extraordinarily sensitive. This was different; it was a clear, directed desire. Something had changed in her, she realized, since they had so nearly come to coupling in the empty chamber.

However, it was not embarrassment that made her look away but amusement, which she did not wish to explain. It was barely possible that her father trusted to her virtue and Walter's self-restraint; however, her mother and grandmother were not so high-minded. Lady Alinor had said dryly, "It would be best to keep your maidenhead for your wedding night if you can, but do not be such fools as your mother and father were and drive yourself and Walter to distraction over the matter. Walter can do for you as my Simon did for me, and no one the wiser." And while Joanna had frowned, she had not contradicted her mother. Walter, Sybelle thought, would be shocked, and in any case, although he might not realize it, he was too tired for such games this night.

There was no sense in disillusioning Walter about the character of the senior lady of Roselynde too soon. "Yes, of course," Sybelle said softly in reply to his remark about her parents. "But William and Ian are gone and all the servants asleep. It cannot be easy for you to take off your clothes with only one hand. I will only help you undress and then go away."

Walter made an inarticulate sound of protest, and Sybelle looked up and laughed.

"Come," she urged, "you will not force me, I know, and I promise to resist."

Walter had to laugh, too. He was very tired, and the momentary urgency he had felt drained quickly away. Moreover, now that he thought of it, he welcomed the notion that he would not need to struggle with ties and laces or, alternatively, sleep in clothing that was clammy and stank with the sweat of his long ride.

"Very well," he agreed, "but only if you promise to resist *fiercely*."

"If I resist fiercely," Sybelle remarked as she unbuckled his cloak and laid it on the traveling basket serving as Walter's clothes chest, "you will fall flat on your face. Sit down on the stool while I get your tunic and shirt off. Your bedrobe is warmed. You can wear that while I look at your knee. I saw you were limping. Did you hurt it again?"

"No. It just aches from the long ride. There is no need to do anything. A night's rest will put it right."

Sybelle did not argue. Walter was probably right, and even if the knee needed attention, it could come to no further harm while he was sleeping. She undid his belt, unlaced his tunic and drew it off, then his shirt, swiftly covering his bare body with the bedrobe. It was fortunate, she thought, that she was behind him and he could not see her face. It had taken all her resolution not to run her hands through the curly red-brown hair that covered him. Apparently it was not necessary for Walter to do or say anything to spark her desire.

"I do declare," Sybelle said hastily, trying to divert herself as she came around in front of him and knelt down to undo his crossgarters and shoes, "that Lady Pembroke and her sister are the silliest women I have ever come across in my life."

"What?" Walter said, his voice constricted. "Why should you say such a thing?"

Sybelle did not lift her head. She was afraid to look into Walter's face. The odd sound in his voice seemed a warning that what she was doing had wakened his passion again. She remembered how violently he had reacted when she had offered to remove his chausses the first time, how he had said she would not have seen a man in *this* condition before. It was true. She had never seen an aroused male member. She recalled, too, the hard bulge along Walter's thigh when they had kissed. Her hands trembled on the laces of his shoes.

"Because now that nearly all the guests are gone," Sybelle gabbled, saying something, anything, to divert them from what she believed was first in both minds, "the only ladies are Lady Pembroke, Lady Marie, Rhiannon, and myself. We spent the day in company, and thus I know they have no conversation beyond dress, and . . . and who is in love with whom that should not be."

Hardly aware of what she was saying in the beginning, Sybelle realized by the end of the sentence that to talk of illicit love affairs could scarcely calm Walter or herself. Her voice trembled over the final words, and she bent lower to peer more closely in the dim light at the laces, which seemed to have taken on a life of their own and were deliberately resisting her efforts to untangle them.

Walter felt frozen with horror. He had forgotten when he left Builth that the situation Sybelle had just described would occur. Once he had shed the worst burden of his guilt, he had put out of his mind the fact that Marie was not behaving like his past mistresses. Then the news that Simon's men had brought had simply wiped the problem of Marie from Walter's mind. The news was far more important to him than the doings of a woman who had thought she wished to play at love and had discovered the game could hurt her.

The mistake Walter made was never to associate Marie with Sybelle at all. Never before had he been fool enough to run triad between a pair of women. Not that he invariably had only one mistress at a time, but never in the same place where they would be forced into close proximity. Walter was a brave man, but he had always considered two women under one roof a form of lunatic bravado. Moreover, in the past the women he had played with had far more to lose than he. It was in their interests to be discreet.

What has that stupid bitch Marie said to you? Walter tried to ask, but his throat and tongue felt paralyzed. All that came out was a wordless croak.

By the time Walter collected himself even enough to try to speak, Sybelle had managed to undo the laces of his shoes and had drawn them off. Walter's rigidity and inability to find words increased the tide of desire that was flooding her in response to what she believed was *his* rising passion. She had promised to resist. Of course, that had only been a jest. Nonetheless, Sybelle knew that Walter *did* wish her to be *virgo intacta* on her wedding night. Thus, though spoken as a jest, her promise to resist was a serious pledge to help him.

There was nothing left to do but run away. Sybelle feared that if Walter laid a hand on her or spoke a pleading word, her resolution might crumble. Both of them would regret bitterly what had happened . . . or, at least, Walter would. Sybelle had her grandmother's cynical words to comfort her, but Walter would blame himself—and perhaps her, also.

She rose suddenly to her feet, keeping her eyes averted from his face, and said, "Wine and cake are on the table beside the chair. It is very late, my lord. I believe you will be able to manage the rest of your undressing, so I will away to my bed."

The last few words were a mistake. Sybelle had meant to say she wished to sleep, but that other phrase had leapt out of her mouth. Her voice broke, and she fled incontinently before her treacherous body or tongue betrayed her even more flagrantly.

Her departure was so sudden and Walter still so frozen in a milling turmoil of doubt and regret, that he just sat staring like the image of a man at the door through which she had passed. By the time he gathered his wits, he knew it was too late to do anything that night. He realized that Marie could not have betrayed their coupling outright. All the ladies had been together. Even if Marie did not mind her sister knowing what she had done, she certainly would not openly expose her fornication to Rhiannon. Moreover, Sybelle's manner indicated doubt and distress rather than outrage.

Perhaps that was owing to the sweetness of her disposition? Amid his anguish, Walter's lips twitched toward a smile. Sybelle was not *that* sweet. He had seen her temper when her property was threatened. No, nor would any woman who cared for a man be sweet enough to ignore his starting an affair with a lady of breeding the very day he had made contract for marriage. Sweat started out all over Walter's body when he realized what he had done. At the time he had not thought about it that way, had not considered how it would appear if it should ever come to Sybelle's ears. All he had been aware of was his dire need for a woman, any woman.

Why, oh, why had he not sought out a maidservant or a whore? Sybelle would have understood that. She might not have liked it, but she would have understood. He was a man, and he *had* to relieve his body. But it was useless to waste time in vain regrets. What he must decide, and at once, was what to do now. Not, thank God, this moment, Walter thought, nearly ready to weep between weariness and worry. He would not need to do anything until the morning. As if deliberately to add to his torment, his shoulder, which had troubled him not at all for two days, began to ache.

Bed, Walter thought. But his bed, while it certainly increased his physical comfort, simultaneously increased his mental anguish. He found, when he had managed to get to his feet, stagger over to it, and crawl in under the blankets, that he did not need to endure the usual few minutes of shivering misery until his body warmed the sheets. The cot was already warmed, and there were hot stones wrapped in cloth against which to rest his cold feet. That was what Sybelle had been doing when he first saw her.

Walter ground his teeth. To lose the tender care, the loving consideration that made Sybelle leave her own bed to warm his . . . And then it came to him that Sybelle's attentions had been offered *after* she had heard what Marie had to say. That meant either that Marie had been sufficiently vague so that Sybelle was disturbed without certainty or that Sybelle did not wish to believe Marie's hints but that they were broad and convincing enough to breed doubt in her mind. But which? What he said and did must be adjusted specially to each case.

Then Walter realized whichever case was true, Sybelle was on his side. Perhaps she doubted, but she wanted to believe in him. Shadows flickered on the ceiling from the unsnuffed candles. Walter became aware of them and thought he should really get up and put them out. But he was warm now, and the sharp aches in knee and shoulder had faded to a dull discomfort that was also ebbing. He lay quietly, hugging to himself the knowledge that Sybelle wanted to believe in him, and, warmed and comforted, he slipped asleep.

There was one consideration that had not occurred to Walter but that was of great importance: Sybelle believed in herself. In fact, the hints Marie had been giving were broad enough to make Rhiannon frown but passed right over Sybelle's head. Not that Sybelle failed to understand; however, by the time Marie found what she thought was a place in the conversation where her hints would really pierce Sybelle to the heart, Sybelle had decided that Marie was not only silly but a deliberate and spiteful troublemaker.

She had reason and opportunity to come to this conclusion because she had discovered that Marie mistakenly believed she had a right to a grudge against Walter. This came about through Rhiannon's efforts to keep Sybelle and Marie apart. During one of the times Rhiannon managed to draw Marie away, Gervase told Sybelle the sad story of Marie's dower lands and how Walter had rejected her after showing her particular favor when Richard refused an adequate dower. She coupled this information with the spoken assumption that Lord Geoffrey would never be so ungenerous, even if his circumstances were straitened by a war, leaving the clear implication that Walter had offered for Sybelle only for her dowry. Naturally, Gervase tried to cover the spitefulness of such a revelation with the suggestion that she made it only to warn Sybelle of her future husband's cupidity so that she could take steps to protect herself.

Unfortunately for Gervase, Sybelle knew that Walter had, more than once, offered to take her with no dowry at all and provide for her out of his own lands by assigning one of his properties to her. Moreover, he had agreed without argument that the property and money which would come with her should remain in her control. Thus, Sybelle was convinced more firmly than ever that Walter desired her for herself alone. Nor was she in the least angry with Gervase, who, she assumed, had been misled by Marie's delusion that Walter was enamored of her.

For Marie, Sybelle felt a mixture of distaste and pity that insulated her completely from any hints, no matter how broad, that Walter was Marie's lover. Marie's manner when she uttered her suggestive little stabs was so spiteful under her simperings that Sybelle dismissed what she said without a qualm of doubt as a desire to make trouble. What kept Sybelle awake for some time after Walter was peacefully asleep was not jealousy but her concern over their mutual desire.

Her urgent physical reaction slowly dissipated, but the memory of it persisted. It seemed plain to Sybelle that something would have to be done, and the simplest and most logical solution to the problem to her mind was to persuade Walter to return to England and marry her out of hand. Although she had no objection to Walter's political association with Richard, she reasoned that Walter could be little use to the earl while his sole support for the rebel cause was his own small troop from Goldcliff.

Would it not be better for Richard, as well as herself and Walter, Sybelle reasoned, if they married and Walter devoted the next few weeks or months to taking hold of his property? Then, if the king had not yet come to terms with Richard, Walter could bring more men and money to strengthen the earl's cause. Of course, Sybelle was not being perfectly honest. She had great faith in her father's wisdom and political foresight. Papa had said that he expected the war to be over soon, perhaps in a matter of weeks. Sybelle did not admit to herself that she expected a truce or even a peace long before Walter had settled his personal affairs and that half her urgency to marry at once was based on her desire to keep Walter out of any further fighting.

She was sufficiently contented with her decision to relax and sleep and to wake in the morning still contented and determined to take the first step toward implementing that decision at once. The first step would be easy, she thought as she washed quickly and sketchily in the cold and pulled on her riding dress. Papa had said Walter intended to summon the castellan of Knight's Tower to come to Clyro. He could do that from Clyro as well as from Builth. Once he was away from all the talk and planning for the war and was already thinking in terms of his own property, it would be easier to divert his mind to concentrate on that. Then there would be chances enough to show him that he would be more useful to Richard as the master of Foy, Barbury, and Thornbury in addition to Goldcliff and Knight's Tower.

Walter woke almost as peacefully and contentedly as Sybelle. Sometime during the night, although he did not recall dreaming about it, he had resolved his problem. Had he been innocent of whatever Marie told Sybelle, he reasoned, he would not have reacted to Sybelle's unstated doubts. He might have been slightly puzzled by the abrupt way she left his room, but that was not important enough to mention the day after. Thus, all he had to do was ignore the whole situation—and get Sybelle away from Builth as soon as possible, that very day if he could manage it.

A single doubt flashed through Walter's mind because the solution seemed so simple and painless. Should he instead tell Sybelle the truth? He recalled her shaking hands and trembling voice and recoiled from the idea of admitting that he had made contract for her, come near to coupling with her, and rushed off to bed another woman. From a man's point of view, the sequence of events was perfectly logical, but it was too much to hope that a young girl would not be hurt. Better never to mention the incident and forget it himself, if he could. The chances were that Richard would rid himself of his wife and sister-by-marriage as soon as he left Builth so that Sybelle and Marie would not meet again in the near future.

That thought started a new worry. Would Richard expect him to take the ladies back to Pembroke? Walter wondered. He shuddered at the thought and nearly leapt out of bed in his haste to go to Richard and tell him he intended to leave for Clyro that very day to begin his attempt to gain control of Knight's Tower.

A call brought a servant to his aid to help him dress, after which he asked at the door of Richard's apartment for him and was admitted at once to the antechamber, where the earl, still tousled and in a bedrobe, listened to his request for leave and his reason for it.

"Yes, go," Richard said, nodding with enthusiasm. "It will serve my purpose very well to have a strong point in that region to which we may retreat in case of need. I do not foresee that need, but a safe haven is never amiss. Lady Fortune's wheel can spin at the most unexpected times."

Since Richard's expression was as cheerful as possible, considering the peeling scabs on his face, Walter recognized the words as a propitiation to those evil forces that seemed to gather around the overconfident rather than a result of any tenuous fears as to the success of the enterprise. He made some reply and started to bow before saying farewell.

"Wait," Richard said. "Come to me—I will be either in

Abergavenny or in Usk—when you know the result of your invitation to this man. If he will not obey you, we must decide how to bring him to heel with the least damage to your property."

"You are too good, my lord," Walter said, startled. "I would welcome your advice, but I hope you do not intend to put aside more important matters to settle my small affairs. I know well that even allies' lands may come to hurt in the raging tides of war. If it is necessary to ravage the lands of Knight's Tower because of the castellan's stubbornness, I will not hold you to blame for that."

Richard laughed, a growling chuckle that he did not permit to pull at his lips. "I am considering my affairs far more than yours," he admitted. "If, God forbid, we have the worse in our attack on Shrewsbury, Llewelyn's men can run back into the hills from which they came, no long distance away. But my men are not the kind who can disappear into a wood, and I have no safe place nearer than Clifford, which is thirty or more miles south of Knight's Tower. Besides, as Knight's Tower is not known as a stronghold friendly to me, to go there might gain us time enough to regroup, since it is so much closer to Llewelyn's lands than is Clifford. And, if we must make a stand there, I do not want the lands burnt over beforehand."

"Very well, my lord," Walter replied, but a frown creased his brow.

Richard, always oversensitive about his rebel state and about drawing others into his trouble, said quickly, "If you are uncertain over this, we will not use the place."

Walter naturally connected Richard's statement with his own doubt and therefore took no offense at it. "It will be easy enough if Sir Heribert *refuses* to obey me," he said. "We can put him out and leave a safe deputy in charge. But, my lord, what if he comes to Clyro full of sweet words, allows us to stay while we are in our full strength, and then closes the gates to us when we are in need?"

Richard realized he had misunderstood Walter, but any regret he felt for the momentary lack of trust was pushed out by an astonishment so strong that it showed even on his battered features. "Do you know Heribert to be so treacherous a dog?" he asked.

"That is my trouble," Walter admitted. "I do *not* know it. I have never met him or spoken to him in my life. For all I know, he may be a worthy man. But Sir Heribert was chosen castellan by my brother Henry. You knew Henry. Can you see why I doubt?''

Since the earl was not one to speak ill of the dead, he did not answer the question directly. He was sure anyway that Walter's brother was in hell or purgatory and needed no further castigation, but did understand what was troubling Walter. ''If the man comes, you must keep him with you.''

''That is just what Lord Geoffrey advised,'' Walter acknowledged, ''and what I planned also, but if I am to come to you . . .''

''Bring him along,'' Richard suggested, then stopped speaking suddenly as he saw the problem.

If Walter brought Heribert along, the castellan could complain to the king that Walter was forcing him into rebel company. In addition to causing Walter's outlawry, which, Richard acknowledged, would probably not trouble Walter at all, but would trouble *him,* King Henry was almost certain to bestow the keep as a direct vassalage on Sir Heribert. The condition of outlawry might be easily reversed by a royal proclamation, but the vassalage could not be dealt with that way. Even if the king returned Knight's Tower to Walter's overlordship, which he would be reluctant to do, Sir Heribert, who had betrayed Walter in the first place, would be unwilling to accept the situation as, most naturally, Walter would not be overjoyed to have such a vassal.

Richard did not go on to detail the further complications to himself. He hastily amended his invitation with ''No, you had better not bring him. Perhaps it would not be safe.'' He stopped there, cleverly implying that Heribert might be a danger to him or to the rebel cause rather than to Walter's future. ''If Heribert comes,'' he went on, ''come back alone—it is not so far from Clyro to Abergavenny or Usk—and tell me what you have decided about the man. Then together we can think whether you should send him back to Knight's Tower alone or go with him and wait there for us.''

''But my shoulder will be healed by then,'' Walter protested. ''Already it gives me little trouble.''

''We will see,'' Richard temporized. ''I am uncertain of my own moves as yet, except that I, too, intend to leave Builth no later than tomorrow. Prince Llewelyn goes today, I think. Simon is coming with me to be near his men and interpret the news they gather.'' He hesitated, then went on: ''But if you desire to go today, will you be able to take Lady Sybelle with you? Will she have time to pack? She is welcome to come with me and her uncle, if you wish.''

Walter did not blanch although he felt appalled. He had not thought of Sybelle's need to have her possessions packed. ''She must come,'' he said. Clyro is, as you heard at our sealing of the contract, her keep. If she cannot be ready, I must wait a day, but . . . If you will give me leave, my lord, I will send word to her at once and see what she says.''

CHAPTER 17

Richard dismissed Walter almost at once, and Walter hurried away, marshaling not only reasons why he and Sybelle must leave in such haste but various ways of implying, without actually saying, that he was innocent of Marie's accusations and that rushing off to Clyro had no connection with her. To his surprise and relief, Walter found that none of the difficulties he feared arose. When Sybelle had come swiftly to him in response to his summons, she had smiled at him sunnily with no shadow in face or manner. Walter concealed a sigh of relief and dismissed the question of Marie from his mind. And when he told her he wished to leave for Clyro that day, she merely asked what time, frowned in thought, not in anger, and said she would be ready then or soon after.

"And for how many men must there be food on the road?" she asked. "The cart with the baggage will have to follow more slowly. Will you assign men to guard it, my lord? Or should I so direct those Papa left for me? There are only ten, but he thought I would not need more since I am in your care."

Instead of answering, Walter said, "I love you."

Sybelle put out her hand to him. What she had been told all her life was true: If she shouldered without fuss her portion of any task her husband had, asking only such questions as were necessary to good performance of her share of the business, this would bind her man closer than any lamenting over the difficulties so that he would know how hard she labored for him. It was irrelevant that her ready response was as much owing to the fact that Walter's order to leave corresponded exactly with her own desire to do so as to her mother's and grandmother's lectures. What was important was that she had experienced a practical example of their teaching.

"Then perhaps I can leave out two portions," Sybelle

teased gently, although her eyes were full of tenderness, "since it is said those in love need no other sustenance. But the men, my lord, are not in our happy condition and must eat."

"And I will continue to love you even if you are idiot enough to believe that people in love do not get hungry," Walter said, grinning. "I am starving right now. However, if I cannot seduce you into sweet talk . . . I do not believe I will take my whole troop. Why should Sir Roland have to feed them? And Richard may have use for the men if the trap he hopes to set is sprung before I return to him. Ten of my men with us and five of yours, and the same with the baggage. All your men, I presume, know the way to Clyro and can serve as guides?"

Sybelle nodded her answer to that question and said lightly that Walter should go attend to his starving condition. There was no sign in her face or voice that she had noticed his remark about the trap Richard was setting and that he expected to return to the earl—doubtless before the trap was set, if possible. It had been said very casually, not as if Walter felt the words to be of importance, but Sybelle had developed a great respect for her betrothed's cleverness. She did not put it beyond him to have arranged this hasty departure just to slip in those words.

As she went about her business, Sybelle considered this problem and how to counter it. If Walter had given his word to return to Richard, she knew she would be unable to stop him. However, if this were some idea of his own . . . Her father had told her that the earl would not be ill pleased if Walter went about his own business. Thus, she would not be causing any enmity between her betrothed and his most powerful neighbor if she induced Walter to remain in Clyro somewhat longer than he intended. With luck, Richard's trap would have already snapped closed and then she could consider the next step.

Sybelle was ready to leave about an hour after Prime. The baggage wain was not completely packed, but their clothing was traveling with them by packhorse and Clyro was furnished, so the time of arrival of the wain was of no importance. To Sybelle's surprise, she had considerable trouble finding Walter. She had expected him to be in the hall, but only Gervase and Marie were there, idling by the fire, and they said they had not seen him. With considerable warmth, they invited Sybelle to wait for him with them, insisted on her company, in fact, but she excused herself with equal determination despite the fury that showed for an unguarded moment on Marie's face.

The next idea that occurred to Sybelle was that Walter would be with Richard, but inquiry proved that also wrong. Then she realized that he must be either in the stable, making sure of the cattle to draw the wain and seeing that their horses were ready, or giving instructions to the men-at-arms. But Tostig, her father's master-at-arms who had been left with her to ensure a wise head for her protection, had not seen Walter, either. Puzzled, she went on to the stable. It was most reasonable that Walter should give orders to have the horses and oxen ready, but how could that take three or four hours?

At first Sybelle thought he was not in the stable, either. The grooms were Welsh and did not speak French; therefore, she tried asking for Walter by saying his name, speaking more loudly than normal in an unconscious effort to promote understanding by raising her voice. This did not have the intended effect, of course, but Walter himself heard her and came out from among the horses.

"I came to tell you that all is ready," Sybelle said, after exclaiming about how he had apparently appeared from nowhere. "I am sorry I am later than I said, but Lady Pembroke and her sister delayed me a little, and then I was so foolish as not to realize you would be here. It must be nearly time for dinner now. Shall we stay and eat, my lord? Since we do not intend to wait for the baggage wain, it can take little more than three hours to ride to Clyro. Even if we leave as much as an hour after Sext, we will still come there in daylight."

Under other circumstances, Sybelle's first expectation would have been correct; that is, she would have found Walter pacing the hall and grumbling about the inefficiency of women that made them so slow over a small matter like retrieving and packing all the items their men had strewn over their chamber, their friends' chambers, the hall, and any other place in the keep they had happened to be. However, Walter had narrowly escaped being caught by Marie.

After he had spoken to Sybelle, Walter had gone to Mass and then to his room to say over his prayers of penance. Coming down to the hall to break his fast at last, he had been so late that Marie and her sister were already at the table. By good fortune, he had seen Marie a split second before she had seen him, so he was already in the doorway on his way out when she called. This permitted Walter to pretend he had not heard. He did not wish to hurt Marie more than he had already hurt her.

Since Sybelle seemed to have put aside whatever had raised doubts in her, Walter's anger at Marie had evaporated. He believed the cause of her spiteful hinting was her own fear that she had soiled herself, but he knew no way to erase that feeling except to devote himself to her, which was impossible. At this moment, however, Walter believed that anything he said or did would be hurtful, unless he expressed deep grief at leaving her and undying affection, which would be crueler in the end. Thus, both for Marie's sake and for Sybelle's—for Sybelle was probably the one at whom Marie would lash out—Walter intended to avoid Marie.

Walter's flight from Marie had prevented him from breaking his fast, and he, too, would have preferred to stay and eat. But Sybelle's mention of Gervase and Marie had reminded him that it was impossible to do so. He blenched slightly at the thought of all of them sitting together at the high table now that they were the only gentlefolk remaining at Builth. Nonetheless, he was hungry and annoyed at being unable to satisfy his appetite on tasteful dishes, sitting in comfort at a table rather than eating travel rations on the road.

"No, we will not stay to eat," he said with slightly more emphasis than necessary. "I will have our horses saddled and have the pack animals brought out. While that is being done, I will speak to the men-at-arms. Do you order your servants to carry out whatever you wish to take with us, and do not linger in the hall chatting with this one and that."

The sharp protest that Sybelle had been about to make was swallowed unspoken as the significance of Walter's final phrase connected with Marie's early predilection for him, with the hints of intimacy she had given the past two days, with his expression of distaste when she mentioned being detained by Gervase and Marie, with his haste to be gone, with his unwillingness to sit down to dinner among those who remained in Builth, with his absence from the hall, with the length of time spent in the stable during which nothing seemed to have been accomplished. Once all these facts came together in Sybelle's mind, she realized that Walter was trying to avoid Marie and also to keep her apart from Marie. With that realization came another: Almost certainly Marie's hints were true; she had been Walter's mistress.

Without a word, Sybelle turned away. It was fortunate that her sense of dignity would not permit her to run. The need to control her body and the brief period it took her to walk to the part of the keep in which her chamber lay gave time for her first raging burst of jealousy to ease and for her to change her mind about refusing to go anywhere with Walter. Then there was the need to give orders about carrying the packed baskets down to where the horses would be waiting and to speak a few last words to her mother's maid, Edwina, who had also been left behind for Sybelle's convenience. During this time Sybelle did not permit herself to think consciously of Walter and Marie. Nonetheless, some process inside her must have been picking over the evidence because when she was ready for riding, booted, gloved, cloaked, and hooded for the long, cold journey, she had reached some very soothing conclusions.

First was that it did not seem possible to Sybelle for Walter to have had any relationship with the woman since he had arrived in Builth. Second was that she herself had seen him discourage Marie from the day he had asked her father for her in marriage. Third, Marie's very viciousness the moment Walter was away and unlikely to hear of it was a strong indication that he had probably broken off the affair. Had he still been sniffing after her, Marie would have acted superior and condescending and would have been far more eager to keep the relationship a secret.

These conclusions did not wipe out the jealousy Sybelle felt, but they gave it a new direction. After all, Sybelle had been taught—indeed, she herself had told it to Rhiannon many times before Rhiannon had agreed to marry Simon—that what a man had done before his marriage was not subject to a wife's criticism. A wife's rights began only after the bonding, and it was the wife's business to make herself so interesting that her husband had no cause to look elsewhere for pleasure and entertainment. Had not her mother reminded her that Walter was no callow boy, that he was a man with a man's experience?

Then his look that very morning when he said *I love you* came back to her and the other times when his expression, his tone of voice, a certain touch proclaimed love even while he spoke of business. Sybelle was still jealous, jealous of the fact that Marie had taken a pleasure from Walter's body that she wanted herself, but she knew herself preferred. Sybelle told herself that if she did not act like a fool he would never again think of Marie.

Certainly everything during the ride to Clyro reinforced this conclusion. Guessing that Walter had missed breaking his fast in his desire to avoid Marie, Sybelle proposed an early stop to eat. Before that, Walter had been silent unless she spoke to him and a trifle snappish when he replied. After he had been fed—and Sybelle had seen to it that they were provided with suitably delicate fare; no hard journey bread and salt meat for her when better was available—his mood sweetened. He began to tease her and jest with the men. In fact, Sybelle thought she had never seen him so lighthearted, as if he had cast off an unpleasant burden.

The only doubt raised in Sybelle during the next few days, while they waited for Sir Heribert to respond to the summons to Clyro, was owing to Walter's refusal to be private with her. He would sit with her in the hall for a little while, but soon he would find an excuse to ask Sir Roland or his wife or both to join them. On the third day, toward evening, when Sir Roland had left them in response to a message from the gate guard, Sybelle asked Walter outright if he found her conversation silly or dull.

"Do not be ridiculous," Walter replied. "I am afraid to be alone with you. Even here, where servants come and go, I cannot trust myself to touch you. When we do not have other company, I begin to desire what I cannot have until we are handfast."

Sybelle did not answer him immediately, but when he started to rise she began hastily, "My grandmother said . . ." and then hesitated.

She was torn two ways. To repeat Alinor's cynical remark might be misinterpreted. Even without misinterpretation, to repeat it was a gross violation of maiden modesty. Sybelle was not much concerned with modesty or with the sin of prenuptial coupling, but the freedom to enjoy her body after marriage was one of the prizes she had hoped to use to induce Walter to come to England rather than return to Richard immediately. On the other hand, if Walter grew too frustrated, might he not think back with longing to the days when he could relieve himself at will with his mistress?

At her words, Walter had aborted his rising movements and settled into his chair again, but not with the relaxation that implied long tenancy. When Sybelle did not continue immediately, he cocked his head at an inquisitive angle. One brow rose, and there was a sparkle in his eyes that betrayed his mischievous amusement. Sybelle wondered how much Simon had told Walter about Lady Alinor and then, considering the amusement, felt sure it was far too much. If she tried to substitute a platitude or wise saw for what her grandmother had really said, Walter would laugh in her face.

"She said," Sybelle began defiantly, her voice angry because she could feel color flooding into her face, "that it would be best if I could keep my maidenhead for my wedding night but not to be such a fool as to drive you to distraction over the matter." And suddenly Sybelle saw a fine bypath opening. Her voice lost its defiance, and her complexion returned to normal. "I had rather," she added, "that you eased yourself on me than spend what is mine on some other woman."

Walter had had to set his teeth to keep from laughing when Sybelle reported her grandmother's counsel. He had, indeed, heard tales from Simon that had indicated Lady Alinor was not overafflicted with prudishness or piety. Thus, once Sybelle had begun with *My grandmother said,* Walter had had a fair notion of what was coming. The last sentence, however, had cut off his amusement as if with a knife.

First came a sense of shock at hearing Sybelle use a phrase in reference to herself that was commonly used for whores. Before Walter could make an angry protest, the end of the sentence hit his brain. *What is mine*. Lord Geoffrey had used the words *mine to me,* but the meaning was the same. Walter heard the fierce sense of possession, although Sybelle's voice was soft and undemanding. But Geoffrey had been talking about the land; Sybelle was talking about *him*.

His natural reaction might have been rage. Men possessed women; women did not possess men. However, Sybelle's tone had changed on the last three words, only a little but enough to tell Walter that she did know about Marie. Guilt immediately cooled rage, and Walter's sense of self-preservation sharpened his perception, which was naturally acute, even further. It leapt into his mind that there was neither blame nor recrimination in Sybelle's statement; moreover, there was no implication of sweet, sorrowful forgiveness. She spoke as of something in the dead past, not forgotten, but of no significance for the future.

There were two sides to such an attitude. It was a relief to know that the peccadilloes of the past, if uncovered, would produce no rages or lamentations or pious mouthings. The calm assumption that it would not, could not, happen again was something else entirely. There was not a shadow of threat in Sybelle's remark—and that was more threatening in a sense than an overt warning not to transgress. One did not threaten to prevent something one knew to be impossible.

It was at this moment, before Walter could decide whether he should laugh at Sybelle's naive overconfidence or be terrified by it—he had just remembered Lord Geoffrey saying *If I am in bondage to my wife . . . I have no desire to cast off that bondage*— that Sir Roland came back, leading with him an armed knight of startlingly handsome appearance.

"Sir Heribert," Sir Roland said.

Surprised out of the thoughts that had prevented him from noticing the approach of the pair, Walter got to his feet, only to be more surprised when Sir Heribert dropped to one knee and offered up his sword, saying, "My fealty, my lord."

There was something in the action that reminded Walter of the mummeries of jongleurs, a kind of overdone height of manner. His instinct was to refuse the gesture, but he knew he could not. Besides, he told himself, as he touched Sir Heribert's weapon and uttered the formal words of acceptance, his mood was scarcely agreeable at this moment. Perhaps at another time the offering might have seemed more natural. Certainly Sir Heribert had come as swiftly as possible in answer to his summons. The formula complete, Walter bade his man rise.

By coincidence, Sir Roland and Sir Heribert were of opposite physical types—Sir Roland short and broad, Sir Heribert tall and slender. But they seemed opposites in everything else also. Sir Roland had harsh features, no wise improved by a nose that had been broken and ill set and a scar that puckered one cheek. His eyes were dark and serious, and his smile rare—but when it came it illuminated his whole face. From the first meeting, Walter had been well pleased. There was a rocklike solidity about Sir Roland that bred confidence, and that confidence had been reinforced by the fact that Sir Roland's children ran to him with glad cries and that his wife bore no bruises and did not cringe when he raised his voice.

In contrast, as he rose to his feet and stood again nearly beside Sir Roland, Sir Heribert could have modeled for the statue of an angel. However, the willowy appearance did not imply feebleness, for Sir Heribert had moved down the hall toward them with an easy litheness under his armor that showed he was accustomed to its weight. Blond and blue-eyed, with a fine-cut nose and perfect lips on which smiles came and went fluidly, Sir Heribert's whole appearance should have given unalloyed pleasure. Unreasonably, Walter suppressed a shudder—and then was ashamed, telling himself that his immediate distaste for so handsome a man could only be a result of envy.

"I have brought with me the full tithing of men from Knight's Tower," Sir Heribert said as soon as he was erect, "since I did not know what your summons portended. You are, I have heard, the Earl of Pembroke's man. Do you call me to war in his party?"

A soft trill of laughter came from Sybelle. "My lord has summoned you for a far happier purpose, to tell you that he is to be married."

Either Sir Heribert had truly not noticed Sybelle because his attention was fixed upon his new overlord, or he wished to seem not to have seen her so that he could now produce an aspect of first surprise and then marveling. This, too, Walter found distastefully redolent of the acting of jongleurs, but Sybelle smiled and lowered her eyes, seemingly pleased with the fulsome compliments. Next Sir Heribert turned to Walter to congratulate him on the capture of a prize of such beauty. Walter had to unclamp his set jaw to respond with civility and to introduce Sybelle, who held out her hand to be kissed with such eagerness that Walter's jaw jammed shut again.

This did not matter for the moment because Sybelle began to prattle and ask questions about Knight's Tower and Sir Heribert's journey. Walter was well aware that his looks were nothing out of the ordinary, and it sprang uncomfortably into his mind that the usual reason for a woman to be indifferent to her man's infidelity was that she herself did not care for him. The sensation this generated in him was so unpleasant that he forced himself to look away from Sybelle's absorbed attention to Sir Heribert's reply to a question. His eyes fell upon Sir Roland's face, which bore an expression of total astonishment.

Instantly, everything fell into place. It was plain that Sir Roland had never seen Sybelle behave in such a fashion. Moreover, Walter knew that he had expressed his doubts of Sir Heribert's trustworthiness to her. Her manner and her reply to Heribert's initial question, Walter realized, were masterpieces. It was just the kind of answer one would expect from a woman, placing personal matters in advance of anything else. Not a word of it was a lie—Walter would certainly be quick to announce to his vassals his imminent marriage to a woman of powerful family. Nor did her reply commit Walter or deny to Walter any action.

In command of himself again, Walter was about to ask Sir Heribert to sit down when he heard Sybelle cry, "So far? Alas, I did not realize. How unkind I have been, keeping you talking when you must be very tired. Sir Roland, do summon your lady to attend to Sir Heribert's needs, and bid her, I beg you, have a full supper prepared for us, with hot pasties and brawn if it can be readied. Sir Heribert must have missed his dinner in his loyal haste, and he will be the better for a good meal after donning a clean, warmed gown."

Without a word, Sir Roland bowed ceremoniously and turned away. That would have worried Walter, since a ceremonious relationship was not characteristic between vassal and lord in Roselynde, but he saw that comprehension rather than anger had replaced the astonishment in Sir Roland's face. Walter used Sir Roland's movement as an excuse to step back, thank Sir Heribert in more collected terms for his prompt answer to the summons, and invite the man to sit down while matters were arranged for his comfort.

Walter gestured Heribert to a chair with its high back to the hall, the one in which he himself had been sitting. In a sense it was the seat of honor and thus fitting for a guest. It faced the fire directly, getting the best and most even heat, and the high back shielded the sitter somewhat from the noise and drafts of the hall. Of course, it also prevented anyone sitting in it from seeing what was going on.

If Sir Heribert felt fear or suspicion, it did not show. Nor did he have much time to worry because he had hardly settled when Lady Ann came hurrying forward with two of the prettiest maidservants in the keep at her heels. Sir Heribert was led away in a stream of apologies for any deficiencies in his welcome that might have been caused by haste.

After his departure there was a little silence. Walter was trying to sort out his impressions; Sybelle sat at ease, but her eyes were on the comings and goings in the hall. There were several faces she did not know among the servants now, passing to and fro, some carrying items of baggage, some seeming to look about for something dropped or mislaid and those, oddly, often passed close to where she and Walter sat.

Perhaps great ladies did not, in general, know the faces of the serfs who did personal service in their subsidiary keeps, but that was not in the Roselynde tradition. From childhood, Sybelle had been trained to know her people, not only the castellans and their families but the servants and, to the best of her ability, those on the land. Since no new servants had been presented to Sybelle, it seemed clear enough that these were Heribert's people. Perhaps their movements were innocent, but it would be unwise for Heribert's servants to hear anything that could imply Walter did not trust him.

As Sybelle reached this conclusion, Walter said, "What do you think—"

"Oh, I think it most charming, so thoughtful, of Sir Heribert to desire to meet me," Sybelle interrupted, in an unnaturally high-pitched voice. "Do you know if he is married? If so, I am sorry he did not bring his lady to meet me also."

Walter blinked once, then realized that although Sybelle's head was turned toward him her eyes were not. She was looking sidelong out into the hall. Walter did not need to be hit on the head to absorb a warning. Plainly Sybelle had noticed something he had not.

"I am ashamed to say," Walter remarked smoothly, "that I do not know. My brother and I were not on good terms, and I have never met Sir Heribert before."

Sybelle replied to that and then made some inconsequential remark about whether they could provide some entertainment, since they now had a guest. "For I will not be able to bear it," she said pointedly, "if all you do is talk about the war. You know, Walter, that you can take no part in it for some weeks longer. Please, do promise me that, at least for tonight, you will not discuss the Earl of Pembroke's quarrel with the king."

Since this was scarcely the attitude Sybelle had displayed up until this moment, Walter recognized another warning. He was a trifle annoyed that Sybelle should think he needed such a reminder until he realized that Sir Roland had reentered the hall and was coming toward them. He nodded, which might have been taken as acquiescence to her request, as Sybelle's quick smile might only have implied pleasure in his agreement; however, what the nod and smile had communicated was that Walter understood the need and intended to warn Sir Roland.

"I think," Walter said to the castellan before he could speak, "that Lady Sybelle has been sore afflicted by our talk of the war and too polite to complain of it." He smiled as he spoke, implying a mild jest. "She has just drawn a promise from me that we must entertain our guest in ways other than with talk of Pembroke and the king."

Sir Roland laughed aloud. His amusement was at the thought of Sybelle being too polite—at least, in the sole presence of her castellan and her betrothed—to say anything she thought. However, his eyes were wary even as he laughed. He was a clever man and had already put together Sir Walter's original distrust of Sir Heribert with that gentleman's almost too-great eagerness to declare fealty, and had come up with a smell of bad fish.

"I do not blame her," he said. "I fear our conversation has been somewhat lacking in new matter. Perhaps Sir Heribert will have news for us."

Walter understood that Sir Roland had taken the cue. Heribert was to be encouraged to do the talking. He said no more, and Sir Roland went on to tell him how he had arranged the quartering of Heribert's men, but Walter listened with only half an ear, nodding when his approval seemed necessary. He was really thinking with warm pleasure of the rapport that existed between Sybelle and himself.

Walter liked women in general, except the few who were deliberately vicious. Those who were silly he had always found amusing; the gentle and pious gave him a sensation of security, of rightness in the world, for gentleness and piety were the prerogatives of women, even if it made them somewhat dull; the lustful he enjoyed without much thought; but best of all he liked the clever ones who could play a rousing game of chess, spar with words, and talk sense. Sybelle had attracted him by her beauty, but his attention had been fixed by her intelligence. Now there was a ripening. He saw her intelligence wedded to his interests and directed to the advancement of his purposes.

Sybelle asked again about entertainment for Sir Heribert, and Sir Roland replied. Walter was content to leave the decision to them. He wondered, now that he had seen so clear an instance of Sybelle's quick perception and devoted attention to his welfare, whether there might be more sense than he had originally thought to one suggestion she had made repeatedly. She insisted that he would be of more value to Richard's cause as the powerful holder of five considerable estates than as a single knight with his troop.

Despite the innocent look and unfaltering voice, Walter had had grave doubts as to the genuineness of the sincerity Sybelle displayed. Love her as he did, Walter suspected that Sybelle was more interested than she would admit in removing him from the rebel cause. Not that he suspected her of favoring the king's purpose. The passion with which she insisted upon the right of landholders to rule their estates as *they* wished was not counterfeit. Plainly Sybelle liked the idea of an absolute ruler no more than he did. However, Sybelle was perfectly willing for others, already engaged in that battle, to continue to fight it without assistance from her betrothed, and Walter's personal loyalty to Richard weighed far less in her scales than other topics.

One was the notion that it was an abomination that land belonging to Walter should remain for one minute longer than absolutely necessary in anyone else's power—and Sybelle made not the faintest effort to conceal this opinion. Walter would have been horrified at his future wife's greed if it had not been apparent that she was not thinking primarily of lost profit. In fact, she had said very seriously, with a worried frown that amused Walter excessively since it implied that she felt she might have to convince him of the truth of her assertion, that if his brother had been so bad a landlord, it might be necessary to put effort into the land for several years before they could hope to draw on it for men or supplies.

However, there was some strong emotion, besides Sybelle's itch to get her hands on the land, that Walter could not identify clearly. He thought of it as Sybelle's reluctance that his association with Richard embarrass her family. It did not occur to him that his betrothed was fearful for his personal safety; she had implied concern only once, at the tournament, and when Walter thought of it, he considered it half a joke, as his reply to her had been. Thus, he assumed that part of the reason she urged him to attend to his own affairs was to prevent an outlawry within a clan that was known for its fidelity to the royal house. Walter was also concerned over this subject, but he felt his earlier commitment to be paramount.

Now he was beginning to wonder whether, despite her prejudices, Sybelle might be right. Perhaps it would be wise to speak to Richard and ask him directly which path would best forward his purpose. Walter grinned crookedly. Richard was no more to be trusted than Sybelle. He would certainly choose what he thought best for Walter—unless Walter's assistance would really make the difference between success and failure. Nonetheless there was good sense in talking to Richard. Walter found Richard far easier to read than Sybelle.

As he was being made comfortable, Sir Heribert cursed himself for judging one brother by another. His late overlord had been so self-centered that he saw nothing beyond what he wanted to see. It had been very easy to encourage Sir Henry in every vicious form of self-gratification, to push him along a path that was rapidly leading to such excesses that even the most loyal castellan might be forgiven for complaining to the king. And such a complaint, when shown to be justified, could lead a clever man into the king's favor and to wealth and power thereby. From all Heribert had heard, King Henry was just such a fool as the Henry who was his master.

Sir Henry's death had closed that door, but the killing had opened another path even easier and more pleasant. Heribert knew from his late master's sneers and curses that Walter was an adherent to the rebel cause. Every day, Heribert had expected to hear that Walter had been declared an outlaw. Then he would only have to go to the king and declare his own loyalty. From there he could make his way upward.

But the king did not declare Walter outlaw. Sir Heribert assumed that Walter had powerful friends who shielded him from the king's wrath. However, Heribert believed if he could get Walter to order him to join Pembroke, he would have the lever he needed. Then he could go to the king, saying he had been forced to defy his overlord because he would not turn rebel. Thus, he would gain vassalage.

Later, when Sir Heribert joined Sir Walter and Sybelle, he was suitably dressed, neither too finely nor too simply for a castellan meeting his new overlord in a private situation; his manner was now irreproachable. Despite the fact that he obviously wanted to talk about Pembroke's rebellion, he gracefully acceded to Sybelle's stricture against that subject. Instead, he gave them the news they asked for from the north Wales border, although he disclaimed wide knowledge of the situation there with due, but not overgreat, modesty. Moreover, without actually speaking ill of Walter's brother, he deplored the exactions he had been forced to make, admitting that the lands he managed were in bad condition.

After a time, Walter began to feel uncomfortable. He liked Sir Heribert less and less, and this disturbed him because it seemed totally unreasonable. Walter was not averse to trusting his instincts with regard to most men, but he knew himself to have been prejudiced against this one from the beginning. It was unfair, he knew, to dislike Sir Heribert because he had loathed his brother and because the man's face was so clean and fine.

Fortunately, Sybelle did not permit the situation to continue for long. Soon after the evening meal had been served, she chose a pause after Sir Heribert had answered a question and Walter was searching his mind for another to ask that had no offensive connotations.

"My lord," she said, "it is not my place to tell you what to do, but I see by your looks that you are not at ease. You know you have not been well. I think you have pain. Will you not go now to bed? And Sir Heribert must also be tired after his long ride. In the morning we will all be fresh." She smiled sweetly, apologetically. "And in the morning, I will betake myself to my woman's duties so that you may speak to each other of what is first in your hearts."

No one made any protest against this scheme. In fact, Walter and Sir Heribert rose almost simultaneously, each murmuring vague agreement. Lady Ann beckoned the maid who was attending Walter and went herself with Sir Heribert to be sure that anything lacking in the chamber assigned to him had been provided. Sybelle and Sir Roland sat together a little while longer, talking softly, first of estate matters and then, very briefly, of the men who had accompanied Sir Heribert. Then they, too, went to bed.

Hours later a door opened slowly and cautiously, then closed. A shadow moved along the wall, hardly visible in the dim light of the night candles that burned near the banked hearth, the hood of a dark cloak pulled forward to hide any gleam of pale skin. At the door of Walter's chamber, the shadow paused, the hooded head turned outward, looking across the hall. An arm slipped out of the folds of the cloak, pale against the dark fabric, to reach behind the body. The door latched clicked, and the figure slipped inside the smallest possible opening.

CHAPTER 18

Many thoughts had chased each other through Walter's mind as he lay abed, but prime among them was his suspicion of Sir Heribert. As often as he thrust the notion out and tried to concentrate on some idea more fruitful or more soothing, it returned. Finally, sighing at his own foolishness, he rose and sought out a long hunting knife, which he slid beneath the pillow, and he caught one side of the bed curtains under the mattress so that there was a little opening through which he could see. He knew that even if his suspicions were fact, rather than founded on prejudice, Sir Heribert would never dream of attacking him in a place where Heribert was the only stranger. Nonetheless, the knife was a comfort, a symbol of Walter's wariness.

The wariness followed him into sleep, into uneasy dreams that kept him floating near the edge of wakefulness. Thus, he stirred at the first click of the door latch in the antechamber. His hand was beneath the pillow grasping the knife before he was really awake, but as his eyes opened he saw the shadow slide in through the doorway to his bedchamber. It then passed out of the range of the opening in the bed curtains, but Walter knew it was moving forward toward the head of the bed. The bed curtain moved gently as a body came against it. Walter raised the knife.

In the next instant three things happened so fast that it was impossible to say which occurred first. A hand gripped the edge of the bed curtain, Sybelle's voice whispered "Walter," and Walter just barely turned the point of the blade so that it slashed a long cut in the bed curtain rather than piercing Sybelle's breast.

"Walter!" Sybelle exclaimed, although her voice was still little more than a whisper.

"What are you doing here?" he asked furiously, but no louder than she had spoken.

"I had to speak to you," she replied. "I have noticed that Sir Heribert's servants pass to and fro listening when he is not by, and I do not think we will be able to be private at any other time without notice being taken of it."

He did not answer immediately, waiting for the passing of a wave of dizziness and nausea, a reaction to what he had almost done because of his baseless suspicion. With it also passed his fury at Sybelle. If he had not allowed himself to imagine what he knew to be ridiculous and impossible, there could have been no danger to her. He put down the knife.

"You find Sir Heribert unwholesome, too?" he asked, levering himself up to a sitting position.

"I do not know," she replied, pushing back her hood and perching herself on the edge of the bed. "When he first came in, his actions seemed strange to me, and the curiosity of his servants still seems excessive, but that could be owing to nervousness on first meeting you or to many other causes." Then she cocked her head inquiringly. "You say 'unwholesome.' Did you find him so even later?"

Walter repeated his doubts of his own impartiality, and Sybelle nodded. She had pushed the bed curtain back when she seated herself so that the glow of the night candle illuminated her face; however, it looked all different in the dim, uncertain light. The eyes were dark and mysterious; the shadows painted hollows in her temples and cheeks so that she lost the fresh bloom of girlhood; and the thrust of her full, moist, lower lip, shining intermittently as the light caught it, was a sensual invitation. In the few hours since Walter had parted from her, Sybelle seemed to have matured into a knowing woman.

"Then what will you tell Richard if you return to him immediately as you said you would?" she asked. "Heribert has, indeed, obeyed your summons to him. He speaks and proffers most fairly. You are not sure in your own mind, you say, whether he is what he seems and you are tarring him with your brother's blackness or whether he has wrapped his foulness in clean cloth. Would it not be most reasonable to write this to Richard and spend a little time with the man to judge him better?"

Sybelle had been delighted when Walter confessed he was

confused by his prejudice. It was the perfect opening she had been seeking to keep him at Clyro until Richard's trap, whatever it was, had been sprung. Thus, she was not being honest when she said she did not know what to think of Sir Heribert. The truth was that she felt Walter's word, *unwholesome,* fitted the man perfectly. However, to admit that she, and Sir Roland, too, agreed with Walter would probably settle the matter in his mind. Doubt, Sybelle felt, could do Walter no real harm, whereas a certainty that would send him off to Usk or Abergavenny too soon might be his death.

Walter heard the words, but it was not the good sense in them that convinced him that a letter would serve his purpose just as well as speaking to Richard in person. Sybelle's lips themselves were a more convincing argument than the sounds they uttered. As if in a trance, Walter leaned forward very slowly until their lips touched. He did not embrace Sybelle nor she him. Their mouths clung together gently, but with great tenacity. After a few minutes, endlessly long and yet timeless, Walter withdrew a hairbreadth.

"Let me love you," he breathed. "I will do you no hurt."

Sybelle made no more reply to this than to move forward the tiny space between them and touch her lips to his again. She had no idea what Walter meant. She remembered vaguely that she had intended to withhold herself as a temptation to marriage so that Walter would come to England and be safe from the war, but at this moment the tenuous contact of lip with lip was stronger than adamantine chains. She could not withdraw. She would think of something else to draw him to England, she told herself, as Walter's fingers found the tie of her night-robe and loosened it.

The cloak was already on the floor, although Sybelle had no memory of Walter's hand undoing the broach that held it. He drew off the robe easily, carefully—and with great skill. *He has done this before, many times before,* Sybelle thought as the toe of each foot pushed off the slipper of the other, but even that thought could not break the hold of their barely touching lips.

Now he put his arm around her bare waist to swing her off the bed, just for a moment while he kicked back the covers with one leg so he could draw her in beside him. Again Sybelle thought how practiced his movements were. She was shivering, but she herself did not know whether it was with cold or with excitement and nervousness. She was not afraid of the act of love—she was eager for that—but she was not skilled. Would she be a disappointment, a failure, compared with those others?

Walter had freed his arm as he pulled her down, and he quickly covered them again, but he made no move to take her, only stroking her cheek, her hair, her arm. It was warm in the bed, and soft. No thoughts were left in Sybelle's head. All that remained were sensations, the delicate thrill of the breath-light kiss, and the warm tingling wherever Walter stroked her.

His hand ran down her arm, down past her fingers, over her hip, down to her thigh. There one finger made little circles. Behind their touching lips, Sybelle sighed. She moved her leg, not away from Walter's touch but to draw it closer to the inner part of her body. He sighed also, or released a breath he had been holding. For some reason that made Sybelle more eager, but his hand slid up her body again, over her abdomen to cup a breast. The hand turned, the fingers ran across her upstanding nipple. Sybelle gasped as a deeper thrill struck her.

That broke the kiss, but Walter bent his head and took the tingling nipple in his mouth. Free now, his hand went down again, between her breasts, along the midline of her body to come to rest at last between her thighs where there was a growing ache. Was it pain or pleasure? There was no telling, and the gentle movement of his fingers made it worse; but Sybelle would not, not for the price of the whole world, have bade him stop. Nor could she lie unresponding. Her hand went out to repeat the actions of his. She felt him draw breath deeply and then emit a shuddering sigh. The next breath he drew he held, and held, and when it was released, it came forth in a long, low moan. Sybelle whimpered and raised her hips toward those tormenting fingers.

Then all at once Walter broke all contact, lifting his head and hand. Sybelle uttered a low cry of protest, but before it ended, he was atop her. Instinctively her legs parted, but he only slid his shaft between them, then drew them back together hard with his own. Holding her thus, he kissed her again, hard now and demanding, and began to move against her body. Surprise checked excitement, but only very briefly. Soon Sybelle began to whimper again and to writhe against him, driven by the exquisite pain to produce more pleasure—or by the exquisite pleasure to produce more pain. There was something more she wanted; there was something incomplete. But she could not stop to think what she desired; she could only respond more and more frantically until the pleasure-pain rose in a crescendo so overpowering that she screamed behind her muted lips.

For a little while she was aware of nothing beyond the ebbing of that fierce sensation, a pleasure in itself, though mingled with a sense of loss. Then she felt Walter still moving, but in a different way, gasping with effort or frustration. She longed to help him but did not know how until she remembered how sensitive her thighs had been. It would not be possible, she thought, to force her hands between them, so she stroked the back and, still remembering, the inner part. Immediately, Walter's muscles contracted, his mouth pulled free of hers as his head bent downward, pressed painfully between her neck and shoulder. He thrust fiercely between her thighs, once, twice, then jerked convulsively, groaning, and at last lay still.

Sybelle lifted her arms and embraced him gently. She felt a kind of wondering bemusement mixed with warm comfort and was prepared to lie embraced for some time despite the fact that Walter's weight made breathing very difficult. Thus, she was startled and a little hurt when Walter pulled her arms away and rolled off her. He did not move far, however, and at once pulled her up and over so that she was partly atop him and partly to the side, cradled in his good arm. This surprised Sybelle even more. What was to happen now? But nothing happened. Walter lay still, breathing hard at first and then more easily.

Eventually curiosity overcame shyness, and Sybelle asked, "Were you uncomfortable, my lord?"

"Not at all," Walter replied, chuckling. "You make a most soft and pleasant mattress, but I wish to wed a well-rounded woman, and you would have been flat as a rush if I lay atop you long. Also, the bed must be wet where you were lying."

So simple an answer. Sybelle giggled. "And are you content?" she asked, growing bolder and teasing.

"No," he said, laughing again, "and I have sinned in spilling my seed abroad. Still, I have not sinned by fornication, so that is even. I suppose I am as content as I could be within the keeping of my word to do you no hurt. And I am more content in knowing that I have much to which to look forward."

There was another short silence. Sybelle remembered how in the midst of her passion she was aware of some lack, some incompleteness in their loving. There was more, then, and Walter was doubtless less satisfied than she, since he knew only too well the whole pleasure. Sybelle felt a prick of jealousy, which she repressed, reminding herself that it was not her business what Walter had done in the past. Instead, she fixed her mind on the fact that she had lost nothing at all in the delight she had found. Not only had she eased her man's need, but from his flattering, if amused, remark she had whetted his appetite for more. She felt him chuckle again.

"And are you content?" he asked, teasing in turn. "Did you get what you came for?"

"But we did not finish talking about Sir Heribert—" Sybelle began, and then blushed.

Had she really come to talk of Sir Heribert? Or had she come because of her worry that if Walter's need for a woman grew too great, he might regret the mistress he had left behind in such haste?

"I did not know that you would. . . ." she added in a very small voice.

Walter's arm tightened around her. "Love, love, I was only teasing you," he murmured. "I know you are innocent. If there is a fault, it is mine, but I do not think it much fault even on my part. How wrong can it be for a man to desire his betrothed wife? Perhaps I should blame the king, for if not for his stubbornness, we could have been wed at once."

"You may blame the king with my goodwill," Sybelle assured him, but the mention of Henry brought back into her mind Heribert's seeming eagerness to take part in the struggle against him. "Why did Sir Heribert bring so many men?" she asked. "I wrote the summons for you myself, and I know there was nothing in it to imply you desired him to go to war."

"I have this thought and that about it—all of them not to Heribert's credit," Walter replied somewhat grimly. "Yet I am not sure. It *could* be that Heribert is hot against the king for some reason of his own. If so, to set mistrust of him in Richard's mind could lose us a useful adherent."

"Then why did he not come forward on his own, when he knew you to be Pembroke's man?" Sybelle asked sharply. Then she could have bitten her tongue. It was her purpose to increase Walter's doubts so that he would stay safe in Clyro, not to agree with him.

"That thought has passed through my mind also," Walter said, "but there could be reasons. We did not talk together very long. I tend to agree with you that I should know him better."

While he spoke, Walter unconsciously stroked Sybelle's arm. There was infinite sweetness in this pillow talk, directed wholly to his interest and his welfare, and in the soft, satisfied languor of his body that had no bitter taint of guilt. It was true that he had missed the ultimate pleasure of penetration in their lovemaking, but that only lent a spice of anticipation to the complete fulfillment that would come in time. For now, despite his teasing denial to Sybelle, Walter was content. He knew she would come again to him this way at his lightest hint, and he did not allow himself to perceive how much that colored his determination to know Sir Heribert better.

By the time Sybelle left his bed to return to her own, they were agreed that Walter would write to Richard and wait at least a few days longer unless Richard asked him to come at once. But the few days passed, and then a few more. Richard did not summon him; indeed, he wrote that they were doing nothing aside from waiting to see what move John of Monmouth would make, that he himself intended to be away from the area for a week or two while he visited keeps and gathered men from the south coast, and that Walter should take his time with Sir Heribert.

But there was nothing at all to settle Walter's doubts one way or the other. In fact, Sir Heribert appeared to be a model vassal. On his own, he suggested that he should send his men back to Knight's Tower since Walter did not need the troop for war. He kept only ten men, enough to ensure his safety in traveling in unsettled times but surely not enough to be any threat to his new overlord.

Walter felt guilty and uncertain—and more and more in love and reluctant to leave Sybelle, even for the few days it would take him to find Richard and report. But he was not the only unhappy member of the party. Sir Heribert had been bitterly disappointed when he could not induce Walter to order him, or even invite him, to join the rebel cause. He assumed Walter had agreed to abandon Pembroke for the price of a beautiful and wealthy wife. Thus, the simple path of betrayal was closed. Either he must think of another way to rid himself of his overlord or he must accept the fact that all roads to power and wealth were shut. He would never be more than a simple castellan of one modest keep.

By the time Heribert went to bed after the third day at Clyro, however, he was sure he would not even be able to keep his position of castellan but would be cast out to sell his sword like a beggar or become an outlaw himself. Heribert had sensed Walter's dislike and Sir Roland's reserve. It was clear that his best efforts had not deceived Walter and that his overlord's pleasant outward demeanor was meant to lull his suspicions until Walter could gather the power to wrest Knight's Tower from him by force. No, not force, Heribert told himself. If Walter intended force there would have been no need to summon him to Clyro. But, then, what was the purpose of the summons? What had been accomplished?

The answer to that was not long in the seeking. The only result of the summons was that Sir Heribert was out of Knight's Tower, leaving no one of any authority in the keep. If Walter should appear at Knight's Tower and demand entrance, it would not be denied. Once in, Walter could easily buy the loyalty of the men-at-arms or even drive them out. Sir Heribert had never made any particular attempt to bind his men's loyalty—he did not believe in loyalty. He paid them well, but Walter, with the backing of the wealthy and powerful Roselynde clan, could offer more.

Despite the warm featherbed in which he lay and the warm covers above, Heribert shook with the terrible chill of fear. He thought first of leaving immediately and rushing back to Knight's Tower, but in the next moment he realized that was useless. As soon as Walter understood his subtle device had failed, he would use force. Heribert knew Knight's Tower could not stand against the army Roselynde could muster. That path would only lead to his own death. Why should he lose everything? Why should he die?

Then terror receded. Why, indeed, should he die? Why not Walter instead? If Walter died before he married and had an heir, there would again be opportunity for advancement. The lands would devolve on the child Earl of Gloucester, who was the ward of the king. Again, there would be an avenue open to King Henry, and Heribert was sure he could manipulate the king.

As soon as his fear calmed, Heribert was able to think clearly and make plans. The first result of those plans was his offer to send his men back to Knight's Tower. Heribert had weighed the chances of being murdered if he reduced the number of men, and decided that if Walter intended to have him killed, the number of men did not matter. After all, Walter could always tell Heribert's men-at-arms that their master had taken sick. And murder did not seem likely in the presence of his betrothed wife and Clyro's castellan. Thus, it was safe to order the men to leave Clyro. But they would not go to Knight's Tower, no, not nearly so far.

Walter had come to Clyro with thirty men-at-arms, including the ten of Sybelle's, but he had sent some of them away. When Walter left Clyro, an ambush could be arranged. The whole country was in a state of unrest. Who was to say by whom Walter had been attacked? As the days passed, Heribert wondered for what Walter was waiting, and then decided he was waiting for his shoulder to heal. He would not want to take the chance of entering Knight's Tower if he could not lead a fight.

By 23 December Sybelle decided Walter's bone was knit. She removed the strapping, but she warned him that the bone would be weak for some time longer. He could use his hand and arm for light things, but not to hold a shield against a blow. Mendaciously, Walter agreed with her—and an hour later was in full armor, striding up and down the bailey to accustom himself again to its weight and calling for his horse to be saddled.

Sir Heribert did not offer to ride out with Walter. Heribert was no coward, but he knew he was no match for Walter man to man, and there would be no chance to summon his men. Moreover, it would be difficult to explain how Walter had been killed, while he had managed to escape. No, he would keep to his original plan.

At first Walter was only enjoying the freedom of not being half-crippled, but by the time he returned to the keep to eat dinner, his conscience was stabbing him. If he had not been able to make up his mind about Sir Heribert in two and a half weeks, he would be no better off in two and a half years unless some incident put the man's loyalty to the test. Moreover, his collarbone was healed; the obvious thing to do was to explain the situation to Richard, but it was not the kind of explanation he could make in a letter. Too many shadings could be lost. Walter knew he himself would have to go and speak to Richard.

So, during the afternoon, he found a moment to whisper, "Come to me," to Sybelle.

Despite Walter's thoughts the night she had ventured into his room on her own initiative, it was the first time he had asked her to join him. Many times, every day and many times a day, the request had been on the tip of his tongue and he had swallowed it for lack of trust in himself and a vague feeling that it was not right to generate so strong a taste for coupling in Sybelle. He resolved, as he spoke, that he would not take Sybelle into his bed that night, either. His invitation was not for play but because he was a little at a loss for an excuse for leaving Clyro without dismissing Heribert and hoped that Sybelle's quick mind would find one for him.

However, Walter was more tired by the exercise he had taken than he expected, unaccustomed as it was, so that he slipped asleep and did not wake until Sybelle's lithe, bare body pressed itself against his. Then, of course, it was too late for good resolutions. Desire overwhelmed caution, and it was only by a miracle that Sybelle retained her maidenhead. However, this did not draw from her praise of her lover's self-control but teasing complaints of deprivation, which Walter answered with laughing threats of the shame of white sheets on her bridal morn. Far from making Sybelle cautious, these brought forth the story of her grandmother's wedding night and the service her husband had done her.

"And you are quite hairy enough," Sybelle purred, running her hands up and down through Walter's luxurious pelt.

"Stop that, you little devil!" he exclaimed. "You will start me off again, and I have a long ride to make tomorrow."

Sybelle's hand froze where it lay. "A long ride! To where?"

When Walter had explained his need to speak to Richard, Sybelle realized that it would not be possible to divert him again. Then an idea came to her. It would not keep Walter from going to Richard, but it would keep her with him.

Perhaps she could yet find some compelling reason for him to take her to England once he had discussed the matter of Knight's Tower and come to some decision.

"Will you leave me to keep Christmas all alone?" she asked. "Can I not come with you and share the feast with Simon and Rhiannon?"

Since Sybelle had not pulled the bed curtains closed, she could see that Walter looked thunderstruck. "Christmas!" he repeated, the stunned expression rapidly giving way to one of apprehension.

"What is it?" Sybelle cried.

"The twelve days!" Walter exclaimed. "I have not one fitting gift for you, let alone twelve."

Sybelle burst into laughter. "Dear heart, you have just given me twelve gifts in one, and all of them rich and fitting," she assured him. Then, more soberly, she went on, "In these hard times of war, such small pleasures as gift-giving must be put aside. I have naught for you, either, except an embroidered collar for a gown that is not made. This feasttide we will make do with kisses."

Walter lifted his brows. "I suppose you will desire that the kisses be generously given? Ah, yes, then we will be in sore straits by Twelfth Day—twelve generous kisses. . . ." His voice faded as a new train of thought entered his mind. "Yes, yes, I will take you with me," he said quickly. "The best excuse I can give to Sir Heribert will be that I must take you to spend the twelve days with your uncle and his wife. We can say that it is a long-promised appointment, and since Simon is Llewelyn's vassal, I can use that as excuse for not asking him to accompany us. That is reasonable." He paused, then went on more slowly. "I do not know why, Sybelle, but I still do not trust him—and yet . . ."

"I understand," she replied. "I did not wish to push you one way or the other, so I said nothing before, but Sir Roland and I feel the same. Sir Roland says that Heribert's men are not just what they should be, either. Not that they are undisciplined, but he feels there is an arrogance in their manner betraying that their master allows them more freedom than is right with the common folk. He thinks, and I do, too, that Sir Heribert did not object as much as he claims to your brother's ways."

Walter nodded. "Sir Roland is no fool. I am glad to know

that it is not only I who cannot swallow Sir Heribert's perfection. I wish I had not accepted his fealty, but I did not feel it fair to reject him when I knew no ill of him except that he had served my brother. Even a good man might be forced to do that for a livelihood. In any case, it is too late to go back. I now must have a reasonable cause to remove Knight's Tower from his care. At least we know he has no wife nor close kin. Sir Roland can ask him to bide here for the merrymaking."

"Yes, and I will leave my maid Edwina here with permission to crawl into his bed if he will take her," Sybelle suggested. "That might keep him fixed. But if he feels our suspicions and will not stay, what then?"

"I will ask Sir Roland to send us word if Heribert leaves, but it does not matter. He cannot cry to the king that I have urged any treasonous proposals on him. In fact, in telling him that I cannot take him into Simon's company, I have done just the opposite. Thus, he cannot harm me. Beyond that, what I do will depend upon Richard."

CHAPTER 19

Owing to his various anxieties, Sir Heribert slept very ill. Moreover, Clyro keep was small and old. The wall chambers, unlike the tower chambers, were tiny and had only arrow slits for windows. With these stopped to keep out the cold, it was needful to leave the door to the hall open when there was a fire in the hearth or else choke to death. Thus, Sir Heribert was wakened early by an unusual bustle in the hall and, by chance, heard Edwina's voice exhorting the menservants to take down the clothes baskets with care.

Heribert sprang out of bed, thinking to arm himself, but then he lay down again. If murder was intended, he was a dead man; he could make no defense. But nothing happened at all. At his regular time, then, Sir Heribert emerged to find his hosts seated at table, wearing traveling clothes, Sir Walter full-armed, and breaking their fast more liberally than usual.

Walter stood up to greet him and invite him to table and, when they were both seated, said, "I must beg your pardon for leaving thus, without due warning, but I lost count of the days—"

"And I did not remind him," Sybelle put in pertly, "for it was a pleasure to me to bide here in peace and good company, and I know the journey to my uncle is no more than a day's ride."

"Sybelle, let me say what must be said in good order," Walter protested. "My betrothed has long given her promise to spend the holy feast day of Christmas with her uncle and his new-wedded wife. I am sorry I cannot ask you to accompany us, Heribert, but you may know that Simon de Vipont is vassal to the lord of Gwynedd, and his wife, Lady Rhiannon, is Llewelyn's daughter. In these times they are not healthy company for you."

"If their company is suitable for you, my lord, it must be suitable for me," Heribert insisted.

Walter shook his head. "I do but accompany Lady Sybelle, who has no part in this conflict and is free to visit her kin in war and peace. As for myself, if you will be so good as to bide here with Sir Roland, I will come again on the day after Christmas and then ride with you to Knight's Tower. I am healed of my hurt, and it is time, I think, to see the lands myself so that we can consult together on how to amend their condition."

Sybelle's eyes opened wide, and her lips parted. In the next instant she lifted her goblet, drank, and then lowered her face over her food. However, Sir Heribert had caught the brief expression of shock. It was immediately clear to him that Walter had no intention of returning to Clyro, and his suspicion was confirmed that Walter intended to take Knight's Tower during his absence and bar him from the place.

"My wife and I will be most pleased if you will give us your company," Sir Roland urged. "Nor need you think that it will be too quiet with only us. Later this very day I expect my brother and two cousins with their families. We will have minstrels also, so we will be merry enough."

In a way, Sir Roland's sudden mention of the arrival of his relations was soothing to Sir Heribert, despite the fact that he saw it also as an additional threat. To Heribert it implied three additional men to keep him prisoner. It was the final spur to his determination to have Sir Walter murdered. However, it also meant that there would be many additional witnesses to the fact that he had been innocently celebrating Christmas in Clyro keep when his overlord was attacked and killed. His men had had their instructions from the beginning. He had only to send a messenger to them to tell them their prey was on the way.

"I thank you, Sir Roland," Heribert replied, smiling. "It is a long time since I have had the pleasure of joining a family party at this festive season. I will be glad of your coming to Knight's Tower, too, my lord," he added, turning to Walter, "but if you will give me leave for a few minutes, I would like to send one of my men ahead to bid them make ready in the keep such poor welcome as a bachelor's establishment may provide. It is a long ride, and the days are short. If

I bid my messenger to go at once, it will save him a little time of riding in the dark."

"What sort of welcome does he plan?" Sir Roland asked the moment Heribert was gone.

Walter shook his head. "If it were an ill one, would he be so open about it?"

"You did not mention this to me," Sybelle said, her voice carefully neutral.

"I told you long ago that I must look over the lands myself," Walter replied. "This may be a very good time for it—or it may not."

Walter's tone was familiar to Sybelle; she had heard it used by both her father and grandfather. It said that argument was useless, that there was a duty to be done. Walter had not mentioned Richard—he did so as little as possible in Sir Roland's presence, not because he was untrusting of Sir Roland's loyalty but because he did not wish any shadow of the rebellion to taint a man beholden to Roselynde. Sybelle knew, however, that Walter's suggestion had been made in case Richard thought it wise to hold Knight's Tower for him from within.

She said no more, even when they were out of the keep and on the road. There was no use in nagging at Walter about an action that had not even been decided. If necessary, Sybelle thought, she herself would speak to Richard, since she was sure Walter would make light of, or not mention at all, the danger of putting himself into Sir Heribert's power. Walter would be fit to kill her for such interference, but better he should be enraged than dead.

It was very cold with a sharp and biting wind so they rode in silence with hoods drawn forward and heads bent. The horses moved briskly, instinctively quickening pace to keep themselves warm, and their hooves clattered sharply on the road where the raw earth had frozen almost hard as stone. No one had much thought of anything besides the weather. They were nowhere near any contested territory, and they were too well armed a group to invite attack by an outlaw band, specially as they had no baggage train to hint at rich loot. There was only one packhorse with clothing and linen for Sybelle and Walter.

Thus, even Walter did not react when they first heard the sound of travelers on the road ahead. He was busy with his own thoughts, and he first associated the sound of the oncoming horses with the guests Sir Roland had mentioned. Also, the road curved, so that even though most of the trees were bare of leaves, it was impossible to see any distance ahead and sounds were muted and distorted.

Suddenly, however, several half-perceived impressions came together in Walter's head. It was much too early for guests to have come this far unless they had traveled all night, which was out of the question during such cold; the sounds he was hearing were of many horses, far too many for a guesting party; most important of all, the horses were coming at a gallop! Walter threw back his hood and shouted a warning. It had not yet entered his mind that the oncoming party was any specific threat to them, but any group riding that fast heralded trouble. Either they were in hot pursuit of someone or they were fleeing pursuit. Whichever was true, Walter did not wish to tangle with a group as large as this one sounded to be, particularly when Sybelle was with him.

Not far behind, Walter remembered, there had been a narrow track leading south into the desolate mountain area. Walter did not imagine it went far, possibly only a few hundred yards to a woodcutters' village, but he was not thinking of seeking shelter or defense, only of getting out of the way of a troop that he was sure had no interest in him. He shouted at Sybelle to ride back, at the men to make way for her, and at Tostig to find the bypath and lead the men into it.

There was barely a minute of confusion before Walter's orders were obeyed. The men were trained to swift obedience, and Sybelle had become aware of the danger at about the same time Walter did. She was through the group, kicking and yelling at her mare, partly to encourage the animal but also because she felt the female voice would inform any war party that they were neutrals. The men closed in behind her, whipping their horses to a gallop. Walter was the last to turn. He had had no sight of the oncoming troop, but he felt from the sound that they were very close, barely around the next turn of the road.

Because he had no suspicion that he was the prey the riders sought, Walter swept his cloak aside to expose his shield. He assumed that even if his colors were not recognized, the blazon would inform pursuers or those who fled other pursuers that he was neither enemy nor target. Moreover, the fact that his shield was in rest position, rather than on his arm and ready for offense or defense, was a signal of intended neutrality. He was thus considerably shocked a few minutes later to hear cries of recognition and threat.

Although Walter could scarcely believe what he heard, he was forewarned. He shouted to the men ahead that they should not stop but ride on, even into the woods if the road ended, and he heard the order relayed to those in front. He also heard the *whir* of one crossbow bolt and then another. The flesh of Walter's back quivered in involuntary fearful expectation, even though his conscious mind recognized that the bolts were wide of the mark. At least the track they now followed was so narrow that most of the danger, that of a mass volley, was eliminated. No more than two could ride abreast, and even then, Walter thought, the horses would jostle each other so much as to reduce nearly to nothing the none-too-great accuracy of the crossbow.

That was some comfort, but if the road opened out into a village or mown fields, they would be in desperate danger. There was also terrible danger in abandoning the road for the woods, for their party was already small. If they became separated, they would be even easier prey. Walter cursed himself bitterly for not foreseeing the danger, but even as he did, he could find no sense in it. Danger from whom? Heribert leapt into his mind as soon as he realized he was the target, but it seemed utterly impossible that the man should be guilty. He had been away from the hall no more than five minutes. He could not have arranged an ambush in that time, and he had not known more than a minute or two earlier that Walter intended to leave Clyro. But no one else had known, either. It must be a mistake; his shield must have been misread for someone else's.

Mistake or not, there was no way to explain, and to flee was no answer, not with pursuers so close behind. They needed a refuge. Simultaneously with Walter's thought of refuge came shouts from ahead warning of a village and a crossroad.

"Longbowmen to the rear!" Walter bellowed. "Tostig, take my lady left on the road, left!"

That was back in the direction from which they had come. And since the track did not simply end at the village, Walter had hopes that it would curve around and rejoin the main road. If the longbowmen could delay the pursuers by shooting some as they came out of the narrow track, the rest of the party might get near enough to Clyro to be seen by the guards on the walls.

Moments later, Walter emerged into the small broadening of the track caused by the crossroad and the clearings around three woodcutters' huts. Sybelle, her escort, and the pack animal had already disappeared up the path—for that was all it was—to the left. The sound of their horses' hooves came back through the trees. Walter wrenched Beau left, then around the nearest hut, and had to bite back more curses when he saw only three men hastily stringing their longbows and nocking arrows, two behind the farther hut and one sheltered by the one he had circled. A fourth man was holding the horses beyond the third ramshackle shelter. Inside the hut Walter could hear a child's scream being muffled and a woman hissing for silence between sobs of fear.

"Take them as they come out," he said to the man near him, "one or two, then mount and follow the others. If you can get in a shot behind as you ride, do that, too, but do not get yourself hit."

He spurred Beau across to the other hut, meanwhile placing his shield on his arm, and repeated his order. Briefly he thought of telling the men to shoot one of the horses, hoping to block the trail, but he could not make himself do it. One arrow, or even three, would not kill a horse instantly, and, if they did not, there was no purpose to harming the innocent creature. The bows *twanged* just at that moment, and the first man out of the tree-sheltered path screamed. However, since shock and pain had caused him to kick his mount, the animal sprang forward and the bowmen had a chance at the second man coming out. They got him, too, more successfully, for he fell from his horse.

The wounded man had regained control of his mount and turned it toward the huts. One of the bowmen shifted his attention from the oncoming men, but Walter shouted at him to keep his aim on the mouth of the road. His sword sang out of its sheath, and he rode out to finish what the arrow had begun. It was no heavy task, but Walter regretted he could not take the man prisoner and wring from him the truth of who had set the ambush and for whom it had been set. However, there was no time for that. Crossbow bolts were flying at him. Most were deflected by the trees, but one or two came very close. Walter killed his man swiftly and sought shelter.

From the hut where the horses were being held, a woman began to screech. The third man out was also hit, but he did not fall, nor, having seen his comrade so quickly dispatched, did he ride toward Walter's archers. Instead, he tried to turn his horse back into the shelter of the trees. Walter's men sent several more arrows flying into the mouth of the track, and then in response to their master's signal ran for their horses, mounted, and followed Walter, who had already started Beau toward the left-hand road. As he went, Walter heard orders shouted and horses crashing through the winter-killed, brittle brush that lined the track. He muttered an obscenity. He had hoped that one of the men in the forefront who had been killed was the leader of the troop, but apparently that hope had been vain.

Walter spurred Beau to an even faster pace, concerned that he might leave the men behind but more afraid that those pushing through the trees would come out on the road between him and the party accompanying Sybelle. That would be a disaster. While he was delayed fighting that group, another could go ahead and attack Sybelle and the men with her. He had no idea of how long they had been in the village. It seemed like only a few minutes, but he could not hear any sound of horses ahead of him at all. How far had Sybelle got? There was more shouting behind him, but Walter could not make out the words, which were distorted by the other noises. He roweled Beau again, hoping the destrier would not stumble on the ruts worn into the track by the woodcutters' carts.

No sooner had the thought crossed his mind than a new twist to the path disclosed a mounted man with wound crossbow waiting ahead of him. Walter bent low over his horse to present the smallest possible target and lifted his legs to strike Beau's sides again in the hope of drawing yet further effort from the beast. But then he heard his own name called and the man-at-arms lowered the bow and turned his mount, shouting that de Clare was coming. Relief mingled with rage as Walter realized that Sybelle had ordered the men to stop and wait for him. Now he heard the horses ahead being prodded forward, but he had to curb Beau sharply lest he overrun them.

The woods, Walter thought, must be thicker than he believed.

Although he could still hear horses coming through the trees, they sounded fewer and more distant than he would have expected. A few minutes later Walter spotted a widening where a forest glade came to the edge of the track, and he shouted for a halt. When they were grouped together, he explained what he wanted them to do if the path should end or if what he hoped were true and the path opened onto the main road they had been traveling.

"And do not be so foolish," he said sharply to Sybelle, "as to stop and wait for me again when I bid you go forward."

She did not reply, but the golden eyes that met his were in no way chastened. And, if there was some fear in them, it was not such as to induce stupid, hysterical reactions. Walter felt ashamed of his criticism, believing that Sybelle, too, must have realized the danger of their parties being separated. But there was no time to take back his words. That would have to wait until they were safe. A single gesture set them in motion again.

Walter had had his ears cocked for the sound of pursuit while he gave his orders, but the resistance they had put up by the woodcutters' huts seemed to have made those who followed them cautious and they started before any pursuers appeared. The track was widening again, and in another minute or two they passed several more huts. Here the road bent left again, not simply another twist but a definite heading northward. Walter shouted a warning that they were likely soon to come upon the main road. "Lady Sybelle in the middle and shields up!" he bellowed, suddenly aware that it was not only caution that had made the sound of hooves behind so faint. There were fewer men following.

Walter had had the thought before, but among his other concerns he had not stopped to wonder where the other men had gone. Now he realized that the leader of the pursuers probably also had guessed that the forest track might come out on the main road if it did not stop at the woodcutters' huts. Likely he had divided the troop and sent some of the men back. They would have made faster time on the broader, smoother road, which would also be straighter and shorter than the track his party was following, and there were the few minutes he had stopped to give instructions. If so, their pursuers could be waiting at the intersection.

Mingled yells of consternation and triumph proved that Walter's warning had come just in time. It was fortunate that the track they were following widened somewhat as it met the road. There was room for Sybelle and the men behind her to turn their horses. Ill, however, was mixed with the good. There was also room for the group on the road to launch a barrage of bolts. Walter heard more than one horse scream, and two bolted off the path directly southward, away from the pain that had struck them.

"Into the woods!" Walter shouted, turning Beau toward the trees, but holding him back.

He saw Sybelle's blond mare crash through the brush. Directly behind her, shielding her as well as he could with his body, came Tostig. Several other men followed, but two of those who had come first to the road had held their horses steady and were charging the bowmen. Walter wrenched Beau around again, calling to the men nearest him to charge. The pursuers, unable to recock the slow crossbows in time, dropped them and reached for their swords. For several it was too late, and the others backed away to give themselves time. Walter and five others were on them, however, and they turned and fled.

"Back! Back!" Walter roared. "Those behind us will take Lady Sybelle."

They rode back into the byroad in frantic haste and, in fact, met the party that had been behind them hesitating as to whether to follow the plain trail that Sybelle and her guards had made into the woods or go up to the road from which sounds of the brief confrontation must have come. Even if Walter and his men had wished to do so, it would have been impossible to check their horses in time. In any case, they did not wish to avoid a fight. All were furious with fear and confusion, and their blood was up owing to the aborted battle on the road. Shrieking blasphemies and obscenities, they charged into the group.

The men who had been pursuing were not taken completely by surprise. They had heard horses coming fast, but they had not been sure, until they heard the yells of rage, that those who were approaching were not the other part of their own troop. Thus, their response was not concerted. Several, who had been carrying wound crossbows on the chance of getting in a shot at the fleeing group, fired their weapons without much chance of aim. Still, because of the way Walter's men were packed close by the trees bordering the byroad, two bolts struck home.

Right beside Walter, one man toppled from his mount without a sound. By chance the quarrel had taken him right in the eye. Behind, another man shouted hoarsely, but the voice sounded more angry than agonized. Since Walter was a trifle in advance of his men, Beau being stronger and faster than the other horses, the falling man struck his destrier on the croup. Startled, Beau leapt forward, and Walter was alone among those whose purpose was to kill him.

CHAPTER 20

Toward evening, four days before Walter decided he must go to Richard and explain that he still distrusted Sir Heribert but could find no cause to rid himself of the man, Siorl had come to report to Simon that John of Monmouth's preparations for war were so nearly finished that Monmouth's army could be expected to move in a day or two. Simon brought the news to Richard, privately wondering if he would need to urge Richard to go ahead with the plan he had made to set an ambush for John of Monmouth's army.

There was, however, no need for urging. On the preceding Thursday, Richard had spent the night at Margam Abbey after a round of inspection of some keeps to the west. There, a brother of the Minorite order named Agnell, an advisor of King Henry's, had come to him and given him a lecture about having "traitorously and unjustly taken arms against the king." Agnell insisted that there had never been "any design against Richard's person or property," and that he had no right to burst out into violence against the king until he had "ocular demonstration" that the king was his enemy. Thus, it was Pembroke's duty and to his benefit to throw himself on Henry's mercy.

Holding his temper with some effort, Richard had asked what terms Henry was prepared to offer. To this, Agnell replied haughtily that he was sure the king would grant him safety of life and limb and would allow him a sufficient portion of land in Herefordshire to support him honorably; however, Pembroke could not make any conditions prior to yielding and must humbly sue for mercy without knowing what terms would be granted him.

Since Agnell was a man of God and they were in an abbey, Richard did not smite the man dead with his fist. He even made shift to answer civilly and at length the charges made against him, citing the violation of the truce agreed to after the attack on Usk and the fact that the king had deprived him of lands and offices by decree, without any trial before his peers, for which he had repeatedly asked and by the decision of which he had sworn to abide. Under the calm exterior, however, Richard was boiling. Even at this late date, he would have seized on any honest and reasonable offer to negotiate an end to the conflict. Far from raising fear and awe in him, which he supposed had been the purpose, the arrogance of both messenger and message had only infuriated him and firmed his purpose.

Thus, when Simon relayed the information Siorl had brought, Richard cursed fluently at the timing but gathered his forces and ordered them to march out of Abergavenny and Usk. Those from Usk came northward along the river valley, but the movement of the wains that carried the great war ballistae and mangonels was slow. That portion of Pembroke's army camped at dusk where a tributary stream entered the Usk. At dawn, the wains continued northward, but most of the men who had started with them were gone. During the night, quietly as possible, they had moved onward along the tributary, eastward toward Monmouth.

From Abergavenny, Richard himself led his men, again with a large baggage train, toward the valley of the Dore. They started rather late in the day and struggled no farther than four or five miles along the difficult terrain of the route chosen, camping near Llanvihangel. The one advantage of that route was that it led nearly due north. Richard hoped that John of Monmouth was sufficiently ignorant regarding travel routes in that part of the country that he would not realize the army could have made better time the longer way round along the Usk valley. However, he decided to chance it rather than take his men so far out of the way of their real objective.

Having given the men time to eat and rest, Richard ordered that the camp fires be left burning. In addition, he gave instructions to the small guard, which would continue north with the carts and siege machines the next day, that all the fires should be fed during the night. After that, Richard led the bulk of his forces on a long, hard march around Skirrid-fawr southward to meet the men from Usk, who had come to rest, according to his orders, south of Wern-yr-healydd. They were nearly dead of exhaustion when they arrived, but Richard was not worried about that. He was sure they would have at least two days and possibly as much as a week to rest.

He was more concerned about the weather, which seemed unnaturally cold. Although Richard had done everything possible to convince John of Monmouth that he had started north to join Prince Llewelyn, he knew Monmouth was no fool. Despite the feint, John of Monmouth would have patrols out. That meant few and small enough fires so that neither smoke nor light would attract attention. And that meant freezing nights and cold and ill-cooked meals.

A brief period of such discomfort would make the men angry, eager to punish those who had threatened their master and thus caused them to be dragged from their comfortable winter quarters; however, too long a siege of cold nights and cold food could turn them sullen and give them the feeling that their leaders were fools who did not know how to plan properly. Thus, Richard toured his camp, speaking to the captains and to the men themselves, commiserating with their condition and showing that he was no warmer and not much better fed than they, while he waited for Simon's Welshmen, who were watching the roads, to report when and which way John of Monmouth would move.

If Pembroke had intended to assault Monmouth, he would not have camped at all but would have brought his army due east to the valley of the Trothy from Abergavenny or along the route that led directly northeast and southwest from Usk to Monmouth. Now Richard's forces lay between those two routes, ready to strike either way, depending upon whether John of Monmouth launched his attack against Usk or Abergavenny.

Until the departure of Richard, his vassals, and his adherents, Abergavenny keep had been very lively. At the invitation of Lady Pembroke, some of the minstrels had followed Richard's party south from Builth, so there had been music and dancing, juggling and mummeries. Gervase had been well pleased, even with these simple pleasures, compared with her previous isolation in Pembroke keep. Thus, she had not only behaved with moderation but actually pleaded with Richard to allow her to stay when he suggested sending her west again to greater safety. And Richard, who was himself taking pleasure in the improved relations with his wife, realized that he would probably never have another chance to save his marriage if he did not yield.

He did not feel there really was much danger in his wife and sister-by-marriage staying. It was conceivable that his ambush would not result in the complete victory for which he hoped, but he was certain that John of Monmouth's force would be badly enough hurt that any attack on Abergavenny would be impossible, at least until John of Monmouth could reorganize his army, and that would be time enough to send Gervase and Marie west.

Marie had also been eager to stay in Abergavenny. Although she had been near bursting with rage when Walter left Builth so suddenly and without a single word to her, she had had much to distract her while Richard and all his men remained in the keep. It was, in a way, as if she were the only woman there. Obviously, no man would flirt with Gervase under her husband's eyes, and Rhiannon's husband was also present. Besides, Marie noticed that many of the men seemed to be afraid of the Welsh woman. When Rhiannon sang and her bell-toned voice filled the hall, all watched and listened in silence. But when the songs were over, the men shook themselves, as if they had been freed from a spell, and few went to speak to her.

Thus, Marie was the focus of attention for every man who enjoyed the company of women. She was too busy and too flattered to dwell on the rage she had felt when Walter left Builth or the hatred she bore Sybelle, who seemed to have snatched out of her hands the prize she desired. However, when the keep was emptied of all except a few men too old to fight or to have any interest in entertaining her, it was rage and hatred that filled her empty hours. In fantasy, she tortured and murdered both Sybelle and Walter; but such fantasies were too empty to bring any satisfaction.

She could not, however, release the notion of making trouble for those who, in her opinion, had insulted and robbed her. Marie now acknowledged that Walter was more powerfully drawn by money and power than by her, and realized seduction would not induce him to forgo his heiress. She had also hoped to infuriate and disgust Sybelle so much that she would beg her father to repudiate the verbal contract or that her jealousy would be poured out over Walter in a stream so bitter that he would back out of the casual commitment.

The plan had failed, in Marie's opinion, because Walter was so greedy he would eat filth if enough wealth and power were offered as sauce, and Sybelle was so much a dog in the manger that she would not let go what she knew was worthless to her for fear another would have it. Disgusting people, Marie thought. They both deserved to be deprived of what they grasped at so greedily. But if neither would let go, what could wrest Sybelle's dowry from Walter's grasp and make her family into his enemies?

As soon as the problem formed that way in her mind, Marie had the answer. If Walter could be shown to have made contract falsely—if there were a claim of prior contract, for example—surely the proud Lord Geoffrey, cousin to the king, would repudiate the agreement. Marie mulled that idea over, and the more she thought of it, the better she liked it. Not only would the whole Roselynde clan hate Walter, but Richard would hate him, too. After all, she was Richard's sister-by-marriage, and it was a gross insult to him that Walter should promise her marriage, seduce her, and then make contract for the daughter of one of Richard's enemies who offered a greater dowry.

Then a snag caught Marie. If Walter had promised her marriage, why had she not spoken as soon as Sybelle began to spread the word that there was a betrothal agreement? She could say, of course, that she had been ashamed and had not wished to make trouble, but then she would have to explain why she was speaking out now. All the next day she wrestled with the problem, unable to find an answer; on the day Walter and Sybelle started for Abergavenny she discovered her flux had begun. At first she only cursed the blood that had stained her shift and tunic, wishing she could be rid of this useless burden, for she had no desire to bear children. And then the thought of children solved her problem.

Obviously, if she had been Walter's mistress and had just discovered she had got with child, she would have had to expose their relationship, despite shame and her willingness to sacrifice herself for her lover's profit. Unfortunately she had already tossed her shift and tunic to her maid to clean, so the girl would know that she was not with child.

Marie's brow wrinkled into a frown. A far greater danger than her maid was that Walter would deny everything, but surely Richard would believe *her*. A woman would not admit to such a shameful situation unless she were desperate. But perhaps Richard would not care. He had been totally indifferent about the injustice done her in France. In that case, Richard might still refuse to annoy Walter to protect her. Biting her lips with chagrin, Marie went to Gervase's chamber. If both of them swore to the promise, Richard would have to listen.

Gervase's pleasure had also been cut short by Richard's departure. Not only had he taken with him the men who had been entertaining her with tales of King Henry's court in more pleasant times, but he had ordered the minstrels to leave also. This had been done in the hope that they would spread the tale that he had gone north to join Prince Llewelyn, not because he desired that his wife be lonely and bored, but Gervase never thought of that and, if she had, would not have regarded it as a sufficiently good reason to deprive her of amusement.

Thus she was again very angry at her husband and delighted with a proposition that would hurt him and cause him trouble. Nonetheless, Gervase was not completely a fool.

"He lay with you only that once," she said. "Are you really with child?"

Marie hesitated a bare second. Richard would not think to question her maid, but Gervase certainly would, and no matter what Marie threatened, the girl would tell the truth because she belonged to Gervase, not to Marie. Again Marie tasted the bitterness of dependency and hated Walter and Sybelle all the more for snatching away her chance for independence.

"No, I am not, but what does it matter?" Marie spat.

"What will you say three months from now when you do not begin to increase?" Gervase asked.

"Do not be ridiculous!" Marie exclaimed. "Next month when my flux comes, I will cry out in pain and lose the child."

"Then you will lose the man, too—if you can ever gain him by this method." Gervase frowned. Although they snipped and snapped at each other and although she resented having to support Marie out of her purse, Gervase was fond of her sister. "Are you sure you should do this?" she asked. "He will hate you. And I am much afraid that Richard will not take your part if Sir Walter takes out his rage by beating you. He might not even allow me to give you sanctuary. I fear—"

"I do not expect to gain Sir Walter," Marie interrupted impatiently. "I will find another. Sir Philip Bassett is not wed, and to speak the truth I find him more to my taste, if not as rich as Sir Walter."

"Then why—" Gervase stopped abruptly.

She knew why. In Marie's opinion Walter had cast her aside for a richer woman, even though he liked that richer prize less. Gervase no longer agreed with Marie; she had watched Walter and Sybelle with eyes less blinded by prejudice than her sister's. Gervase no longer thought Walter was marrying Sybelle for her dowry, and the loss of a woman he desired would not be forgiven.

Marie's statement that she did not intend to marry Walter removed Gervase's doubts. She did not like the women of Roselynde. The fawning devotion of Lord Ian and Lord Geoffrey to their wives infuriated her, and the mild contempt Sybelle could not hide when Gervase had told her Walter was greedy had added to the dislike she already felt. Gervase would not mind making Sybelle and the whole Roselynde clan unhappy, not at all. Nor, in her present mood, was she averse to placing Richard in a position that would doubtless embarrass and infuriate him.

The idea of infuriating Richard gave Gervase second thoughts, however. She did not wish his wrath to descend upon her. The outcome of that would be that he would send her back to Pembroke and keep her there, or in some even more isolated castle in Ireland, forever.

Marie had been answering Gervase's aborted question, but Gervase interrupted abruptly, saying, "I cannot lie to Richard for you. No, do not be angry, Marie, I would do it gladly and I will gladly say all that I know is true, such as that he courted you when he came to Pembroke and on the road to Brecon, but I cannot say I heard him offer you marriage and I cannot say that I knew he lay with you."

"You fear him," Marie sneered.

"In a way I do fear Richard, and so should you," Gervase admitted, although her lips thinned with irritation and her resolve hardened not to sacrifice herself for so ungrateful a sister. "Think what will happen if I prove so ill a keeper for my sister that I consented to such an arrangement."

"Why should you not consent if you had heard him offer marriage?" Marie whined. She had caught Gervase's look and realized the sneer had been ill-timed. "Betrothed couples may be excused for a little love play. I am no maiden who should show red sheets on my marriage morn."

"That may be true, but Richard will blame me for permitting such freedom before he had approved the match, and he will say that if we cannot be trusted in company, we had better go where there is none."

Marie, whose mouth was already open to accuse Gervase of selfishness and lack of pity, swallowed her words. It was too likely that Gervase was right. She began to weep. "Am I to have nothing," she sobbed, "not even revenge for so cruel a hurt?"

"I do not know," Gervase said in a softer voice, for she understood her sister's rage and did sympathize with her. After all, Gervase had herself suffered from impotent rage. "It is for you to decide whether to take the chance. I swear I will do all I can to help you. But there is another problem, even more important, that you have not considered. It can do no good at all to make this accusation unless Sir Walter and Lady Sybelle are both here. If you tell Richard and he writes to Sir Walter, the chances are that Sir Walter will reply by letter or, if he comes, he will come alone. How, then, will those of Roselynde hear of Sir Walter's prior contract?"

"He would have to tell them of a prior contract that would make his marriage to that bitch invalid," Marie said. "Or if he does not, Richard would have to tell them. Or I will write to Lord Geoffrey myself."

Gervase shrugged. Marie seemed to have made her decision in favor of attacking Walter at any cost, regardless of the difficulties involved, but she herself was growing more and more doubtful of the efficacy of the claim Marie wished to make. Even if Richard believed Marie, Gervase doubted that he would rate her claim high enough to quarrel with a friend over it, especially after she said she had miscarried the child. However, there was no sense in arguing with Marie, who would only scream and cry and grow sullen. It was bad enough being alone in the keep again without that. And the whole thing might come to nothing anyway. For instance, if Richard were away for several months, it would be self-evident that Marie was not pregnant.

"Well, nothing can be done until Richard returns, and God knows when that will be," Gervase said, hoping that Marie would understand that hint. "Consider well, Sister, the cost and the reward, and be sure the latter is worth the former."

Beau's sudden leap into the troop that had been following Walter and his party along the road shouldered aside the lighter mount of the man to Walter's left, giving Walter a moment to launch a mighty blow at the opponent on his sword side. The parry was in time, but a man-at-arm's sword was not of the same metal as a knight's fine-tempered blade. The weapon snapped short, and Walter's slash went on to cut into the man's arm.

The victim howled, as much from the pain in the hand that had been holding the sword hilt as from the wound; the cut was not deadly deep, since much of the power of the blow had been absorbed by the broken sword. Nonetheless, that man was out of the battle for the moment, and he could not back his horse because of his comrades hemmed into the narrow path behind him. Nor was he willing to go forward, weaponless as he was, and face the blades of Walter's oncoming men. Thus, he was a protection to Walter as he struggled to turn his excited horse into the trees to get out of the way.

To Walter's left, a second brief impasse had developed. When Beau's powerful shoulder struck one horse, that animal had collided with a second whose rider was attempting to thrust himself between Walter and his men. The confusion lasted less than a minute, but in that time the four remaining men of Walter's troop had come up and Walter was no longer isolated. Their onslaught was so furious that both the men to Walter's left were wounded and overthrown. The man whose sword Walter had broken had withdrawn and another had taken his place, but his fate was worse than his comrade's. He had missed his parry, and Walter's stroke had cleaved through platelets and leather to shear flesh and break ribs.

This time Walter's luck had turned. One of the men downed had been the group's leader. Thinking him dead and faced with such successful and determined opposition, the remainder of the men lost their enthusiasm and backed away. This drew victorious shouts from Walter's party, but a sharp order stopped the attempt at pursuit. Walter had not forgotten Sybelle, fleeing south through the woods, or the fact that the group on the road might well reorganize and come to the assistance of their comrades.

He drove Beau through the brush already broken by Sybelle's mare, and his men followed, cursing first because they had to leave the second fight unfinished and then because the cold stung the minor wounds two of them had received. One looked back, but the man who had been hit in the eye by the quarrel lay as he had fallen. Two prayed for him as they rode, but his body would have to take the chance of being found if those who had attacked them would not collect it with their own dead for decent burial.

This time Sybelle had not stopped, but the land rose sharply no great distance from the byroad and slowed the pace sufficiently that Walter soon caught sight of her. Tostig had turned to face the sound of oncoming horses and had recognized Walter by his armor, since none of the attackers wore knight's mail. At his word they all waited, and the two groups joined.

"Can we go back, my lord?" Sybelle asked.

Walter looked back through the woods. There was no sound of pursuit now, but they had left a clear trail of broken brush and torn earth, and the attackers must know that they would do so and could be followed at leisure. He tried to remember how many men there had been in the attacking party and how many they had killed or wounded, but it had all happened too fast for accurate memory. He was sure that there were still many more opponents than the men he had, and four of his party were wounded, although not seriously. Still, it would make them slower. Another thing he was sure of was that every effort would be made to prevent his party from regaining the road.

Had Sybelle not been with him, Walter might have considered returning and bursting through the guard on the road. He did not think there had been enough men to do more than patrol, but he knew they would patrol with wound crossbows, and the idea of a bolt finding its way into Sybelle's soft and silken flesh made him shudder.

"No," Walter replied to Sybelle's question about going back. "They will guard the road. I do not know who they are or whom they hunt, but sight of my shield did not turn them away. They are too well armed and well disciplined to be outlaws. Also, whomever it is they hunt, they want that person dead. And from the lack of care with which they launch arrows, I would say that they probably do not mind who else dies with him."

"Then we must find a stream of some size to follow," Sybelle said calmly. "I do not know this land as I know that near Clyro, but I know that there are hills here no horse can climb. Only along the bed of running water will the slopes be easier. I know also the streams run north and south, or almost. Then to find one we must go east or west, but I have no idea which way would be better."

"Nor do I," Walter admitted. "And I do not have any idea how far east we have been driven, but I do not believe it to be far. Also, I think they will expect that we will try to work our way back to Clyro. Let us go west."

The choice turned out to be a lucky one. Although at one point they were forced back almost to the byroad by a projecting cliff that even a mountain goat would have found too much for it, in a way that was lucky, too. Angry voices came to them through the trees. At the distance they were, they could make out no words and only knew the voices were angry from the fact that they heard them at all; however, it was warning enough. They went carefully, without speaking, making as little noise as possible, and any doubts Walter had had about not going back to the road were put to rest.

Very soon after that, they found their stream. Walter sent most of the men through it still farther west to make a false trail, bidding them come back exactly as they went. Tostig returned with the excellent news that they had actually come out onto the byroad so that if the trail were followed, it would seem as if their party had escaped that way owing to the inattention of the guards.

"Then perhaps we could do that," Walter said.

Tostig shook his head. "We did not come out onto the road, and I heard voices not far from where we were, only two or three men, my lord, but I think they are part of a regular patrol."

"We can kill two men. We are not so crippled we cannot do that," one of the men-at-arms who had been wounded growled.

This time it was Walter who shook his head. "They would not stay to fight, and we have only two bowmen now, so our chances of shooting them as they run are small. We cannot take the chance."

His eyes went to Sybelle, and the faint murmur that had risen among the men, who were angry at being hunted, died. If any harm at all came to the lady, those of them who survived would be the *unlucky* ones. Lord Geoffrey would have them apart muscle by muscle and bone by bone, and Lady Joanna would make sure each muscle and bone suffered separately.

Thus, with one accord they turned south and began to follow the stream. It was slow going, for brush and trees grew thickly along the edges. When they could, they rode away from the banks themselves, but there were places where the water had cut its way down through sheer rock. There they were forced into the water, and the horses jibbed and stumbled in the shifting, rocky bed. Moreover the stream was growing smaller and shallower, and the terrain was rising higher and higher.

"I fear I have chosen ill," Walter said to Sybelle. They had found a small, level spot and had dismounted to let the horses rest.

"Oh, no," she replied cheerfully, although she was stamping her feet and beating her hands together to warm them. "We must get over the ridge if we wish to go south. We will have to lead the horses from here, I think, but there is nearly always another stream on the other side going down."

Walter knew that, but he had wished to give Sybelle a chance to relieve her fears, discomforts, and frustrations by railing at him. He stared in wonder at the face turned up to his. There was neither fear nor petulance in it. Indeed, the eyes were bright, the lips parted and curved upward in a half smile. With a sensation of mingled irritation and joy, Walter realized that Sybelle was now heartily enjoying herself.

He sent one man up along the stream to see how the land lay, and one each east and west. The last two came back soonest, reporting that there was no way for horses in either direction. Along the stream, travel was still possible for the animals, so they went that way, hoping they would not be driven back in the end after wasting more time. Now that they were all afoot, Walter set the wounded men to leading several horses so that the others could flank them left and right.

Hope of finding a passage was all but dead, for they could see a sheer cliff ahead where, most probably, the springs that fed the thread of water to which they clung trickled out of the rocks. However, the man eastward cried that there was a slope in that direction. How far it went and whether it ended in another sheer drop they did not know, but it was a chance and they took it. And it was the devil's own work getting the horses along. The beasts did not mind climbing up and, although they liked it less, would go down steep slopes, but getting them along sideways was a nightmare. Horses' legs are not made to accommodate ground a foot higher on one side than the other. So it was necessary to lead them three paces up at an angle and then three paces down at an angle to advance one pace forward.

The men said things in English that made even Walter raise his brows. He did not check them, knowing that they needed some outlet for their feelings and believing that, although she spoke English, Sybelle would not understand. However, he learned otherwise when Sybelle giggled and then, when they stopped to rest, asked one to repeat a phrase. Tostig exclaimed in protest and the man turned red, so she did not insist, but she asked Walter with innocent gravity in French if what she thought she had heard were humanly possible. Resisting one impulse to reprimand her sharply for comprehending such language and another to laugh himself silly, Walter replied with what dignity he could muster that he did not know, never having thought of trying it.

However, a few minutes after they started out again, Walter himself said something almost as obscene when he realized that not far ahead there were no trees. The disaster was not as complete as they had feared. When they came to the edge, it was not a sheer drop they found but an area of scree. Somewhere above, the whole side of the mountain had loosened and fallen; earth and rock had roared down, taking with them trees and topsoil and leaving a narrow river of unstable, unsettled ground—not a complete disaster but a serious check. The horses would never get over that. Walter sighed. Oh, well, there were plenty of trees, and war axes could be used for more than one purpose.

It took hours, but they bridged the earth river at last—although not without cost. Two men went down and were retrieved much bruised and battered, one with a broken leg. Sybelle set it and splinted it, but of course the man would have to be carried in a litter fashioned of branches and a blanket until they reached sufficiently level ground for him to stay in the saddle with only one foot in the stirrup. And that meant that there would be three extra horses for the remaining men to lead uphill and down. But there were no complaints; all were too fearful that the bridge would not hold to say a word.

One of the men—in fact, it was he who had not wished to repeat to Sybelle what he had said—volunteered to lead his horse across first. The bridge held. Then Sybelle said she would go. Walter opened his mouth to protest, but she shook her head.

"It is the safest time," she said steadily, "before many crossings have weakened it. My mare and I are both lighter than those who went first. And you must follow just after me, my lord. I will have your word upon it before I go. You are necessary to all our safety. God forbid any should fall, but if one must, it must not be you."

Walter smiled at her. "I love you," he said. "There can be no woman in the world your equal. Go, then. I will follow."

Sybelle crossed without difficulty, murmuring to her mare comfortingly as the beast was coaxed to put one fearful foot before the other. But after her came not Walter but the two men carrying in a litter the third who had broken his leg. They were all muttering under their breaths, but it was prayers this time, not blasphemies. Sybelle bit her lip. She had again forgotten Walter's cleverness. He had said he would follow, but not when. Sybelle understood. There were three men at risk, and all of them together weighed less than Walter and Beau. But after them, Walter started Beau over.

Midway, the stallion jibbed. The bridge groaned, and trickles of scree rolled down the slope. Sybelle closed her eyes and prayed. She heard Walter's voice, firm, easy, chiding Beau for foolishness. The bridge groaned again, and Sybelle heard pebbles skittering. The prayer went out of her head; in her terror she could not remember words she had said thousands and thousands of times. Then her chin was tipped up, and her lips were kissed, and she heard Walter laughing.

"You can open your eyes now, you goose. Why do women always close their eyes then they do not want something to happen?"

Later Sybelle remembered that although the men had been clustered close around her, she had not heard a normal breath in the entire time it took them all to cross the bridge over the scree and also bring across the three extra horses and the packhorse. Either there was no sound of breathing, as all held their breath during a crossing, or there were gasps and sighs as one was completed. But that thought only occurred to her when there was no longer any need for held-in breath.

Beyond the scree they found the slope easier, and following along the gentlest path, they soon came to another stream, already well developed, not rising from the mountain they had crossed but from some other to the north and east. In no long time they were able to mount their horses again. However, by now a new concern was filling all minds. It had taken so long to build the bridge and cross the scree that most of the day was past. The sun was dropping and the cold growing more intense. This was plainly no night to be sleeping in the open. In addition, all were very hungry. While they had labored and endured danger, no one had thought of food. But both danger and labor tend to hone the appetite when the effort is over.

All were very relieved when Walter suddenly pointed and said, "Look. There is an ax mark on that tree. There must be at least a woodcutter's shelter not too far."

CHAPTER 21

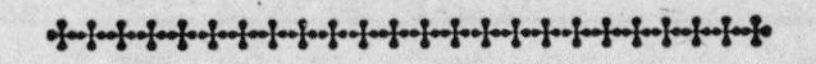

Fatigue had kept Walter and Sybelle from discussing the ambush they had escaped after they had found the huts of the woodcutters and helped themselves to food and shelter. There was no complaint from their startled hosts, for Walter paid liberally for what they received. This was less owing to generosity than it was a form of insurance, since he did not wish to set guards that night and need to check on them himself for fear they had fallen asleep. With money in hand to replace whatever food for the humans and fodder for the horses were consumed and extra as a reward, there was no likelihood that the woodcutters would take the desperate chance of attempting robbery or that they would betray the presence of the party to a possibly unfriendly local lord.

The next morning, however, while they were eating the coarse but filling barley gruel provided for their breakfasts, Sybelle voiced her suspicion that the men who had attacked them were Sir Heribert's minions.

"I thought the same," Walter admitted, "when I showed my shield and they seemed to recognize it and still pursued, but it cannot be."

He then explained his reasoning: how Sir Heribert could not have had time to organize an ambush, that it must have been a mistake, some local quarrel, perhaps, involving a minor vassal of the de Clares who had adopted the chevrons and colors of the family.

After a dissatisfied wrinkling of her nose, Sybelle sighed. "It might be so. Clifford is close by. I thought I knew all the relatives of Aunt Isobel—I mean Richard's Mama, of course, not his sister—but it is possible there were some black sheep that she did not recognize. And in these times when de Clare is so divided . . ."

"There are not enough of us to be divided, only poor little

Richard, who has no say in the matter, and myself. But you are right. I myself had forgotten that there must be a good sprinkling of Strongbow's bastards' children holding manors around Clifford."

Walter's voice was easy, but he was annoyed with himself. Why should his first thought on being pursued be that Sir Heribert had tried to ambush him? Then he put the matter out of his mind. He would talk out the problem of Sir Heribert with Richard. It could not be long now until the attack was made on Shrewsbury. At that time he would gain a clearer picture of Sir Heribert's loyalties.

When they finished eating, they rode south again. The track was rough, but compared with the difficulties of the previous day, it was easy. The only complaints were Sybelle's, as she scratched flea bites and wondered if the relative warmth of the woodcutter's hut was worth the trouble she would have in ridding herself and her clothes of the creeping, biting pests they had collected. The woodcutters had moved out of the hut, but they had left behind many, many small inhabitants it was impossible to evict. However, she was only teasing, offering Walter laughing sympathy because, similarly afflicted, he was unable even to scratch because of his armor.

The light mood lasted until they came to the meeting with the main road at Llanvihangel. The village was in an uproar. First they had the news that the Earl of Pembroke's army and siege equipment had passed through two days before. Sybelle feared that Walter might order her to go on to Abergavenny with the men and pursue Richard's army north alone, but he did not ask which way they had gone. His only questions were about Henry's men. Had there been patrols, and were they likely to meet any such patrols on the road? Then they discovered that the frantic activity they had noticed was not owing to Richard's passing.

The villagers had scarcely replaced the few valuables they had and called their young women out of hiding after Richard's men were gone than they had word that an army was on its way from Grosmont. They were now preparing to abandon their village entirely, since they feared a battle would be fought right over it if Pembroke's men returned. Even if there were no battle, the villagers knew they would be safer in the woods. Then the worst that could happen, provided they could get most of their supplies out, was that their houses would be burnt. That would be very bad in this bitter cold, but for most, except the old and the very young, not catastrophic.

As soon as Walter understood, he urged Sybelle and the men onto the road at the best pace they could make. Despite the cold, all the men had rolled their cloaks and had their shields on their arms. They expected any moment either to meet or to be pursued by foreriders of the king's army. However, there was no untoward incident for several miles. Indeed, they were so close to Abergavenny that Walter thought it safe to slow the pace to spare the horses, when they rounded a curve and saw an armed party drawn up in defensive array.

Convinced this was the patrol of foreriders they had been expecting, and unwilling to lose the impetus of forward movement, Walter asked no questions and called no challenge. He dug his spurs into Beau, at the same time bellowing, "Sybelle! Fall back!"

Instantly, rising above a cat's ferocious yowl, a woman's voice called out an order in Welsh, and then, in French, "Walter, stop! It is I, Rhiannon."

As soon as he heard the cat's squall, even before Rhiannon had spoken his name, Walter had lowered his sword and shield and begun to fumble for Beau's reins, which he had wound round his pommel just as he spurred the destrier forward. He found them and pulled, but it was impossible for Beau to stop. However, Rhiannon's men moved their horses aside and a collision was avoided. The men behind Walter, somewhat slower to charge, were able to come to a halt before more dodging was necessary.

"What in the world made you run at us like that?" Rhiannon asked as Walter came round and stopped Beau beside her mare, Cyflym.

"We heard in the village up the road that an army is on the move from Grosmont. I thought your group was foreriders. Where is Simon?"

A shadow passed over Rhiannon's face, and her voice trembled slightly. "Simon is with the army. But how do you come from a village on this road?"

"Never mind that. Sybelle will explain. Lend me a man to take me to Simon or Richard. I must tell them that there will be an army on this road as well as—"

"No!" Sybelle cried. "Do not leave us."

For just a moment Walter looked startled. It was not possible that Sybelle could feel she needed his protection for the short distance to Abergavenny in the company of Rhiannon and double the number of men. She had understood the danger of meeting a patrol and had followed every order he gave quickly, but she had shown no sign of fear. Then he realized that she was afraid for him. It was sweet to know, a warm comfort to carry into the coming battle. He smiled and shook his head at her.

"I must go, and quickly," he said.

"You will break your collarbone again and be useless in ten minutes," Sybelle countered.

"I will take care," Walter assured her, smiling fondly, but his eyes and voice were inflexible.

Knowing the outcome of such an exchange, Rhiannon had not listened to it but had explained in Welsh to her men that one of them must guide Sir Walter to Simon or, if he were gone on some scouting mission, to Lord Pembroke. Efan, who had a word or two of French, said he would go, and Rhiannon turned back to Walter and Sybelle just in time to hear her say, "Then God go with you, my lord."

Sybelle's voice was calm and her eyelids lowered. She had been well schooled. She knew when argument was useless, and she knew how to part with a man. She had seen her mother and her grandmother part with their husbands often enough. She had not known, however, how much it hurt, how hard it was to force quiet words through a throat constricted with terror. It would not always be so bad, she told herself, barely aware that Walter was already riding back up the road, as she prodded Damas into a trot beside Cyflym. She was only frightened because Walter's bone was still weak, and if it broke, he would not be able to hold his shield properly. But Richard would know that; surely Richard would know and either would order Walter not to fight or would protect him.

"I am afraid also," Rhiannon said, her voice high-pitched and trembling. "Sybelle, should we go back? We could stay in the camp with the boys and the servants."

Fear called to fear. Sybelle turned her head and saw how staring-wide Rhiannon's eyes were. "You know we cannot do that," she said. "You know how great a danger we would be to our men if . . . if the battle should go ill.'' Her voice began to waver, and she stopped and steadied it and went on firmly, ''You promised Simon you would bide safe if he kept you close until the eve of battle—you told me that. No harm will come to either of them. Think how often they have fought and come safe away. And . . . and if one of them should be hurt and both of us taken by Monmouth, who would tend the hurts?''

Rhiannon sighed, and the fixed staring of her eyes misted over with tears. ''I do not like to be afraid,'' she whispered.

Sybelle did not like it, either; however, the fear saved her from an even more futile agony. When she heard Sybelle had ridden into the keep, Marie was nearly beside herself with joy. She sat by the fire and polished the words with which she would destroy Sybelle's betrothal, and she stabbed her needle in and out of her embroidery as if it were Sybelle's heart instead of cloth in the frame. But anxiety made it impossible for either Rhiannon or Sybelle to sit quietly, so Marie had no chance to say her piece.

She did try, however; as soon as Rhiannon and Sybelle came in and made polite curtsies to Gervase, Marie said she had something of great importance to impart to Sybelle. Thinking she knew the range of Marie's news—some new scandal—Sybelle said as politely as she could that she would come anon to hear it but that her men had been wounded on the journey and she must see to their hurts. For once Gervase did not cry out against a fine lady soiling her hands on the common men-at-arms. Had they been less disordered by fear, both Rhiannon and Sybelle would have noted this as unusual and understood that Gervase wanted them gone. As it was, they would hardly have noted it if Gervase had been dancing naked on a table.

Desiring only something to do, something on which to fix their minds, they went to collect what simples Rhiannon had carried in her baskets and then to examine what stores the castle leech kept. From there, they progressed to the area in the men-at-arm's quarters set aside for the sick, where they consulted so anxiously over each cut and bruise that they frightened the poor men, who earlier had thought nothing of their hurts, none of which was serious.

As soon as they were gone, Gervase said, ''Sister, I beg

you to say nothing to Lady Sybelle about your . . . er . . . situation until you have spoken to Richard.''

''Why?'' Marie cried. ''You promised to help me. Is this your help?''

''I will help,'' Gervase responded somewhat mendaciously, for the more she thought of Richard's reaction to what Marie planned, the less she liked the scheme.

The two years in Pembroke, compared with the festivities at Builth and the mild interests and pleasures of residence in Abergavenny, had taught Gervase a lesson. She had complained of isolation and boredom when Richard was at war in France, but there had always been some visitors, some coming and going, moderate-sized towns with fairs and markets, and other simple amusements. Pembroke, as far out in Wales as one could go, was different. Whether or not it had been intended so, it had been a prison. Gervase did not wish to suffer such isolation again, particularly not for her sister's petty revenge.

''You have not thought,'' Gervase continued. ''If you tell Sybelle your tale and she believes you, she will not sit and weep. Have you not seen she is not that kind? She will go back to her keep in Clyro, probably write to her father and very likely to Sir Walter. But Sir Walter is with Richard and can tell him anything—and you will not be there to defend yourself. In addition, Lord Geoffrey is the most likely person to mediate between the king and Richard. You yourself must have seen how often they spoke together at Builth. It is true that Sybelle may write ill of Sir Walter to Lord Geoffrey, but do you think it is Sir Walter that *Lord Geoffrey* will blame? When does a man blame another man for playing with women? He will blame *you,* and if he will no longer speak for Richard to the king, Richard will kill you rather than support you.''

Marie stared at her sister, her face pallid with rage. ''I will have my revenge on him for playing with me, for using me. I will!''

''And I will help you,'' Gervase assured her, knowing that Marie must be quieted or her spite would override her fear. ''But you must work through Richard. If you wait for him and tell him your story in private, little blame can fall on you beyond that for the weakness of a woman who believed the lies of a man she had reason to trust. Richard is your warden. It will be his duty to act to protect you.''

"And what if he will not act?" Marie cried. "He let my lands be taken, although it was his duty to return them to me."

"Then . . . then we will see," Gervase answered, fondly hoping neither Richard nor Sir Walter would return to Abergavenny until long after it was possible for Marie to claim she was pregnant with Sir Walter's child; in which case, no matter what Marie said, Richard would laugh at her. "But we will do *something,*" Gervase added, hurriedly seeing the fury in Marie's face and desiring to pacify her.

She might not have been successful in her attempt to keep Marie quiet if Sybelle and Rhiannon had come to sit with them, but they did not. When every bruise had been salved on the men-at-arms, they were reminded by the tolling of the church bells that it was Christmas Day. Forgoing dinner, for which neither had the smallest appetite, they hurried to the church. No day seemed more appropriate to prayer.

To whom Rhiannon prayed, Sybelle did not ask. Rhiannon made the proper responses during the Mass, but afterward she whispered softly in her own tongue. In fact, Sybelle was glad of it. It mattered not a pin to her if the power that preserved Simon and Walter were approved by the church in which she worshipped. If the old gods still had strength here in Wales, she was glad Rhiannon knew how to appeal to them. Sybelle would have prayed to them herself if she had known how—or to the devil for that matter. But being in church, she did what was best known to her, giving silver to the priest and making offerings at every shrine.

Then, without a word spoken but knowing what the other wanted, Sybelle and Rhiannon made their way up to the walls. The guards were surprised but did not say them nay, and they stood long there, staring eastward despite the cold and bitter wind. They went to Mass at Vespers, too, and then back to the wall. But no sign came, and, at last, the light failing, they went within to stand shivering by the fire.

By then Marie's first rage had faded, and Gervase had managed to instill in her a sense of fear and caution. She looked hatefully at Sybelle, but she would have had to stick a dagger into Sybelle's side to draw her attention. There was little talk as they ate the evening meal, and after that, Rhiannon sang. She did so to ease her own heart, for her music was her comfort, but so compelling were her songs that all listened, even Sybelle, even Marie.

When Rhiannon grew too tired to sing again, Gervase and Marie went to bed; Sybelle and Rhiannon sat by the fire, waiting, waiting. But no news came, and at last they were forced to admit that their trial was not over. No battle had been fought that day. They must endure through the night and then through another day. Clasping hands, they, too, rose to go to bed, but neither could bear the thought of lying alone through the sleepless hours, so they lay together in Rhiannon's chamber, comforting each other as best they could until, near dawn, both slept.

It had been a bitterly cold night for Richard's army, for they did not dare light fires. Nonetheless, the men were in good spirits, for they knew their time of penance was over and they were warmed by the thought of the booty they would take. Dawn was a welcome sight, however, and there were few who needed to be roused by their captains. By Terce all were in position, eagerly awaiting the first sight of John of Monmouth's troops.

The noblemen had suffered less from the cold; braziers of charcoal warmed their tents, and furs protected their bodies. They were less sanguine than the men, however. Walter's news had not been welcome—although, of course, Richard was glad to be warned. There would be more men than they expected, and that fact hinted that John of Monmouth might not be as unaware as they had hoped of the ambush laid for him. Still, Simon's Welsh reported that few precautions had been taken in Monmouth's camp.

Walter spent the night with Simon. The Welsh were assigned to keep pace with the very forefront of Monmouth's force and let loose with their bows to stop the advance when the signal came. On hearing this, Walter offered to add his troop to Simon's to provide an even more complete blockage. Richard, whose face was healed and showed no more than lighter, pinkish patches where the scabs had fallen off, wrinkled his brow and asked whether the bone Walter had broken was yet strong enough for fighting.

"Sybelle says not for jousting," Walter replied, "but there will be none of that."

That was not what Sybelle had said, but Richard did not

know, and he was glad to have Walter and his men to steady the Welsh. He had learned to appreciate their abilities, but he still did not trust them. In that—at least for the purposes of a set battle—there was some justice. The Welsh were not known for standing their ground and slogging it out. Lightly armed, light-footed, and few in number, they were prone to fade away before too strong an opposition, harassing their enemies as they fled until pursuit became too costly. However successful this method was in defense, it would not serve in this case.

Richard did not want any chance that his enemies would break through the front of the lines, re-form, and come back to hit his forces from the rear. He had intended to assign a troop of better-armed men to support Simon's Welsh archers, and Walter's offer was the ideal solution. Although Walter's troop was from south Wales—and therefore hardly to be considered human by Simon's men, and vice versa—each group still preferred the other to Bassett's Saesones. And their enemies were Saesones also—or mostly. Thus, the whole party was in the highest spirits when they left the camp to take their places for the battle.

Waiting, Walter and Simon talked quietly until, in the middle of a remark, Simon's voice stopped abruptly and he cocked his head to listen. Walter could hear nothing, but a moment later there was a birdcall, and Simon put on his helmet and swung his shield into position. Without question, Walter did the same. To him, the birdcall was just a birdcall, but Simon's reaction indicated it was a signal he recognized. A few minutes passed, and then Walter heard vague sounds in the distance, a low rumble punctuated by an occasional higher note.

"We must wait for the signal," he murmured.

Simon grimaced, but nodded. They had tried to set themselves far enough ahead so that if they had to move, it would be forward, toward the oncoming army. It was more difficult to remain unnoticed when one had to follow along or move just in front.

Suddenly there were sharper sounds, horses closing quickly at a trot. Simon whistled three piercing notes, warning his archers to let the foreriders go by. To attack the foreriders would warn the main force. The foreriders themselves were not a serious danger. Even if they heard the battle once it started and returned, Simon's archers could pick off most of them. Once Walter's troop was actively engaged, the archers could not volley for fear of shooting their allies, so a group of them could watch the road behind.

They waited tensely for another twenty minutes while the dull rumble sorted itself out into the thud of many feet, the plodding of slow-moving oxen and horses, the grind of wheels on hard earth. Now they could hear the higher notes even more clearly, the screech of axles, shouted orders, the whinny of a protesting horse. Simon and Walter glanced at each other. This was both good luck and bad. The presence of the wagons proved that their ambush was unsuspected, but they would have to order the men to move back. Walter nodded, and Simon pursed his lips to whistle a signal—but it was drowned out in the blare of horns and trumpets from farther down the road.

Walter saw flickers among the trees in which they were hidden and knew that Simon's men were running forward to where they could shoot. He waited until he felt they were clear and shouted orders to his own men to move, but they went along the road, and Simon came with him. Once the Welsh were launched, there was little he could do to direct them, and Simon was by training a knight who fought on horseback with lance and sword—only neither he nor Walter had a lance. Those were not easy weapons to maneuver among trees, and they did not expect the mounted men accompanying Monmouth's siege weapons to be carrying spears, either.

When the vanguard of the army came into sight, they were already in dreadful confusion. Richard's signal had warned them of a coming attack, and they had drawn together to protect the wains. This move, although useful against footsoldiers and even against mounted men, was an invitation to disaster when the attackers were Welsh bowmen. Simon's men were picked for their skill, but even had they been only fair bowmen, they could hardly have missed the target presented by the close-drawn enemy troops.

A first hail of arrows, loosed at the signal of a single whistle, wreaked havoc, striking victims above and below the round footmen's shields, and, although the captains immediately began to shout orders for the formation of turtles, some men were demoralized, others unable to comply. A second volley followed the first with almost as dire results. A few men broke and ran. Siorl shouted in Welsh to let them get away, at least some distance before picking them off, to encourage others to run. A few more did, but not many, for the troops were not raw levies but mercenaries who knew their business.

The turtles began to form, some men kneeling, others standing, presenting a wall of shields against the arrows, which even the yard-long shafts of the Welsh bowmen could not pierce. To volley against such a target was useless. Only single arrows were loosed now as one Welshman or another saw an exposed head or limb. Then, before the captains could decide whether to turn back or try to move forward, Walter and Simon appeared at the charge at the head of the footmen.

At first it was a May-Day fair for Walter, Simon, and the men. Monmouth's troops, shocked and caught between protecting themselves against the archers and fighting the oncoming swordsmen, fell like grain before the scythe. But they were well disciplined and did not break. And then, all too soon, the foreriders were back. The Welsh took some of them out and cried warning, but there were ten or twelve mounted men opposed to Simon and Walter alone, and then another mounted troop began to force its way past the stalled wains and the battling footmen—and they bore lances.

CHAPTER 22

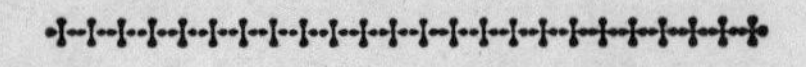

Because they had fallen asleep only near dawn and were exhausted by effort and worry, Sybelle and Rhiannon slept late. Both were also unconsciously deceived by the warmth of each other's body in the bed. In sleep, neither was aware of the feminine nature of her companion and was soothed by the false conviction that her male partner was beside her. Thus, the rest that came was deep and long.

Gervase and Marie were not naturally early risers. When they did come into the hall and did not see the other ladies, they assumed they were long since risen and doing some vulgar "business," so they did not inquire. Thus, by the mercy of God and the normal devices of nature, Sybelle and Rhiannon were spared many hours of mental agony.

It was well beyond Terce when Rhiannon stirred, reached out to embrace Simon, and found her hand tangled in the long, thick hair that lay upon Sybelle's shoulders. The touch wakened Sybelle, and both started up, crying out in surprise, and then laughing when they recognized each other. Both thought immediately of Simon and Walter, however, so that fear came hard on the heels of laughter. But it was less sharp than it might have been; the immediate presence of a dear friend who shared the emotion was a help. Nonetheless, both leapt from the bed without a moment's delay and ran to the door, snatching up bedrobes to preserve decency. There was no reason to come out, however. When they opened the door and listened, there were only the soft sounds of common activity in the hall. It was clear that there was as yet no news of the battle.

Gold eyes met green, and both girls sighed. The minutes and hours of this day would be very long. Still, they must be lived through, and the best way was to be busy. Almost simultaneously Sybelle and Rhiannon moved to their clothing and began to dress. There were the wounded men to see to and the church to pray in. Then Rhiannon went to talk to the castle leech and Sybelle to see what was being prepared in the kitchens; there would be wounded coming back to Abergavenny even if Richard's army was victorious and pursued Monmouth's men to the very walls of Monmouth keep.

Dinner, though not much of it for Sybelle and Rhiannon, was eaten in virtual silence. Gervase was very annoyed. She did not much care for either Sybelle or Rhiannon, but any company was better than none—or so she had thought until she found herself dining in the presence of what seemed to be a pair of deaf mutes. Marie was actually in a better mood than her sister by then. She realized that nothing she said to Sybelle would have made any impression and also that she had been mistaken about Sybelle's distaste for Walter. That would make her revenge doubly sweet. Sybelle would lose something she did want, something it would cause her more pain to lose than mere hurt pride.

After dinner, they all sat for a little longer than an hour by the fire. Sybelle, trained to the manners of the lady of a keep moreso than Rhiannon, actually tried to make conversation, but her mind wandered so badly that Gervase found Sybelle's effort at politeness more annoying than Rhiannon's silence. Marie grinned like a cat that had caught a pet bird that had been irritatingly out of reach for years. Well before None, however, all had had enough of each other's company. Rhiannon said abruptly that she would go out. Sybelle leapt up, fearing her wild friend meant she would ride out toward the battle, and she begged Rhiannon not to break her promise.

"I will not," Rhiannon said harshly. "It does not matter. If Simon comes not, I will go swiftly to meet him in the land of Annwn. We cannot be parted long."

It was the first time Sybelle had heard Rhiannon's voice other than clear and musical. And, although she had never heard the name Annwn, she knew from the way Rhiannon spoke that it was what the Welsh called the world of the dead. "There is no bad news!" she exclaimed.

Rhiannon shook her head. "I do not despair," she assured Sybelle. "I am only impatient of this waiting." Then her voice softened. "It must be worse for you. I have no ties except Simon to bind me to this earth. My mother and father love me, but their lives are their own. I can go when I wish, free. But you are tied to your land, are you not?''

''Yes,'' Sybelle whispered. ''I am bound to the land more harshly than any serf. I am not free, nor ever will be.'' Then she lifted her head higher. ''But this is foolish talk. The advantage is all with our men. It is sitting with those . . . those ghouls, who do not care about Richard's well-being or success or, perhaps, even hope for his ill-doing that has made us uneasy. Come, let us go up on the walls again. They must come soon. Surely, they will come or news will come soon.''

In fact, it was soon. Before the chill had reached through their cloaks and heavy woolen clothing, the guards on the walls saw mounted men in the distance. They called warnings and then politely, but with strong emphasis, bade the ladies go down. Sybelle and Rhiannon gave no argument, knowing their presence would be a hindrance to defense if defense were necessary—although what defense the few men remaining in Abergavenny could make, they did not know. But it was only a few minutes before the riders the guards had seen were crying out their identities and assurances of a great victory.

The guards relayed the message to the gate guards so that the drawbridge could be got down. Sybelle and Rhiannon heard. They were at the gate to question the foreriders, but these men had no word of Simon or of Walter. Gold eyes locked again with green. Unspoken in both was the desire to ride out and look for their men. Oddly, it was the bolder Rhiannon who shook her head.

''The road will be blocked and the woods full of stragglers,'' she said. ''And if our men are unhurt, they are like to be as far as the gates of Monmouth keep.''

''And there will be work for us now,'' Sybelle agreed.

Rhiannon nodded. The wounded would be the first to return, having been sent on ahead. Sybelle and Rhiannon then withdrew to a vantage point where they could watch the bailey, which was now becoming crowded and a scene of utter confusion. Oxen lowed, horses whinnied, men shouted orders and imprecations, the wounded moaned and screamed. However, it was not quite the chaos it looked. The old knight left in charge of Abergavenny knew his business. Sybelle and Rhiannon threaded their way through the servants and men unloading the wains, leading away the animals, and carrying or helping along the wounded.

"Will you look to the arrangement for the men or shall I?" Sybelle asked.

Rhiannon laughed. "I will," she said. "The word is about that I am a witch. If I smile and say all will be well, it may give a few enough heart to survive, but in this weather the weakest will certainly die."

Sybelle nodded unsentimental agreement with that and turned away toward the keep where the noblemen who had taken hurt would be carried, while Rhiannon moved toward the shelters that would be used to house the wounded. The common leech and those selected to assist him were already there; servants were laying out straw for the men to lie in and bringing in fleeces with which to cover them—at least the lucky ones. If there were many, there would be only more straw for a blanket.

As the men were carried in, the leech looked at the wounds. The worst wounded were only laid down; since there was little chance for their survival in any case, it was not sensible to waste time with them while others who might be saved grew worse. Rhiannon spoke to those who called to her or looked to her for help, offering what comfort she could, but she did not stay long since everything seemed to be in good order. Her skill was too precious to spend on these common folk, at least until after all those of the higher orders had been treated. And if Simon had been hurt, he would be in the keep. Rhiannon moved faster, controlling her fear.

But there was no sign of Simon in the keep, nor of Walter. Nor, for that matter, was there any sign of Gervase or Marie, who had retreated to their chambers when the bloody wounded were brought in. Great lords could afford chirurgeons, and their ladies did not soil their hands with such work. Sybelle had noticed they were missing and had curled her lip with contempt, but she had more important things to think about. When Rhiannon came in, she called to her to look at Philip Bassett, who had a long slash on his back where a blow strong enough to break his mail had landed. It was not deep or serious. Sybelle stitched it up, and Rhiannon brought a salve to help the healing.

He was the first of many. Soon torches and candles were lit, but neither Rhiannon nor Sybelle noticed. They were not aware of the passing of time nor of fear until, suddenly, there was Simon, with dried blood on his arm and knee, patiently waiting his turn. Rhiannon shrieked aloud with joy and in the next instant cried, "Where is Walter?"

Simon laughed. "In hiding, I think. He *did* break his collarbone again and does not wish to hear what Sybelle will say to him."

Needless to say, Sybelle uttered not a word except the sweetest that love and relief could bring to her tongue. In fact, she had great difficulty holding back a paean of joy, as it was almost certain the attack on Shrewsbury would take place before Walter's shoulder could heal, and that would mean that he would take no active part in the fighting.

In this, Sybelle was not disappointed. The ambush had fulfilled Richard's highest hopes. John of Monmouth himself had escaped, but the slaughter among his men had been enormous. The casualties among Richard's troops, on the other hand, had been very light. Indeed, Simon and Walter had withstood the hardest of the battles. For a few minutes, between the returning foreriders and a group of mounted men-at-arms who were trying to break away forward, it had been a near thing, but Richard Siward's men had been hard on the heels of the escaping troop. It was in the few minutes of hard fighting that Walter's collarbone had given way, but he had sustained no other hurt and had remained with his troop, guarding the captured wains and prisoners and eventually directing them toward Abergavenny.

That was what made him and Simon so late in returning. Richard did not come back until the next afternoon. Since his casualties had been so few, he had reorganized his sound troops and pursued Monmouth's men nearly to the gates of the keep, looting and burning all the way. So the land was empty, the people fled, and at least half of Monmouth's army was dead, wounded, or prisoners. Monmouth would not be able to organize another—even if he had the money and will to do it—in less than a few months. No help would come to Shrewsbury from the king's men in the south.

As soon as he returned to Abergavenny, Richard plunged into plans for starting his fighting men north. The siege engines and war machines should already have reached the agreed-upon rendezvous with Llewelyn's forces. Marie asked to speak to him privately on the very afternoon he arrived, but Richard turned her away brusquely; and when she insisted, saying the matter was urgent and of great importance, he laughed.

"Nothing a woman could say could be urgent or of great importance now," he stated. "Do not plague me, or I will send you back to Pembroke just to keep you out of my way."

Marie turned toward Gervase, but she shook her head as she drew her sister aside. "If he sends us to Pembroke," she murmured, "you will have lost all chance of revenge. Wait until his plans are made. Perhaps there will be a time of quiet before he is ready to leave."

Angry as she was, Marie recognized the truth in what Gervase said. To work off some of her spite, she attached herself to Sybelle and Walter, although there were now plenty of men who would have been glad to be in her company. To both, her speech was honey-sweet, but filled with sly innuendos for Sybelle and long, languishing glances at Walter. Sybelle missed neither; now that Walter was safe, her mind was able to focus on what was going on around her. However, she was uncertain of what it meant, and there was no one with whom she could discuss the problem because Simon and Rhiannon left Abergavenny at dawn on the twenty-eighth to join Llewelyn.

There was, Sybelle felt, no real reason for jealousy. Plainly Marie was trying to revive the love affair, and equally plainly Walter did not wish to do so. He made answers that changed the meaning of the innuendos to comical or innocent; he did not return the glances cast at him; he clung to Sybelle, unless he was surrounded by men talking war, as if she were a lifeline and he dangling off a cliff. On the other hand, he made no effort to drive Marie away or to discourage her. He was unfailingly polite, and not coldly but pleasantly.

Although there were two obvious reasons for such behavior—Walter might be sorry for Marie, and Marie was the Earl of Pembroke's sister-by-marriage—Sybelle did not think either of the reasons wise or compelling. To be kind at the termination of a love affair might be more cruel than a sharp rebuff; it was apparent to Sybelle that Richard was unlikely to take offense if Marie complained of insult. However, Sybelle was not a hasty person unless her temper was aroused or her feelings deeply hurt, and the present situation was not of that kind. It was not her business to tell Walter how to behave to a past mistress, so long as he did not love her or seek her bed.

As it was, Marie was with them when Richard approached and said, "So, Walter, what of this castellan of yours of whom you had such doubts?"

"The doubts remain," Walter replied. "Yet I have not a thread with which to spin them into cloth."

Richard frowned. "Can it be only because he was your brother's man?"

"My lord," Sybelle put in, "my castellan at Clyro felt the same about Sir Heribert, and he did not know Walter's brother." She did not mention her own feeling. Most men would regard that as irrelevant or even as a mark in Sir Heribert's favor.

"I never knew you to take a man you did not know in aversion," Richard said to Walter, also nodding at Sybelle to acknowledge what she had offered. "It can do no harm to be cautious. Where is this Sir Heribert now?"

"I asked him to remain at Clyro, and it seems he has done so because Sir Roland would have sent word if Heribert had gone. I said I would return there and that we would then go together to Knight's Tower."

Richard looked at Walter's arm, which was bound to his side again. His lips twisted into a grin. "You told me that the bone was healed, except too weak for jousting. More the fool I was to believe you."

"But it *was* a lance blow that broke it," Walter protested. "It was no set battle we were to fight. I did not expect to be charged by spearmen."

Richard's expression showed a strong doubt about Walter's defense, but he just shrugged. "Well, truth or not, you are crippled again, and I do not think it wise for you to be in the power of a man you do not trust when in such a condition. Write to Sir Heribert and tell him that you cannot come now but that you will meet him at Knight's Tower on the first day of January. You need not say that the whole army will be with you."

"I am not likely to do that," Walter assured him dryly. "And since I will be of no use to you as I am and my men have had some hard knocks, too, what I will do is send the garrison of Knight's Tower with your army and let my troop guard the keep. Thus you will have some fresh men, I will be safe, and you can be certain Knight's Tower will be open for refuge if—God forbid—you need it."

"And Sir Heribert himself?" Richard asked.

"Let him make his own choice. He has been neutral thus far, and I have no right to push him into the rebellion. However, he came to Clyro with a large troop, saying he believed I wished him to join your party in the war. If he refuses to go with the army, would that not be a sign that his earlier eagerness to be urged to become one with us was a trap for me?"

"So it would seem to me," Richard agreed. "Not enough to merit his dismissal, perhaps, but a sign—yes."

Marie had not said one single word, but she was listening intently. The way Walter refused to be separated from Sybelle and his steady rejection of her own advances had fanned the red coals of her hatred to white heat. Her mind was quick and had seized immediately on the fact that Walter suspected Sir Heribert of being an enemy. Whether or not this was true made no difference. Marie thought it would not be difficult to make suspicion into fact. If she warned Sir Heribert that Walter intended to dismiss him, very likely he would seek to save himself. Whatever action he took might make trouble for Walter, and Marie passionately wished to make all the trouble she could.

A brief discussion on what would be adequate cause for dismissal of Sir Heribert passed over Marie's head while she was thinking of ways to implement the idea that had come to her, but her attention was caught when she heard Richard saying, "I will take Gervase and Lady Marie to Clifford. There can be no danger of attack on so strong a place now, and they will be more comfortable there and also closer to hand if the king should have a change of heart. If you would like, I can include Lady Sybelle in our party or I could take her to Clyro, which is only a few miles out of the way."

"I thank you, but I will accompany Walter to Knight's Tower," Sybelle said firmly. "There has been no lady in that keep for some years, and I felt no conviction that Sir Heribert was the kind to keep the women's quarters in good order. The sooner I take matters in hand there, the better."

''When do we leave for Clifford, Brother?'' Marie asked. ''If it is soon, I must tell Gervase so that we can pack.''

''Tomorrow,'' Richard replied, looking somewhat startled, as if he had not previously thought of the problem of his wife's packing. Then he glanced at Walter, whose face was so carefully blank that it was clear he was appalled. Richard cleared his throat. ''Perhaps *I* had better go and tell Gervase,'' he said, and turned away.

Marie seemed to follow him, but she hastened into her own chamber. So they would be at Clifford, only a few miles from Clyro; that was very interesting. Perhaps Sir Heribert would have time before he rode to meet Walter on the first of January to pay a short visit to Clifford. She need not say everything in her letter, only enough to bring Heribert to her if he really was Walter's enemy. And if he came, that would be proof he wished Walter ill. Perhaps between them they could devise something that would satisfy them both.

First she sent her maid to see if she could discover who would be sent as messenger to Clyro; if not, Marie could send someone herself, but she liked the idea of Walter's messenger carrying her letter. Then she set herself to write it as if it came from a man rather than a woman, saying that the writer had reasons, which ''he'' would not name, to wish Sir Heribert well and wish Sir Walter ill. Thus, overhearing talk between Sir Walter and the Earl of Pembroke concerning Sir Heribert and devising his downfall, the writer wished to warn him of it.

It was dangerous to say more or to identify the writer of this letter, which might not be delivered into his hand, ''But,'' Marie wrote, ''if you will come to Clifford, calling yourself Sir Palance de Tours, and ask for Lady Marie de les Maures, you will learn more. She did not write this letter and knows not what is in it, but out of gentle pity for me, she is willing to pass to you another letter containing information that may save your life and lands.''

The ease with which Marie's maid was able to pass the letter to Walter's messenger, who was in haste and did not even inquire from whom it came, lifted Marie's spirits and made her feel her luck had turned. This feeling was confirmed when, early in the evening, a servant came to tell her that Richard was at leisure and ready to grant her private audience, as she had requested. She was surprised that Gervase was not there, having believed it was her sister who reminded Richard of Marie's desire to speak to him, but in this she wronged her brother-by-marriage. He had remembered on his own.

Doubts flashed across Marie's mind; she would be confessing to a great sin. Would Richard change his mind about taking them to Clifford and send them instead back to Pembroke? If so, Gervase would make her life a hell for her. But he looked particularly good-humored, and Marie knew she would not have another opportunity to use this device. The attack on Shrewsbury might take weeks, and Richard might not return to Clifford but go on to some other action in the war. Also, Sybelle was here with Walter and would have to be told.

Clasping her hands nervously, she said in a quavering voice, "I have a great trouble to confess to you."

Richard's expression did not change. "I did suppose so," he said calmly. "I did not think you needed a private talk with me to tell me of a great joy. Well, what is it?"

"I . . . I am with child," she whispered.

She expected a roar of rage, but Richard only lifted his brows. "That is no great surprise, either," he sighed. "What other great trouble is a woman likely to need to confess?"

Marie gasped with outrage. "I am no whore," she cried. "He promised me marriage!"

Now for the first time, Richard frowned. Likely, Richard thought, that fool of a woman had become enamored of some penniless but clever popinjay, who had got her with child because he believed that would force Pembroke to give permission for the marriage and then support them both. Any honorable man interested in marriage would have come to him first for permission. Or perhaps it was a young fool, and Marie had convinced him this was the only way to wring a livelihood from her niggardly guardian.

"So? Who is it?" He growled.

"Sir Walter de Clare," Marie snapped defiantly. "And since you would not offer enough, he went elsewhere for more. Now I am shamed and dishonored."

There was a moment of stunned silence. Then Richard got precipitately to his feet. "You lie!" he roared. "Bitch whore! You lie!"

"I do not!" Marie shrieked, and forgetting caution in her rage added, "I can prove he lay with me. Summon him and ask. He will deny it. Then I will bring my proof. Let us see who lies."

Richard's fists clenched, and Marie shrank back fearing that he would strike her, but he did not move. He had remembered that Walter had seemed interested in Marie when he first met her, and that he himself had warned him she would not make a suitable wife. But promised marriage? No, that could not be true. Doubtless Walter had said he loved her or some such nonsense, and she had taken that as a promise of marriage. *Stupid bitch!* Richard thought, but with weary patience instead of rage. Still, if she were with child by Walter, the child would be Walter's responsibility. He nodded curtly to Marie and went to the door to send someone to look for Walter.

Fortunately, since neither Marie nor Richard had a word to say to each other, Walter was in the hall and came in a few minutes. The smile of greeting with which he entered Richard's chamber froze on his face when he saw Marie. He stared at her for just a moment and then looked at Richard. "What is amiss, my lord?" he asked.

"My sister-by-marriage says she is with child by you," Richard replied.

Walter's complexion turned pasty gray. "My God," he breathed, "never has so much ill come from so brief and joyless a sin." He turned to Marie, holding out his hand. "My dear, I am so sorry. I gave you no pleasure, and now this has come upon you. What can I do to help you?"

She slapped his hand away and spat at him. "You lied to me," she shrieked. "You promised me marriage."

"Marie!" Walter exclaimed, shocked. "You know I did not. I even told you that I had offered for Sybelle. You do not need to use such a lever on me. If you say it is my child, I will acknowledge it and care for it."

"You told her you had offered for Sybelle?" Richard said suddenly. "But that was not until you came to Builth. When you spoke to me after you had left Gervase and Marie in Brecon, you would not name the woman you desired because you had not her father's permission. So when did you have time . . ."

Walter closed his eyes for a moment. "That afternoon in Builth before I went with Simon to Abergavenny to meet with the men watching Monmouth. Curse me, I needed a woman and Marie . . . perhaps she was teasing, but I . . ."

"Or perhaps she was with child already and needed some honorable fool to acknowledge it," Richard growled. "How likely is it that one coupling will set seed in a woman?"

"No!" Marie cried.

Richard looked at her coldly, his face set like flint. "It is easy enough to discover the truth of that. We need only ask your maid the time of your last flux."

"No," Marie gasped, backing away, "no."

"Please," Walter pleaded, "do not torment her by questioning her maid and adding to her shame. I do not believe Marie had any other lover."

That statement was based on Walter's memory of how little pleasure Marie had taken in their coupling, but his voice faltered as he realized the same effect could have been based on her desire for another man rather than her limited enjoyment of sex. Would he be raising the bastard of some man-at-arms or groom from Pembroke?

Walter had dropped his eyes as the doubt crossed his mind, but Richard had been staring all the while at Marie. Richard did not know much or care much about women, and he had never tried to understand them, but the blazing hate in Marie's face told him a great deal. That Marie should hate *him* was reasonable, but her gaze, to his surprise, has been fixed on Walter. There was no need to understand women to fathom that. Man or woman, one does not hate a person who is a willing dupe.

"You nasty bitch!" Richard exploded. "You are not with child at all. You desired to make trouble between Walter and Sybelle."

"No, not to make trouble," Marie cried, seeing a way out of her predicament. "I wanted him, and I thought he wanted me and took Sybelle only for the greater dowry. There was no written contract. Why should I not try to gain him?" And she lifted her hands to her face and wept.

"Oh, God," Walter breathed. "I am sorry. I am so sorry. I did not know. I thought you understood and only wished to play. Richard knew I had exchanged kisses of peace with

Sybelle's family. That is as ironbound to me as written words. I thought surely Richard had told you.''

Unlike Richard, Walter had not seen the hatred in Marie's face, and now he recalled how she had tried and tried again during their lovemaking to bring him to say he loved her. He even remembered that she had said she would be willing to live in poverty so long as they could be together. He nearly wept with her in sorrow and remorse. However, Richard, having seen what he had seen, was totally unmoved.

''She loves you like boredom and death,'' he said. ''She only wishes to make you suffer. Do not be a fool. Marie, you deserve a whipping for this meanness and stupidity.''

''No!'' Walter exclaimed, stepping in front of Marie.

Richard looked at him and slowly shook his head. ''I had not thought you so vain,'' he remarked dryly. ''However, reserving the punishment may serve a better purpose. Come, step aside so Marie can see me.'' He fixed his eyes on her broodingly for a moment and then said, ''Take your hands from your face. I have already seen what you were too slow to hide, and by now you have had time enough to paint sorrow where hate sat. Out of mercy to Walter, who would suffer more than you, I believe, if you had the treatment you deserve, I will do nothing and say nothing of this disgusting scene.''

''In God's name, Richard,'' Walter protested, ''if anyone has done wrong, it is I.''

''You were led by the nose, like the jackass women make of most men, and are still being led by it. Hold your tongue or go. Marie is my responsibility.'' Richard's eyes moved back to Marie. ''Hear me, Marie. I said I would do and say nothing. I did not say I would forget. If one person other than the three now in this chamber should ever hear one whisper of the lie you told, I will whip you bloody and I will set you in Pembroke keep without the right to leave your chamber unless special approval under my seal is given by me. And there you will stay until I can find some man—who will be told every word of this so that he knows your evil intent and foul treachery—to take the care of you out of my hands.''

''You wrong me,'' Marie whispered. ''I meant no harm. I only wanted Walter.''

''Do not repeat that again,'' Richard growled. ''I know

better. However, you *are* only a woman. If you behave yourself, for Gervase's sake I will permit you to go with her to Clifford and live as you have lived. Only remember my warning. One hint that Walter was ever anything to you but a partner for mild flirtation and you will be mewed up tighter than any eremite. Now do not speak to me again, lest I forget the sensibility of this fool whose heart is wrung for you. Go."

CHAPTER 23

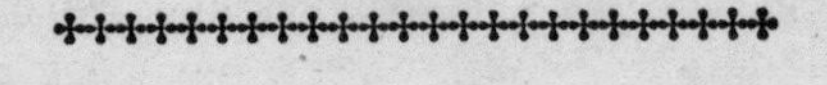

Clyro was separated from the area in which the second battle of Monmouth had taken place by the range of mountains over which Walter and Sybelle had struggled. None of those who fled ran northward, or, at least, not so far north as Clyro. Thus, the twelve days of Christmas were being celebrated there with high spirits in total ignorance that King Henry's cause had suffered another violent setback or that the Earl of Pembroke's army was about to march north to attack Shrewsbury.

Sir Heribert received Walter's letter and Marie's at just about the time Marie entered the Earl of Pembroke's chamber. Long before the lie she had told Richard was exposed and the whole matter unraveled, Sir Heribert had resolved on his course. In truth, since he did not know Walter had been incapacitated again or of the planned attack on Shrewsbury, he believed he did not have much choice.

He had had word—his "messenger returning from Knight's Tower"—of Walter's escape from their ambush, and he had bade the men lie in wait near the road to watch for Walter's return and have a second try at him. However, he had never had much hope that would work.

Sir Heribert had feared that Walter had recognized the ambushers as his men. He had been living in momentary expectation that Walter would send orders to Sir Roland to imprison him, but he did not dare leave Clyro because his remaining was a proof of his innocence. Thus, when he received Walter's letter, he understood that it was a trap. He believed Walter had decided to turn Heribert's own methods against him. Either there was an ambush waiting for him on the road to Knight's Tower or once he was in the keep, Walter would find some other way to eliminate him.

Heribert had no intention of returning to Knight's Tower

until Sir Walter was dead or no longer controlled it. Yet he had no chance that he could see of achieving either of those conditions on his own. The other letter the messenger had handed him held out the only hope of retrieving his position or even of saving himself from Walter's future vengeance. Of course, the second letter might also be a trap; it was unsigned and sealed only with formless blobs of wax. However, a long evening of thinking—in between the infuriating attempts of Sir Roland and his family to include him in their entertainments and conversation—and a sleepless night made him decide to clutch at this one hope.

Since Heribert had already showed Sir Walter's letter to Sir Roland, he knew there would be no difficulty about his leaving on the morning of 31 December. It was most convenient that Clifford was in the same direction Heribert would go if he had been returning to Knight's Tower. He had noticed when coming south that there was a ford of the Wye to the northeast and that another road ran southwest from that ford. Once out of Clyro, Heribert sent one man to tell the remainder of his troop to abandon their watch for Walter and meet him at the ford, where he would await them.

Half a dozen times on the road he went over the dangers of what he intended to do, but each time he was on the edge of abandoning the attempt, he realized that he had nowhere to go. There was money in his purse and saddlebags. In fact he had cleaned every coin and jewel out of Knight's Tower as a precaution, but it was not a large hoard. Cheating Walter's brother had not been easy; Heribert had not dared to withhold much, and the amusements his overlord demanded had often been costly. He could not live long on what he had, and he had few friends. Nor was it likely they would remain friends when he was penniless and powerless. It was Clifford or a life of penury. Faced with that choice, since Sir Heribert was not a coward, he would dare whatever danger he must.

However, there was no apparent danger in Clifford keep. Sir Heribert was welcomed with due caution, as any stranger might be in time of war, and asked his business. The name he gave according to instructions, Sir Palance de Tours, raised no alarm, although his men were confined between inner and outer walls and could have been killed or taken prisoner without any trouble. And, when he said he wished to see

Lady Marie de les Maures, he was escorted to the hall by an understeward, not by men-at-arms. Refreshment was offered while a maid went to tell the lady of his coming. That promised well, Sir Heribert thought, relaxing a little. Surely if treachery were intended he would have been disarmed and guarded.

The fury Marie had built up in Abergavenny against Walter and Sybelle after Richard and his men left was a poor, pale thing compared with the burning rage that ate at her vitals after her confrontation with Richard and Walter. Her total impotence added bitterness, and the anger and bitterness were intensified because they had no vent. Marie could not even void her spleen to her sister because, at this time, Gervase was very pleased with Richard and would not hear a word against him. He had flattered her deeply, not only by expressing a concern for her comfort and suggesting the move to Clifford but by taking her to Clifford himself rather than sending a deputy with her and leading his army personally, as usual.

Although she had taken Richard's threats to heart in that she would not dare repeat her lies about Walter, Marie's rage blinded her to other dangers. As soon as the name Sir Palance was brought to her, she saw the first crack in the chain of impotence that bound her. Heribert had come; therefore he hated Walter as much as she did. Every restraint of caution flew out of her mind. All she could think of was that she had a tool, a weapon to use against the men who had foiled her and shamed her.

Her first sight of Heribert was an additional jolt. Marie was not a particularly sensual woman, but his beautiful features awakened a warm interest in her.

She came forward in a rush, thanking God that Gervase was not yet in the hall. "Sir Palance," she cried. "How glad I am to see you. It has been so long since you visited my husband and myself at Maures. Had you heard that Pierre died and I am now a widow? Oh, of course, you must have. It was more than two years ago. It is so kind of you to come to see me now that I am no more than my sister's, Lady Pembroke's, companion."

"A lady so lovely as yourself is never 'no more than,' "

Heribert replied smoothly, understanding the need to make him seem an old friend. He was shocked, to learn that he was in Pembroke's keep, but he said evenly, "Yes, I had heard of Pierre's death. It saddened me greatly that I could not come to you at that time. But you ask if I knew! Did you not receive my letter?"

That, Heribert hoped, would be a hint for her to bring the promised letter out of her sleeve or from wherever she had concealed it. Instead, she put a hand on his arm and urged him to come into one of the wall chambers.

"But we have no company," she said, reading the flash of suspicion on his face, "and you are welcome to choose whichever chamber best pleases you."

Heribert pointed at a door at random, and they moved toward it together. Since there could not be men in every room, it could not be a trap, and, indeed, the chamber was empty.

As soon as Marie closed the door behind them she said, "Sir Heribert, I have a confession to make. I did write the letter you received. I did not wish to lie, but you must see that I needed to protect myself."

"That is perfectly reasonable," he replied, much more at ease but still cautious about committing himself.

In the next few minutes, however, it became apparent to Heribert that all his fears and worries had been unnecessary. Lady Marie had a violent hatred for Sir Walter and the Earl of Pembroke, and she told him everything she knew about Walter's plan to take over Knight's Tower and to send Sir Heribert's garrison and Sir Heribert himself to aid in the coming attack on Shrewsbury. Because it was past and she understood so little about war, Marie did not mention the terrible defeat Monmouth had suffered.

When she had emptied her budget, Sir Heribert thanked her profusely and then asked, "What would you have me do?"

The animation began to fade from Marie's face and the glitter from her eyes. "Is what I have told you useless?" she asked. "Can you not somehow use it to avenge us both?"

"I can try," Heribert said. "I think I know a use that will cause de Clare to be outlawed and that would benefit *me* greatly, but what if another effect is Pembroke's downfall? Will that not harm you and your sister?"

"No," Marie answered without hesitation. "We will simply go back to France, from where we were dragged against our wills. Richard's downfall or death would benefit us as well as Sir Walter's will benefit you."

Sir Heribert thought privately that she did not know what she was talking about or that she so hated her brother-by-marriage that the emotion had disordered her wits, but it mattered little to him. He had his lever to oust Walter from his overlordship.

"Then if you have no objection, I will take my information to the king," Sir Heribert said. "When King Henry has this proof of Sir Walter's treason, he will disseisin him. He will lose all his estates. Will that avenge you?"

Marie nodded, although she was not completely content. That Walter should lose his lands was good; but if he felt the contract was ironbound, could it be irrevocable to Sybelle's parents also? Marie was as much interested in destroying the betrothal as in reducing Walter to a pauper—like herself.

Then the doubt cleared. Lord Geoffrey would have to break the contract; he could not have his daughter betrothed to an outlaw. Or if he could not break it, Marie thought that Walter would be regarded with loathing for bringing outlawry and penury into the family instead of honor and a good estate.

"Yes," she agreed, "it will serve my purpose. But you will not leave me in doubt, will you? Will you not return and tell me how you fared?"

"Indeed, I will," Heribert said heartily. "And to give you proper thanks for your kindness to me, for which I have not time now because I must be in Gloucester as soon as possible to make this news of value to the king."

"Then I will not keep you," Marie said, putting out her hand. Her voice held quite sincere regret, because Sir Heribert's handsome face and smooth voice appealed to her.

Heribert kissed the extended hand with considerable grace, and his lips lingered just fractionally longer than they should, indicating that the salute was more than a common, indifferent courtesy. In fact, Heribert did think that Marie was an attractive woman, but his hearty agreement to her request, the lingering of his lips on her hand, and his glances of admiration were no more than a hedge against future trouble. If it were useful and expedient, he would return; if not, Heribert was totally indifferent to any desire of Marie's.

• • •

Despite the bitter weather, Sybelle enjoyed the ride to Knight's Tower. They went the long way around past Builth and west of Gilwern Hill to meet Simon and Rhiannon at Cefnllys with the main force that Llewelyn was sending to meet Pembroke's army. There they spent the night. In the morning they turned northeast toward Penybont and joined Richard's army south of Glog Hill. The forward units, unencumbered with supply carts, moved swiftly under Richard's direction and reached the gates of Knight's Tower within an hour.

Walter asked for Sir Heribert, and when told he was not in the keep, he and Richard exchanged significant glances. Then Walter simply demanded entry as overlord. The master-at-arms knew the name de Clare and knew that the previous overlord was dead. He looked out at the sea of men waiting in the fields that stretched around the keep; he thought of the men-at-arms available to defend Knight's Tower. He knew that even if Sir Heribert returned, there was no way he could muster any force to oppose the army behind de Clare. He called a welcome and bid his men open to their new master.

Walter spoke him fair but made clear that he and his men were to go with the Earl of Pembroke while Walter's own men took over the defense of Knight's Tower. Walter knew nothing against the man, and it appeared that he had done his duty, for the men-at-arms were disciplined and obedient. They gathered their equipment and marched out in good order, apparently not ill-pleased at the idea of some action and the chance of loot.

The servants were not in such good case, being dirty, frightened, and clearly ill-fed, but Walter suspected that condition was of long standing. Whether the master-at-arms had encouraged it or added to it mattered little since he and his troop were going with the army. Those who returned after the Shrewsbury campaign would be sent down to Goldcliff, where they would soon learn new behavior or be turned out.

The next day, Richard and the army marched on, and Walter and Sybelle turned their attention to a detailed investigation of their new possession. Both were busy all the day and found more and more cause to be satisfied with their choices of mates. From living alone for many years, Walter appreciated more than most men the duties of a woman in a keep. He was very glad to be able to hand over to Sybelle the accounting of supplies, the problem of ordering the duties of the servants, management of the stillrooms, gardens, dairies, kitchens, and clothmaking. But he was also interested in hearing about the condition of these necessary functions, for he knew Knight's Tower would not be self-sufficient without them. And any keep that was not self-sufficient was less economical to run and less able to withstand a threat.

On the other hand, from being trained to manage her own properties completely, Sybelle understood far more than the ordinary woman about the defensive armament of a castle, about the smithies and their products, about crops and herds, about hunting dogs and horses and the breeding of such animals, and about trade and the management of the towns and villages beholden to a keep. Thus, she was as interested in what Walter had to say as he was in her talk of her daily duties.

Although they were alone and free to do as they liked, they came together only once—and that time to no purpose. Since there were no other gentlefolk in Knight's Tower, Sybelle came boldly into Walter's chamber. He welcomed her gladly, but soon after, as they stood passionately embraced before the fire, Walter drew back.

"Love, we should not," he said. "We are tempting fate. I will forget myself." A wry smile twisted his lips. "And you have long since failed in your promise to resist me."

Sybelle might have protested, but she was puzzled by his reference to "tempting fate." Although she felt they could not be more married by the words of a priest than they already were by the contract that had been sealed and by their commitment to each other, she was uneasy about something in Walter's manner. She was aware that he was truly disturbed, torn between desire and some fear he did not wish to confess.

It was clear he would yield and make love to her if she tempted him because, although he said they should not, he had not relaxed his tight hold on her. In fact, he was still pulling her hips against him so firmly that his swollen shaft, hard and ready, pressed into her abdomen. He had broken their kiss to speak, but now despite what he had said, his face was coming toward her again, the lips very full and a little parted.

Sybelle had come to Walter's chamber ready to make love, but still she was not as sexually aroused as he—and that reminder about her promise of resistance, that was a plea for help. She turned her face fractionally aside.

"You are not happy, dear heart," she sighed. "That is no way to join in love."

Slowly, reluctantly, Walter's good arm loosened and rose from her hips to embrace her shoulders lightly. "Your parents left you in my care, and I have not been such a guardian as they expected," he said.

Walter stroked Sybelle's cheek, but he was thinking of Marie and the unhappiness he believed his unbridled lust had caused. He was by no means as sure as Richard that Marie was not with child. She had never actually admitted she was not, and it was clear she was terrified of her brother-by-marriage. She might have backed down out of fear. And whether she was pregnant or not, it was bad enough to have brought sorrow to her by the sin of lust. To chance that Sybelle might be punished for the same cause was unbearable. Better they both suffer the minor torments of chastity until their mating was no sin. Walter was sure their marriage could not be long delayed if the attack on Shrewsbury was a success.

Although Sybelle was young, she had considerable experience with every male reaction to trouble. In the loving and open family life of Roselynde, Sybelle had seen and heard a great deal. Simon usually laughed and ran away. Ian and Adam raged and roared. But her father locked his trouble inside himself, smiling with his lips while his eyes were dark and shadowed. So Sybelle was able to recognize the signs; Walter was hiding something. She suspected she could pry it out of him by a combination of sexual temptation and pleading, but Walter was too clever to fail for long in understanding what she had done. That was too high a price to pay, for he would end by distrusting her and himself.

There would be time enough, Sybelle decided, to discover what was troubling Walter without pressure or subterfuge. Most likely they would stay at Knight's Tower for some time, definitely until his shoulder healed. It was apparent to both that Sir Heribert's statement that the property was in poor condition was all too true. The serfs were sullen and half-starved, the headmen of villages sly and evasive, the servants dishonest and ill-trained, seeking to do as little and steal as much as they could, each blaming another for every evil. Moreover, the conditions would be difficult to amend, since every attempt at correction would be taken as a new sign of oppression.

They were already standing a little apart. Sybelle looked into Walter's troubled face. "My parents are not such dragons," she said lightly, "but if you are so proper and prudish, I will not tease you."

"I love you," he said, with such intensity, although his voice was low, that tears came to Sybelle's eyes. "I would not for any prize on earth, nor for the hope of heaven, do anything that might hurt you. I fear this lust we have for each other, not that the desire in itself is wrong but that our easy yielding to the temptation, when we both know it will be soon enough that we can join with the blessing of God, will bring some trouble that will cause you grief."

That statement worried Sybelle even more. In Clyro, Walter had made a jest about the cancellation of his sins—one the spilling of his seed "abroad" and the other, which he had not committed, fornication. It was clear he had not been troubled by the results of their "lust" at that time, aside from the practical consideration of wishing her to remain a maiden. But plainly between then and now something had happened, and it must have been in Abergavenny—and if it happened in Abergavenny, it must have something to do with Marie.

Nasty bitch, Sybelle thought, she must have caught Walter alone and said something or threatened something that had put this nonsense into his head. Doubtless since she and Walter would marry only when there was peace, or at least a truce, between Richard and the king, Marie could expect to be at their wedding because Richard would certainly be invited. Could Marie have threatened to throw a shadow on their marriage by contesting it or saying at the morning ceremony that the blood on the sheets was not Sybelle's?

Whatever poisonous growth Marie had planted, Sybelle was determined to weed it out, but this was not the time. Let the memory fade a little.

"Love between a promised man and wife cannot cause grief—unless you mean the grief of parting or loss." Sybelle smiled. "But I cannot wish to avoid that, except by the joy of having you with me always, and that joy is well worth the fear of pain. Is it not so for you?''

''Before God, it is only your pain I fear, not my own,'' Walter said fervently.

''I know that,'' Sybelle replied, ''but as long as you live and love me, you need fear no other pain for me.'' She leaned forward and kissed him on the cheek, then turned and left the room.

CHAPTER 24

Sir Heribert rode for Gloucester at his best speed, but when he arrived he realized it would have made no difference how he had dallied on the way. His news was no news. Spies had brought word weeks before that the Earl of Pembroke meant to attack Shrewsbury. Worse yet, that information was now considered to have been no more than a trap to make John of Monmouth believe that Pembroke was no longer in south Wales and that his keeps were thin of men and supplies.

Instead, Pembroke had been lying in ambush and had not only nearly destroyed Monmouth's army but had so looted and burnt the land all around Monmouth and for miles east and north that there was hardly a head of cattle or a bushel of wheat to support life in the area. It made no difference that Heribert knew that Pembroke had now really gone north to attack Shrewbury. King Henry had no men, no arms, and virtually no money. Pursuit or aid of any kind for Shrewsbury was impossible. Thus, to bring the king news of the attack on Shrewsbury would only be rubbing salt into a wound.

Sir Heribert had been fortunate enough to discover this before he approached Henry. He had come into the hall, seeking some officer of the court to whom he could apply for audience with the king; however, Henry had been there already, with the bishops of St. David's, Chichester, and Hereford. In alternation they were describing to the king the shambles to which the countryside had been reduced, the corpses of the slain, almost numberless, lying unburied and naked in the roads and fields, defenseless against tearing and dismemberment by carrion birds and beasts. The stench, Hereford sighed, was so great that it corrupted the air, and the dead would soon thereby slay the few remaining living.

"Of your graciousness and mercy, my lord king, let this

madness end,'' Ralph of Chichester pleaded. ''I know the Earl of Pembroke—''

''Do not say that name to me!'' Henry bellowed. ''For the people, I have pity. If I could, I would ease their state, but not by bowing down to that traitor. I will have no dealings with him, not unless he come naked before me, creeping on his knees with a halter around his neck and acknowledging himself a foul, treasonous destroyer of me and of my kingdom.''

Sir Heribert made himself inconspicuous, cursing Marie for sending him on a fool's errand and for being such a fool herself that she had not mentioned the serious defeat the king's forces had suffered. It was clear to him that Henry was nearly rabid between frustration and fury—and both the emotions were intensified by an underlying fear, which the king consciously denied. But Heribert was not willing to yield his one hope without any attempt to better his condition. Later he found an attendant of Peter des Roches, Bishop of Winchester, and begged for an interview, which, somewhat to Heribert's surprise, was granted without much delay.

The bishop was a worried and shaken man, not willing to turn away even one minor knight for whom he might conceivably find a use. Ordinarily the defeats suffered by the king's adherents would not have made him desperate. The losses in men and materiel had been great, but England was a rich nation and there were enormous resources that had not yet been tapped. In the long run, Winchester knew, the Earl of Pembroke could not win. The trouble was, Winchester had recently come to realize, that Henry was not a man for long runs.

The king was impetuous and impatient. Winchester had presented to him an ideal, a nation in which the king was so strong that the nobility lived at peace with each other because a just and merciful king could arbitrate their quarrels without war. In such a nation all the wealth and power could be turned against external enemies or inward toward the betterment and beautification of the realm. But Henry could not move slowly toward this purpose; he leapt and grabbed, offending those who should have been led imperceptibly and unknowingly along the path until they understood that they would benefit by yielding what they now thought of as their rights and privileges.

Thus, Winchester had been trapped into the attempt to break by force the will of those nobles who opposed absolute power for the king. It had not been the path he would have chosen, but he did not fear it in the beginning. He had believed that it was only necessary to remove or to destroy Richard, Earl of Pembroke; the rest, seeing the mightiest fallen, would bow down willingly. Winchester had therefore encouraged Henry in just those acts that would most offend and infuriate Richard Marshal, first hoping to catch and imprison him and, thus, leave the rebellion headless.

When that had failed, he had still been confident, certain once Pembroke was brought to cry defiance that the army of foreign mercenaries the king had gathered would take Pembroke's keeps one after another. But the war had not followed any normal pattern. Welsh raiders had ravaged the baggage trains, and Pembroke had burnt over his own land so that his enemies could not find sustenance on it. The defeats would not have been important, except for Henry's attitude. While success supported him, the king could be firm; but he would not hold steady in the face of defeat.

Winchester had already moved to rid England of the Earl of Pembroke in another way. He had written to the nobles of Ireland—to Maurice Fitz-Gerald, who was the king's justiciar there, to Walter and Hugo de Lacey, and to Geoffrey de Marisco, some of whom were supposed to be allies of Pembroke's—that the earl was now an outlaw:

> We therefore order you on your oath, as faithful subjects of our lord the king, to seize [Pembroke] if he should happen to come to Ireland, and bring him, dead or alive, before the king; and if you do this all his inheritance and possessions in the kingdom of Ireland, which are now at the disposal of our lord and king, will be granted to you to be divided amongst you and to be held by you by hereditary right. And for the faithful fulfillment of this promise to you by our lord and king, all of us, by whose advice the business of the king and kingdom is managed, will become securities if you bring the above design to effect.

Lazy and indifferent, Henry had signed and sealed that letter without knowing what was in it—Winchester had not dared tell him. Henry was too unpredictable. He might be furious and frightened enough to approve, but equally he might be utterly horrified at such a treacherous plan. However, Winchester was certain that once Pembroke was dead or a prisoner, the king would not question too closely how his enemy had come to that condition.

Before that letter had gone out, Winchester had by various devices fomented unrest within the earl's huge Irish domain and attacks upon Pembroke's lands by every enemy the Marshal family had. Gilbert, Richard's brother, who ruled the Irish lands in Pembroke's name, was beset by more trouble than he had ever remembered. Unaware of the treachery intended, he had sent messengers to beg Richard to come himself and see if his presence would stem the restlessness and rebellion. Winchester had been aware of Gilbert's request, and John of Monmouth's attack was intended to be launched after Pembroke had gone—but Pembroke had not gone, and some victory was needed to calm the king, who, though he ranted and raved of revenge, was growing more and more fearful. Thus, all—even Winchester himself—had leapt at the news that Pembroke was going north, and another disaster had befallen them.

Winchester was by no means blind to the acuteness of his danger. He had misjudged Henry in several ways, but he had not forgotten the king's habit of casting the blame on others for any unpleasant result of his own activities. If the tide of war did not turn very soon or the rebellion was not broken in another way, say by Pembroke's death, Winchester knew Henry would turn on him with the same ferocity he had turned on Hubert de Burgh, the preceding chancellor. So when Sir Heribert told the bishop's secretary that his business concerned Walter de Clare, Winchester made time in his busy day to speak to him.

"How may I help you?" The bishop asked after Sir Heribert had been ushered in.

"I do not know," Sir Heribert answered truthfully, too clever to pretend he was selfless to a man as shrewd as Peter des Roches. "I came to bring the news of the attack on Shrewsbury, but I discovered that it was no news here. I came, also, because my new overlord, Walter de Clare, is an open rebel and has put the keep of which I was castellan,

Knight's Tower, at the service of the Earl of Pembroke and sent the garrison with him toward Shrewsbury."

"Walter de Clare is not proscribed," Winchester said.

Sir Heribert shrugged. "He should be, and proof of his treason would be easy enough to get."

Winchester thought for a moment, calling to mind everything he knew about Walter. One fact leapt to the forefront: de Clare was long and intimately connected with Pembroke. But almost immediately that was overridden by the memory of a recent rumor that de Clare had been accepted by Geoffrey FitzWilliam as husband for his eldest daughter. That was not so good. Henry had a deep fondness for Lord Geoffrey. In Henry's present mood, the bishop knew, he had only to present Sir Heribert, and de Clare would be an outlaw. But although the king was very angry with Geoffrey just now and would not care if he hurt him by punishing de Clare, Henry's delayed reaction at hurting a member of his family would be ten times as bitter.

Yet Winchester felt it would be unwise to give away the possibility of "discovering" de Clare was a traitor. There was the chance, Winchester thought, of using the rage generated in the king by the evidence of a new defection—although de Clare had been a rebel by intent from the beginning—to provide a few days' grace if Henry seemed about to turn on him. But this was not the time for a measure that might have desperate repercussions. Just now Henry was angry enough, and not yet sufficiently afraid of losing his kingdom altogether, to give up his dreams of glory. In fact, evidence of de Clare's open support for Pembroke might tip the scales the other way and terrify Henry into rejecting Winchester and all he stood for.

"This is no time for more proscriptions that will further enrage the barons," Winchester said, "but I suppose your absence from Knight's Tower at this time will have been noted by Sir Walter?"

"He bade me return," Heribert replied, "and I have failed. He knew I had no love for the rebel cause." The statement was not true, but Heribert preferred that lie to admitting that he had given Walter cause to desire his death. "Thus I believe I have lost my place and my livelihood."

Again Winchester considered for a moment. Then he said,

"You meant well to King Henry and have lost thereby. I cannot do much for you now. However, in the end the king must triumph because he has the wealth and power of the whole nation. When that time comes, there will be an accounting, and those who were King Henry's enemies, whether avowed or secret, will be exposed and punished; likewise, his friends will be rewarded."

"So do I hope," Heribert said bleakly, "but until then what am I to do? I have near fifty men in my troop. How am I to feed them? If I turn them loose—"

"That will not be necessary," Winchester interrupted. "For the present, I will take them—and you—into my household."

Sir Heribert relaxed and smiled. "Thank you, my lord. Be sure that I will serve you in any way I can, and gladly."

At the time the agreement was made, Sir Heribert was delighted. He knew the bishop was the most powerful man in the kingdom. Although from time to time the king liked to play at ruling, it was no secret he soon grew bored with the details of governing. Thus, in all but name, Winchester ruled England as Hubert de Burgh had ruled before him. Sir Heribert thought he had put his foot on the first rung of the ladder of success.

He was so pleased that he actually felt apologetic for the curses he had called down on Marie's head. Stupid though she was, she had started him in this direction. Then he recalled that he had promised to send her news of what had happened. *Why not?* he thought. She would be angry if he broke his word, and she might be useful again in the future. There could be no danger to Sir Heribert if Sir Palance de Tours wrote a letter to Lady Marie de les Maures.

So the letter was sent, vague enough so that anyone who read it could determine no more than that Sir Palance had gone where he said he would when he spoke to Marie and had been well received there. "The business you desired me to perform," he wrote, "cannot yet be done. However, I have received a promise from the bishop himself that he will urge it as soon as the opportunity presents itself." And, being that there was space on the sheet he had chosen, Heribert filled it with warm thanks and flowery compliments. They cost nothing.

Some ten days later, Heribert was far less pleased with his

situation. News arrived of the burning and looting of Shrewsbury and the ravaging of the whole area. Heribert began to wonder whether he had attached himself to the right party, and his doubts grew stronger when word came that Pembroke was turning south once more, and the king's reaction was to order a retreat to Westminster, leaving only bare garrisons to protect the strongholds in the west. Winchester had spoken glibly enough about the king's strength, but Heribert saw no sign of it, and, anyway, no amount of strength is sufficient to someone who fears to use it.

One thing Heribert did not regret was the letter he had sent to Marie. From her dress and the way the servants obeyed her, it seemed that her brother-by-marriage did not hate Marie as much as she hated him—or that her sister had sufficient influence with Pembroke to protect Marie. But if the king were driven to yield to Pembroke, Marie would be on the winning side.

So Sir Heribert might be destroyed and disappear, but Sir Palance might do well enough with Lady Marie's goodwill. Before Heribert left to travel east with the Bishop of Winchester's household, he wrote again to Lady Marie. His excuse was to apologize for not yet being able to perform the charge she had given him, but the letter was far more full of compliments of her manner and person than of business.

A little over two weeks later, Sir Heribert was thankful that he had one hope left. On 3 February, Sir Palance wrote again to Lady Marie, stating that there was no longer any chance that he could fulfill the charge she had laid upon him. At the council held at Westminster on the Purification of Mary, the Archbishop-elect of Canterbury, Edmund of Abingdon, had bitterly reproached the king for his differences with the Earl of Pembroke. Edmund said plainly for all to hear that the counsel King Henry received from the Bishop of Winchester was evil counsel, that Winchester and his adherents hated the English and had estranged the king from his people, and he had begged the king to dismiss these evil counselors. Nor had Henry flown into a rage or denied the archbishop-elect's arguments. He had only begged a respite from taking the advice given, saying humbly that he could not dismiss his counselors so suddenly, at least not until he had from them an account of the money entrusted to them.

Perhaps all was not lost, Sir Palance continued. It might be possible to achieve Lady Marie's purpose in another way. He was returning to the west and would stay at Craswall Priory. If she wished to pursue the business they had discussed, she could write to him at that place and he would come to her at her convenience or meet her at any place she chose to name. He added a sentence or two to indicate that he would be only too happy to see her even if she no longer wished to transact business.

Sir Heribert allowed his letter to imply that he was really coming west for no other purpose than to see Marie again. In fact, he was coming because he wished to be as far away as possible from Winchester when he fell from power, and he had to leave before the final crisis. Heribert had discovered that the bishop planned to use him to ignite Henry's wrath against the rebels again; Winchester had discussed with him what he must say and how to say it.

However, Heribert had felt the temper of the court and sensed the growing despair of Peter of Rivaulx and Stephen de Seagrave, Winchester's most important adherents, and he guessed that the bishop's use of him was an act of desperation that had little hope of success. Moreover, it would cost Winchester nothing. Heribert would be the sufferer if the attempt failed, because the king *would* be angry, and if Henry did not choose to vent his anger on the rebels, he would doubtless vent it on those who tried to make trouble between him and his "loyal" subjects.

There was nowhere but west for Heribert to go. He knew no one at all in the east of England, and he clung to the hope that Marie had not forgotten her spite. Somehow, he might still use her to destroy Walter. If he could do that, he might manage to recover Knight's Tower. The king did not know that he had ever been associated with the Bishop of Winchester.

Two other letters went out the same day, with faster couriers mounted on better horses. Geoffrey wrote to Richard a far fuller accounting of Edmund's lecture to the king and a far more perceptive analysis of what might be expected. Since these confirmed what Richard had hoped when he heard that King Henry had abandoned the western strongholds and returned to Westminster, he promptly put into effect plans he had made for responding to his brother's appeals as soon as leaving England would not damage the rebel cause. The day after he received Geoffrey's letter, Richard and fifteen knights set out for Ireland.

Richard did not take Gervase and Marie. For one thing, Grevase pleaded to stay at Clifford and he knew she could make no trouble for him in England, where she had no property and no friends to whom to appeal. For another, Richard did not expect to have time for her in Ireland, nor did he expect to be there for long. They had been getting along so much better since she had been released from Pembroke that Richard had again begun to hope for an heir. It would be stupid to make Gervase turn sullen and need to put up with her whining and bad temper when she would be safe enough in England.

Geoffrey's second letter was much shorter and went to Sybelle and Walter in Knight's Tower. It said only that peace was at hand and that Geoffrey had obtained King Henry's permission for the marriage of his daughter to Walter de Clare. Geoffrey urged Walter and Sybelle to make all haste to Roselynde, where he would explain more fully how the king had been induced to change his mind. If it was agreeable to them, he continued, they could be married at once in a small, private ceremony because this was no time for large, joyous gatherings. It would be most unfortunate, he ended, if the king should mistake their happiness in being united for a victory celebration.

If Geoffrey's first letter was received with satisfaction, his second was received with an enthusiasm that amounted nearly to hysteria. Although both Walter and Sybelle had tried hard to control it, the sexual tension between them had mounted painfully. While they were in the same keep, Walter would not seek relief even from a whore. Partly he felt it was unfair for Sybelle to suffer desire when he could quench his; partly he knew the quenching would be ineffectual—he had tried that before with Marie, and it had not reduced his desire for Sybelle; but mostly he did not try the expedient because he was relatively sure Sybelle would notice and her jealousy would be aroused.

And Walter's frustration sparked Sybelle's. Had they been apart, she would have missed him more for the companionship he provided than because of sexual need, but the avidity in his eyes and the way he avoided touching her was a constant reminder of his desire and her own. Twice, over the month they were in Knight's Tower, Sybelle had touched him and said, "Please." And it was all she needed to do. Walter was frantically eager, but afterward, even though he had not forgot himself as he feared, he was uneasy, the shadow of worry in his eyes more pronounced.

Fortunately, they were not alone for long. After Shrewsbury had fallen, Simon and Rhiannon had returned, bringing back the old garrison of Knight's Tower. After allowing the men-at-arms to rest a week and making clear that his ways were far different from Sir Heribert's, Walter had sent south to Goldcliff those who said they were willing and had dismissed the others.

The presence of Simon and Rhiannon had somewhat mitigated the sexual tension between Walter and Sybelle. Nonetheless, Geoffrey's letter was greeted with the joy and reverence one would normally have expected to be accorded to a heavenly vision. Simon and Rhiannon were no less happy than Walter and Sybelle, because the strain of acting as buffers was telling on them, too. That very day all the arrangements were made—Walter left Dai in command of Knight's Tower with orders to keep everyone out, and Sybelle and Rhiannon drove the maids and themselves until all the packing was finished. They left the following dawn.

The worst of the cold had broken on the same day that Edmund had protested the evils of the civil war and Henry had all but agreed to make peace. Many took this as a token from God of better times to come, and it might have been, but its immediate effect was to make travel much more pleasant. There were some drawbacks, as the thaw filled rivers, made fords dangerous, and turned parts of the road to bogs. However, the party moving toward Roselynde had no baggage wains and were able, despite the conditions, to make excellent time. And even checks and delays were taken lightly, for everyone was in the highest spirits. With the end of their trial in sight, the pressure had lifted from Walter and Sybelle. They could touch and laugh and even kiss; they were eager, very eager, but the frustration was gone.

The family was already gathered in Roselynde when they

arrived. Sybelle was greeted with fond embraces, and Walter was pounded on back and shoulders with such enthusiasm that Sybelle complained that Adam, Ian, and her papa among them would unseat for a third time his newly healed collarbone. Then it was the turn of the vassals, the closest of whom had also arrived. They greeted Walter with less exuberance but with considerable respect and deep interest, for they knew that it was he with whom they would deal most often. Ian made no pretense about the fact that he tired easily, and Geoffery was so tied to the king and court that he had little time for local problems. Walter, for all practical purposes, would be the new overlord of Roselynde.

CHAPTER 25

"Have you invited anyone else to this wedding?" Geoffrey asked when the first furor of greeting was over and the men of the family had drawn together in relative private.

Walter laughed. "I am afraid I was too eager to stay a moment longer than necessary, even to write invitations." Then he shrugged. "I have no one to invite, really. My parents and brothers are dead, young Richard . . . I do not even know where he is just now, and Richard—oh, a pox on all these Richards—Pembroke is either gone off to Ireland already or will be leaving any day. He will be sorry not to see me married, but Gilbert has been begging him to come for two months, at least, and when I spoke to him last he said he would go as soon as Wales was safe. I suppose I should have written to Richard—damn! I mean, Cornwall—and Isabella, but—"

"He could not have come," Geoffrey said. "He would not leave Henry at this time because Winchester still comes to the king constantly for one reason and another, and he is not like de Burgh, who made his own case worse each time he spoke to Henry. Winchester is as smooth and sweet as fresh cream, and he has a hundred new plans for conciliating the barons. Richard, I mean Cornwall, must constantly remind his brother that *nothing* except Winchester's dismissal is acceptable now."

Walter's brows rose. "Is Cornwall the right person for this purpose? He is the best man in the world, kind and just and wise also, but Henry's indecisiveness can drive him into a rage faster than good sense can hold him back."

Geoffrey looked slightly uneasy, but Ian said quickly, "We have all warned Cornwall to be careful, and all signs show the king to be firm despite Winchester's devices. When Henry stopped in Saint Edmund's, where de Burgh's wife is in sanctuary, he not only visited her and bespoke her most kindly but returned to her eight of the manors belonging to de Burgh that he had previously confiscated. He cannot pardon de Burgh until peace is made, but to regrant the manors at this time is surely all but a promise to do so. And you know how in the past he would not even allow anyone to say de Burgh's name."

"That is true," Geoffrey agreed, "but I confess that part of my haste to see you and Sybelle married is so that I can return to the king."

Walter laughed again. "You cannot be in more haste than I, although my reasons are more private than public. And if you asked me whether I expected guests in order to know how long we must wait—I expect none, and I am willing to be married right now if Sybelle will agree to it."

"But the child must have a chance to prepare," Ian protested. "She will be disappointed if she does not have a fine new gown and some special festivities for so important a day."

The eager expression faded from Walter's face. "You are quite right, Lord Ian. What is worse, I do not have so much as a brass pin with me to give her as a wedding gift. Dolt that I am, I never thought to send to Goldcliff for my strongbox."

Adam's bass rumble of laughter rolled out. "Ask Sybelle," he suggested, remembering that Gilliane had not even waited long enough to *change* her dress, much less tarry for a new one to be sewn, but had married him on five minutes' notice with no more than two vassals as witnesses.

"It is not fair." Walter's voice was uncertain.

"No!" Geoffrey exclaimed, appalled. He was afraid Sybelle would not be willing to forgo every special privilege of a bride and that Walter would be hurt.

But Simon was laughing, too. "Faint hearts!" he cried. "If you will not ask her, I will."

And he was away toward the women grouped around Alinor before either Walter or Geoffrey could catch him. They hastened after him, but it would have taken force to stop him and that would have raised questions, the answers to which would have exposed his purpose in a way more embarrassing to all.

"Sybelle," Simon said, "are you willing to marry Walter today, right now, without more ado than calling Father Edgar and walking into the chapel?"

"Simon!" Joanna cried. "Whatever has got into your head?

We are in haste, yes, but not such haste as this. A few days cannot make any difference."

But Sybelle was not looking at her mother. Her eyes had gone to Walter as soon as Simon said "marry," and she had seen the real anxiety behind the surface irritation with Simon's mischief. "Of course I am willing," she said, smiling calmly at her betrothed and stretching a hand toward him.

Walter came over to take her hand and lifted it to his lips. His color was higher than usual. "It is only Simon's jest," he said. "I am unready, for I have no bride gift for you nor a decent gown with which to do you honor."

"As to the bride gift"—Sybelle's face and voice were grave, but her eyes glittered with laughter—"we had some talk of gifts at Christmastide, if you remember. I do not think I will need to complain of any lack." Walter emitted a strangled choke, but Sybelle ignored it and continued, "And, as to the gown, I am sure Adam will have one grand enough that will fit you. You can borrow a gown, if such a thing troubles you."

"Oh, by all means," Adam agreed. "We can wait long enough for you to change from your travel dress." Then his deep chuckle rumbled out. "Only I suspect that Sybelle would just as soon take you naked."

"Adam!" Gilliane protested, but her lips were twitching to restrain a smile.

"It is ridiculous!" Joanna exclaimed.

"No," Alinor said, "it is not ridiculous. You know that the king's intention is balanced on a knife-edge. On the one hand, he sees disaster looming and is nearly convinced that the archbishop spoke the truth. On the other, it is very hard to give up the notion of being all-powerful and even harder, no doubt, to remember his rash words about how Pembroke must crave mercy on his knees. He must feel that all his vassals are laughing behind their hands. I believe that all of us who have previously avoided the court should now attend on the king, showing him that we honor and respect him the more for his decision—and the sooner we come to court, even by hours, the better."

Geoffrey uttered a sigh of relief and put his arm around Sybelle. "Dearling," he said, "we do not wish to take from you any of the joy of being a bride, but your grandmother does speak the truth. If you are willing to delay until peace is made, we can have such a wedding as will be remembered for years, or even a court wedding, if you desire—''

''No,'' Sybelle interrupted. ''I do not wish to be put on show. Will our vassals deny the aide they owe on my marriage if they are not invited?''

Geoffrey smiled and shook his head. ''We can invite them to the christening of your first child,'' he said.

Sybelle turned to look at her grandfather. ''You do not think that any of your vassals will object to Walter, do you?''

''Certainly not,'' Ian replied, and Alinor agreed decisively.

''Then as to the exact time . . .'' She hesitated and looked at Walter.

''Will you blame me,'' he asked, smiling, ''if I take you at your word and say, let us marry now, this very afternoon?''

''You see?'' Simon said. ''You have all made a great deal of talk about nothing. You could have sent for Father Edgar as soon as Sybelle said yes.''

''Be quiet, you mischievous idiot.'' Alinor laughed. ''I am truly glad that Sybelle and Walter agree, but we will have some ceremony. Gilliane, will you speak to Father Edgar and see that the chapel is bedecked? Joanna, go down to the cooks and ask what they can give us for the evening meal—I think you will find they have delicacies ready, for I warned them there would be need. Rhiannon and I will see to dressing the bride, and I am sure we will find clothing—'' Alinor stopped abruptly, then smiled and said, ''The contract is ready. Geoffrey, if you will show it to Walter, I will take care of the rest.'' She rose quickly, with no sign of stiffness. ''Sybelle, come with me.''

She led her granddaughter up to her own chamber and went to a chest Sybelle had never seen opened. ''These are your grandfather Simon's gowns,'' she said. ''No man has worn them since he died, but men's gowns are no different in fashion now than they were then, and I have cared for them. There is no weakness in the cloth nor tarnish in the threads of the embroidery. If you are willing and you think Walter would take pleasure in the gift, you may have them. They will befit Walter well in size, but they are all of one color—gray.''

''Grandfather Simon's gowns?'' Sybelle knelt and began to lift them gingerly from the chest. She was a little startled at the magnificence that could be achieved in a monochrome, accustomed as she was to the brilliant colors commonly worn by men and women alike. Her eyes opened even wider as she examined the embroidery and realized that real tiny emeralds and rubies made the eyes and tongues of the fantastic beasts worked among the silver leaves of the trees that climbed the fronts and circled the collar of one heavy silk robe.

"You did not strip out the gems?" she asked, amazed.

"I could not." Alinor's voice shook. She was herself startled by the pang of loss that stabbed her. Simon had been dead for over twenty years, and she loved Ian deeply and passionately. But Simon was her first, and he had taught her the strength and wisdom that made Roselynde what it was. Then she smiled. "We are rich enough. If we had needed them, I would have taken them, but no need came."

She paused, watching Sybelle lift and shake out the gown, which was of a rich, heavy silk that retained few creases, and thinking of the many, many times over the years that she had taken it from the chest to air. Simon had only worn it three or four times. Over the period that John had been king, Simon had not needed court dress, and the gown was too rich for such ordinary affairs as meetings with neighbors and vassals. But with care in the cool damp of the keep, the cloth had not aged.

It was superstition, perhaps, to give the gown to Walter, but Sybelle was young and she would need, very badly, the kind of strength, humor, and wisdom that Simon had provided for a young Alinor. The whole weight of Roselynde, Alinor feared, would soon fall upon those slender shoulders, for her own time must come soon and Joanna would be tied to Geoffrey and the court.

"Tell me, Sybelle," she asked suddenly, "are you yet a maiden?"

Sybelle blushed. "Yes, but . . ."

Alinor's laugh acknowledged the meaning of the blush and the "but" and relieved her granddaughter of the need for completing her statement. "Yes," she said, "take the gowns. More and more your Walter reminds me of my Simon. That one you hold, Simon wore at our wedding. It was my gift to him."

"And it will be ours to Walter," Sybelle said eagerly. "Thank you, Grandmama."

She turned to leave the room, carrying the gown, but

Alinor said, "Send a maid with it—and with a note, if you wish. The men will be busy reading over the contract. You will have to read it over, too, but that may be at your leisure since I wrote it. You may be sure your interests and those of your children are safeguarded."

Sybelle nodded acceptance, only asking, "Where have you put us?"

"In the south tower." Alinor smiled. "You will be more private there. Edith will wait upon you, and you may keep her and her daughter, Adele. The girl is not trained yet, but Edith knows her work."

Sybelle nodded again and went out into the antechamber, where she found Alinor's writing desk and penned a few lines to explain the gown to Walter. Then Rhiannon came up, followed by maids and menservants carrying the bath and hot and cold water to fill it.

"Why," Sybelle moaned, as she shivered before she stepped into the tub, "does this whole family marry in winter?"

"Because the nights are longer," Alinor said with a wicked chuckle. "You will have compensation for shivering now by being well warmed later."

A similar exchange, although in different words, passed between Walter and Simon about an hour later in the main chamber of the south tower, where Walter was also bathing before the fire. He actually had more reason to complain, since the fire, although as large as the hearth could hold, had only been laid when his party arrived and had not yet really warmed the room, whereas that in Alinor's apartment burnt night and day all year. Under the circumstances, Walter's ablutions were brief, no more than a dip to satisfy the need for ritual cleansing. Sybelle, he thought, as Adam and Simon vigorously rubbed him dry, would not care. She had made no objection to his unwashed condition in Clyro or Knight's Tower.

The thought was as warming as the friction generated by the cloths Adam and Simon wielded, and more comforting. He had been somewhat dismayed by their reaction to the magnificent gray gown and the note he had found when they arrived in the tower room. Both had regarded the garment with awe, and then had looked at him with almost equal awe—and awe was not a common state to either Simon or Adam. Apparently there was a greater significance in the gift than the value, although that was great enough by itself. However, neither Simon nor Adam told him more than what was in Sybelle's note, that the robe had belonged to Lady Alinor's first husband.

Nor did dressing in it provide any enlightenment, beyond the fact that it was remarkably warm for a garment so light when compared to a woolen gown. A second shock came when Walter entered the hall and Ian sprang to his feet, crying, "Simon! Simon!" In the next instant, before Lady Alinor could catch at his arm or Lord Geoffrey had exclaimed, "No, Ian, it is Walter, Sybelle's man," Ian himself had shaken his head, laughed, and come forward with his hand outstretched.

"Do forgive me, Walter," he said, smiling. "I had just been thinking about my lady's first husband, wondering what he would have said to Henry—for Simon was honest, but very wise—and suddenly it was as if he had appeared before me. You are very like him in body and in the way you walk."

"And hopefully in the way he thinks," Lady Alinor added, coming up beside her husband. "It is my fault, Ian. I meant to tell you that Walter would wear Simon's gown. I thought the color would suit him, and it does. But you and Geoffrey distracted me with the problem of our greeting to the king. Let us put it aside now. It is time to see the children handfast."

Walter had had no chance to say anything, and it was just as well, for his impulse was to deny any association with a being who seemed to be venerated by every person in Roselynde. The silk gown, which only moments before had seemed so light, suddenly weighed upon him ten times heavier than his full armor as the significance of the gift became clear. Ian was old; Adam was tied to his own great estates and had no doubt been subtly taught almost from birth that Roselynde was not his concern so that he would never contest his sister's right to the lands; Geoffrey was bound by blood and by political necessity to the court and to the lands for which he was king's castellan, and he would have little time for the management of so great an estate as Roselynde; Simon had always said he would have no part in the responsibility for Roselynde.

It was the first Simon who had initially taken up the burden, then Ian had carried it, and now, Walter understood, it was being handed to him. But he was a third son; little had been expected of him, and until he set eyes on Sybelle, he had led a carefree life, responsible for nothing beyond his small estate. Even after Geoffrey had told him that Roselynde and the honors beholden to it passed in the female line, Walter had not really thought about it, except to feel relief because Geoffrey was in the prime of his life and he had mistakenly believed it would be many years before the lands would be dropped into his hands. His attention had been on the civil war and on the property that had come to him upon his brother's death.

For one panic-stricken moment, Walter was tempted to tear off Simon's gown, feeling as if the soft folds of silk were strangling him. Then Lady Alinor and Lord Ian turned and stepped apart, one to each side of him, and Walter saw Sybelle. The golden goddess, Llewelyn had called her, and Walter had raised a brow. Now his breath caught.

Her underdress was of golden silk, so finely finished that it shone like the metal; the outer gown was a darker gold and glittered with metallic thread. Her bronze hair outshone them both, hanging loose as bridal custom decreed, and falling over shoulders and back to midthigh. Topazes around her throat and in the circlet that held her hair glowed richly, but not so richly as her eyes.

For a frozen instant, Sybelle seemed as unreachable as a priceless image of a virgin saint, but then her warm, red lips curved upward in a smile and Walter remembered her body moving under his. Virgin, yes—but neither image nor saint. Certainly not saint, he thought, as a gentle prod from Lady Alinor, who had taken one arm, and Lord Ian, who had taken the other, urged him forward. The glow in Sybelle's eyes might be caused by fervor, but not for the delights of celibacy or of heaven, where it was said there was no marriage.

Walter was headed toward Sybelle, but a tug on one arm and a push on the other turned him to the right. He almost pulled away to maintain his direction toward his lodestar when he saw Geoffrey and Joanna fall in beside Sybelle as Alinor and Ian walked with him, and then the vassals form up behind. It was at that point in the proceedings that Walter realized they were headed for the chapel, and he remembered Geoffrey saying, "You may obtain Sybelle *and* Roselynde, but not one without the other."

The heavy jeweled hem of Simon's gown seemed to tangle

at his ankles and the weight of it dragged at his shoulders, but the afterimage of Sybelle burned behind his eyes and Walter knew he would, like Atlas, lift the world on his shoulders if that was what he must do to have Sybelle. And in that moment, the gown was only light and warm, the smooth fabric a sensuous pleasure where it touched his skin, and he himself wondered what a man both honest and wise would say to him at this time. But then he was facing the priest, and Lord Geoffrey placed Sybelle's hand in his.

Sybelle looked up into the plain face of the man about to become her husband and felt as if nothing could ever go wrong for her again. There might be no great beauty in Walter's features, but Sybelle felt that everything she needed or desired was there: knowledge and strength and steadiness of purpose. Walter had felt the weight of responsibility fall upon him suddenly, but Sybelle had carried that weight with her all the years of her life. She had been molded and fitted to carry the burden, but it was a heavy burden nonetheless—and now she felt half the weight lifted from her. Her hand lay trustfully in his, and with joy and with relief she repeated the words that would bind them together.

For her, the wedding was perfect. Sybelle had attended state weddings and had shuddered inwardly at the thought of being in the bride's place during the days of public display. If it had been required of her, she would have done her duty with a smiling and serene face—as she performed so many duties that caused her inner qualms—but the quiet ceremony, witnessed only by those she most loved and a few vassals whom she knew and trusted, gave her great happiness and comfort.

The family and vassals cried *Fiat!* and the servants—all those who could fit having crept into the chapel—made a joyous noise when she and Walter gave each other the kiss of peace after the vows had been exchanged. Then they went out to supper, a quiet, cheerful meal, albeit considerably grander than the usual few dishes served. Rhiannon sang the story of Geraint and Enid, a most tender tale of love, although it held a strong warning against the foolishness of male pride and female reticence. Then, at last, Sybelle and Walter were alone in the south tower.

Sybelle had been displayed naked to her husband, but it had been no great trial when all those present were so well known to her and Walter had already seen all there was to see and was clearly well content. There had been no crude jests, nor was every second or third phrase a salacious innuendo. Not that Sybelle was prudish or so silly that she never saw there was a ridiculous side to making love. She could call a spade a shovel with the best—but she had never felt that the tender time in which two people were united for life was the proper moment for such sallies of wit.

When the last good wish and kind word was uttered, the bed curtains were drawn, and the wedding party left the chamber. As he heard the door close, Walter got out of bed and pushed the curtains back. "I like to see what I am doing," he said, looking with approval at Sybelle, whose golden glow of hair and eyes was softened but not extinguished in the dim light of the night candle. "And now for my gift to you."

Sybelle smiled slowly. "Was it immodest to remind you of those words?"

"Yes," Walter replied with mock seriousness, still standing by the edge of the bed and staring down at her, "of course it was, but I did not choose you for your modesty."

"For what, then?" Sybelle teased. "My great inheritance?"

She felt his eyes on her but she did not look up to catch his expression. There was no need. She was watching his shaft thicken and harden and start to rise. It was a thing she had never seen before, since Walter had always been fully ready by the time she saw him naked. But the process stopped abruptly at her last words, and Sybelle raised her head in time to see Walter shudder.

"Do you know that when I came into the hall and I understood what your gift to me signified, I wanted to run away," he said. "Every man thinks he desires to be rich and powerful before he considers what that truly means, but I am not a fool, and of a sudden I saw that it is harder by far to rule than to take orders. I wanted no part of it. But then I saw you. . . . You may not believe me, Sybelle, but I swear that even before I thought clearly of what it meant to be husband to the lady of Roselynde, I offered to take you with nothing."

"I believe you," she murmured, leaning toward him and encircling his hips with one arm so that she could rest her head against his abdomen. "My father told me. Do you think

I would have made such a jest if I had a doubt? And I have felt the burden all my life."

"You?" The single word held a wealth of surprise. "But you are always so sure. . . ." His voice trailed off as Sybelle tilted her head back to look up at him.

"I shake inside," she said simply, tightening her grip on him. "There are so many duties for which I have been taught the right words, and yet I do not understand in my bones what I say." Then the anxiety in her expression changed to confidence. "But now you will explain to me and share with me. . . ." Worry flickered briefly in her eyes. "Have I done you ill instead of good, my love? Am I asking too much?"

But his arms were around her before the words were out, pulling her even closer. "If I have you, no burden is too great."

And his body gave proof that he meant what he said, for Sybelle could feel the hardness and heat of his swollen shaft between her breasts. His skin was cold, however, rough with the goose bumps of chill. Sybelle relaxed her grip and turned her head so that she could bend it down, pushing away from his hold just enough to kiss the rosy head straining upward.

"Come," she murmured, sliding across to make room for him in the spot she had warmed, "you have promised me a gift. It is time for the giving of it."

CHAPTER 26

When Sybelle and Walter had agreed to be married so quickly, most of the arrangements for a wedding celebration were put aside. However, Alinor had not wished to deny the common folk their pleasure, and she had sent out word to all the farms and villages within a day's walk that the next day was to be a holiday and that there would be food and drink for the taking in the town of Roselynde. While Walter and Sybelle had enjoyed each other, cattle, pigs, and sheep had been slaughtered, roasting pits had been made ready, and permission granted to cut wood for use in them. The town bakers had mixed ten times the usual batches of dough for bread and cakes, brewers had rolled out kegs of ale and beer, and vintners had broached casks of wine.

In the morning, the wedding party returned to the bedchamber of the bridal couple to examine the sheets. These were properly bloodied, but after they were displayed and carried away to serve as evidence in case the bride's purity should ever be questioned, gravity and dignity departed.

"It is just as well that blood is blood and no one can tell from whom or from where it came." Sybelle giggled. "You have capped your other gifts with the saving of my good name. But what a shame it is that we did not know I was like my grandmother and had no maidenhead to broach. Think of your trouble to bring me untouched to my wedding bed—all wasted."

Walter had been laughing also. He was in no doubt as to his wife's virginity despite the fact that he had found no impediment to entry into her. In fact, he knew he had caused her considerable pain although he had taken time enough to make her eagerly ready, and it had not been easy to deliver the gift he had promised. It had been necessary for him to withdraw and to ease his passage with one of the unguents

Sybelle used to soothe the skin of her hands in winter. It was plain to Walter that he was penetrating a way previously unused. Their second coupling, just after they woke near dawn, had been less difficult. Still, her last words sobered him.

"It was not for that, Sybelle," he said.

Walter's voice held so odd a note that Sybelle stopped and turned back toward him. She had been about to go to the door and shout down for Edith and Adele to come up and help them dress. "What is it, my lord?" she asked, no longer laughing.

He shook his head. "Nothing. Nothing to do with you, my beloved wife. We are blessed in being able to share our love and our pleasure without shame or sin in the sight of God and all men." A brief expression of regret passed over his face, but then he smiled. "We had better dress if we wish to attend Mass. And I think we are supposed to ride into the town and show ourselves to the people there. Also, I must talk to your father and grandfather. I cannot leave Dai with the charge of Knight's Tower in his hands. I will have to have a new castellan, and he will need to be a man of experience."

"And also a man with a wife who knows how to manage a keep," Sybelle agreed briskly.

But a chill had passed through her when Walter had been unwilling to tell her what troubled him. She forgot it during the busy day that followed, for the regret did not recur and Walter was obviously happy. There was no sign that he felt the duty of being displayed to the people a burden. Nor was there any uncertainty or unease in his manner of dealing with the merchants of Roselynde town or with the serfs and fisherfolk who had flooded into it to enjoy the largess provided.

In fact, this type of duty was not what had troubled Walter. As a son and later brother of the Earls of Gloucester, he was accustomed to deputizing for them at such functions and well practiced in dealing with all levels of the commons from mighty guildmasters to the meanest serf. It was decision making that worried Walter, not the carrying out of decisions. However, that question had not yet arisen.

The afternoon and evening were spent in making plans for the immediate future. They decided to leave the next morning, hoping to catch the king at Oxford, for Geoffrey knew that Henry had intended to move west again after performing his devotions at Bromholm. Rhiannon offered to travel with the court and soothe Henry with her singing, which he admired almost to excess. If Henry accepted her, it would be another stitch in the patch over the tear in the fabric of Henry's relationship with his barons, since she was Llewelyn's daughter.

At this point Walter raised the problem of Knight's Tower. Geoffrey and Ian agreed at once that Walter's need to take hold of his property was immediate. There was no necessity for him to stay with the court.

"I have just the man for you," Geoffrey said when Walter asked about a suitable castellan. "Sir John is a man of middle years with a most capable wife. Moreover, he has a son who can take over the management of the keep he now governs. This will give young John experience, and it will be only a temporary arrangement. When Knight's Tower is ready you can choose a man of your own, and Sir John can return to Odiham. I am almost certain I will have a place for his son by then, so we will all benefit."

"Yes," Ian said, "and the need to install the castellan will be reason enough for you and Sybelle to make only a brief stay with the court. But you must also write at once to Barbury, Thornbury, and Foy for the castellans to come and do you homage. God forbid that this should be only a lull before the renewal of the conflict, but if so, your lands should be firmly in your hands before any new trouble starts."

"Good," Geoffrey approved. "Sir John can meet us at Oxford. I will send a messenger out today. Odiham is no great distance."

"If you are going west," Alinor put in, "do not forget to stop at Clyro and have Sir Roland do homage to you, Sybelle."

"Surely there is no need for haste in that," Sybelle said. "Sir Roland already knows that Clyro is part of my dowry, and he is loyal."

"Certainly, but it never hurts to renew oaths of fealty," Gilliane suggested.

"That is true, Gilliane," Alinor agreed, smiling fondly at this daughter-by-marriage, who had once been a brutalized pawn and was now fit to rule a kingdom, should one fall into her hands. "However, that was not my main purpose. If I remember the country in the west aright, Knight's Tower is the northernmost of all Walter's keeps and Goldcliff the most westerly. Clyro will be at least a day's travel closer than either of those to Thornbury and Foy. Barbury you need not consider, as you can summon that castellan to the manor at Braydon."

"You remember the country in the west aright, Lady Alinor," Walter said, "and to summon the men to Clyro is wise for another reason than distance. Not all of them may be as fearful or, perhaps, as treacherous as Sir Heribert. There is even a chance that one or more are decent men. There is no need to add to their unease by having them see that I have already changed not only the castellan of Knight's Tower but also the garrison."

"And it will be most natural to summon them there at this time," Sybelle added, "for you must announce our marriage to them and they may serve as witnesses to Sir Roland's homage to me—at which time you can point out that Roselynde's strength is behind you."

There was a murmur of agreement from the family. Walter settled himself more easily into the cushioned chair that had been added for him to the group near the fire. He had wondered during the early part of the discussion, which had centered so wholly on national affairs, whether his personal interests were so small in comparison that they would be pushed into the background. Now he understood that having been absorbed into Roselynde, nothing of his would ever be forgotten. He grinned, remembering Simon's exasperated description of his mother and sister as women who would cheerfully give away ten bushels of grain, but only after counting every kernel on every head and calling out a major court of inquiry if even one kernel should be missing.

Actually, Walter could see no fault in that. He found Simon's attitude more incomprehensible; having offered to play their parts at court, he and Rhiannon had lost interest in mere details and had wandered away. But Walter did not like to be cheated himself, and he was not averse to putting effort into determining that he would not be. And as he looked around the group, his satisfaction grew even stronger. He could see no fault in anything this family—now *his* family—did.

All was decent and in order. Despite the fact that every woman in the group was far richer and more powerful than her husband, only Lady Alinor sat in a chair, and that was lower and less elaborate than Lord Ian's. Moreover, her age gave her that privilege. Joanna, Gilliane, and Sybelle occupied stools at their husbands' feet, which was proper when there were not enough chairs, just as if they were ordinary, subservient females. That was soothing, although Walter was well aware that it was utterly meaningless. Then he corrected his thought; it was not meaningless because each wife leaned confidingly against her husband, as Sybelle was resting against his legs. Gilliane was playing with the fingers of Adam's hand, which lay on her shoulder; Geoffrey absently stroked Joanna's cheek with one finger. It was trust and self-confidence that permitted these women to act the role of meek wives for the sake of appearances.

They did not find the king at Oxford. He had gone, a clerk of the Exchequer told Geoffrey, whom he regarded as a trusted friend of Henry's, to Huntington, west of Hereford, not far from Painscastle. Geoffrey thanked his informant and joined his family for a hurried and worried consultation. Henry's move so far west seemed to be a deliberate challenge or temptation to the rebels.

"And it may be taken up," Walter said. "With Richard gone to Ireland, it is Gilbert Bassett who controls Pembroke's men. Bassett has no love for the king, and I think a large part of Richard's army, at least all that is not needed to garrison the other keeps, is at Clifford."

"It is that snake Winchester's doing, by my guess," Geoffrey snarled. "If Bassett attacks Henry and the king must flee, his anger and shame may overpower his desire for peace."

"I will go to Clifford to warn Bassett," Simon offered.

"No," Walter said, "I will do that. You and Lady Rhiannon will be of more use in Huntington. Your presence will be a strong sign to Henry that Prince Llewelyn had no part in any attack if I should come too late or if Bassett will not listen to me."

"And I, my lord?" Sybelle asked. "Will it serve your purpose best if I come with you or go to court?"

"Neither," Walter replied after a moment's thought. "Or, rather, I will ask you to follow me at the best speed that Sir John and his lady can make. They do not know the country and cannot be left to travel alone. In any case they could not go to Knight's Tower without me because Dai will not open for them unless I am there to order it."

Walter hesitated, aware that Dai would open for Sybelle. Then he told himself that it would not be convenient because he would have to travel north to meet Sybelle and then take her south to Huntington. It would not matter if Knight's Tower was without a castellan for a few days more. Below the conscious thought, however, there was a small uneasiness generated by the notion that the real reason for not sending Sybelle on to Knight's Tower was an unwillingness to be parted from her for the extra day or two that such an arrangement would necessitate. But the uneasiness surfaced in a completely different interpretation. The last Walter had heard was that Lady Marie would be staying in Clifford with her sister.

"Do not come to Clifford," Walter went on quickly. "I do not wish that Sir John's loyalty to the king should be open to challenge, owing to a visit to a rebel stronghold before peace is actually signed. Go on to Clyro. I will come to you there."

What Walter said was completely logical, and Clyro and Clifford were so close that he could ride back and forth, if that were necessary, without trouble. Still, there was something in his voice, in the haste with which he had amended "follow me" to going instead to Clyro, that reminded Sybelle of the flash of regret Walter had displayed the morning after their wedding. She, too, knew that Lady Pembroke and her sister, Marie, would be in Clifford. Was that why Walter did not want her in Clifford?

There was time for a single pang of jealousy before Sybelle called to mind her husband's steady tenderness, his eagerness in coupling, how he had clung to her whenever Marie appeared while they were in Abergavenny. It was nonsense to be jealous of a brainless doll who, Sybelle thought, not being afflicted with false modesty, was not nearly so beautiful as herself. Moreover, the comforting thoughts were reinforced, as Sybelle agreed calmly to her husband's order, by the fierceness of his farewell embrace, and his whispered urging that she hurry Sir John and his lady as much as she could so that they would be reunited the sooner.

By driving the horses and men with him nearly to foundering, Walter arrived at Clifford late the following night. To his intense relief, Bassett was there, innocently asleep, and unaware of the king's intended destination. Although he was not too happy to be routed out of bed, Bassett greeted Walter's news with enthusiasm. This was somewhat tempered by Walter's reminder that Richard would be ill pleased by any attack that might cause a renewal of the conflict—particularly while he was out of the country. However, since it was too late to do anything that night and it was clear that Walter was having difficulty in staying awake, further argument was suspended until the following morning.

Owing to his fatigue, Walter slept late, but Bassett rose at first light to pass the news he had received to Richard Siward. There was nothing secret about it, and Bassett discussed the matter with his brother-by-marriage at considerable length while they broke their fast.

Neither paid any attention to Sir Palance de Tours, a guest of Lady Pembroke's sister. They had become accustomed over the last few days to seeing him hanging about. He was pleasant enough, decently modest, not intruding but ready to join in any sport or game of chance when he was invited. However, he was unimportant to them, and neither noticed the haste with which he disappeared when Sir Walter's arrival was mentioned.

By the time Walter joined Bassett and Siward, Heribert had managed a hurried conference with Marie and had left Clifford with the intention of returning to Craswall Priory. If she would send him news of Walter's movements, he told her, he would assist her in any way he could to obtain the revenge she desired. Marie assured him most sincerely that she would send any information she obtained, but by now her interest was as much in keeping Heribert in attendance as it was in injuring Walter.

Marie found it very pleasant to have a knight at her beck and call. His deferential manner pleased her mightily, since her late husband had not encouraged his friends to regard her with much courtesy. She did not for a moment consider Heribert for a husband, despite his charm and good looks, because he simply had not sufficient rank or wealth nor any prospect of gaining them. However, his compliments and attention were pleasant, and as the weather grew milder, it was very convenient to have an escort who would take her anywhere she wished to go.

It was a satisfactory arrangement all around. As Marie's guests, Heribert and his men were housed and fed at the Earl of Pembroke's expense. However, that was so small an addition to the present wartime garrison of Clifford that no one raised any objection. Marie had not sense enough to realize that the situation would change when peace came, nor did she stop to think that if Heribert gained his purpose of depriving Walter of his estate, Heribert himself would regain control of Knight's Tower and return there. In fact, Heribert spoke so constantly of Marie's revenge—as if his only interest in Walter were through her—that he had thoroughly obscured in her mind the fact that he had his own reasons for hating Walter.

Thus, Marie's first reaction to the news of Walter's arrival was not satisfaction that Walter was within reach of her vengeance but irritation for depriving her of her *cavalier flagorneur*. Had he left immediately, she would simply have sent word to Heribert to return and said she could not discover where Walter planned to move next. However, Walter had no intention of leaving Bassett and Siward to their own devices, particularly when he knew Sybelle could not yet have reached Clyro. So when he woke, he settled down to discuss what moves, if any, could be made that would push the king toward peace.

Marie had thought she would simply ignore him for the brief time he was in Clifford. This she expressed by an icy glance and a turned back in answer to his soft greeting. It was most unfortunate that she did turn her back, for she would have misinterpreted Walter's stricken expression of guilt for sorrow or regret. That, plus her own self-conceit, might have convinced her that Walter was longing for her and suffering, dissatisfied with the choice he had made of staying with Sybelle. In her present mood, that might have been satisfaction enough.

However, she did not see, and her seat near Gervase was close enough for her to hear snatches of the conversation among the men between the desultory comments Gervase made to her. From those snatches, Marie managed to determine several unpleasant facts: One, Walter had already married Sybelle, and to Marie he sounded as swollen with pride as a cock on a dunghill. He spoke of what "we of Roselynde believe" as if that family were the pivot of the sun and stars. Two, Walter seemed to be urging Bassett and Siward to some action in the war, and that meant all the men would leave and she and Gervase would be bored to death again. Three, it did not seem, after all, that Walter's stay would be brief. Apparently he intended to remain at Clifford until his bitch of a wife arrived at her keep and then to ride over from Clyro every day.

Marie was by now thoroughly infuriated. In her mind, Walter was an abomination on the face of the earth. He spoke to her with so casual a mien, as if nothing special had ever passed between them; that was an insult. He was an evil influence, desiring a renewal of the war—which Marie knew everyone else wanted ended; that was treason. He was a nuisance, for as long as he was in the neighborhood, Sir Heribert would have to hide at Craswall; that was the greatest evil of all because she would be left to beg favors from Gervase every time she wished to ride out or have a note carried instead of telling Sir Heribert what she wanted and having it done. Walter would have to be got rid of.

Walter was distressed by the way Marie responded to his greeting because it indicated she still had strong feelings about him. All his previous affairs, except those terminated because of excessive greed on the part of his mistress, had ended by mutual consent, with no stronger emotion than mild regret. When by chance he met those ladies again, they were pleasantly, if distantly, friendly. Thus, Marie's refusal even to acknowledge him increased his sense of guilt. He believed he had misjudged her and caused her pain, and he felt an obligation to make up for that.

However, Walter knew there was no recompense that he could offer, and he tried to bury the guilt in concentration on the political problem at hand. His first suggestion was to ignore the king's presence altogether, since Henry was offering no threat to them. This, however, neither Bassett nor Siward would accept. Both wished to strike a telling blow.

"But not at the king," Walter warned. "You know that Richard would not consider that, even when Henry was sitting outside his gates at Usk. Nor even when the king had broken his oath and offered greater insult could anyone persuade him to attack his liege lord directly. If you move on Huntington, you will have Richard for an enemy. In Roselynde we spoke of the fine edge upon which Henry's purpose is balanced. Is there some way we can show our contempt for his ministers and our respect for his own person?"

"Respect!" Siward sneered.

Bassett sighed. "He *is* the king, and it is true that Richard would not agree to any thrust at him."

"Lord Geoffrey says that this desire for absolute power is only a fever raised in Henry by Winchester's poisoned words," Walter pointed out, "and I believe it, because my father and brother complained often that the king cared too much for beautiful churches and too little for government, leaving all in the Earl of Kent's hands. Thus it is at the king's ministers we should strike, not at the king."

"But if—" Siward began, only to be interrupted by Bassett saying, "Wait, wait, let me think. Something is in the back of my mind, something that falls in with what Walter just said. To strike at the king's ministers . . . I have it! Not more than two miles from Huntington lies the manor of Almondbury, and that belongs to Stephen de Seagrave. If we attack that, the news of it will come soon enough to Huntington."

"Very good," Walter agreed, and smiled. "Yes, that will be perfect. Henry will know that you could just as easily have moved on Huntington, which would have yielded richer spoils. Thus, that you did not will show your respect for his possessions and your contempt for Seagrave's. What a pity my men are at Knight's Tower, but I am sure—"

"I do not think you should come with us," Bassett said. "Have some sense, Walter. If your colors should by mischance be reported among the raiders, your father-by-marriage will have some difficulty explaining to the king how he happened to give his daughter to a man who, not a week after his marriage, is out raiding with a passel of outlaws."

Walter opened his mouth and then shut it.

Richard Siward put a hand on his shoulder. "This, as you said yourself, is no time to raise doubts in the king's mind, and Geoffrey FitzWilliam is blood-bound to Henry. It is enough that you came to tell us. You need not fear we will think your loyalty wavering."

Bassett endorsed Siward's sentiments wholeheartedly and then began to discuss more specific plans for the attack. Walter said no more, but he was painfully aware that he had not come to offer these men an opportunity but to prevent them from acting in a way those loyal to the king disapproved. He tried to consider dispassionately whether what he had done would actually forward the cause of peace or would merely salve the king's pride and make him worse in the future. It was irrelevant that the arguments he had used to dissuade Bassett from attacking Henry were true. Walter knew that Richard would not have approved of threatening the king, but Richard's conscience was often too tender for his own good.

Or was it? Was it not wisdom that made Richard insist on avoiding any direct confrontation? After all, they would have to live with Henry after peace was made; hatred held down only by fear was no happy base on which to build a future. That was a comforting thought, but Walter did not trust it or himself. It sounded very much like something Geoffrey would say, but would he be thinking this way if he had not married Sybelle? It did not matter, Walter told himself firmly. He had done what he knew Richard would have wanted, and that was his proper duty. It was not his right to decide what was best for the Earl of Pembroke in his absence.

Having repressed his doubts, Walter entered into the planning of the raid. Bassett regretted that none of Simon's men was available for spying, and Walter agreed heartily but then suggested that since Clifford and Huntington were so close—no more than about five miles apart—it was possible that huntsmen from Clifford knew some of their own kind from the king's forest. This was found to be so, and the men were dispatched to learn what they could.

By dinnertime, Marie had reconsidered her original idea of refusing to notice Walter's presence. If he planned to remain in Clifford, or spend much time in the keep, such behavior would become noticeable. Although Gervase would understand, Bassett and Siward would surely wonder and perhaps report to Richard. Marie was flattering herself, as the gentlemen had far better things to wonder about and more important ones to communicate to Pembroke, but Marie saw life from her own point of view.

Unfortunately, as she thought about Walter, Marie's rage reawakened. She wished to be coldly disdainful, as if he were one of the lower orders, but she did not dare, fearing he would grow angry and be crude and boorish enough to make a public jest of her desire to marry him one month and her coldness the next. The result of the varying emotions that boiled in her was a most peculiar manner—a gush, followed by a withdrawal, a titter of nervous laughter for no reason, a few hesitant words with lowered eyes, which lifted suddenly in a flashing glance.

Walter was distressed by these further signs of what he mistook for lingering desire. He did his best for Marie, pretending not to notice anything unusual and attending to what she said with a grave courtesy that held no suggestive overtones. However, his voice was soft with guilt and his eyes troubled. This, Marie took for regret, but it was too late for that satisfaction to content her. That Walter suffered was not enough; Sybelle must suffer, too, must learn to hate the husband she now loved so that life would be a hell for both of them.

After dinner the huntsmen returned, and Walter excused himself with considerable relief to listen to what they had to say. Marie made no protest. She was eager to be alone, for she needed to plan. Sybelle had not reacted to any of her hints about her relationship with Walter, so something stronger than words were needed. Marie decided that she and Walter must be caught in so compromising a situation that it could not be ignored.

But that would ruin her as surely as Walter. No, it need not. Not if she said she had appealed to Walter for help and then claimed that he had responded by seizing her by force and raping her. If she said she could not live without one more passage of love to remember and pleaded with him, surely he would be fool enough to take her to bed. And even if he would not, she could tear her own clothes and scream for help.

Of course she would need a reliable witness, but she was certain she could trust Sir Palance—no, Heribert—she called him Palance in public so that she often forgot his real name—and he was perfect because he and Sybelle knew each other. Heribert, Marie believed, was clever enough to find an explanation that would satisfy that fool Sybelle for not coming to Knight's Tower when he was expected.

The timing might be difficult, for Marie was uncertain just how long Walter intended to remain in Clyro after Sybelle came. In any case, it would be best if Walter came to her soon after his wife arrived. That way, it would be a greater insult. And where should they meet? It must be near but not here in Clifford. No one would believe Walter would try rape in Clifford.

Then Marie remembered that after the cold had broken and before Richard had left for Ireland, they had ridden out and visited a manor house at Hay. The bailiff there would remember her and raise no objections to her spending a few hours and using his bedchamber—and even if he did not remember her, he would not dare protest if she were accompanied by Sir Heribert and his men. And Hay was very close to Clyro, a mile or a little more. They had passed Clyro when taking a longer route back to Clifford.

Then she bit her lip with chagrin. How could she be accompanied by Heribert and his men when Heribert was in Craswall? If only she were at Craswall . . . Well, why not? All she need do was tell Gervase that she could not bear to be in the same place as Walter and that she wished to retreat to the priory. Gervase knew what had passed between her and Richard when she tried to claim to be with child by Walter. Now that peace was near at hand, Gervase was intent on remaining on good terms with her husband so that he would take her to court when he went. She would not wish to take a chance that Marie would cause trouble; she would rather do without her company for a few days.

Marie jumped to her feet. There was still time to get to the priory today so that Heribert could send for his men tomorrow. Walter had said he did not expect Sybelle until the day after tomorrow. Heribert could send some men to watch for her arrival. One could ride back to warn Heribert and herself, and another could deliver Marie's letter. Marie giggled. If Walter did not happen to be in Clyro, the letter might be handed to Sybelle. If she read it . . . If she read it, all kinds of additional possibilities for making trouble would arise.

Since Gervase had been uncomfortably aware of Marie's peculiar behavior at dinner, she was not at all averse to her sister's request. If the thought that Marie was more interested in obtaining Sir Palance's company than in avoiding Walter's crossed her mind, she made no comment about it. She was aware of the attention Sir Palance paid Marie and that Marie enjoyed it, but she understood her sister and was not in the least afraid that Marie would get involved too deeply. The fact that Sir Palance had returned to Craswall so suddenly had puzzled her, but Marie said glibly that Sir Palance did not wish to become involved in the war and had retreated to avoid being asked to accompany Bassett and Siward on the proposed raid. That seemed reasonable enough to Gervase, and with no more than a cynical lift to her brow, she bade Marie enjoy her retreat.

Gervase's request for a party to accompany Marie to Craswall naturally was referred to Bassett, who said several things not quite under his breath about Richard's sister-by-marriage and her desire to visit the priory just when he needed every horse for a more important purpose. Walter overheard and was filled with a combination of guilt and relief. He had been considering riding to Clyro rather than spend an evening in Marie's company, but he did not wish to go to Clyro. He had just thought of how it would be possible to accompany the raiders—he could carry a shield with colors other than his own—and he wanted time to argue Bassett into accepting his idea. Thus, although he felt guilty for having driven Marie away, he was also grateful to her for going.

When Marie rode into Craswall Priory, Sir Heribert was startled and at first rather alarmed. He was aware that Marie was not yet sufficiently enamored of him to have followed him just to be with him, and he feared that some emergency had arisen. However, as soon as she made known her plan, Heribert was delighted. Naturally, he had no intention of simply accusing Walter of rape—he would never have been believed. He intended to kill Walter when he caught him naked and unprepared in Marie's bed.

Heribert was not afraid that Marie would betray him as a murderer, for he could place the entire blame upon her. He had heard enough of the Earl of Pembroke's fondness for Walter to make logical the threat that Marie's brother-by-marriage would either kill her or immure her forever if he discovered she had been instrumental in the murder of his friend. Once Walter was dead, Heribert would make clear to Marie that they would sink or swim together. She would have to keep the secret of how Walter came to die or be adjudged as guilty as his killer.

However, Heribert said nothing of his private plans, merely agreeing that the device should certainly cause a new, young wife much pain. He tried to convince Marie that it would be safer to send her letter to Clifford, since it would be more likely that Walter would get it. Sybelle might destroy the letter, he pointed out, if she received it before Walter arrived in Clyro.

Marie laughed. "Then I will send another, tearfully asking why he did not respond to my first letter, which will surely make him ask what happened to it. Walter is not the man to take kindly to a wife's interfering with his life. He may come a day or two later, but he will come all the same, and Sybelle will be all the angrier."

Sir Heribert was about to argue further, for it was essential for him to know when Walter would arrive. Marie would be comfortable enough inside Hay, but he did not wish to camp out for several days in winter weather. Then it occurred to him that he could not, without detection, keep a large troop of men near enough to the manor to be sure of getting at Walter, and he raised that question.

"You will not need a large troop," Marie said. "How many men will it take to overpower a naked man? And why should you camp out? You and ten or fifteen men or even twenty can come to the manor as an escort."

Heribert shook his head. "Where would you get such an escort if you have quarreled with your sister? If Sir Walter sees the men, he will be suspicious, and if we try to hide the men, the bailiff will certainly think it peculiar and might even warn Sir Walter to avoid trouble in his house."

But in spite of his arguments, Marie would not be moved. She insisted that the letter go to Clyro so that Sybelle would know of it. Eventually Heribert yielded because it came to him that Sybelle's knowledge of Marie's letter would be evidence beyond his assertion that Marie had devised the plan that led to Walter's death. It would be an extra insurance that she would be silent.

He could bring two or three men, Heribert thought. The bailiff would think nothing of that, nor would he think it odd if the men made themselves scarce after they arrived. He might be no match for Sir Walter alone, but three or four of them should be enough to hold him, particularly if Marie could manage to get him unarmed and into bed. A man stationed near the road could gallop off to bring the rest of the troop as soon as he saw Walter arrive, and the troop should be at the manor house in plenty of time because Heribert assumed it would take as much as half an hour for Marie to do her part. If Walter came at all, for whatever reason, he would come prepared to talk for a while. Then, even if Marie had overestimated her power to bring him to Hay without an escort and tempt him into bed—Sir Heribert had his doubts about that, having seen how beautiful Sybelle was—the troop should arrive in time to kill Walter and the men he brought with him.

Although some of Heribert's doubts were justified, Marie was not really taking any chances. She was not altogether a fool and did understand that to tell a man she was certain he could not resist her was to waken that resistance. Despite having misinterpreted the reason for Walter's softness toward her, she knew how to use it; her letter was a masterpiece of hints and fears. It had taken her all the rest of that day to compose, but was well worth the effort.

While she was engaged in that task, Heribert rode back to Clifford and, with due care not to run into Walter, instructed his troop to ride out at the same time as the raiding party left. Thus, hopefully, no one would notice their going. They, however, were to take the opposite direction, pass Hay, and take over the shepherd's shelter about a mile farther down the road. They could take their ease—whatever ease they could find in so rough a lodging—for that day and the next morning, but after that they were to be armed and ready to ride back to Hay at a moment's notice.

The following day the letter was sent off with two men—one to deliver the missive as soon as Sybelle was known to be in the keep and then ride back to tell Sir Heribert, the other to carry the news of Walter's coming. As soon as Walter arrived in Clyro, Marie, Heribert, and three of his men would move down to Hay.

Sybelle and her party started for Clyro soon after Walter left Oxford. Sir John had protested mildly that there was no urgency; it would be better, he thought, to leave the next day because only a few hours of daylight remained. In response, Sybelle pointed out blandly that the weather was fine at present and one could not rely on good traveling weather at that time of year. It was good to take advantage of dry roads while it was possible. Sir John and his wife exchanged glances, and the lady sighed. They knew Sybelle; this would be no easy journey, and Sir John's wife was sure she would be very saddle-sore and tired of riding pillion before they arrived.

The next day was also fine, and Sybelle had them out on the road before the sun was up. The third day on the road was a repetition of the second, but the weather broke that evening. The rain, however, did not in the least diminish Sybelle's determination to reach Clyro the next day. Determination notwithstanding, it was clear by the afternoon that it would be impossible for the baggage wagons to get so far before dark. The reasonable thing, then, was to turn back to Hereford and stay the night there, but Sybelle could not bring herself to do it. Nor did she wish to examine closely the reasons for her behavior. She told herself she was simply eager to be reunited with Walter and that he had urged her to come as soon as possible.

Nonetheless, she did not wish to inflict hardship on Sir John's lady. Thus, she offered to go on alone with only a few guards. But Sir John would not hear of that, so eventually the mounted party rode ahead, leaving the baggage wains with some men-at-arms to follow as quickly as they could. Sybelle soon regretted her foolishness, but not soon enough to make returning to Hereford a possible alternative. It was a miserable ride, and far longer than she had expected; it grew dark earlier than usual because of the rain, and they had to pick their way along the road very slowly for fear of wandering off it and becoming lost.

When they came to the place where the road forked left to Clifford, Sybelle was tempted to give in and go that way; Clifford was only about a mile farther, whereas there were still more than five miles to go to Clyro. However, she held steadily to the right fork. Walter had specifically told her not to go to Clifford. Doubtless he wanted to protect her from Marie's nasty tongue. Sybelle sniffed contemptuously at the thought. She could have turned Marie into jelly in five minutes if she had not wished to avoid shocking Walter and if the woman had been worth crushing. And anyway, Walter would be waiting in Clyro.

But Walter was not in Clyro. Despite Sir Roland's warm welcome, despite the blazing fire and dry, warm clothing, Sybelle felt chilled to the bone. Walter had not come to Clyro at all, had not even sent a messenger to warn Sir Roland to expect her. It was as if he had forgotten her existence.

As her first shock of disappointment wore off and Sir Roland and his lady exclaimed in surprise when they heard how quickly her party had come so far, Sybelle told herself not to be a fool. Although Walter had asked her to come as swiftly as she could, he probably had not believed she would arrive so soon. Moreover, he had business with Bassett in Clifford. Perhaps he was having difficulty in persuading Bassett not to attack the king. Sir Gilbert was very bitter against Henry.

Good sense almost prevailed against a suspicion Sybelle would not even admit she felt. And she had little time to brood. They went early to bed, and fatigue won out over her smothered doubts. She slept soon and well, and if she dreamed, she did not remember any unpleasantness in the dreams. The next morning Sybelle was caught up in a discussion about Sir Heribert and the conditions in Knight's Tower.

Sir John was naturally curious about the keep he was to manage. He had asked a few questions on the road, but it was difficult to sustain a conversation while riding, and now he pressed Sir Roland and Sybelle for all the information they could supply. Sir Roland had a few points to make about Sir Heribert himself, but he had never been to Knight's Tower. Thus, it was Sybelle to whom most of the questions were addressed. She was far more able than most women would have been to answer, but unlike her mother and grandmother, who could have replied with half their minds on some other subject, she was sufficiently inexperienced that she had to concentrate on what she said.

It was not until after dinner, when Sir Roland and Sir John went off together to look at the war machines on the walls and to discuss attack and defense, and their wives betook themselves to the nursery to talk of babies, that Sybelle had time for her own thoughts. These, as she worked over the embroidery of cuffs to match the collar she had finished for a gown for her husband, were not pleasant, but they were not jealous, either.

It had occurred to Sybelle that if Walter had not been able to dissuade Bassett and Siward from an attack, he might have decided to accompany them in the hope of exerting some control over what the men did. She was counting over the days, trying to calculate how long it might take to organize an attack, and when Bassett would be likely to strike if he were going to do so—and in general engaging in a series of mental gymnastics, useless owing to a total lack of information—when a servant approached her with a letter in hand.

Sybelle reached eagerly for the folded parchment before the servant spoke, hoping the letter was from Walter and fearing it was from Bassett to say her husband was hurt or dead. In fact, in her anxiety she almost broke the seal before looking at it, but as her nails caught at the wax, she remembered that it was most likely of all that the letter was not for her but for Sir Roland, and she looked questioningly at the servant who said, "For the lord or lady, and the messenger did not wait."

"The lord or lady" did not answer the question of whether the letter was for her or Sir Roland, but it immediately relieved any fear that what she held announced that harm had come to Walter. Sybelle looked down at the device on the seal, but it meant nothing to her and she did not study it closely. Doubtless the letter was from a friend or relative of Sir Roland. She turned it idly as she began to lay it on the small table that held her embroidery silks so that the superscription caught her eye. The letter was for Walter, and the handwriting was almost certainly not that of a scribe.

Curiously, Sybelle turned it over again to look more carefully at the seal. Who would know that Walter was expected at Clyro? Whose seal would be unfamiliar to her? It was a small seal, too. Sybelle hesitated, thinking that it might not be her business to know who was writing to Walter, and then shook her head. Nonsense. All of Walter's business was hers, and hers his. They were married, one flesh and one blood now. What if the letter were from young Gloucester or from some friend appealing for help? Sybelle carried the letter to where the light was better and looked carefully at the outlines in the wax. Then her lips thinned to a hard line. The seal was small, but it had been pressed carefully, most carefully, into wax of just the right consistency. *Les Maures*, although bent around a curve, was easy enough to read.

CHAPTER 27

Meanwhile, from the time Marie had left Clifford, Walter began to enjoy himself. Gilbert Bassett only laughed when Walter said he wished to change his shield and accompany them, agreeing that if Walter wanted to go for the sport and what loot he could snatch, he was very welcome. And, although he was consulted in the planning, Walter felt a delightful lack of responsibility about it. It was a great, if temporary, release to need to give thought to no one but himself, not even to the small troop he had led for many years.

Just as he got into bed, and a prick of longing for Sybelle's lithe body reminded him he missed his wife, he began to laugh. Tomorrow's raid would be his last wild fling. He would probably never again be engaged in an action in which he was free to do as he pleased without any consideration for the effect of his behavior. He lay back thoughtfully with his arms behind his head and reflected on his new situation in life. He had feared the wrong loss of freedom when he had first offered for Sybelle. It was the weight of responsibility for Roselynde he should have dreaded, not the vow to care for only one woman.

He remembered how he had asked himself, after Lady Joanna and Prince Llewelyn had warned him of Sybelle's jealousy, whether he was no longer to be in control of his own life. Now Walter wondered how he could have been so foolish. From the first time he had laid eyes on Sybelle, he had desired no other woman. To be faithful to his wife—at least, for any period in which they were not parted for long—would be no harsh trial. Besides, he had not seen a hint of jealousy in Sybelle, and Marie had given her reason enough to be jealous.

The thought of Marie made Walter uncomfortable, but only

momentarily. He would not need to see her again for some time if peace were made. Richard would take his wife to court, no doubt, and then settle her somewhere while he restored order to lands disorganized by war. Meanwhile, Walter would be busy on his own estates and visiting Roselynde lands.

Again a wave of oppression passed over him, but more lightly, and it was mixed with a sense of pride. It was a great thing to be thought worthy by such men as Lord Ian and Lord Geoffrey. Anyway, if peace came, the burden would not be dumped on him. He would have time to get to know the people and ease slowly into the duties.

Walter turned on his side and pulled the covers up over his shoulders. It was all in the future, and the future was in God's hands. Tomorrow alone was close enough to count on what would happen surely, and tomorrow would be a day of freedom and amusement. They should be back in Clifford by dinnertime, and after eating he would ride over to Clyro. Probably Sybelle would not arrive until the next day, but Sir Roland would not mind his coming earlier. A frown creased Walter's brow briefly. Should he have written to Sir Roland to warn him of their coming? He yawned sleepily. It was too late now, and he would be too busy in the morning. Sir Roland knew him well enough not to be troubled by an unannounced visit.

And, indeed, the first part of the morrow held exactly to the plan made for it. All the men Bassett could mount rode out of Clifford soon after Lauds, which Walter attended with a distinct sense of pleasure since he had no duties among the men. Their arrival at Almondbury was timed to coincide with the early confusion of breaking fast and morning tasks, and they succeeded even better than they expected, reaching the manor just as the gates were opened to permit the entry of a small herd of cattle. Not that they had been worried about the simple gates of the manor, but not to need to breach them saved time and labor and, perhaps, a few wounds from arrows.

They charged across the fields, shouting and laughing, driving the cattle before them so the few defenders of Almondbury could not close the gate. After that it was all as easy as a brawl at a fair. They cut down the few who dared resist, ransacked the house and the buildings, loaded all the carts they could find with the contents, and drove out the animals.

Then, serious business done with, the men-at-arms were free to take their pleasure. Some scoured house and grounds for whatever small things of value had not yet been taken. Others seized those women who appealed to them, most to play with at the moment, a few, the youngest and most comely, to be dragged back to Clifford. The air rang with terrified screaming, and wails of grief and pain mixed with the shouts and laughter of the victors.

The knights, although not above disporting themselves as rudely as the men-at-arms when the spirit moved them, were not so disposed this day and still sat upon their horses, as did a small group of men-at-arms specially detailed to guard against counterattack and the squad captains who were responsible for rounding up their men when it was time to leave.

Bassett cast an eye over the young men and children of the manor, who at his order were herded before him by a few of the captains, but he saw nothing interesting enough to bother carrying away. The bailiff was dead, and the blacksmith and carpenter had already been dragged out. He turned to Siward and Walter, who had also rejected the group of serfs as worthless.

"Are they worth killing?" Bassett asked.

"I do not think so," Siward replied. "What do you think, Walter?"

"It would take too long and serve no purpose," Walter replied. "These are nothing and can be replaced so quickly that it is not worth the effort of lifting a sword to dispatch them. In fact, they may do more harm alive to Seagrave. If they are left starving, he will have to feed them or they will steal from the surrounding farms."

"Now that is a wise thought," Bassett agreed, and shouted an order to the men-at-arms to let the people go and to start burning the buildings, adding a jovial threat that those who dallied too long with the women might find themselves afire before they even got to hell.

However, Bassett and Siward were not really in any hurry. The coincidental opening of the gate had made the taking of Almondbury so easy that there was a feeling of incompleteness about the raid. They took time to douse the walls with those kegs of oil that had not fit on the wagons and to drag the most flammable materials close around the buildings so that even what was made of stone would collapse. Nor did they ride away when the fires were set, but lingered to reignite anything that seemed likely to go out. Then Siward conceived the idea of sending out groups of men to burn any shepherds' shelters or woodcutters' huts in the vicinity and collect the sheep from the fields and the hogs from the woods.

"And if the swineherd is stubborn," Siward said, "just shoot him. The pigs will soon go wild and terrify the whole neighborhood."

Walter laughed. "Yes, and if there is peace and this land goes back into the king's hands, we may be invited to hunt the hogs down and thus have good sport."

Being unable to think of any further ways to create havoc, the three knights were waiting somewhat impatiently for the small parties they had dispatched to return, when one of the guards who had been watching from a small rise of land shouted a warning and came galloping back toward them. A large party of armed men led by a mailed knight was coming from the direction of Huntingdon.

"I hope we have not lingered too long," Walter said worriedly.

But he was the only one who was worried. Bassett and Siward with large, vicious grins on their faces, shouted orders to their men to form for battle. They had agreed not to attack the king directly because they knew Richard would not approve, but if Henry was fool enough to ride out and contest their winnings, they were prepared cheerfully to whip him and his men until they fled like beaten curs.

Although he knew it to be hopeless, Walter was about to protest against this unnecessary clash. They had accomplished their purpose and would lose nothing at all by retreating from the area. Then he realized that whoever was leading that party, it would not be Henry. The king was not a physical coward, but the barons and ministers now with him would never permit him to risk himself in defense of a minor manor that was not even crown property. Walter laughed as he ranged Beau beside Bassett's destrier and fewtered the lance he had not used in Almondbury because he took no pleasure in skewering defenseless serfs. There had been no fighting worth the name in taking the manor. This would round out the morning perfectly.

However, Walter and his companions were not to have the pleasure of a brisk passage at arms. As soon as the oncoming party became visible, Bassett roared an order to charge, and the whole troop spurred their horses forward, the three knights well to the fore. They were at a slight disadvantage because their opponents had worked up a greater velocity, and Walter gave a single anguished thought to his weakened collarbone and what Sybelle would say to him if he broke it a third time.

Then, in unison with his comrades, Walter loosed an unbelieving roar. The oncoming troop had suddenly fallen into utter confusion. The knight who led it had screamed something at his men and turned his horse suddenly to the side when he saw Bassett's group charging toward him. His desperate move fouled the path of the men-at-arms who followed him, so that the most forward of them collided with each other in trying to avoid him, and those behind came to skidding halts to keep out of the tangle ahead. Those even farther back were also turning aside.

Walter, Bassett, and Siward instinctively headed their horses in the same direction, but it was not, as they suspected, an inept attempt to flank their line or to spread out the better to combat them. Leader and men continued to turn until their backs were toward Bassett's group and they fled incontinently in the direction from which they had come. For a little while Bassett pursued, but it was clear they could not overtake quickly, and Sir Gilbert was too experienced in war to allow himself and his men to be spread out as they would be by a long pursuit and, perhaps, drawn into a trap. He drew up, calling to Walter and Siward to do the same, and shouted orders to regroup.

"It must be a trap," he said. "I suppose they wished to draw us into a larger force on unfavorable ground."

"Should we go now?" Siward asked.

"No, let me ride forward and see whether they have stopped, now that we are no longer pursuing," Walter suggested.

He did so, but from the rise of land where the guard had been stationed he saw only the stragglers of the group riding away as hard as they could. And although he waited for some time, expecting to see a much larger force coming to attack them, there was no indication of any further opposition.

Eventually Siward came to join him and tell him that the loot they had taken was well on its way to Clifford. Since there still was no sign of any threat, they rode back to the smoldering ruins of Almondbury and, after a puzzled conference about the abortive attack, which none of them could fathom, made their way quietly to Clifford.

Walter dined with his friends and enjoyed the meal, his appetite having been honed by his morning's exercise. Although the conversation centered on the final event, no one discovered any explanation of what had happened. Nor, after they talked it over, did it seem very important. Walter collected his share of the portable loot, arranged to have the cattle and sheep owing to him driven over to Clyro when convenient, and took his leave.

He was in high good humor as he rode the few miles to his wife's keep, and when he heard that Sybelle was already there he dismissed the servant who wished to announce him and rushed up to the hall glowing with pleasure. No small impediment arose to annoy him. Sybelle was sitting by the fire embroidering, and he strode across, pulled her into his arms, and kissed her soundly before everyone there.

"I have missed you," he said, kissing her again, "but to speak the truth, I am glad I did not know you had come so soon. I have been out with Bassett and Siward. How did you get here so fast? Did you fly?"

"I wish we had," Sir John's wife replied comically. "If we had, I would not need to be sitting on extra cushions."

Sybelle could not help smiling at that, and she said collectedly, "You said as soon as possible, my lord, so I kept the pace hot."

But she was cold inside again. Walter had never greeted her in such a way before. To her, the public warmth of his embrace seemed false, as if he were overdoing a show of love to hide something else. All she could think of was Marie's letter, yet she could not bring herself to give it to him here, where everyone could see her face and his. Her mind seemed numb, and she could not think of any way to suggest that they should go apart—at least, any way that would not give rise to jests, which, at this moment, she could not bear.

Walter had no time to notice that there was something wrong with Sybelle. Although he did realize that she had not really responded to his kisses, he put that down to surprise and to the fact that there were onlookers. But his attention was drawn from her almost immediately by Sir Roland, who had caught the significance of the words "been out with Bassett and Siward." As he rose to offer his chair to Walter, he asked anxiously what Walter meant by that remark.

Usually, Sir Roland knew, a civil war was no easy place for neutrals, who, rather than being protected by not taking sides, were more often targets for both antagonists. Thus far, Clyro had been safe because Richard Marshal would not hear of any attack on the property of his "aunt" Alinor and "uncle" Ian, particularly when he knew they would make no move against him. But Pembroke was now in Ireland, and Sir Roland did not have the same trust in Richard's lieutenants. If the war had caught fire again, he wanted to know.

Walter's reply calmed Sir Roland's momentary anxiety, but led to a lively discussion of the raid itself and then on to a more serious one about whether peace was really imminent and upon what terms that peace would be made. Sir John expressed the hope that Pembroke would not be kept in Ireland too long, since the king might be induced, during a long period of quiet, to change his mind yet again.

"I do not think so," Walter replied to that. "For one thing, from what Lord Geoffrey told me about the archbishop-elect, he will not give over his exhortations—and he is a truly holy man whom the king fears and respects. For another," he added, his lips twisted, "there will not be so much peace that Henry will be able to think his barons have forgotten their distaste for the Bishop of Winchester and his minions. I am quite sure this will not be the last raid on lands beholden to them." He paused and frowned. "But I wish I knew the reason why that troop would not close with us, but turned and ran."

"Could they have been allies?" Sir John asked.

"Then why not call their name and loyalty and ask what we were doing?" Walter countered.

"They could have feared they were overmatched," Sir Roland offered.

"I suppose so." Walter sounded doubtful. "They could have feared a trap or thought that many more men were with the booty we had taken and would come to our support if we were put to the worse. But I still cannot see why they would not try to come to grips with us. There was a clear road behind for them to flee if we were too strong.'' Then he shrugged and smiled. ''We will never know, I guess, and I do not think it important, but it is a question that teases the mind.''

While this discussion had gone forward, Sybelle had been uncharacteristically silent. Ordinarily she would have been as interested as any of the men in the political significance of Walter's suggested policy of attacking the property of the king's ministers while sparing that of the king himself and even of those barons loyal to the king rather than to Winchester. The truth was that since she had received Marie's letter a few hours before, she had not been able to think of anything except its probable contents. She had hardly heard anything that was said, her mind skipping from wondering what Marie wanted to wondering how she would get Walter away from everyone else.

The latter problem at last was solved when Sir Roland's wife, in a pause in the talk, said hesitantly, ''My lord, Sir Walter must be very tired and uncomfortable. Do you not think it would be well to let him unarm—''

''Indeed it would,'' Sybelle interrupted, springing to her feet. ''Pardon me, my lord, that I should have neglected your comfort. If you will come above to our chamber, I will see to it at once.''

Walter rose with alacrity. While he was talking about the raid and its probable consequences, he had been aware that Sybelle was unusually quiet, and he had been delighted yet again with the myriad perfections of his wife. He assumed her modest manner was devised to show him off in the best light to his new castellan, Sir John. His eagerness to be unarmed was far less owing to any discomfort than to a desire to be alone with Sybelle and tell her that he understood and appreciated her behavior. This, of course, was true, but Walter also hoped by showing his pleasure to encourage a like modesty in her at other times. He had learned to accept her bold entry into male conversation in her own family but was concerned about its effect on others less accustomed to Roselynde ways.

It was impossible to speak on the narrow, winding stair, and Sybelle preceded him with such speed to the principal bedchamber—yielded by Sir Roland and his wife to their overlady and her mate—that Walter had not been able to say a word. One does not shout compliments at the back of a woman two or three paces ahead. But Walter was not at all annoyed. In fact, he was rather amused by Sybelle's haste. They had been apart for four nights, and she had shown sufficient delight in the joys of the marriage bed that he wondered whether she intended to slip in a short coupling. Thus, he did not lengthen his stride to overtake her, wishing to allow her time to arrange whatever seemed suitable to her.

Unfortunately, this most laudable intention had a dire effect on Sybelle. To her, it seemed as if Walter were lagging behind out of reluctance to be alone with her. The cold within her struck deeper, and she picked up Marie's letter from where she had laid it out of sight of the other gentlefolk in the keep and turned, extending it toward Walter at the full length of her arm as he entered the room.

"This letter came for you soon after Sext," she said.

"A letter?" he echoed.

Walter could not guess who had written to him, but his wife's rigid stance implied trouble, and he seized the parchment with an anxiety that appeared to Sybelle as eagerness. Nor did he bother to look at the seal before he broke it. This was, of course, reasonable. Walter could discover who had written the letter much faster by reading the opening than by trying to make out the device on the seal. However, to Sybelle it seemed as if he must not only know the writer but have been eagerly expecting the letter.

So strong a pang a grief pierced Sybelle that tears filled her eyes. But pride would not permit her to allow Walter to see such weakness. She turned away, walked to the fire, and stood beside it, rubbing her hands together. However, the cold was inside her, and no external heat could warm it. Worse yet, her movement prevented her from seeing her husband's expression, which changed from a frown of displeasure when he saw Marie's name to the pallor and rigidity of horror when he read what she had written:

> I have no right, I suppose, to address you, but I no longer know where to turn for help. Despite the command the Earl of Pembroke gave to me to tell no one what passed among the three of us, he informed my sister of it, and she, in her terror of being again immured away from all life, ordered me not to recognize you. I tried to obey her, as you know, but, alas, my feelings

overcame my caution when I saw that my coldness troubled you. I did not believe that such innocent talk as passed between us in open company would offend Gervase, but she took this as a sign that I intended to flout her order. She ordered me out of Clifford, and when I begged her permission to return after you were gone, she would give me no answer.

I do not write to ask you to intercede for me; in fact, I beg you not to speak to Gervase at all. To plead for me can only increase her anger, which, if left to abate of itself, may fade. I can only pray that my sister will not abandon me completely. She knows I have no home except by her charity, my dower property having been unjustly seized by my late husband's brother, and I cannot believe that she would permit me to starve.

What has driven me to write to you is the fear that even if Gervase permits me to return, she may drive me out again. I have another trouble, not great now, but which must increase with time and cannot long be hid from my sister. Perhaps you will not believe me or will choose to believe the foul calumnies uttered by my brother-by-marriage. I can only say that when the earl accused me so harshly of misconduct, I was so terrified by an attack from him, who is supposed to be my stay and comfort, that I could not defend myself. Moreover, I was stricken by such pain that I was sure I would lose that which was to me both a joy and a dread. It is our curse, my sister's and mine, to be unable to retain the fruit of our wombs. Yet it did not happen and, although I cannot swear that it will not happen at any time, especially when I am so distraught of spirit, yet if it does not—what am I to do? Perhaps the earl will turn me out, even if my sister will not.

I swear to you on the souls of my father and my most beloved mother that I have had ado with no man since my husband died except for you. I dare not approach you openly for fear of the Earl of Pembroke and my sister, nor do I desire to make trouble between you and Lady Sybelle, your wife, yet I am near insane for at least a word of comfort, if you can offer me no more than that. Thus, I have come down from Craswall and am staying at the manor house of Hay. I do not know how long the bailiff will suffer my presence before he asks Gervase if it is by her will that I am here.

Thus, I beg you to come to me in secret as soon as you can. It is scarce more than a mile from Clyro. Do not, I beg you, bring any escort or make known to any person whom it is you visit. If my trouble should pass from me, none need know of it or that I disobeyed my sister, and perhaps she will forgive me. But I must see you. Again, I beg you to come to me, even if only for a few minutes, even if only to say that you do not care whether I live or die and you do not wish to be troubled by me ever again.

"I must go out again," Walter said.

Sybelle whirled around, her hands gripped hard together. "Go out? Where?"

"To Hay," he said, his eyes were on the letter he was carefully refolding and his mouth was a hard, bitter line, but Sybelle did not see that because his head was bent.

Red fury mingled with the ice of pain in Sybelle's heart. "I read the seal," she said. "I know that letter is from Marie de les Maures."

"Yes."

Walter was stunned by this resurgence of a problem he had thought dead and buried. He wished he could thrust Marie's letter into Sybelle's hands and ask her what to do. Surely she would pardon one single mistake that had such a tragic result. She must realize that there was no real intention of infidelity on his part. And if Sybelle's family would be willing to shelter Marie until the child was born and then care for the babe, the worst misery for all could be avoided. But he could not reveal Marie's trouble to Sybelle without her permission.

And what if Marie would not agree to let him ask Sybelle for help? He could send Marie to Goldcliff, but she would be miserable there, in a little keep almost as isolated as Pembroke. And how could he explain her presence in his keep to Sybelle if Marie would not permit him to expose the whole story? Would she prefer to take refuge in a convent? If so, which one? And would she wish to use a name different from her own? And after that, what? With his mind whirling, Walter said no more than that flat monosyllable. He thrust the letter up his mail sleeve and turned toward the door.

"Walter!" Sybelle's voice was sharp. "Have you no more to say to me than that?"

"Not now," he replied. "I must speak first to Marie." He was so distraught that he did not realize how such a remark could be misinterpreted.

Sybelle gasped with outrage. "You must speak to Marie before me? I am your wife. I do not know how other wives feel about such things, but I know you have been warned that I am not the woman to share my husband with another."

"Do not be a fool," Walter snarled. "I do not care a broken groat for Marie. I have done her an injury and have an obligation to redress it. That is all."

"You are a fool," Sybelle snapped back. "Can you not see that the woman cares nothing for you, that her one desire is to make trouble between us?"

"Do not speak ill of her," Walter said coldly. "I have wronged her, not she me. Nor has she done you any ill, nor wishes to."

"Oh, you are right, I *am* the fool," Sybelle cried. "From the first, in Builth, I saw there was something between you and Marie, but I deceived myself that it was me you wanted. I believed you spoke the truth when you offered to take me with nothing, but I see that it was Gervase who spoke the truth when she said you wanted me for my wealth and power. That was a clever feint you made. You knew that I would not be given without Roselynde, so it was safe to offer to marry me without a dowry."

"Sybelle, I do not have time for this nonsense," Walter snapped. "You know as well as I that I cannot profit by our marriage except at your pleasure. Would I be such an idiot as to spite you if it were your lands I wanted?"

"Love makes idiots of people," Sybelle spat. "It has made one of me."

"Well, it has not made one of me!" Walter bellowed. "And I do not propose to stand arguing with you while it grows so late that I will have to ride back from Hay in the dark."

"Walter." Sybelle's voice was level and cold as ice. "If you go to your mistress now, you do not need to worry about riding back after dark. You will not be permitted entrance into this keep or any other place where I am."

"Do not threaten me," he snarled, thoroughly aroused. "You jealous fool, you will destroy us over a debt I hate, over a woman I care for only because I have hurt her. I love you and only you, but if you think that I would lie for profit, then you also think I am not worth having. You need not fear. If you lock me out, I will make no effort to force a way in to you." He stood staring at her for a moment, then added softly, "I swear I love only you, but I will not be made a rag to wipe spittle with. I would explain this if I could, but as I cannot, you must trust me or be done with me."

CHAPTER 28

Walter left the room; Sybelle remained, frozen between rage and anguish. For some time she stood absolutely still, unable to believe that he had really gone, straining her ears to hear his footsteps returning. Then she flung herself down on the bed and wept, and the rain of tears cooled the fire of rage, leaving a sodden misery behind. But it was not a blank misery. Her mind kept saying, *He has gone to her, he has gone to her,* and each time it did, she reheard his answer, that he loved only her and that she must trust him.

"Men lie," Sybelle sobbed softly to herself.

But Sybelle did not really know any men who lied. She had heard secondhand many sad tales of deception and cruelty, and, of course, she was familiar with the songs and stories that minstrels related of fair maids abandoned—and of faithful lovers cast off, also. Her personal experience, however, was exactly the opposite. All the men in her family were loving and faithful husbands. They did not lie to their wives, and even when they ran free among the women before they were married—even then they did not lie. Sybelle knew that Simon, the most notorious of lovers, had never promised any woman love or constancy except Rhiannon—and to her he had given them without deception.

Sybelle wiped her eyes and sat up. Why did she think the worst of Walter? Had he ever given her cause? And if he wished to lie, why had he not lied? Sybelle knew her husband was not a fool, that he had a glib tongue and a quick mind. Surely he could have made up some reasonable explanation instead of saying he could not explain. And there had been no light in his eyes. Sybelle had seen Walter's eyes alight with love and with anticipation of love, but then they had been fixed on her.

Was she only a jealous fool? How could she ever know?

What had Walter said? That he had done Marie an injury and he must redress it. What kind of injury could a man do a woman? Sybelle knew there had been no damage to Marie's reputation. Marie was known as a flirt, but no worse than that was said of her. It was an injury that would make him ride out again after he had fought, however lightly, in the morning and only just returned to his new-wed wife. Sybelle's mouth hardened. Either Walter was totally, utterly, madly in love with Marie—and that was utter nonsense, for he could have offered for her and married her with Richard's blessing—or . . . it was something else.

Sybelle nodded as everything fell into place. A debt he hated. . . . Of course Marie had probably written that he had got her with child.

Sybelle jumped off the bed. No, Walter must not hate that innocent debt. Her own father was a bastard, and a word wrongly said could still make him wince, although God knew Grandfather William loved Papa dearly, and his stepmother, Lady Ela, loved him also. And if Walter had spoken the truth and loved only her and their marriage was destroyed by that debt, he might, indeed, hate the child.

With an exclamation of distress, Sybelle ran and got her cloak. It had not taken very long for her to reason out the problem. Walter would have to wait for whatever men he took with him to saddle up. Perhaps she could catch him, tell him that she would take the child and raise it. It was his child, after all, and to leave it to that vicious bitch Marie . . .

By the time that last thought entered Sybelle's mind she was down the stairs and about to enter the hall. Sir John and Sir Roland and their wives still sat talking near the fire. At once, Sybelle became aware of her tear-raddled face and the need to escape questions. She drew the hood of her cloak up so that it hid her features and pulled it closely around her. If she passed swiftly, well away from the hearth, she might be taken for a maidservant with an urgent task.

The maneuver was successful; at least, no one called out to her to ask where she was going, and she ran across the bailey to where the riding horses of the gentlefolk were stabled conveniently close. There she halted, sobs catching her breath again as she saw that Beau was gone. The last words in her mind before she was distracted returned to it . . . *vicious bitch*.

Sybelle stood staring at an empty stall. Whatever Walter said, Marie *did* intend to make trouble between them. God alone knew what she would say to him or what demands she would make. And her own jealous accusations, Sybelle knew, would make any evil hint seem more true. Fool that she was, why had she not said she would go with him as soon as he stated he had done Marie an injury? If she went now, would it not seem that she was spying, seeking to catch him in adultery? And what if all this reasoning was nothing more than her own desire for him blinding her to the real truth, that he *had* lied, that he *did* love Marie, and now that she herself was fast bound in marriage he no longer felt it worth his while even to lie?

Then it will be better to know, Sybelle told herself. But she did not feel fearful or sad, as if she expected a bitter disappointment. She felt excited, eager. Walter would be furious, simply furious, but she did not fear that, either. She was following with open hands to offer help, not blame. Let that nasty bitch try to turn awry her offer to raise her husband's child and her reason for it—her own father's bastardy.

Sybelle called out for a groom to saddle Damas and then went herself to speak to Sir Roland's master-at-arms. Casually, she asked how many men had gone with Walter, not wishing to incure blame by riding out unattended, particularly in view of the attack upon them in the vicinity. It was a dreadful shock to hear that her husband had gone alone; in fact that he had angrily refused to wait until an escort could be mounted to accompany him.

For a frozen moment every doubt of Walter's fidelity returned and was magnified. Why should he go alone unless to an assignation? But that question was countered at once with another. Why should Walter tell her openly and without hesitation that he was going to Hay if his purpose was dishonest?

Atop those questions came a sudden, icy fear. There was no reason for it. Walter had ridden safely from Clifford to Clyro only an hour or so before with no more than the three men-at-arms who had accompanied him from Oxford, and the attack on them had been more than a month ago and had come miles farther down the road to the southwest. Nonetheless, all Sybelle's uncertainties immediately resolved into self-blame. It was her fault, Sybelle believed, that Walter had been so impatient and angry that he refused to wait for an escort. If ill befell him, it would be because of her unreasonable jealousy.

After Marie broached her idea to Heribert, he had considered setting an ambush for Walter on the road between Clyro and Hay. He had abandoned the plan because killing Walter on the road might not implicate Marie sufficiently to keep her mouth shut. Besides, the trap at the manor was certain to result in Walter's death even if he did bring an escort. The men would not accompany him into the house and possibly could be disposed of quietly one at a time. And, if the fool did come alone, Marie was probably right about him and they would find him utterly helpless, naked in her bed.

Sir Heribert's reasoning was faultless; nonetheless he was completely wrong. So preoccupied was Walter between his misery over Marie's situation and his misery over his quarrel with Sybelle, that a small child with a slingshot could have disposed of him on the road between Clyro and Hay. It was lucky that Beau was sagacious, or Walter would have drowned in the fording of the river that ran across the track between Clyro and Hay because aside from urging his horse into the water, Walter paid scant attention to the stallion's progress.

Heribert had instructed his men to tie up and gag the stableboy and take his place so that no hint of extra horses or men should come by chance to Walter's ears, but that, too, was unnecessary. It was unlikely that Walter would have noticed a whole army encamped in the stable yard, not to mention four extra horses at the far end of the stable.

It was not until Walter entered the house and came to Marie, who was sitting beside the fire in the main chamber, that any fact penetrated his distress. There had been no one to open the door for him or announce him, but he did not wonder at that, supposing that Marie had sent everyone away. As he crossed the floor, he let his shield down from his shoulder and leaned it against a table, but his eyes were on Marie.

He did not see what he had expected, a miserable huddle of woman, beblubbered by tears. Marie looked as pretty as ever and was dressed even more seductively than usual. As soon as he laid eyes on her, Walter suffered a shock of revulsion. He had rushed away from Sybelle without even trying to calm her because he had envisioned Marie in dire agony of mind, feeling every minute an hour while she waited to know whether he, too, would cast her off. Instead he found her sufficiently self-possessed to have given several hours to her dressing, if he was any judge of appearances.

As soon as the thought passed through Walter's mind, he castigated himself for lack of charity. Women, too, had pride. It was sufficiently humiliating that Marie should have to approach him, after such a scene as had been played before Richard. Naturally she would wish to show herself as unaffected as possible. But the thought of the scene with Richard reminded Walter of Richard's first accusation, that Marie had been with child before their coupling. That was clearly not possible, for if it had been true, she would be showing considerable sign of increasing by now. *At least,* Walter thought, *I will not be nurturing the brat of some baseborn lover.*

Marie was standing to greet him at that moment, and Walter could not help noting how unaltered and graceful was her figure. The dress she had chosen was designed to show her body to best advantage, and it succeeded admirably in that purpose, for the cloth was very soft and its gentle folds clung to her. Unfortunately, Walter's mind was fixed on one aspect of the body only, and it struck him that from 3 December to now, nearly the end of February, there should be some sign of the child she carried. That brought Richard's second accusation to mind—that she was not with child at all. *Ridiculous,* Walter thought. *Why should she say such a thing if it were not true?*

To make trouble—both Richard and Sybelle had claimed that was her purpose. Walter shook off the thought and said, "I am sorry you are in this trouble, but I will not fail you."

"I knew you would not," Marie replied, and smiled.

The smile disturbed Walter anew. He told himself it was a brave gesture, but he was uneasy. "I will do what I can," he assured her. "I have thought of several different ways to provide for you until the child is born, and you—"

"Come into the inner chamber," Marie said hastily, taking his hand and trying to draw him with her.

"Why?" Walter asked.

"The bailiff will return, or his wife, or one of the servants. Do you think I wish to speak of these matters where all can hear?"

Then she had not specifically sent everyone away? Where, then, were all the household? Walter could not remember ever having seen a house utterly deserted as this one was. The hairs at the back of his neck prickled. Instinctively, he pulled away and looked back at the door.

"What is wrong?" Marie cried, her voice shaking. If Walter uncovered the trap before he fell into it, he would betray to Richard what she had done, and her life would be over.

"Nothing. Nothing at all," Walter responded, ashamed of himself for having alarmed her.

Doubtless Marie had asked the household to leave her alone for some stated length of time, but he had come later than she expected. He remembered that Sybelle had said the letter came around Sext. Marie had not known that he intended to stay at Clifford and join Bassett and Siward on the raid. She had probably expected him soon after she sent the letter out. Then there was a sound outside the door, the scrape of a foot. Marie gasped.

"Come," she begged, "please come."

She does not want anyone to see me, Walter thought, and he snatched up his shield and followed her. It seemed as if his assumption was correct, for once he was in the room she drew the door shut and leaned back against it, smiling. She seemed much less nervous, too. That seemed odd because they had not yet decided anything, which meant that the unpleasant part of their meeting was still ahead. However, Walter dismissed the small oddity. All he wanted was to settle with Marie as quickly as he could so he could go back to Clyro and calm Sybelle—if she would let him in.

Walter closed his eyes and swallowed, recalling the level, icy tones of his wife's voice when she said if he went to Marie just then she would not permit him to come near her again. Those were not the insensate shrieks of rage or the shrill ones of peevishness; it was the voice of a deep and bitter anger well under control. If he lost Sybelle over this . . . Walter bit his lip and opened his eyes. His wife was a reasonable woman. She would not destroy their marriage over a single slip, and Richard would confirm his story about Marie's pregnancy.

Marie had to bite back a chortle of glee when she saw Walter close his eyes and look so unhappy. She took it as a compliment to her, as an effort to resist temptation. The fool was so busy being noble that he had not noticed she had not really shut the door. Now Heribert could listen at the crack and know the exact moment to break in and discover Walter "raping" her. It was so satisfying that she nearly did allow herself to laugh, to tell Walter that all she felt for him was contempt. Then she remembered the bland, self-satisfied look Sybelle had worn in Abergavenny. If she sent Walter away, he would soon forget his desire and Sybelle would not suffer at all.

"I am not angry with you," Marie said. "You need not be afraid to approach me."

Walter stared at her, but his mind was still with Sybelle and he made no particular sense of her words. "I will tell you what I think would be best," he said. "If you would give me leave to broach this problem to—"

"I do not wish to think about that yet," Marie said, coming forward. "I have not yet carried any babe to term. I only wished to be sure that you would not desert me if I had need, and I see that you will be true."

"Yes, certainly," Walter agreed, "but this time it is near three months already, and it is less likely, I believe, to lose a child after that time." What he thought was that because no one wanted this misbegotten babe, the pregnancy would be sure to hold. "If you will only permit me to—"

"I will permit you anything," Marie interrupted. She took two quick, short steps, which, because Walter had not moved far into the room, brought her so close she was almost touching him, and she took his hand and held it between her breasts. "There is nothing I would deny you to thank you for your swift coming at my request."

The movement, gesture, and tone of voice finally got through Walter's preoccupation and the muscles in his jaw bunched briefly as he gritted his teeth over a wave of sickness. She still desired him, he thought, but then he remembered that she had taken no real pleasure in their coupling. This was no desire of the body. He backed away, but not far because Marie still held tight to his hand. To Richard she had spoken of love—but that was hopeless. Could Marie be so enamored that she wished to be his mistress? No, there was a false note in that. A mistress seeks either gold or the pleasure of the body. Then he thought he understood. Marie did not really trust him. She was offering the only thing she had to pay him for continued support.

"There is no need to thank me," he said gently. "Indeed, you have more cause to curse me. I made this trouble and I will extricate you from it. In any case, the child is mine, and I will care for it."

"I am not thinking about the child," Marie murmured, resisting Walter's first gentle effort to draw his hand away. "I am thinking of you. Let me unarm you so that you may be at ease." *What a nuisance the man is,* she thought contemptuously. *Why cannot he behave like any other man and take what he wants without all this ado?*

Although Walter was still heavily aware of guilt, he was beginning to be annoyed also. He had acknowledged his debt and his responsibility, and Marie's repeated offering of her body was becoming insulting. Moreover, although he fully intended to see that Marie suffered as little as possible from their sin, he did not intend to have her hanging like a millstone around his neck for the rest of his life. Even if she thought she was in love with him, a continued association would be the worst thing in the world for her. If they could manage to keep this child of sin a secret, Marie would be able to marry and live with honor. She must understand that any relationship between them in the future was impossible. Nonetheless, he hated to hurt her more than he had already.

Walter withdrew his hand from its position against Marie's breast with some effort, his irritation increasing because Marie would not take a hint; it was necessary to pull away with force, and she persisted in holding on to his fingers. He did not wish to wrench himself free and would have used his other hand to unloosen her grip gently, but it was supporting his shield, which he had not yet had an opportunity to set down anywhere.

"I have no time to unarm," he said, trying to keep any sharp note from his voice but determined to be firm. "I must go back to Clyro, and I do not wish to ride in the dark. Will you return to Craswall Priory? If you need money, I can send it to you there. If you do not wish to make any plans at this moment, tell me what I may do for you at this time and let me go."

Outside the door, Sir Heribert cursed silently. It was not to be so easy after all. He had been tasting the sweet flavor of revenge and of winning back his holding with no more effort than plunging his sword into the back of a man sleeping or engaged in the act of love. Walter's soft protest to Marie's first suggestion sounded to Heribert like a formality, and he had expected Walter would enthusiastically accept her invitation to unarm him. His insistence on returning before dark to Clyro did not promise so well.

Heribert considered bursting in at once, for his three best men were with him, but the rest of his troop probably would not arrive for another quarter hour. He could afford to wait until Walter actually said farewell. Perhaps Marie would succeed in getting him to change his mind. She was certainly trying. Heribert heard her cry out against Walter's cruelty and beg him to be kind.

"But I do not believe it is kind for me to linger," Walter said.

Sir Heribert relaxed while he listened to Walter trying to explain that for her own good Marie should think of him only as a friend who cared sufficiently for her to protect her, to think of him as she thought of Richard—a person bound to consider her well-being and that of her child, but not . . .

At that point Marie interrupted furiously, to deny that Richard considered her well-being and to profess undying love for Walter. "Come to me," she cried. "I must have you, I must. Even if you never come again, let me have this one time."

Again the hairs lifted on Walter's nape. The outburst against Richard had been sincere; he had heard the ring of true feeling in Marie's voice. Following it so immediately, her profession of love and her plea for a coupling were patently false.

"What is it you want from me?" he asked harshly.

Sir Heribert sprang to attention. He knew that tone of voice. Marie had betrayed herself in some way, and Walter had become suspicious. If she tried sweet words again, he would leave without further delay. Heribert imagined Walter turning toward the door. Should he allow him out into the main room? The larger space would favor him and his men, since they could more easily surround Walter. Still, although the bailiff had been told to stay away, he was somewhere about, and there were other men working in the yard of the manor house. If they heard sounds of conflict, they might run in. It was much less likely that the people of the manor would hear a fight taking place in the inner room, where the two narrow windows, closed for the winter anyway, opened only on the garden.

He had hoped he could kill Walter quickly and quietly, get his body out of the place without drawing attention, and dump it somewhere on the road. The body would soon be found, but there would be no evidence about how or by whom the murder had been committed. In that case, when his troop rode in they would do no harm but merely accompany him away from Hay. However, if the murder could not be carried out in secret and the folk of the manor became aware of what was happening, Heribert was prepared to have his troop sack Hay and kill every person who was there.

As the last thought passed through his mind, Heribert decided it was not a choice he favored. There was always a chance of someone escaping his men or someone seeing his troop coming or leaving. He and three men should be capable of finishing off Walter. He discounted Marie's presence. She would hold her tongue, owing to her complicity in the crime.

There had been a brief silence after Walter's angry question during which Heribert made his decision, and then Marie cried out, "I want nothing, only to love you."

Heribert signaled his men and threw open the door at which he had been listening, but he had not realized that Marie was still so close to it. The door struck against her and then rebounded; it knocked Marie off balance, so that she staggered a step or two sideways. But that was warning enough. Walter had been uneasy from the moment Marie had urged him into the inner room. The sense had ebbed and flowed in him but had never disappeared. Thus, in the moment granted him by the rebound of the door, he lifted his shield and drew his sword.

Marie had screamed wordlessly when the door struck her, but as Heribert and one man leapt into the room she screeched, "Heribert, not now! It is too soon, you fool! Oh, you fool!"

Naturally neither Heribert nor his man paid her any mind, particularly as Walter had surged forward to meet them, thrusting so hard with his shield that Heribert's own shield hit him in the face and he himself was shoved back into the main chamber. His man launched a blow, however, which Walter caught on his sword, and a second man slid around

Heribert, who was shaking his head to clear it, and slashed at Walter's head. Walter stooped to avoid the swing, chopping with the bottom of his shield at the man's unprotected knees.

Had the blow connected as meant, the man would have been crippled, but Walter's defensive dodging worked against his offensive move. Unopposed, the weight of the attacker's sword swung him around so that Walter's shield only caught the edge of his calf. He grunted with pain, but had taken no great hurt. The motion that had saved him, however, endangered his fellow man-at-arms, since his sword came around directly at his comrade. In backing away, he trod on the third man, who was coming in.

The tangle in the doorway gave Walter time for one telling blow. It was not as successful as he hoped, for it struck the first man's sword, rather than his hand or arm. Nonetheless, it was sufficiently powerful that the weapon was knocked from the man's hand and fell clanging to the floor. By that time the second man had recovered his balance, and the third pushed his weaponless companion to the side and came forward. He lashed out, but Walter was able to parry with the backswing of his sword, and he struck again with his shield, desperately trying to keep the men blocked in the doorway so that they would be unable to come at him from the sides.

Marie was screaming again, having realized that this attack was no part of her plan to trap and expose Walter in an act of rape. These men meant murder. She wanted no part of that. Having been the one who brought Walter to the house, she could only believe that she was to be blamed for the crime.

Meanwhile, Heribert had cleared his head and, seeing his chance as one of his men lunged forward, slid past him into the room. He paused for one moment, seeking an opening to thrust at Walter from the side, but Marie's hysterical shrieks distracted him. Thus far there were no shouts of alarm from the people outside the house. The clatter of weapons in the room was loud, but, dulled by the walls, it might not draw any notice because the sound of metal clanging against metal was common and could be owing to many causes. Marie's screaming, on the other hand, once heard, could not be misunderstood. Heribert turned away from Walter and struck Marie heavily across the face, knocking her to the ground.

"Shut your mouth," he snarled. "I will have him dead,

but you wrote the letter. If you make another sound, I will strike you witless."

Then Heribert whirled away toward Walter, and not a moment too soon. His intended victim had disarmed one man, who was dodging around the edge of the group trying to grab his weapon from the floor without getting himself killed or getting in the way of his companions. Another of Heribert's men-at-arms was bleeding from a wound in the thigh. The third had just set his foot on the sword on the floor and was toppling backward, which saved him from the full force of the blow Walter had struck at him.

CHAPTER 29

Sybelle stared wide-eyed at Sir Roland's master-at-arms. "Sir Walter went alone?" she echoed. "But it is not safe! We were attacked not far from here, and those who pursued us shouted recognition of his shield. I will not have it! Call out twenty men to arm and saddle."

She turned and ran back toward the entrance to the keep, ignoring the cries of the master-at-arms about where the men should go. She did not wish them to leave without her and also did not wish to become involved in the argument she knew would ensue if she said she would accompany them. If there was danger, she was wrong to expose herself, but she could not be sure of that, and to send the men without her, without the excuse that she wished to offer a home and suitable upbringing to Walter's child—and even offer sanctuary to Marie, if necessary—would be an inexcusable offense.

It took only minutes for Sybelle to tear off her gown and replace it with a riding dress. By the time she came down into the bailey again, Damas was waiting. The groom helped her mount, and she rode to where the men were forming up. The master-at-arms cried out in protest, as she had expected, but she did not answer him, calling out, "Follow me!" and laid her whip on Damas's sleek side so that the mare leapt forward across the drawbridge and out on the track that led down to the road below.

Sybelle was light; the mare was fleet and strong. No lesser horse such as those ridden by the men-at-arms had any chance to catch her or to stop her. They knew she was their overlady, that she was prized above any jewel by her parents and grandparents. If ill befell her, worse would befall them. They followed fast and hard, spurring and beating their mounts. The mile along the track that ran between Clyro and Hay flashed by, but there was the river to ford.

By then it was too late to talk of sending Sybelle back, although they knew their goal must be the manor house at Hay. A few men went before to test the ford. Then a line formed downstream so that if Damas stumbled, there would be a man at hand to catch the mare or catch Sybelle. Despite her haste, Sybelle did not protest. The few minutes extra spent in fording safely were nothing in comparison to the time that would be wasted if she should fall into the river.

Besides, most of Sybelle's anxiety had passed. Her specific fear, bred of her previous experience, was that Walter would be ambushed on the road. But there was no sign of that. The pace she had set had not prevented her from looking at the ground as they passed, and it was plain that no large troop had come that way. Thus, they assembled on the bank and turned left from the ford toward Hay at no more than a trot.

It was no great distance, but as they sighted the gates to the manor house, which, Sybelle saw with relief, were open, the master-at-arms shouted a warning. A larger troop was coming north on the road toward them at a faster pace. Sybelle cried out and again laid her whip onto Damas, who sprang ahead. The men roared in protest and spurred their mounts forward.

Sybelle and her men were somewhat closer to the gate of the manor, and the sound of a woman's voice confused the leader of Heribert's troop. The only woman he knew to be involved was Lady Marie. Had he arrived too soon? he wondered. If so, and if he and his men were seen by the man their master wished dead, he might take alarm and flee. It was obvious that the men following the woman were not knights, nor did they wear the colors of the one their master sought. The whole troop slowed as the leader held up his hand and pulled back on his rein, puzzled and undecided, while Sybelle and her men swept into Hay manor. Only when he saw the gates closing behind those who had entered so hastily did Sir Heribert's man understand that he had guessed wrong and some unexpected element was disrupting his master's plans.

The few serfs of the manor who were working in the yard near the gates cried out in fear and drew together when they saw the troop of armed men ride in. They were ignored by Sybelle's men, however. Some dismounted to shut and bar the gates, others rode around the house to explore those parts of the limited courtyard they had not seen, and a third group, swords drawn, began to investigate the interiors of the outbuildings. Sybelle directed Damas toward the cowering manor serfs and asked when Walter had ridden in. One began to stammer an answer, but before he could finish a man-at-arms came running around the corner of the house from the stable.

"He is here, lady," he called. "The lord's horse is here, and the stableboy is bound."

"Inside!" Sybelle cried, gesturing those four men who had swung the gates shut toward the house as she lifted her leg over to slide from the saddle.

"Do not dismount," the master-at-arms shouted. He had not originally intended to go, since he had arranged that a reliable and experienced captain lead the men. However, when Sybelle rode out, he had seized a horse from one of the other men and followed.

"You defend the gate," Sybelle ordered. "That troop will probably try to batter it down as soon as they reach it."

He knew she was right, and he also knew that he should not permit her to go into the house where there might be grave danger—but he had no idea of how to stop her, since restraining her by force was unthinkable. And at that moment a pair of men came from the small smithy, herding the smith and the bailiff between them. Moreover, shouts of anger could be heard as the troop they had seen arrived outside the walls, which proved that Sybelle had judged right. The troop intended entry into Hay; they were not passing by coincidence.

A blow struck the gate. It was nothing, probably two or three men kicking it to see if the bars had been set in place, but it was another sign that the men outside intended to force an entrance. The master-at-arms spent another second shouting a plea for Sybelle to be careful, and then turned his attention to the bailiff, trying to calm him and convince him they meant no harm, that far from intending to sack Hay and kill him, they wished to defend the manor against attack. Another blow struck the gate.

"One does not bring a lady on a raid," the master-at-arms pointed out, exasperatedly. "We ourselves are seeking shelter."

At last the bailiff's fear diminished enough for him to listen. He remembered the woman's voice, and she had said to defend the gate. He began to answer the master-at-arms questions about the defensive armament of the manor. A third blow struck the gate, this one much heavier. The master-at-arms's head came up alertly. Somewhere the men had found a log or a beam that they could use as an improvised ram. He shouted orders to look for any farm carts and roll them in front of the gates. The bailiff, understanding, bade the serfs drag out any building stone available, plus unworked lumps of iron and whatever else was heaviest to fill the carts.

A fourth blow struck the gate; the bar groaned.

Inside the bedchamber, Walter's sword was in full extension forward, his shield was warding off the wounded man—and his back was fully exposed and unprotected. Sir Heribert took three quick steps, his sword rising in his hand as he went, exultation in his heart. Heribert had promised a rich prize to the man who killed Walter—to encourage his men to fight hard. The fact that he would not have to pay it would make the pleasure of killing Walter himself all the greater.

But Heribert's first stroke at Walter's back went awry. Somehow Walter sensed him and twisted away so that the edge of Heribert's sword did not strike true. And then Walter turned and slashed at Heribert, a blow that numbed Heribert's shield arm, although he had managed to ward it off. A second blow would kill him, he feared, but one of his men thrust past Walter's shield and a second struck him on the light basinet helmet he wore, so that he went down on his knees.

Even then Walter was not finished. He lifted his shield to protect his head and swung out low with his sword, catching the man bending to stab at him so hard that his ankle was sheered. The second man leapt into the air to avoid the backstroke, and Heribert lifted his sword again for the *coup de grâce,* his blow once more aimed at Walter's unprotected back. This time Heribert knew Walter could not dodge because he was on his knees.

Sybelle had allowed the four men to precede her into the house, and the moment they opened the door, they heard a clash of metal and a yell of pain. All of them shouted in response.

Sir Heribert paused with his sword uplifted and shrieked, "In here! In here!"

Heribert was ready now to pay out the prize he had promised. Despite the fact that Walter was nearly finished, when he heard the male voices in the main chamber, Heribert was very glad of help. His confidence had been shaken, but now it was restored. His shield slipped a little sideways and, sword raised to strike, he paused to call to those he believed to be his men.

From the time the door burst open, Walter had had no time to think. He had reacted as a trained fighter, making all the right moves. Rational thought processes were too slow for the physical responses necessary. Motions, shadows, sounds, all seemed to go directly from eyes and ears to the muscles that countered the threats. At no time had Walter worried about dying. What small part of his mind was free of the necessary ingrained process of defense, almost as automatic as breathing to him, recorded successes. He had disarmed one man and wounded another. Although there were still three against him, one of those was slow, owing to his wound, and the unarmed man was often in the way of the others as he tried to retrieve his weapon.

Even when he was beaten to his knees and wounded, Walter felt no despair. The cut that severed an ankle took another man out of the fight, immediately and for good. He was subliminally aware of Heribert somewhat behind and to his right, preparing to strike again, and he got one foot beneath him, ready to turn and dodge. But when he heard the voices in the outer room, he gave up hope. And since he would die anyway, he was determined to take his enemy with him.

With no further thought of protecting himself, Walter shook off his shield as he twisted and came up from the floor, seized his sword in both hands, and drove the point into Heribert's gut with such force that it not only pierced through his mail but slit it upward and finally lodged in the breastbone. Walter knew there was no freeing his sword in time to parry any blow, and he no longer had a shield to present against the two men behind him. Now, in the endless instant in which he waited for a deathwound, he understood the trap Marie had set.

But there was no deathwound. Behind him he heard new shrieks of pain and fear rise above the moans of the man he had maimed. The screams were brief. Sybelle's men made short work of the others who were already tired, hurt, and thunderstruck at the death of their master.

A trained fighter may expect to die, but his body goes on

struggling for life. Even as the skin and flesh of his back tightened against the expected pain, Walter's foot was pushing Heribert's body off his blade and he was turning to try to face his opponents. He succeeded just in time to see Sybelle appear in the doorway. Eyes and mouth both opened, but further action was impossible. Walter was paralyzed by surprise. At that moment any assassin could have cut his throat slowly with a dull knife, and he would not have made the smallest objection.

Sybelle was not inhibited by surprise. She pushed past one of her men, who was just straightening up after cutting the throat of the last living assassin, leapt lightly over the bodies, and clutched at Walter, crying, "Beloved, are you sore hurt?"

And Walter said, "I did not break my collarbone again." He then blinked at the words that had come out of his mouth and roared, "What are you doing here?"

The volume of his voice, despite the trickle of red that was running from his side under his left arm, assured Sybelle that her husband was essentially intact. She was much tempted to say *Saving the life of an idiot,* but she was aware of the troop outside the gate, which Walter was not, and knew this was no time to start an argument.

"We are beset," she said, instead of answering Walter's question. "I brought twenty men, but there is a larger troop outside trying to fight their way in."

"We need not fear them," Walter began, guessing they were Heribert's men and that, their contract and all hope of future gain being terminated by their master's death, they would go quietly away when informed of that fact.

However, as he said it he became aware that both Sybelle and he had been shouting to make themselves heard over a woman's hysterical shrieks. Sybelle seemed to come to the same realization at the same moment, and both their heads turned in the direction that the men-at-arms were already looking.

"Shut that accursed bitch's mouth for me," Walter said to Sybelle, "while I go out and tell those men Sir Heribert is dead." He started out, then turned back, recalling the expression on Sybelle's face when she looked at Marie. "Do not kill her," he warned. "Just stop her screeching."

Sybelle went over to Marie, who was backed against the wall, staring at the dead bodies and the sea of blood on the floor. Her eyes were nearly starting from her head, and she screamed on a single high note until her breath gave out, gasped in more air, and began to scream again. First Sybelle grasped her shoulders and tried to pull her away from the wall, but she was rigid as steel. Then she gestured to a man and said, "Carry her out into the other chamber."

Until Marie's staring had fixed her own attention on the scene, Sybelle had been too busy, too concerned for Walter, to notice. She was not unaccustomed to blood, but this was a bit too much, and the sight of Heribert's pale pink guts slipping through his pierced belly was doing unpleasant things to her own inner workings. Heribert? Sybelle's mind caught on that. How did she know it was Heribert? He was wearing a closed helmet, not a simple basinet. Then she remembered that Walter had said it was Heribert. As her man-at-arms lifted Marie, still rigid as a statue and shrieking, and carried her out, Sybelle noticed that the device on the dead knight's shield was not the same as that Sir Heribert had used.

She dismissed the problem from her mind, following the man and bidding him hold Marie steady. Then she delivered several stinging slaps on Marie's face. The shrill screech checked, Marie's breath caught, and then she would have crumpled to the ground if Sybelle's man had not been holding her.

"Put her in a chair," Sybelle directed.

The limp body would have fallen over, but Sybelle gripped it by a shoulder and waved the man away. She was paying little attention to Marie. The door to the main room of the manor house had been left open when she and her men rushed in. Through it she could hear Walter bellowing at the top of his lungs words she could not quite make out above the thud of the ram. Then the heavy *thwack* of wood on wood stopped. There was another exchange, longer and even more indistinguishable because the voices were lower. Marie began to stir. Her breast heaved, drawing air.

"Do not begin to scream again," Sybelle said loudly. "There is nothing to scream for anymore. I will slap you silly if you yell again."

Her lips tightened on the last words because Walter walked in just as she said them, but he did not even look at Marie.

"The men are leaving," he told Sybelle. "I thought they might have some idea of holding us for ransom, but I think they realized that news of their attack on Hay would get to Clyro or to Clifford before they could get in. I will wait a little while and then send out to Clyro for more men to be sure they do not make any attempt on us while we are fording the river." He paused, staring at Sybelle and asked once more in no gentle voice, "What are you doing here?"

She had looked first at the trail of blood on his left side, but it was dark and drying already. The wound he had taken was no great matter. She lifted her eyes to his face and smiled mischievously. "Saving the life of an idiot?" she suggested.

Walter's mouth hardened with temper, and he stepped toward her, but Sybelle did not quail. She laughed softly, only there was no challenge in the laugh or in the expression. Her eyes showed only trust that he was not a man to punish others for his own mistakes. Walter burst out laughing, too, strode over to her and caught her, into a hard embrace.

"Saving the life of an idiot," he agreed. "Did you know this was a trap set by that nasty bitch?"

For a moment Sybelle leaned her head against her husband's shoulder. "No," she admitted. "But when you said I must trust you, I knew I must. And then I asked myself what kind of injury you could have done her and put that together with the debt you hated. . . ." She pushed out of his arms and looked up into his face anxiously. "Oh, Walter, if she is with child, you must not hate the babe. It is bad enough to be born a bastard, like Papa was, but to be hated also is too terrible. I will take the child and love it. I swear I will. That was what I followed you to say."

He pulled her back into his arms. "Dearling, dearling, you are so sweet and good. There is no child. Look at her. It was just the bait to draw me, for she knew I would come to her for no other reason. What would I want with *her* when I have you?"

"But why did she want you dead?" Sybelle shuddered and clutched at her husband. "If she desired you, she might want me dead, but why you?"

Walter looked down at Marie who was sobbing louder and louder, working up into full-throated wails. His mailed hand seized her shoulder and the fingers gripped so that she shrieked with pain. "I never saw the face of the man who fought me, but you called him Heribert. How did you come to know my late castellan, Sir Heribert?"

"You are hurting me," Marie screamed.

"And you tried to have me killed," Walter replied.

"No! No!" Marie shrieked, seeing death in his merciless face.

"Walter . . ." Sybelle whispered, frightened herself by his implacable expression, although she had not feared his anger.

"Why?" he demanded inexorably of Marie.

And so the whole ugly story spilled out. And as he listened, Walter's hand relaxed its cruel grip and the hardness went out of his face, leaving only disgust and contempt. At the end he shrugged and said Marie was not worth bothering with, bent his head to kiss Sybelle as if that contact could clean his mouth of the taste of the petty dirtiness of Marie's tale, and went out to send two men to Clyro for a larger escort. From the sounds coming in through the open door, he judged the obstructions had been cleared from in front of the gate.

Trembling, thoroughly cowed, Marie looked up at Sybelle. "What will you do with me?" she whispered.

"As for me, nothing," Sybelle replied. "If Heribert had succeeded and killed my husband, I would have hunted you to your death—and it would have been no easy death. But since Walter is not hurt nor any other harm done except to my husband's enemy, and since in his mind Walter will spit on your name when he hears it in the future, I have no interest in you. I will send you to Clifford, if you wish, or to Craswall if you prefer."

"Will you tell Richard?" Marie whimpered.

"I will tell no one except my mother and grandmother so that they will know where to look first if ill befalls me or Walter, but the tale will go no further than their ears. We of Roselynde are not gossips."

"Let me go before he returns," Marie pleaded.

"As you will," Sybelle replied indifferently, and went out to tell two men to get Marie's horse saddled and to escort her wherever she wished to go.

Marie fled the house and hid herself in the stable, and when Walter came back inside with a half-dozen serfs to carry out the bodies of the slain men, she fled from the manor. Walter did not care when Sybelle told him what she had done. For him, Marie no longer existed. Nor did he react when the bailiff came in and knelt before the chair in which he was sitting, pleading for mercy, begging Walter to believe that he had not known what evil was intended. Walter accepted that, said he would make no complaint, and dismissed the man.

Sybelle watched her husband anxiously. His easy indifference seemed unnatural. At last she asked him if he had taken some other hurt than the cut on his left side. He smiled and shook his head, saying he did not believe that Marie or Heribert would have confided their plans to a bailiff and if the man was innocent, there was no purpose to blackening his name with an investigation.

"I am tired," he admitted. "What with the ride to Almondbury and the lively time I had in that inner room, I am most eager to see the troop from Clyro."

They had no long time to wait. Scarcely half an hour passed before a shout, and the sound of the gate opening, and then of horses in the yard drew Sybelle to the door. She cried out, and Walter jumped to his feet in alarm, but Sybelle ran out, and a moment later Geoffrey came in with her. For a little time there were many questions and no answers, Walter fearing a political disaster and Geoffrey asking why so many men were needed. At last, however, each determined that there was no emergency and full explanations could wait until they were back in Clyro and Walter was more comfortable.

Thus, it was not until the evening meal that Walter's tale was told—with suitable deletions, for although he had no desire to protect Marie, he did not wish that Richard should be embarrassed by the bad behavior of his sister-by-marriage. He would have said nothing at all, except that it was necessary that Sir John know he need not watch for treachery seeded in Knight's Tower by Sir Heribert.

Then Geoffrey explained the reason for his coming was the raid on Almondbury. He wanted to know who had conceived the idea.

"If it is blame, you had better blame me," Walter said. "I could not persuade Bassett and Siward to ignore the king's presence at Huntington. They *would* do something, so I said it was Henry's ministers who were to blame for the trouble and that it was they who should be punished. That set the notion into Sir Gilbert's head; he remembered Almondbury was Seagrave's land."

"Oh, no one is seeking a scapegoat," Geoffrey chortled, "not even the king. We had word that there was burning in the direction of Almondbury, and Seagrave sprang up and ranted and raved about the lawlessness in the land and how it must be corrected. Henry did not speak, but he did look very black. Then Adam said, most innocently, that if it were *his* lands under attack, he would be there already to lesson those who dared offend him."

Sir Roland and Sir John, both knowing Adam, laughed aloud, and Sybelle said, "If he were not there ahead of time, having incited the raid just so he could have the sport of defending the property."

"He is not so irresponsible as that," Geoffrey protested, but he was smiling also. "In any case," he went on, "it was the exact right thing to say."

"A miracle, in Adam's case," Sybelle teased.

"We will never hear the end of this story if you do not hold your tongue," Walter remarked dryly, "and I have the feeling the end of the tale is worth hearing."

"Indeed it is," Geoffrey agreed, "for the king picked up Adam's remark and offered Seagrave the use of the men-at-arms in Huntington. I do not think Seagrave was too well pleased with Henry's generosity, but he accepted with due thanks. I never saw a man take longer to make ready. I suppose he hoped you would be gone by the time he came."

Walter explained how easy the taking of Almondbury had been and the odd sense of incompleteness they felt, which had caused them to linger somewhat longer than they ordinarily would have done.

Geoffrey lifted a brow. "God's hand was in this, then. When a herd of cows and a few minutes' time come together to bring about such a great good, I must believe it was a thing ordained and not a result of chance alone. In no long time after he left—as you must know—Seagrave came pelting back. He told Henry there was a whole army under Bassett and Siward ravaging the entire district and urged Henry to flee. Ian and I were a little worried, fearing you had not been able to control Bassett, but then I thought the attack would have come directly at Huntington. Adam, of course, wanted to stay and fight, but Simon had the best sense of all for once in his life and had sent out some of his men to follow Seagrave."

"Army!" Walter exclaimed. "I do not think there were a hundred of us. That was all the horses Bassett could gather from Clifford and the nearby farms and manors. He did not wish to wait another day to collect more horses or to rest those brought from farther afield for fear the king would move.''

''So Simon's men reported,'' Geoffrey agreed. ''That is, they said there was only a large troop at the manor itself and a few groups of three or four men each, burning shepherds' huts and driving the flocks and herds southward. As you know, Henry is no coward—at least, not for things of the body. He has fought well the few times he had the chance. But, Walter, you do not seem at all surprised by this news. Were you there? Simon's men said nothing—but perhaps he told them to hold their tongues.''

Walter had nodded when Geoffrey mentioned that Henry was no coward. It was true the king was willing and even eager to fight, but his skill was less than his courage because of lack of training and opportunity. Moreover, being so surrounded by his nobles on the field, Henry seldom was given any chance to engage. But the nod also served as preliminary to his answer to the question of whether he had been at Almondbury.

''I was there,'' Walter admitted, the confession somewhat muffled by a huge yawn. ''But Bassett and Siward suggested I change my shield—and so I did. With a closed helmet, even Simon's men would not know me.''

Geoffrey laughed and shook his head at Walter's admission but he did not comment on it. ''Thus,'' he continued, ''when he heard the truth, Henry laughed immoderately at Seagrave's timidity, but he was disgusted. Later, when we were in private, he said to me that he would be glad to be rid of such cowardly counselors and officers.''

''That is good news,'' Sir John said with enthusiasm.

''Yes.'' Geoffrey smiled with satisfaction and relief. ''I do not believe there is any longer any chance of influencing the king to change his mind. He spoke to me also of going east again to ask Edmund of Abingdon and the Bishop of Chester to arrange peace terms with Richard.''

''Chester is a good choice,'' Walter began, and was interrupted by another jaw-cracking yawn. ''I am sorry,'' he said, smiling. ''I assure you I do not find the subject dull.''

That raised a laugh. ''Go to bed,'' Geoffrey suggested. ''You have had a busy day.''

"Yes," Walter agreed, "but I want to know—" and was interrupted by still another yawn. "I want to know if I may pass this news to Bassett and Siward."

"By all means," Geoffrey approved. "One of the reasons I came was that they should know the success of what they have done. I would like to see the land restored to peace entirely, but if Richard's supporters cannot be persuaded to give up all activity, let them prey upon Winchester, Rivaulx, and the others. The king is no longer a combatant. For Henry, the war is over."

"Thank God for that." Sybelle sighed.

There was a universal murmur of assent. It was one thing to pick a quarrel with one's neighbor and to raid back and forth or even, in a case of greater bitterness, to besiege his keep. Sometimes by a stroke of good fortune one could gain a second property by such means, but usually the overlords of both came and made peace before too-great damage was done on either side. Or, if the overlords were enemies and looked to be ready to join the fight, the king came and made peace.

For the king to be at war with his great barons was something else again. Only catastrophe could ensue from such a condition. All except the youngest members of the party vividly remembered the bloodbath at the end of King John's reign, when some barons became so bitter that they invited Prince Louis of France to be king. Before he was got rid of, the whole country had been laid waste. Of course, there had never been any danger that the Earl of Pembroke would invite any foreign king, but many robber lords who cared nothing for the rights and wrongs of the barons or the good of the realm took advantage of the general unrest to burn and pillage. A private war was good sport, but civil war was a disaster.

"Tomorrow," Walter began, but Sybelle rose from the stool near him where she had been sitting and said, "Tomorrow will best be arranged tomorrow. Papa is going to stay the night, and you will make much better sense of what he has to say if you are not half-asleep while you are listening to him. Come above to bed now, my lord."

"Yes, go," Geoffrey urged. "I have said everything of importance already—except that the king knows that I have come here—so I need not hasten to return to Huntington. I can even stay another day if you think Bassett and Siward would like to come to Clyro to speak to me."

Since by now every bruise Walter had received had stiffened and he ached all over, he did not argue but rose slowly from his chair and straightened carefully so that he would not pull the fresh stitching of the cut on his left side. He said thank you again to his father-by-marriage, who had, of course, been offered the principal bed and bedchamber and had refused. Walter was grateful, knowing in his sore condition he would be more comfortable in a large bed.

Sybelle had gone ahead, and by the time he had climbed the stairs, she had candles alight and maids warming the bed. At first Walter did not think about anything, only glad that he did not need to bend and twist to take off his shoes, untie his crossgarters, and pull off his clothes. It was such a relief and pleasure that he was hardly aware who served him. However, when Sybelle had shepherded him into the warm bed, she bade him turn on his belly so she could again anoint the huge bruise across his back where Heribert's sword had come down.

The sound of her voice reminded Walter that Sybelle had not spoken a word to him when they had been alone since they had returned from Hay. He turned his head, but could not see her face. It occurred to him also that, although she had sat beside him and been as pert as usual in her father's presence, she had not leaned back against him confidingly as she had in Roselynde.

''Do you still think it wrong for me to have gone to speak to Marie?'' he asked suddenly.

Sybelle started. ''I thought you asleep already. Am I hurting you?''

''No, you are giving me pleasure—but you would give me more by answering a question when I ask it.''

''Does a silly question need answering? Wrong? No, of course you were not wrong. Being a man, and she having been your mistress—''

''She was never my mistress,'' Walter interrupted. ''I am not so much a fool as you think. If I had had any long association with her, I would have known her too well to be drawn by her bait. I had her once only—and I deeply regretted it. She had all the warmth of a fish dead a week.''

Needing to see Sybelle's face clearly, Walter turned over and hissed with pain as he pulled the stitches and his bruised muscles twinged. Sybelle, who had been about to say several sharp things about the idiocy of believing Marie's letter, which Walter had shown her, under such circumstances, exclaimed instead at his unwise movement and bent over him to look at his stitches. He pulled her upward and lower.

"And that is a thing I could never say of you," he suggested.

"You are all sore," Sybelle murmured with her lips against his.

"I will be stiffer and more sore tomorrow," Walter hinted, "and we have been long apart."

"Only four days," Sybelle said, but her hands were undoing her girdle as their lips came together again.

Walter said no more, but he assisted her undressing by pulling off her headdress and wimple, which were in easy reach. Having been helpful, he then proceeded to be a hindrance, even while encouraging a swift disrobing, by kissing her ears and neck, which he had managed to expose.

"This is not wise," Sybelle protested feebly.

"But we have gone too far to stop." Walter laughed. "I am already wounded, and you would not wish me to suffer a severe congestion, which could cause grave complications if not relieved by the proper treatment."

"I wonder," Sybelle giggled, "if a contusion on the head is not the proper treatment for this congestion?" But her threat was greatly weakened by the fact that she had rapidly cast off the remainder of her garments. However, as Walter lifted the covers to welcome her and she caught sight of his battered body, she hesitated and looked concerned again. "You will hurt yourself," she murmured.

"No, I will not," he assured her. "I will do nothing. My hips are sound. Sit astride me while I make you ready. Then you can mount me."

Sybelle blushed. "I am ready," she whispered, then giggled again softly. "And I see that you are also."

"Then mount me," he urged, holding his staff so she could the more easily impale herself.

Athough Sybelle was as surprised as Marie had been by Walter's suggestion, she accepted it with a good deal more enthusiasm. So much, in fact, that she was too soon contented and Walter had to bid her continue her ride. And, because he was really very tired and in some pain despite Sybelle's care not to rest too heavily on him, she was doubly satisfied before his release came. They lay, then, for a little while in quiet, but after that, Sybelle started to slip out of the bed.

"Where do you go?" Walter asked.

"Hush, go to sleep," she replied, surprised by the anxiety in his voice. "I only wish to fold our clothing, snuff out the candles, and the light and night light. What troubles you?"

"I love you," he said.

Their coupling in that manner so soon after he had made the assertion that Marie had never been his mistress had kept the whole thing in his mind. Instead of sleeping, as he expected, Walter had been thinking that Sybelle had not made any reply to his statement. Her willingness to make love was probably answer enough in her mind, Walter knew, but he wanted the slate wiped clean by a clear acceptance of what he had said.

"I cannot bear that there should be any doubt between us," he added. "I must be sure you know that what happened with Marie was only a mistake. I would not have gone with her, only that I could not have you and . . . and I needed a woman. I wished to tell you, but it seemed unfair to her and I had been warned so straitly of your jealous nature that I thought it wiser, since I had no intention of renewing the encounter, to forget it."

Sybelle looked down at him. "I was wrong to mistrust you," she said slowly, "for I knew you to be an honest man. And I was wrong to threaten you this afternoon when you told me you must go to Hay. For that discourtesy I ask pardon."

Walter made a gesture of dismissing the need for any apology, but he saw that she had more to say and did not speak.

"Perhaps I am also wrong," she continued, "in asking more of you than is a wife's right to ask, but I do not know any other way to live. I must tell you that no man of my family thinks himself free to have any woman besides his wife."

She hesitated, and Walter said soberly, "So I have been told."

But Sybelle shook her head. She might not have had the courage to begin the discussion, but since it was started she wished to say everything and be done. "I am willing to do anything you ask of me," she said earnestly, "to give you pleasure in any way you wish. Teach me. You will find me an eager learner. No mistress could ever be more desirous of pleasing you than I am now and always will be. But Walter, I cannot share you. The threat was wrong, but it came from the center of my being. If you cannot be wholly mine, I do not want any part of you—not even if it be the greatest and most important part."

Sybelle's voice was trembling, and her eyes filled with tears by the time she finished. Walter took her hands and kissed them. The fragrance of the unguent that she had been using to rub his back was still on them, and the odor brought into his mind all the tender care Sybelle lavished on him, which led to a memory of how she had happened to come in time to save his life. The quick understanding, the willingness to admit herself wrong did not deceive him into thinking she would overlook a real and deliberate departure from her standards. But he himself had changed. He was willing to accept Sybelle's standards now.

Her hands unfolded under his kiss and cupped his face, and Walter thought back with amazement on the resentment he had felt only a few months previous, when Llewelyn had told him that Roselynde women cleaved like welded iron to their men but demanded faithfulness of the men in return. Joanna had warned him also. Perhaps those warnings had made all the trouble to begin with. He could not believe that even without warnings he could ever have been such a fool as to risk what he had for an ephemeral physical pleasure.

"You need not fear me," he said. "I love you, and I am wholly thine, for now and for all time."

GLOSSARY

AIDE: a formal payment by vassals to their overlord on specific occasions, such as the knighting of the eldest son and the marriage of the eldest daughter.

BAILEY: any open area surrounded by the walls of a castle.

BAILIFF: a person charged with administrative duties of an estate; the agent who collects rents and manages an estate or farm for the landlord.

BED CURTAINS: heavy material, usually velvet, silk damask, or wool, fastened above the center of the bed, stretched over a four-sided frame work, and extended to the floor. These curtains provided both warmth and privacy.

BEDROBE: a loose gown, capable of being donned quickly and easily; what we would call a bathrobe.

BETROTHAL: the engagement of a man or woman in a contract of marriage (a legal condition far more binding than a modern "engagement").

CASTELLAN: the governor or constable of a castle, assigned at the will of the "holder" of the castle and liable to removal at that holder's will. (There were some cases of hereditary castellanships.)

CHAUSSES: a garment much like modern pantyhose, except that chausses were sewn, not knitted, and therefore were not form-fitting;

they were tied at the waist with a drawstring and fitted to the legs with crossgarters.

COMPLINE: one of the canonical hours, about 9 P.M., but earlier in winter and later in summer.

CROSSGARTERS: long, thin strips of cloth or leather that were wrapped crosswise around the leg and tied below the knee to prevent the chausses from bagging excessively.

DEMESNE: the land held and possessed by the owner and not rented or controlled by any subordinate, such as a vassal or castellan.

DESTRIER: a war horse, a highly trained animal.

DISSEISE: to put out of possession; to dispossess a person from his estates in such a way that his legal heirs are also disqualified from inheriting; the term was usually used when the dispossession was wrongful.

FEWTER: a rest on the saddle into which a lance was set in preparation for jousting. (The fewter was not yet developed at the time of this book, and here the term is used as a verb to describe the act of holding the lance between arm and body supported by the hand.)

FOREBUILDING: an addition to a keep that sheltered that stair which went up to the entrance. (No keep had an entrance on the ground floor for reasons of defense.)

HAUBERK: armor; the mail shirt made up of linked rings or chains of metal; it had a hook that went over the head and could be laced at the neck and extended a little below the knee, being split in the middle, front and back, almost to the crotch so that a man could mount and ride a horse.

HEADDRESS: small, round pillbox hat pinned to the top of the wimple; could be embroidered or bejeweled for ornamentation.

KEEP:	technically the innermost, strongest structure or central tower of a medieval castle, the place that served as a last defense; in general used to mean the whole castle.
LAUDS:	one of the canonical hours; sunrise (4:30 A.M. to 7 A.M., depending upon the season).
LEECH:	a person who treated injuries and sometimes illness, sometimes combining this with the profession of barber; not a learned physician but a doctor of sorts.
LIEGEMAN:	a vassal sworn to the service and support of his superior lord.
MATINS:	one of the canonical hours, very early morning, between midnight and sunrise.
NONE:	one of the canonical hours; early afternoon, about 2 or 3 p.m.
OVERLORD:	a lord superior; one who is the lord or ruler of other noblemen.
PRIME:	one of the canonical hours; morning, after sunrise.
SEXT:	one of the canonical hours; about 12 noon.
SQUIRE:	a young man in training to be a knight; a squire attended upon a knight, exchanging personal service (like a combined valet, secretary, messenger boy, and body guard) in exchange for lessons in manners, fighting techniques, and military tactics.
SURCOAT:	an outer garment, commonly of rich material; when worn over armor the surcoat was often emblazoned with the heraldic arms of the wearer.
TABARD:	a loose upper garment without sleeves or with short sleeves, open at the sides, worn over the armor and emblazoned on the front and back with either heraldic arms of the symbol of a group—such as the cross of the crusaders.

SIT IN JUSTICE: literally to act as a judge in both criminal and civil cases, originally the duty of the "holder" of an estate.

TERCE: one of the canonical hours, morning, about 9 A.M.

VASSAL: a nobleman who held his lands on conditions of homage and allegiance, which included military service, from an overlord. Vassals might be very great lords who held many large estates from the king or could be minor knights who held one small estate from another nobleman. In any case the tenure of a vassal was permanent and heritable by his children. The property could not be taken away from them legally except for high crimes, such as treason.

VESPERS: one of the canonical hours, also called evensong; sunset.

WAIN: a large open vehicle, usually four-wheeled, drawn by horses or oxen and used for heavy loads.

WIMPLE: a veil of linen or silk worn by women and so folded as to envelop the head, hair, chin, sides of the face, and neck.

Dear Friends and Readers,

I have received so many letters asking me about my next book in the ROYAL DYNASTY Series, I thought I would take this opportunity to tell you about it. The title is *Fire Song*.

The book continues the saga of the Marlowe family begun in *Siren Song* and developed in *Winter Song*. Volume Three, *Fire Song,* centers around the marriage of Aubery of Ilmer, William of Marlowe's stepson and his daughter Alys's childhood friend, to Fenice, Alys's stepdaughter, the natural child of her husband, Raymond d'Aix. At their first meeting, Aubery and Fenice seem well suited and mutually attracted, but ghosts and secrets from the past plague their marriage—secrets of murder, treachery, shame, and unworthiness. Each carries the burden of the unhappy past alone, fearful that exposure will drive out love.

Fenice and Aubery's problems are intensified by a rebellion in Gascony, the English king's vagaries, and a royal wedding in Castile, and their marriage is nearly destroyed by political turmoil in France. It takes Alys's sharp tongue and William's mature wisdom to set the passionate but disturbed lovers on a path that will lead to a joyful future.

I am very fond of Aubery and Fenice and delighted to visit again with my friends in Marlowe keep, Tour Dur, and Blancheforte. I enjoyed writing *Fire Song* and hope you will enjoy reading it.

Roberta Gellis